Jenny Holmes has been writing fiction since her early twenties, having had series of children's books adapted for both the BBC and ITV.

Jenny was born and brought up in Yorkshire. After living in the Midlands and travelling widely in America, she returned to Yorkshire and brought up her two daughters with a spectacular view of the moors and a sense of belonging to the special, still undiscovered corners of the Yorkshire Dales.

One of three children brought up in Harrogate, Jenny's links with Yorkshire stretch back through many generations via a mother who served in the Land Army during the Second World War and pharmacist and shop-worker aunts, back to a maternal grandfather who worked as a village blacksmith and pub landlord. Her great-aunts worked in Edwardian times as seamstresses, milliners and upholsterers. All told stories of life lived with little material wealth but with great spirit and independence, where a sense of community and family loyalty were fierce – sometimes uncomfortable but never to be ignored. Theirs are the voices that echo down the years, and the author's hope is that their strength is brought back to life in ma— characters represented in these pages.

THE AIR RAID GIRLS: WARTIME BRIDES

Jenny Holmes

PENGUIN BOOKS

TRANSWORLD PUBLISHERS
Penguin Random House, One Embassy Gardens,
8 Viaduct Gardens, London SW11 7BW
www.penguin.co.uk

Transworld is part of the Penguin Random House group of companies
whose addresses can be found at global.penguinrandomhouse.com

Penguin
Random House
UK

First published in Great Britain in 2022 by Bantam Press
an imprint of Transworld Publishers
Penguin paperback edition published 2022

A CIP catalogue record for this book
is available from the British Library.

ISBN
9781529176520

Typeset in 11.5/14pt New Baskerville ITC by Jouve (UK), Milton Keynes
Printed and bound in Great Britain by Clays Ltd, Elcograf S.p.A.

The authorized representative in the EEA is Penguin Random House
Ireland, Morrison Chambers, 32 Nassau Street, Dublin D02 YH68.

Penguin Random House is committed to a sustainable
future for our business, our readers and our planet. This book
is made from Forest Stewardship Council® certified paper.

For Olga

CHAPTER ONE

April 1942

Lizzie Harrison thrust her spade into the heavy black soil then tilted her head to feel the warmth of the sun on her face. It had been a long, hard winter, and this Sunday morning in early spring she and her sister, Connie Bailey, had jumped at the chance to work on the family allotment alongside their father Bert.

'Shift out of the way.' Connie shoved Lizzie to one side and carried on working. They had a job to do – a trench to dig and seed potatoes to plant – and dawdling was not Connie's style. Her shirtsleeves were rolled up and her dark, wavy hair was tamed by a bright red scarf tied Gypsy-fashion around her head.

'Watch what you're doing.' Lizzie staggered then regained her balance. She caught sight of their father stooped over the workbench inside his shed – scrawnier than ever since his heart attack just before Christmas. His grey hair was slicked back and his faded blue overalls hung loosely from his spare frame. When Bert attempted to lift a heavy pallet of seed potatoes Lizzie rushed to take it from him.

1

'Nay – I can do it,' he objected half-heartedly, though he let her carry the tray nevertheless.

'I know you can, Dad, but you've been given strict orders to take it easy,' she reminded him. She was glad that she hadn't put on too many layers this morning – simply a short-sleeved Aertex shirt and a pair of khaki dungarees, tightly belted around her slim waist. 'This spot of sun is grand – why not sit there on the bench for a while and tell Connie and me what we're doing wrong?'

'The trench isn't deep enough. You're putting the spuds in too close together and upside down.' Connie mimicked their father's flat, gravelly voice as she listed their likely shortcomings.

'Go on, take the mickey all you like,' Bert grumbled as he took up position on the bench. He still felt breathless at the least exertion, darn it. His arms were weak and his legs trembled as he sat down. 'But I've been winning prizes for my spuds – not to mention my carrots and onions – since before you two were born.'

Lizzie lifted her spade again, ready to take instruction. She didn't mind the heavy work or the stench of horse manure emanating from the steaming heap by the gate, but as the blade sliced into the earth she couldn't help smiling to herself. 'Other girls spend their Sunday mornings filing their nails or reading the latest Daphne du Maurier, not knee-deep in horse muck,' she commented.

'Or else sitting at their sewing machines making dresses for their weddings.' Connie gave her sister a meaningful glance as she stood up straight and eased the crick in her back. 'How are the preparations for the big day coming along, by the way?'

'Grand – St Joseph's is booked and we've got the date we were hoping for, the sixteenth of next month.'

'With the reception in the church hall afterwards?' Connie was to be Lizzie's maid of honour. They'd chosen a forget-me-not-blue satin for her, and the bride's dress would be made from salvaged parachute silk trimmed with lace. At home on Elliot Street the pattern pieces were pinned to the delicate fabric, ready to be cut out then stitched.

Lizzie's face glowed with a mixture of pleasure and nervous apprehension. 'Bill and I want to keep it small. He doesn't like a fuss.'

'Typical bloke,' Connie grunted as she returned to her methodical digging, placing her foot on the lug of the spade and using her full weight to ram the blade in deep before lifting and turning the glistening earth to one side. Her own pre-war wedding to John Bailey had been a quiet affair too. *My, but that seems a lifetime ago. How young I was, how blithe and hopeful.* 'I take it you've told Bill he'll have to wear a suit.'

'Don't worry, it's all in hand.' Lizzie's fiancé, Bill Evans, wasn't a suit-and-tie man – in fact, he was usually to be seen in his trawlerman's outfit of heavy Guernsey sweater, oilskin trousers and rubber boots. 'Yesterday I dragged him kicking and screaming to Moss Bros to get measured up.'

Connie grinned. 'Well done, you. Who'll take charge of catering for the do in the church hall?'

'I've asked Aunty Vera and her group of WI ladies. She's already started saving food coupons for the big day.'

'Damned rationing,' Connie grumbled. It had started in January 1940 with bacon, butter and sugar and had since spread to meat, tea, jam, biscuits, cheese, eggs, lard and milk. You name it; there was now a national shortage thanks to Herr Hitler's blasted blockades.

'Less yacking, you two,' Bert growled from his bench. 'At this rate those spuds will never get planted.'

'Something tells me I came along at the right moment.' The allotment gate swung open and Pamela Carr arrived, dressed for action in green corduroy trousers, white blouse and a fawn V-necked jumper. The Harrison sisters' fellow warden from the Air Raid Precautions team carried a garden fork and a pair of stout gardening gloves. So slight that it seemed a gust of wind would blow her clean over, Pamela's light brown, stylishly cut hair and wide grey-green eyes added to the impression that she would be more at home on a catwalk than a muddy allotment.

'Hey up, here comes the cavalry.' Fearing that there would be no end to the yacking now that a fresh volunteer had shown up, a sarcastic Bert retreated inside his shed.

'What can I do to help?' Pamela hovered by the edge of the Harrison plot. Every allotment within the fenced area behind St Joseph's School was freshly dug and mostly bare at this time of year, with prickly gooseberry bushes and raspberry canes cut hard back and brave rhubarb shoots just nosing through the dark, wet soil.

'You can spread some of that horse muck around the rhubarb for a start.' Connie knew that the smelly job would test the mettle of their more refined friend. 'There's a wheelbarrow by the shed.'

But Pamela didn't flinch as she fetched the barrow

then stuck her fork into the heap of fresh manure. 'Kelthorpe is due a visit from King George,' she announced from the far side of the allotment. 'Did you know that, Mr Harrison?'

'Since when?' Bert had emerged from the shed and stood with his gnarled hands in his overall pockets, watching the three girls work.

'It was on the wireless this morning. He and Queen Elizabeth are scheduled to make a tour of bombsites up and down the north-east coast – us included.'

'Poor old Kelthorpe.' Connie had reached the end of her trench and paused to gaze across the allotments at the spire of St Joseph's Church and beyond that to the dockside area, where a dozen or more steel cranes were visible against a clear blue sky. Many of the warehouses lining St Stephen's dock had been damaged during recent Luftwaffe attacks on vital North Sea ports. 'To be honest, I doubt that a visit from Bertie and his missis will do much to raise morale round here.'

'I'm not so sure,' Pamela argued. 'To my way of thinking, we're all in it together, rich and poor alike.'

'Not quite.' Connie stuck to her guns. 'The royals aren't forced to spend their nights cowering in damp, smelly air raid shelters like the rest of us. They swan off to Windsor at the first sign of trouble. And did you know that the Queen gets over twelve hundred clothing coupons per year compared with our measly sixty-six?'

'Now, now, you two.' Lizzie wasn't sure whose side she was on, though that many clothing coupons did seem a bit much. She crouched down to set the potatoes in the bottom of her trench.

Bert chipped in with his two penn'orth. 'Say what you like, the one we have on the throne now is a darned sight better than that useless article we had before. Him and that Wallis Simpson woman would've been worse than useless at a time like this.'

'That's true,' Connie conceded. 'Anyway, they've shipped him off to the Bahamas, out of harm's way.'

Pamela grew warm as she deftly forked manure into the barrow. 'Anderson's is on the list of places,' she said, referring to the timber yard where she worked as a secretary.

'What do you mean – what places?' Lizzie enquired.

'That's due a royal visit this coming Wednesday.'

'Oh my!' Lizzie stood up and shouted to her father, who had disappeared behind the shed. 'Did you hear that, Dad? Pamela here will most likely shake hands with the King!'

There was no reply so, mystified and a little worried, all three girls went to investigate. They found Bert standing stock-still with his back turned and both arms raised in warning.

'Stay where you are,' he muttered through gritted teeth, slowly lowering one hand to point to a tangle of brambles at the base of the paling fence that separated the allotments from the school yard. There, nestled among the thorny tendrils, inert and silent, was the unmistakable, cone-shaped nose of an unexploded bomb. 'Don't make any sudden movements.' Bert scarcely breathed. 'The least little thing could set if off.'

'Oh!' Pamela gasped. The ugly steel object made her blood run cold. 'How long has it been there, I wonder?'

'God knows.' Connie studied the sinister weapon. The last tip-and-run raid had taken place three nights before, when Jerry had offloaded his spare bombs over Kelthorpe on his way back to base after an attack on York.

'It looks like a Hefty Hermann,' Lizzie said, identifying the massive SC1000 – hundreds of kilograms of high explosives named after Field Marshal Göring.

'What do we do?' Pamela whispered.

'Don't move!' Bert insisted.

'One of us should telephone for a reconnaissance team.' Lizzie repressed a shudder. 'And the others ought to evacuate the nearby houses.'

After the first shock had passed, Connie's training as an air raid warden came into play and, despite being off duty, she quickly took charge. 'Back away slowly, Dad. That's right – one step at a time.'

'I know the drill,' he replied tersely. Bert had acted as head warden at the Gas Street sector post until illness had put a stop to that and Connie had taken over. He of all people was aware that the least vibration could cause the bomb to detonate and blow them all to kingdom come.

Pamela held her breath as she too edged backwards, feeling her way around the shed and waiting for the others to join her.

'So far so good,' Bert murmured. 'There's a telephone box on the corner of College Road. I'll get on the blower to the report centre. They'll send out the reconnaissance boys.'

'We three will raise the alarm and stand guard,' Connie decided. 'Pamela, head for the church – it'll be crammed with worshippers for the morning service. Tell the vicar to get everyone out pronto. Lizzie, knock on all the doors on Maypole Street and warn them.'

'What will you do?' Lizzie asked as Bert and Pamela set off on their urgent missions.

'I'll keep watch here.' Connie gritted her teeth and tried to ignore the tight band of fear that had formed around her chest. Luckily, no one else was on the allotments at present, but other keen gardeners were likely to show up as the morning wore on.

'You're sure?' Reluctant to leave Connie alone, Lizzie hesitated.

'Yes – go!' Connie pictured the sequence of events: houses within a quarter-of-a-mile radius would have to be evacuated and the area sealed off, perhaps for days, as the brave BROs carried out their work. Police would be needed to redirect traffic, while gas, water and electric supplies would be cut off. It would be a massive operation. Finally, lorry loads of sand would be brought in to muffle a controlled explosion of the deadly device. *Rather them than me.* Connie pictured the conditions for the disposal team – all volunteers like her – who would be risking life and limb. 'Go!' she repeated to Lizzie. 'There's not a moment to lose.'

So much for a quiet morning planting spuds! Reluctantly, Lizzie followed her sister's orders, crossing the street to begin knocking on the doors of the terraced houses that faced the allotments.

'What the heck . . .?' A red-faced man in shirtsleeves and a waistcoat answered Lizzie's heavy knock. He was collarless and in need of a shave.

'We're in the middle of our breakfasts, I'll have you know.'

'UXB,' Lizzie explained as she pointed frantically in the direction of the threat. 'SC1000, a big one. You and your family need to get out of here fast.'

'What's up?' the woman at the next house demanded as she flung open her door and glanced up and down the street. Three small children peeped out from behind her skirt, their faces smeared with the remains of toast and jam.

'UXB!' Lizzie told her. 'Go straight to the underground shelter on College Road. Don't stop to gather any belongings. As fast as you can.'

She hurried to the next house, knocked then waited impatiently.

'Hold your horses – no need to break the door down.' A frail, stooping woman in her eighties answered Lizzie's knock with a trembling hand and an anxious look. 'Yes, what is it?'

'There's an unexploded bomb on the allotments,' Lizzie explained carefully. 'Are you able to make your way to the shelter on College Road?'

'Don't worry, I'll look after her.' The harassed young woman from next door herded her three girls out on to the street. 'Come along, Jessie, take my arm. You'll be safe with us.'

A lump came into Lizzie's throat as she saw the small group make their way towards the shelter – the young and healthy assisting the old and infirm. But there was no time to stand and watch. On she went, knocking on doors and delivering bad news, praying that the street would be cleared without loss of life.

*

'Unexploded bomb!' Pamela burst through the doors of St Joseph's Church. Sunlight streamed in through the stained-glass windows and organ music rose to the rafters.

'"Holy, holy, holy, Lord God almighty! Early in the morning our song shall rise to thee."' A twelve-strong choir in crisp white choristers' smocks led the congregation, and the mellifluous sound of their singing drowned out Pamela's warning.

She ran down the aisle to intercept the vicar as he approached the pulpit. 'Stop the service. Empty the church. There's a bomb on the allotments.'

Gerald Greene looked at her in alarm. 'Are you sure?'

'"Merciful and mighty, God in three persons, blessed trinity."'

Pamela tugged desperately at the wide sleeve of Greene's surplice. 'Quite sure. You must evacuate everyone this instant!'

Sensing a disruption, the organist swivelled in her seat to see a slip of a girl in corduroy trousers and muddy wellington boots engaging in a rapid exchange with the vicar. Greene caught the musician's eye and signalled for her to cease playing.

'"Holy, holy, holy! All the saints adore thee . . ."' The pipes wheezed then fell silent and the choir and congregation trailed off. Dust motes danced in the sunlight and the brass eagle on the lectern gleamed bright. A hundred parishioners held their breath.

The vicar – a rotund man with a shiny, bald head and a florid complexion – appealed for calm. 'This is a red alert – follow procedure,' he instructed. 'Leave quietly by the main door. Don't run.'

'What the bloody hell for?'

'What's going on?'

'I didn't hear any sirens.'

Confusion reigned – was this a daytime raid or what? People nudged and pushed, muttered and swore.

Pamela ran up the steps into the pulpit and raised her voice above the hubbub. 'Listen, everyone! A bomb has been discovered on the allotments – a big one. I'm an ARP warden and we're taking steps to evacuate the area as a safety precaution. The bomb reconnaissance squad is on its way.' Her voice was loud and confident, though her body shook and her hands gripped the lectern until her knuckles turned white. 'You must take cover. Those who have Anderson shelters at home, go straight there and wait for the all-clear. For the rest of you, there'll be room in the College Road shelter.'

'Blimey O'Reilly – let me out of here!' A tall man in a grey mackintosh and brown bowler hat began to shove his way past women and children. A younger man in a similar coat and hat followed hard on his heels.

Pamela acted quickly by hurrying down from the pulpit and laying a hand on the older man's shoulder. 'Wait your turn,' she ordered sharply.

'Says who?' The older man, who had a stubborn, unmovable presence, shrugged her off and proceeded to push regardless.

'Says me.' Bert had ended his phone call to the town hall control centre then quickly made his way to the church, entering through the vestry door in time to hear Pamela issue clear instructions. Now he squared up to the bullies in the bowler hats. 'I know you two of old, always putting yourselves first.'

Though Ben Simmons and his son Lionel were both younger and more strongly built than Bert, they avoided the old man's gaze, ducking their heads and muttering as they backed down. Sullenly they took their places in what was now an orderly queue filing from the church two at a time.

Once outside, Pamela quickly shepherded the jittery congregation across the graveyard with its blackened tombstones and leaning stone crosses and from there on to College Road, past Barbieri's fish and chip shop and on again past the bombed-out *Gazette* building.

'Nearly there,' Pamela said briskly as they passed Cynthia's hair salon then Harrison's Bakery. At the entrance to the underground shelter, she joined Lizzie beneath arrows indicating ladies to one side and gentlemen to the other. A pungent smell of disinfectant and bleach emanated from the cubicles below.

'Careful there – mind how you go,' Lizzie said as she marshalled the residents of Maypole Street to the safety of the underground public conveniences.

'Thanks, love,' the woman with the three children murmured as she passed by with frail Jessie in tow.

'One at a time, no need to push,' Pamela cautioned Ben Simmons, who was once more elbowing others aside; every man for himself.

Bert brought up the rear. 'Save your breath,' he said with a scornful curl of his lip in Simmons's direction. Then he too descended the steps.

'All present and correct?' Pamela asked Lizzie, her

heart pounding. Their job was done. Now all they had to do was wait and pray.

'Except for Connie,' Lizzie reminded her friend with a nervous smile.

'Oh my goodness – Connie.'

Pamela and Lizzie's minds flew back to the allotments and to Lizzie's sister standing solitary guard over the deadly SC1000.

Every nerve in Connie's body was stretched to the limit as she watched the bomb reconnaissance vehicle screech to a halt at the end of Maypole Street. Five men clambered down from their lorry, dressed for action in dark blue battledress with stout canvas belts and steel helmets stencilled with the letter 'R' for Rescue. Connie raised both arms to signal the position of the bomb. 'Over here!'

The BROs climbed the allotment steps with the utmost caution. The leader of the specialist team – a middle-aged chap with short grey hair, glasses and a lantern jaw – ordered Connie to back away from the danger zone.

'Gently does it,' he said, scarcely moving his lips. 'By Jove!' he breathed when he saw the size of the problem nestled among the brambles. 'A Hefty Hermann – Jerry meant business, all right.'

'St Joseph's Church and Maypole Street are being evacuated to the College Road shelter,' Connie reported. Her minutes on guard had seemed like hours, each second ratcheting up the tension until it reached an almost unbearable level. She'd stared at three crows perched in the bare treetops overlooking the allotments, desperate for the ominous-looking birds to stay where they were, aware that one beat of their wings, a single disturbance of the air currents surrounding the bomb, could bring disaster.

'It's a good job you've got your head screwed on. You're not an ARP girl, by any chance?'

She nodded. 'I'm Connie Bailey, head warden at the Gas Street post.'

'I'm Charlie Bishop. I know your dad.' The head of the reconnaissance squad had his eyes fixed on the UXB while the rest of the team stood by the pile of horse manure, awaiting instructions. 'We'll need bobbies to divert traffic,' he continued coolly. 'The whole of Maypole Street and a section of College Road will have to be cordoned off. Have you got that?'

Connie nodded again. 'I'll go straight to the police station and pass on the message.'

'Tell them we'll detonate the bomb in situ – it's too risky to attempt to move it. We'll dig trenches around it and fill them with sand.'

Hearing this, two of the men hurried back to their lorry to fetch spades and pickaxes.

'Right you are.' Bishop's tone made it clear that it was time for Connie to make herself scarce. 'Plenty of sand,' he added as an afterthought. 'From Dixon's builders' yard. Can you organize that for us?'

'Leave it to me,' she assured him, descending the steps two at a time. She passed the parked lorry and ran on along a deserted Maypole Street towards the Gladstone Square police station. A glance over her shoulder told her that the reconnaissance team was already at work on the trench, with helmets off and sleeves rolled up. *A thousand times rather them than me,* she thought again as she sprinted on. One false move, one jarring strike of the spade against stone, one fatal vibration . . . Connie breathed hard as she ran to deliver her messages. *What a way to spend a Sunday morning! When, oh when, will the bombs stop falling? Will our spuds get planted this spring and will the good folk of Kelthorpe be able to breathe easy ever again?*

Five large barrage balloons – serene and beautiful – were strung across the mouth of the Kell estuary, reflecting the warm pink light of the setting sun. They were tethered by steel cables to Scammell winches mounted on the decks of old river barges securely anchored a quarter of a mile offshore and were designed to ward off German dive-bombers who flew in low to wreak havoc on the small fishing port and the docks close by. The balloons also discouraged enemy attempts to lay mines in the estuary; they had proved successful in this respect at least.

'Listen to that.' It was later that same evening and Lizzie cupped a hand around her ear to pick up the tune made by the wind whistling against the taut cables. The high, haunting sound sent a shiver down her spine.

Turning up their collars as a protection against the chilly breeze, Pamela and Connie continued to chat.

'Honestly, some people!' Connie was saying. Pamela had described how the Simmons pair had attempted to barge their way to the front of the queue earlier that day and Connie's response was suitably irate.

Lizzie added to the picture. 'They were the limit,

pushing and shoving their way down the steps even though I'd warned them not to.'

Pamela frowned at the memory. 'I'd a good mind to go down after them and order them back up to pavement level, see how they'd have liked that.'

'Listen!' Lizzie said again. The silver blimps fascinated her; the way they tugged at their cables and rolled and dipped like whales in a tempestuous sea.

Connie paid attention at last. 'I don't like them,' she said with a frown. 'All that hydrogen hovering over us – it's enough to give you the heebie-jeebies.'

'But they're amazing,' Lizzie protested. She'd read up about the blimps in a Ministry of War pamphlet. 'Made of two-ply, rubber-proofed Egyptian cotton finished with aluminium powder to give them that sheen. They're the length of three cricket pitches, did you know, and filled with twenty thousand cubic feet—'

'That's enough, Einstein.' Connie cut her sister off in mid-sentence. 'Picture something that size being struck by lightning or by enemy gunfire. Boom!'

Pamela studied the silent dirigibles tugging and straining at their cables. 'I agree with Lizzie – they are beautiful,' she decided. 'And I hear that the RAF is going to install two of the LZ variety on the headland.'

Pausing for a moment on the broad, straight promenade where they strolled, Connie and Lizzie glanced up at the rocky, heather-covered promontory that separated the old town from the new. 'LZ?' Connie queried.

'Low Zone. I only know because Uncle Hugh has offered billets to two RAF men at Sunrise. His house is on the seafront and it's big enough to take in a couple of extra lodgers. They'll be on hand to operate the balloons whenever there's a yellow alert.'

'Can't we talk about something more cheerful?' Lizzie came between Pamela and Connie and linked arms. 'Here we are dressed up in our Sunday best on a glorious sunny evening.' Connie in her bright red coat and matching beret, Pamela in a blouson-style green windcheater and Lizzie risking a summery pale blue cardigan over a floral printed frock.

'You mean, ignore the blimps and the barbed wire and pillboxes lining the beach and the fact that there's a Hefty Hermann still ticking away on Dad's allotment?' The morning's events had left Connie feeling unusually down in the dumps.

'Yes, and think about Tom waiting for you in the Harbourmaster's Inn instead. That should cheer you up.' Lizzie winked at Pamela and waited for her sister's reaction.

At the mention of her sweetheart's name Connie's expression brightened and her pace increased dramatically. She strode on along the prom, past the bombed ruins of the Royal Hotel – now a giant heap of burned roof beams, broken slates and bricks – towards the pub. The wind caught her hair and a new, eager light appeared in her brown eyes. 'And while we're at it, let's hear more details about your nuptials,' she reminded Lizzie. 'Who's doing the flowers for you? Do you still want a bouquet of pink carnations? And why not borrow my white satin shoes that I got married to John in to save on coupons?'

Lizzie shook her head. 'Aunty Vera's in charge of

flowers as well as food. She says she can get hold of pink carnations for my bouquet. And no ta – your feet are a size bigger than mine.'

'You could pad the toes with tissue paper,' Pamela suggested. 'Connie's shoes could be your "something borrowed".'

'But they might bring me bad luck.' Connie's marriage to John Bailey had been far from happy and had ended with his tragic death in an accident at the timber yard. 'No thanks, Con – it's new shoes for me, if it's all the same to you.'

'Have it your way.' Reaching the wide glass door of the Harbourmaster's, Connie swanned in ahead of Pamela and Lizzie to find Bill Evans, Fred Miller and Tom Rose propping up the bar.

Tom turned his head and gave Connie his broadest smile. He strode towards her and greeted her with a kiss.

Spying Pamela, Fred followed suit, putting his arm around her waist to guide her in his gentlemanly way to a table by the window.

And then came Bill: Lizzie's Bill, with his long, loping stride and smiling eyes and with one unruly dark lock of hair straying down over his forehead. 'What kept you?' he asked as he took her hand. Eyes for her and no one else, his one and only.

'We're not late,' Lizzie insisted, her heart racing at the sight of her beloved. 'We're bang on time.'

'What will everyone have to drink?' Tom stepped up promptly to take orders.

As the sun sank below the headland, on this beautiful Sunday evening in spring, the three air raid girls sat with their drinks and their sweethearts in the smartest bar in town, at a table with a view of the sparkling sea – a trio of young couples in love. What better way than this to bring an eventful day to a close?

CHAPTER TWO

It was the pearl necklace that caught Pamela's attention – a triple string nestling above Queen Elizabeth's ample bosom. Each perfect pearl glinted in the morning sun as she accompanied her husband, His Majesty King George VI, decked out in his army uniform with all the bells and whistles but looking serious and gaunt. The Queen wore a lilac coat edged with bands of deeper purple. Her hat was perched precariously on the side of her head, its upturned brim held in place by a spray of silk flowers. She had mauve kidskin gloves, a matching clutch bag and shoes – all perfectly coordinated.

Pamela had been taught to curtsey by her mother. 'Place your weight on your right foot, left foot tucked in behind – just a small dip and quickly up again.' Edith Carr had made sure to read up on royal etiquette and her instructions had been specific. 'Don't speak unless spoken to.'

Come the hour, Pamela was prepared. She'd dressed in her smart royal-blue two-piece with white peep-toed shoes, and taken special care with her hair and make-up. Now she stood next to her uncle, the owner of Anderson's timber yard. As the King and Queen approached across the asphalt yard, escorted by high-ranking police officers and anonymous men in suits, she was struck by how small and dainty the Queen was in real life as opposed to the close-up pictures you saw in newspapers. Her complexion was pale and flawless, her dark hair carefully curled beneath the asymmetric hat.

The King shook hands with Hugh Anderson. He asked about damage to the yard – since German bombing had commenced two and a half years earlier, one of the cranes had been destroyed and several consignments of valuable pitch pine from Scandinavia set on fire. The private rail terminal shared with Freeman's grain yard had been out of action for a week and a storeroom overlooking the dock had been damaged beyond repair. Fortunately, Anderson's vast cutting shed and the brick-built office block had not so far taken a direct hit.

'Very good.' The King nodded, then an aide gestured for Hugh to escort His Majesty down the line.

'My secretary, Pamela Carr; my office manager, Harold Carr; my bookkeeper, Fred Miller; my foreman, Keith Nelson . . .'

Queen Elizabeth, following hard on her husband's heels, smiled sweetly at Pamela but didn't speak. It was just as well – nerves had scrambled Pamela's brain and she could scarcely have summoned a sensible reply.

'What would I have said?' she asked Fred later, after the royal personages and their entourage had moved on from the docks to inspect Kelthorpe's fish market and harbour. Fred and Pamela sat in the canteen dissecting the morning's events over a plate of stew and dumplings. 'I just about managed to curtsey without falling over.'

Fred grinned as he gestured with his knife towards the rows of crowded, noisy tables. 'The whole place is abuzz. Frankly, I've never understood the way the English continue to kowtow to the monarchy.' His early upbringing in Berlin had been free from all that rigmarole. 'We got rid of our Kaiser twenty-odd years ago.'

'Yes, and look what you got in his place.' Fred's mention of his German childhood had taken Pamela by surprise. For weeks after they'd met, he'd kept his status as an enemy alien a closely guarded secret; even now he rarely talked about it.

Their paths had first crossed when they'd shared a boarding house on Elliot Street. Pamela's handsome fellow lodger had struck her as polite but guarded; they'd scarcely got beyond a formal good morning and good evening before a chance meeting in the town library had revealed a shared love of reading. After that, there had been a few shy moves towards romance – a Sunday walk to local landmark, Raynard's Folly; a ride along the coast road on borrowed bikes and a first tender kiss.

'What a catch!' Connie had declared during one of her, Lizzie and Pamela's cosy confessionals. 'Fred Miller is better looking than any of the current crop of film stars. Watch out, William Holden!'

'Do you like him?' Lizzie had asked Pamela more seriously.

'He's clever and well mannered,' she'd replied. And Connie was right – Fred was extremely handsome, with his dark hair, clean-cut features and a particular, searching way of looking at you as if your answers to his questions mattered.

'Yes, but do you actually *like* him?' Lizzie had persisted.

At that time no one in Kelthorpe had known Fred's background – how his Jewish family had been forced to abandon their jewellery business in the German capital and flee from the Nazi regime, how they'd sought refuge in London where they'd fallen foul of Oswald Mosley and his Blackshirts. The family's bid to escape their past had ended in tragedy: Fred's mother and father had died in a fire started by the fascists and Fred had narrowly escaped with his life. After that he'd parcelled up his grief and attempted to wipe the slate clean – Friedrich Müller had become Fred Miller and he'd headed north to find work at Hugh Anderson's timber yard. He quickly became a perfect employee: good with figures, quiet, meticulous and hard-working.

'I like him a lot,' Pamela had declared shyly.

'Your uncle was on tenterhooks too,' Fred observed now over a rice pudding dessert. 'But in the event, everything went perfectly – he impressed the King with his detailed knowledge of imports from Sweden and he charmed the Queen by venturing a question about the princesses Elizabeth and Margaret Rose.'

'It was a big moment for him.' As the klaxon signalled the end of the dinner break, workers rushed to deposit crockery and cutlery on the trolley by the door. 'Duty calls,' Pamela said with a smile. 'Uncle Hugh has asked to see me at one o'clock on the dot – I'd better not be late.'

She and Fred joined the hurly-burly at the exit. 'I'm not working at the report and control centre tonight. How about you – are you free?'

'Sorry – no. I have a last-minute evening shift at Gas Street. Connie needs extra wardens to patrol Maypole Street.'

'Ah, yes – the SC1000.' Fred knew that the bomb squad were still working to decommission the dangerous UXB that Bert Harrison had discovered the previous day. 'After your shift finishes, perhaps?'

'Yes,' she agreed gladly. 'I'll drop in at Sunrise for half an hour.'

There was a brief exchange of affectionate smiles and a murmured 'see you later' as the young lovers went their separate ways.

'Ah, Pamela.' Hugh Anderson looked up from his desk and motioned for her to sit. He cut quite a dash in his pinstripe suit and starched white collar, with his thick grey hair and moustache freshly trimmed and a diamond and gold pin glittering against a dark red silk tie. 'I've been considering your position,' he began.

Perched on the edge of her seat, Pamela drew herself upright. Was this a good thing or not?

'How long have you worked here as my secretary?'

'A little over five months.'

'And you had a baptism of fire, if I remember rightly.'

'Yes.' There'd been spiteful gossip to contend with; accusations that she'd only been given the job because of family connections, and worse, that she was a despicable traitor, the lowest of the low, for associating with Fred Miller who turned out to be

Friedrich Müller and an enemy alien. There'd been threats and more than one brutal attack in broad daylight.

'But the situation has eased?'

'Yes.' Since Hugh's bossy and snide senior secretary Betty Holroyd had handed in her notice, the atmosphere had improved no end.

'It strikes me that you've had to take on the workload of two people,' Hugh went on. 'Which is why I've put an advert in this week's *Kelthorpe Gazette* for a replacement secretary.'

'I see.' Secretly, Pamela had enjoyed having an office to herself and didn't relish the prospect of another Betty ruling the roost.

'No need to look so crestfallen,' Hugh assured her. 'My intention is to promote you to the position of senior secretary and to put a junior girl under you.'

Pamela's eyes widened. 'Oh, Uncle Hugh – I mean, Mr Anderson – that would be marvellous.' Just wait until she told Fred, and her mother and father, and Lizzie and Connie! Excitement made her light-headed and she took in little of what followed.

'This is not a question of favouritism,' Hugh continued. 'It's something you fully deserve. The promotion will come with an increase in salary.'

Better and better! She clasped her hands tightly in her lap.

Hugh's face relaxed into a smile. 'Don't you want to know by how much?'

'Yes, please!' It hardly mattered; she would have taken on more responsibility without a pay rise. But it was important to seem professional.

'How does an extra seven shillings and sixpence a week sound?' he asked.

'It sounds marvellous,' she enthused as her uncle stood up and reached over the wide desk with an outstretched hand. She shook it firmly before making for the door.

'Make sure you don't let me down.' Hugh's brief parting shot echoed in Pamela's head as she swiftly made her way along the narrow corridor and into her cramped and cluttered office. There were invoices to be sent, requests for late payments to be made, wage slips to prepare; a whole host of things to be done before she was free to share the news of her good fortune.

'Our navy lads bagged another U-boat earlier this week,' Tom informed Connie on their way to the Gas Street post. As a part-time volunteer for the Royal Naval Patrol Service he paid close attention to battleship activity in the North Sea. 'U207, to be precise.'

'Good riddance.' She felt no scrap of sympathy for the German submarine's doomed crew. 'I read in the *Daily Express* that poor old Malta is still taking a dreadful beating, so we needed some good news to cheer us up.'

Tom squeezed her hand and smiled. 'I reckon this bunfight will carry on for a while yet, even with the Yanks on our side.' He was a level-headed realist – a perfect foil to Connie's more fiery nature – and he'd seen enough action while carrying out RNPS minesweeping duties to know that the Allies were in for a long haul. Besides, being hit by a torpedo and watching your boat and your best pal disappear beneath the waves was an experience that stayed with you. For days afterwards, Tom had believed that Bill was drowned. He and Connie had had all on to console a grief-stricken Lizzie, and then when it turned out that Bill had resurfaced and managed to cling to an upturned lifeboat before being rescued by a Dutch trawler, there had been enormous relief. *Sea Knight* was gone for good, leaving both Tom and Bill adrift as far as war service was concerned, so Tom had rejoined the Air Raid Precautions team as a warden and Bill had taken up his first-aider role once more.

'You may be right – you usually are,' Connie conceded as they rounded the corner of King Edward Street and saw Pamela emerge from her boarding house wearing ARP battledress and ski cap and with a gas mask slung over her shoulder.

They quickened their pace to catch up with her.

'What have you got to look so cheerful about?' Connie asked after they'd exchanged greetings.

'Am I?'

'Yes, like the cat that got the cream.'

The trio hurried on towards Maypole Street, where they were forced to make a detour down an alleyway to avoid the BRO blockade. The dark ginnel smelled of damp bricks and stale urine and was a dumping ground for a pram without wheels and a dustbin overflowing with rotting rubbish. 'Damn, I'd forgotten about the Hefty Hermann,' Tom muttered.

Pamela's smile broadened in response to Connie's question. 'I've been promoted at work, that's why I'm smiling.'

'Good for you.' Tom was genuinely pleased for her. 'You deserve it.'

'Have you told Fred?' Connie asked.

'Not yet. I'm seeing him later tonight.'

'And how will you celebrate, I wonder?' Connie's wink was loaded with innuendo.

Pamela hid her blushes by rushing on ahead.

They emerged from the ginnel opposite the gasworks – an ugly conglomeration of buildings comprising a brick-built retort house, massive condenser pipes and a purifier building, all dominated by a giant metal gasometer where the coal gas was stored. From here it was a brisk five-minute walk past warehouses and Dixon's builders' merchants to the sector post.

'It's not often that you shake hands with royalty and receive a pay rise all in one day,' Connie continued to tease. 'Let's hope you don't get too big for your boots.'

'Take no notice.' Tom stood up for Pamela. 'Of you three girls, you're the one with your feet most firmly on the ground.'

'Tom Rose, what are you saying?' Connie pretended to be offended. 'Are you calling me and my sister flighty flibbertigibbets?'

'I wouldn't dare,' he said with a chuckle as they approached the entrance to the old cobbler's shop that had been requisitioned by the ARP and now served as a sector post.

Pamela stopped outside the boarded-up shop window, next to a barrier of sandbags and a blackout-time sign that had to be altered on a daily basis. As the evenings lengthened, so the white hands on the clock face crept forward. A tattered Union Jack fluttered above the door: a gesture of defiance that had hung there since Christmas. 'After you, Head Warden Bailey,' she told Connie with an exaggerated salute.

'You're late.' The barked greeting from daytime head warden Brian Bellamy wiped the smiles off their faces. He shoved a pile of paperwork across the shop counter towards Connie then reached for his cap hanging from a hook behind him.

'Only a minute or two.' Connie was nettled by Bellamy's accusatory stare. He was one of the old guard who had served on the Western Front in the Great War and had a tendency to lord it over younger members of the Civil Defence teams. Overweight and self-important, he made a point of picking on women volunteers in particular; in his view, female wardens couldn't be relied upon not to faint at the sight of blood, they behaved illogically and were prone to panic in an emergency, on top of which they didn't have the requisite brawn to shift rubble or raise casualties from the debris of their bombed homes. All the usual out-of-date prejudices were rolled together in one unattractive, portly package.

'Here's the latest from report and control.' Bellamy thrust a final piece of paper at Connie. 'The roadblock at the end of Valley Road has been removed but the Leisure Gardens are still closed until further notice. Looters have been spotted in the grounds of the Royal Hotel.'

Hiding her irritation, Connie continued the takeover while Tom and Pamela sidled past Bellamy into the small storeroom at the back where helmets, eye shields, gauntlets, torches, axes and rattles were kept. As wardens, the handbook instructed them that they must be jacks of all trades, ready to guide the public to shelters in the event of an attack, to assist with casualties, to carry messages between sector posts speedily and with clarity, and, above all, to set an example of coolness and steadiness.

'Let's hope those blimps do their job this evening.' Tom chose a pair of rubber boots and a helmet from the racks. The barrage balloons were relatively new additions to the defence measures put in place in Kelthorpe, ordered there by the head of RAF Balloon Command, Air Marshal Gossage, because the Yorkshire port was now considered a key Luftwaffe target. 'I fancy a quiet night checking household registers and such like.'

'There are worse things than being bored,' Pamela agreed.

After Connie had exchanged curt goodbyes with Bellamy, she poked her head into the storeroom. 'Honestly, he's the limit!' she exclaimed. 'I've a good mind to tell the pompous so-and-so a few home truths.'

'Such as?' Tom loved to see Connie fired up: as she flung her arms wide in exasperation her beautiful face came alive. She seemed to fizz with energy.

'Such as, women wardens are better than men in many cases.'

'Thanks a lot.' It was Tom's turn to seem put out.

'You know I don't mean you.' Connie had seen the man she loved run into blazing buildings without a second's hesitation and deal with incendiary bombs as if they were mere jumping jacks on Guy Fawkes

30

Night. 'But we women get to the heart of a situation faster than men do. When we go into a house, we see straight away who was there when the bomb dropped and whereabouts in the building they were. It's little details that tell you. For instance, if the kettle's on the hob we know that the occupants were downstairs and hadn't gone to bed. If there's a cot in the bedroom, there must be a baby somewhere.'

'Get it off your chest, why don't you?' If they hadn't been on duty this was the moment when Tom would have grabbed Connie by the waist and showered her with kisses.

Sounds from the main shop told them that other wardens had arrived. Connie heaved an exasperated sigh then left the storeroom and began to dish out tasks for the evening: Eddie Fraser was to check that all phone boxes in the district were in working order, while his brother Simon had the job of updating the list of recent arrivals at the Women's Voluntary Service centre next to the grammar school. 'And, Pamela, I'm putting you on sentry duty at the entrance to the Leisure Gardens.'

'What about me?' As the others set off, Tom waited patiently for his instructions.

'Check the grounds of the Royal, would you? Brian mentioned looters in the vicinity.'

Tom pictured the unlit, lonely walk around the base of the headland with a sheer cliff looming overhead, then his arrival at the start of the broad esplanade with its starlit view of the open sea. A little way along he would reach what was left of the town's premier hotel. 'What are the looters looking for?' he wondered aloud.

31

Connie shrugged as she picked up the telephone. 'Scrap metal, perhaps.' Pausing before making the call, she blew Tom a kiss. 'Your place or mine later on?'

'Mine,' he decided as he set off. 'And by the way, I'll have some good news of my own to share soon.'

'Tom Rose, that's not fair.' Connie replaced the receiver in its cradle then rushed out from behind the counter to prevent him from leaving. 'Tell me now!'

'No time – I have looters to apprehend,' he teased, with the twinkle of gentle humour that she loved. 'You'll just have to wait and see.'

Metal water bottle – tick. Haversack containing small, medium and large dressings – tick. Rubber gloves – tick. Four small splints . . . Where the heck were they kept? Lizzie searched the high shelves in the storeroom of her first-aid post until she discovered the wooden splints. Six card labels and an indelible pencil – tick. Last but not least, a small pair of scissors attached to a lanyard, which she strung around her neck.

'Ready?' Bill asked. He'd arrived at the ambulance depot on King Edward Street with a few minutes to spare before the start of his shift, leaving him enough time to check the contents of the ambulance: four metal stretchers, eight blankets, reserve haversack.

'Yes, all present and correct.' Slinging the rucksack containing her kit over her shoulder, Lizzie hurried to take up position behind the wheel of the specially adapted Bedford van parked in the yard of a disused brewery that currently served as a first-aid post for Kelthorpe Old Town. The yard was overgrown with weeds, and the soot-stained brewery building was covered in ivy. A pile of wooden barrels and two carts that had once been pulled by pairs of magnificent dray horses had been left to decay. Only a small annexe was in use, staffed by the doctor and nurse who oversaw a team of first-aider volunteers.

Bill climbed in beside Lizzie. 'Hang it!' he declared before jumping down again and sprinting across the yard to grab the King's harness proffered by the nurse in charge. Taking the canvas and leather contraption used to keep unconscious or badly wounded patients safely strapped in place, he loped back again, opening up the back door of the ambulance and tucking the harness under a metal bench. 'My name would have been mud if I'd left that behind.'

'Where to?' Lizzie turned on the engine.

'Valley Road. There's an old chap at number eighteen who's tumbled out of bed. He needs to be taken to hospital. By the sound of things, we're going to need that harness.'

She nodded then steered her ambulance under the wide brick archway on to the cobbled street. It wasn't unusual for ARP vehicles to be used in domestic incidents such as this. She only hoped that the injury wasn't too bad and could be easily dealt with by her and Bill.

Meanwhile, dusk was falling and the blackout coming into force.

'Put that light out!' The street wardens' familiar cry rang out from the far end of the street. Blinds were drawn and the pavements fell silent as inhabitants disappeared inside their houses.

The route took Lizzie and Bill through the town square then on along College Road towards Valley Road. Bill smiled to himself at the sight of the ruby and diamond ring on Lizzie's slender finger. It was still hard to believe that she'd said yes to tying the knot. Blimey; the wedding was less than six short weeks away – a fact brought home to Bill when she'd dragged him off to Moss Bros for a fitting.

'What are you grinning at?' she challenged as she stopped at a junction.

'You. Us,' he replied enigmatically. A yes from Lizzie Harrison – the prettiest, sweetest, kindest girl for miles around. And modest with it: he'd learned not to compliment her on how beautiful she was because she said it embarrassed her. She would blush to high heaven and grow flustered then change the subject. So, drop the flattery – Bill would just kiss her instead. Kind? Yes, she would just about accept that. But sweet? No.

'Sugar is sweet,' she'd pointed out on one occasion. 'And so are syrup and honey. You can easily overdo sweetness if you're not careful.' Lizzie preferred to see herself as a girl in the centre of the action who could keep calm in any crisis and who never made a fuss. Bill didn't argue with that; it was one of the reasons he'd fallen in love with Lizzie Harrison. That and her deep brown eyes, her wild, wavy hair, her tender touch. His hand strayed towards her thigh and the sway of the van as it turned on to Valley Road brought his shoulder into contact with hers.

'I'm expecting a bit of good news,' he dropped in casually.

'Oh?' Lizzie pulled on the handbrake outside number 18: a tall, imposing terraced house over-looking the Leisure Gardens.

'Yes, fingers crossed.'

'Well?'

'Forget I said that.' He frowned and pursed his lips. 'I promised Tom I'd keep my trap shut until the deal's done.'

'What's Tom got to do with anything?'

'You'll see,' Bill promised as he jumped down on to the pavement.

Lizzie followed him up the garden path. 'Why mention it if you're not going to tell me?'

He knocked on the door. 'Sorry, it just slipped out.'

'That's not fair.' She clicked her tongue against her teeth then resigned herself to being kept in the dark. *All in good time,* she promised herself.

The door opened and a prim, harassed-looking housekeeper let them in. 'Mr Goodman is upstairs, second door on your right,' she told them in clipped tones. 'Be warned, the old devil swears like a trooper when he's had too much to drink. His room smells like a brewery at present, so watch out.'

CHAPTER THREE

Leading Aircraftman Reggie Nolan breezed up the front path of Sunrise and rapped sharply on 'the wide-panelled door. Chirpy and smart in his RAF battledress, with a starched white collar and dark tie, he thrust out his chest and waited for a response. Close behind him, Aircraftman Sidney Donne took in the neatly maintained lawns and shrubberies then the intricate stained glass of the windows to either side of the door.

'Not bad,' Sid remarked, dropping his heavy canvas kitbag with a thump before flicking his cigarette on to the tarmac path and grinding it underfoot.

'We've known worse billets,' Reggie agreed, his mouth twitching impatiently beneath his dark moustache. The sooner they got settled in the more time they'd have for exploring this godforsaken northern town and locating the best watering holes. He anticipated finding at least a couple of pubs that weren't too bad, though Kelthorpe was definitely the back of beyond and distinctly lacking in night life, from what he'd seen en route from the railway station.

'Are you sure this is the right house?' Sid glanced over his shoulder and glimpsed the promenade through the open gate and the grey, flat expanse of sea beyond. The dull day and a long train journey from their squadron base in Norfolk had dampened his spirits. 'They're taking their bloody time if it is.'

Reggie knocked again. Sounds came from inside the house, then a slim, middle-aged woman in a neat grey twinset adorned with a pearl brooch opened the door.

'Yes?' Edith enquired with an edge of suspicion.

'Is this Hugh Anderson's house?' Reggie didn't bother with polite preliminaries.

Taking in the callers' RAF uniforms, Edith relaxed. 'It is indeed. My brother has been unavoidably detained on a business matter. My name is Edith Carr. You must be the two airmen to whom Hugh has kindly offered rooms.'

Swallowed a blooming dictionary! was Reggie's first impression of Edith. That and the fact that her thin face was pinched into an expression of superiority. *Don't go looking down your nose at me, lady*, was his second swift thought. He gave Sid a surreptitious nudge with his elbow. 'That's right,' he confirmed with a self-important air. 'We've been put in charge of the two new kite balloons expected later today. We're the chaps who'll make them ready whenever there's an alert and we bed them down again after an attack.'

Sid stepped forward. 'I'm Sidney Donne and this here is Reggie Nolan. Can you show us to our quarters?'

'By all means. Your rooms are in the attic. Please follow me.' Finding the men too rough and ready for her taste – the smaller one with the puffed-out chest reminded her of a cocky robin redbreast, and his taller, lankier and more lugubrious companion had a well nigh impenetrable sing-song accent – Edith led them across the hallway and up the stairs to the first-floor landing where Fred came out of his room as they were passing his door. Names were exchanged and hands shaken.

'I hope you soon settle in,' Fred told the two RAF men. He wore a tweed jacket and woollen scarf and was setting out to meet Pamela for a brisk morning walk along the prom. 'Sunrise is handy for Musgrave Street – that's the road up to the top of the headland where your LZs will be situated.'

Sid gave a suspicious frown. 'Says who?' he muttered.

'It's common knowledge,' Fred assured him. 'Besides, I'm an ARP executive officer in the town hall control centre so I get plenty of advance warning of any new defence measures that Balloon Command puts in place. It was me who suggested to Mr Anderson that we could find billets for you here.'

'Did you now?' The new lodgers took their time to size Fred up and in the end it was Reggie who broke the silence. 'It's a cut above the usual Nissen hut barracks, I'll give you that. Now then, Fred – you seem to know your way around. I don't suppose you can tip us the wink about the best places to find a decent pint and a pretty girl or two?'

Edith stiffened and clasped her hands across her waist.

'Try the Anchor overlooking the harbour,' Fred suggested. 'The beer there is first class.'

'And the girls?' Reggie persisted with his cheeky line of enquiry.

'Er-hum!' Edith cleared her throat. 'This way, gentlemen.' Without giving Fred time to shape a reply, she led Sid and Reggie up a second flight of stairs then gestured towards two open doors to small attic rooms originally intended for servants. Each contained a single bed and was plainly but adequately furnished with a utility-style wardrobe and a chest of drawers. An easy chair had been placed beside a small fireplace and under the sky-light there was a washstand complete with bowl and pitcher. 'Take your pick,' Edith invited. 'The beds are freshly made and there are towels on the wash-stand. The house bathroom and WC are down on the first floor.'

With a cheery thank you, Reggie promptly opted for the nearest room. Sid nodded and disappeared without a word into the second one.

'I hope Hugh has laid down some house rules for them to follow,' Edith said to Fred as she descended the stairs. 'Otherwise I envisage noisy comings and goings at all times of the day and night.'

'Don't worry – I'll keep an eye on things,' Fred promised.

'Talking of Hugh . . .' Edith pricked up her ears at the sound of her brother's car crunching up the gravel drive. She hurried down to greet him as he entered the house. 'Your RAF men are here,' she announced. 'They're scarcely what I expected.' To her, the Royal Air Force meant clean-cut, upright young officers in smart barathea uniforms with stripes on their arms and eagle-wing insignias above their breast pockets.

Fred had followed her downstairs. 'We have a

leading aircraftman and an aircraftman first class,' he informed Hugh. 'Non-commissioned ranks.'

'Very good.' Taking off his hat and coat, Hugh fended off his sister's no doubt lengthy critique of the new lodgers by making straight for his study. 'Forgive me – I must make a telephone call.'

'I'm sorry for you, Fred dear.' Edith sighed and patted his hand. 'You're used to peace and quiet.'

'I don't mind at all.' His own stay at Sunrise had begun after he'd been attacked and badly beaten by a gang of thugs who had set upon him on the lonely footpath at the base of the headland. Barely conscious, Fred had managed to crawl as far as Hugh Anderson's house, where he'd collapsed on the doorstep. Hugh had taken Fred in and had invited him to stay on after his recovery. An affectionate bond had quickly formed between the two men and they were now more like father and son than employer and employee. 'I'm glad that the spare rooms are being put to good use.'

Unconvinced, Edith sighed again. 'Come across to the bungalow whenever you like, dear. You're always welcome.'

Fred opened the door then stood aside and watched her cross the lawn to the modern single-storey building where she and Harold had taken up residence after their own house on Musgrave Street had been destroyed during a bombing raid. *Deep breath,* he told himself. Edith's snobbishness was hard to take but there was a kind and loyal side to Pamela's mother as well. Tying his scarf into a loose knot, he braced himself for a breezy walk along the seafront.

And here was Pamela, right on time, stepping out past the wrought-iron shelter where an elderly woman with two Cairn terriers sat gazing out to sea. Pamela waved gaily and broke into a run when she saw him.

'You look wonderful,' Fred told her above the yapping of the dogs as they embraced. *Feel wonderful, smell wonderful . . . what a lucky chap I am.*

'Do you like the hat?' She tapped her recent purchase, a stylish apple-green beret adorned with a crimson felt rosette.

'It's wonderful.' *Wunderbar, herrlich, wunderschön.* Fred seized her hand and they began to walk along the busy promenade.

The breeze caught at the skirt of the floral dress that Pamela had chosen to match the beret. Conscious that she was showing too much leg, she flapped at the skirt with her free hand. 'And the shoes?' she asked. 'I borrowed them from Lizzie. What do you think?'

'Won-der-ful.' Fred kissed her quickly on the cheek between each syllable.

'Everything is wonderful with you today!'

'Because I'm with the girl of my dreams,' he declared with a final kiss. 'And because it's our day off and we don't have a care in the world.'

Hand in hand, the young couple stopped to lean against the promenade railing and gaze out to sea. Grey clouds were lifting and patches of blue appearing. The tide was coming in and waves crashed against the headland and on to the sandy shore of the bay to the north. Shrieking herring gulls circled overhead, swooping down to steal a picnicking family's sandwiches – peck-peck with their fierce, bright orange beaks, flap-flap with their strong wings, then off again with their spoils. Only the long coils of barbed wire and a row of concrete pillboxes ranged along the beach as far as the eye could see reminded Fred and Pamela that the world was not as carefree as they would have wished.

When the couple turned to retrace their steps, movement on the top of the craggy headland caught their attention. A lorry had pulled up and a group of men had started to unload bags of sand and cement.

'Who are they? What are they doing?' Curious, Pamela turned to Fred for an answer.

'It's the RAF. They're here to build storm beds for the new LZs.'

'Tell me in plain English,' a puzzled Pamela demanded.

'Storm beds are sturdy slabs with metal bars set into the concrete. It's for when there's a high wind – the balloons must be lowered to ground level then anchored to the slabs with the nose facing into the wind. We don't want something that size and filled with highly flammable hydrogen floating free over Kelthorpe.'

Recalling Connie's similar fears, Pamela shuddered. 'No, quite right.'

'They'll have to wait for the concrete to set before they attach the balloons. In a couple of days they should be up and running.' Fred went on to tell her about the arrival of Reggie and Sid. 'You remember that your uncle offered them a billet at Sunrise?'

'Yes, of course.'

'It turns out that they're not your mother's cup of

tea.' Fred raised one eyebrow. 'Reggie is from Liverpool and Sid is from the Black Country – there's no mistaking their accents. And they're both a little rough around the edges, shall we say?'

Pamela tried to excuse her mother's narrow mindedness. 'She can't help it. She was brought up in the lap of luxury, and old habits die hard.'

'What about me?' Fred said, fishing for a compliment that he was fairly sure would come his way.

'What about you?' She sidled nearer and slid her arm around his waist. Close up, his good looks overwhelmed her. His smooth skin, dark eyebrows and bright, piercing eyes sent her weak at the knees every time.

'Am I her cup of tea?' He looked down at Pamela; how young, how fresh, how innocent.

She elbowed him sharply in the side. 'You know perfectly well you are.'

He staggered sideways, clutching his ribs – the ones that had been cracked when he'd been attacked. 'Ouch!'

Her hand flew to her mouth and she gasped. 'Oh, I'm sorry – I forgot . . .'

Fred righted himself then grinned. 'I'm kidding!'

'Fred Miller!' Pamela tried to shove him again, but he stepped aside and she overbalanced. Fred caught her by the wrist then whisked her along the prom. They were in step as they strode into the long shadow of the headland. 'Did I tell you,' Pamela said as they turned into the drive at Sunrise, 'Lizzie has asked me to be her bridesmaid along with Connie? There's only five weeks to get everything done – dresses to make and shoes to buy, not to mention saving up food coupons for the reception afterwards. It'll be a miracle if we're ready in time.'

Later that morning Bert arrived at the family bakery on College Road with news that Connie and Lizzie were relieved to hear. 'The bomb squad's finally detonated the Hefty Hermann,' he announced as he took off his cap and slapped it down on the top of the glass counter. 'Did either of you hear the bang?'

'I thought I heard something.' Connie made a show of lifting his cap to wipe the surface with a damp cloth.

'No – when?' Lizzie asked. Saturday was half-day closing. She had recently returned from her last delivery of the day and was carrying empty wooden trays from the van into the shop.

'Half an hour ago,' Bert explained. 'I stood and watched them from the end of Maypole Street. They gave the order for everyone to stand back . . . five, four, three, two one – boom! I don't know how many tons of sand and soil shot thirty feet into the air then down again with an almighty thud. My shed never stood a chance. Flattened, it was.'

'Oh dear.' Connie came out from behind the counter and patted his hand. 'Never mind, Dad – we'll ask Pamela to scrounge some buckshee timber from Anderson's and build you another.'

'I'm not complaining. The BROs did a grand job – no one was hurt and now everyone on the street is allowed back into their houses at last. Normal service is resumed.' Bert followed Lizzie into the hot, airless bakery behind the shop, where the appetizing smell of recently baked bread lingered. He watched as she stacked the trays against the side of the ovens. 'You made sure to drop off those six extra loaves at the Harbourmaster's?' Since his illness he'd been less involved in the early-morning firing-up of ovens and the strenuous task of kneading dough and baking bread, scones and teacakes, but Bert still liked to keep a beady eye on orders and deliveries.

'Yes, I dropped them off on my way back from North Street. A band's playing there tonight so they expect a good turnout. It'll be a shilling to go in and they're putting on refreshments – it should be a good do.'

'Did I hear the word "band"?' Connie called from the shop. 'Will there be dancing?'

Lizzie took off her calico apron and hung it from a hook. 'Yes, but don't get too excited – we're both booked in to do shifts tonight, remember?'

'Drat, I forgot!' Disappointed, Connie brought down the shop blind with a forceful snap.

'Watch what you're doing,' her father grumbled. 'I paid good money for that roller blind.'

'Wait – I've had an idea.' Connie rushed to join Lizzie and Bert in the back room. 'Norman Riley owes me a favour. I switched shifts with him last week – maybe he'll do the same for me tonight. And you, Cinders – who can you switch with so we can both go to the ball?'

Lizzie thought hard. 'I suppose I could ask Sam Billington or Jim Turner. One of them might not mind switching to a Saturday night.'

Bert shook his head and tutted his disapproval.

'Don't be like that, Dad,' Connie remonstrated as she put her plan into action by returning to the shop and picking up the phone. 'You know what they say about all work and no play.'

'I'll do a shift tomorrow night instead,' Lizzie promised. 'Shall we tell the boys about our plans?'

'Do they deserve to be told?' Connie replied with a wink. 'They've been sitting on their big secret for days now. Perhaps it's time we kept a small one of our own.'

Lizzie grinned. Her mind had already raced ahead to what she would wear and how she would style her hair for the dance. 'Don't be too hard on us, Dad.'

Bert grunted. 'You're only young once, I suppose.' Young and bright-eyed, glossy and eager, jumping at the chance to have a bit of fun. You couldn't blame them.

Lizzie beamed, then planted a kiss on his wrinkled cheek. Yes; Jim Turner was her best bet – a veteran ambulance driver who lived alone and was always glad to step in when needed.

'Hello, Norman? This is Connie Bailey. Do you happen to have anything on tonight . . .?'

Dance, dance, dance! With the blind down and no danger of anyone watching, Lizzie took hold of her father and gently waltzed him around the bakery out into the shop. One-two-three, one-two-three, between the ovens, past the empty counter and across the freshly swept floor.

Tom tucked his recently acquired BSA motorbike behind Bill and Lizzie. It was third- or fourth-hand and not in mint condition, but he was proud of it all the same. It felt grand to be riding along the winding coast road with Connie on the pillion seat and the wind in their hair.

'Where are we going?' Lizzie had asked when Bill and Tom had turned up unexpectedly at the shop. She and Connie had just locked up and stepped out on to the street.

'Wait and see,' Bill had replied with a mischievous grin. 'Hop on the back and hold tight.'

'You too,' Tom had told Connie. 'Get ready for a mystery tour.'

Connie and Lizzie had exchanged what-are-they-up-to glances. Could the invitation be something to do with the good news the boys had been keeping from them?

'Are you coming or not?' Bill had revved his engine.

'You'll be sorry if you don't,' Tom had teased.

So the girls had bought into the intrigue and hopped on to the backs of the bikes. And now here they were, with their arms around their sweethearts' waists, leaning in as they approached bends and feeling the thrill of increasing speed as they coasted downhill.

The sea to their right sparkled under a bright blue sky. To their left was Raynard's Folly: a stone beacon high on the moors whose original purpose was lost in the mists of time. Rumour had it that it had rarely been used as a lookout point and that a wealthy land-owner had set his labourers to build the tower during periods when they would otherwise have been idle; hence the name. Five miles ahead lay the small fishing village of Raby.

The two motorbikes swooped down into a dip then roared up the next hill. Connie laughed out loud with exhilaration – one of these days she would persuade Tom to let her ride the bike solo; she was sure she could get the hang of it with a bit of practice.

Bill crested the hill and pointed to the next promontory. Beyond it lay the village, tucked into a narrow bay with twenty or so red-roofed houses perched precariously on rocky ledges overlooking a small harbour and a short stone slipway.

'Yonder!' he announced with the same gleeful expression.

Lizzie turned her head to yell at Connie. 'Hold on to your hat – we're heading for Raby!'

Down again and twisting this way and that, they caught glimpses of a restless sea with small boats bobbing; of high, white clouds scudding across the sky and the inevitable gulls soaring on wind currents, following the noisy bikes' progress with apparent disdain.

So the girls knew their destination, but what was the reason behind the jaunt? Connie remained puzzled, and the mystery only deepened when Tom pulled up behind Bill in a small lay-by half a mile short of the village. 'What now?'

'You'll see.' Tom parked the bike then offered her his hand to negotiate a steep cliff path that led down from the lay-by. Bill and Lizzie were a few yards ahead, nimble as goats as they skipped down worn wooden steps. At the bottom of the cliff lay a sweep of beach much frequented by fossil hunters.

'Don't tell me – we're on the hunt for ammonites,' Lizzie guessed.

'Wrong!' Bill jumped the final couple of steps and landed in the soft, dry sand.

'I'm glad I wore trousers,' Connie commented. 'How long is this going to take? Only, Lizzie and I have plans for this evening.'

'Do those plans include Bill and me?' Tom's feet sank into sand as he landed on the beach behind her.

'Maybe,' Connie teased. 'Actually, there's a dance at the Harbourmaster's if you're interested.'

'Come on, slow coaches!' Bill strode ahead with Lizzie in tow.

Tom and Connie ran to catch up, their feet sinking into the sand and hindering their progress. Eventually, the small group rounded a headland and entered a narrow inlet known as Wren's Cove. Here they found two men at work on a wooden trawler that had been beached above high tide in the shadow of towering cliffs to either side. The forty-foot boat had seen better days – part of its deck was rotten and the faded blue and white paint on the hull was flaking to reveal bare planks beneath.

Lizzie and Connie made out the name on the bow – *Annie May* – and noted the rusty metal winches to port and starboard.

'Now then, Arthur.' Tom went forward and shook hands with the older of the two men, a gnarled and weathered sailor with leathery skin and white hair cropped close to his skull. He wore faded overalls over a dark blue jersey and his pockets bulged with the tools that he was using to repair the boat.

The dark-haired younger man ignored the new arrivals. Dressed in a cable-knit Guernsey sweater similar to the old trawlerman's, he kept his back turned as he went on sawing away at a section of deck.

'That's my lad, Ron,' Arthur Butcher explained. 'He's good with his hands but not so hot as far as manners go.'

You can say that again! Connie could practically see waves of hostility rising from Ron Butcher. He worked with his head lowered as if his life depended on cutting through a rotten plank and casting it on to the beach where it joined others, leaving a gaping hole in *Annie May*'s deck that would have to be filled with new timber stacked neatly under the bridge. 'What's eating him, I wonder?' she murmured to Lizzie while Tom and Bill circled the boat, examining the state of the hull and the wooden rudder.

'This hatch needs a new frame,' Tom commented as he climbed a ladder to inspect the deck.

'What do you expect?' Arthur said. 'She's an old girl, built back in 1906 when steam was just taking over.'

'The bulwark supports seem sound, though.' Bill continued his inspection, brushing away sawdust and knocking with his fist at sections of the hull to test their soundness. 'This outer frame is three inches thick and the inner one's not much less.'

'Aye, they built them to last in those days.' The old man knew every inch of his boat – her strengths and weaknesses and exactly how she handled in various weather conditions. It would be a heck of a wrench to let her go.

Lizzie noticed the swollen joints in Arthur's hands

and the forward hunch of his shoulders. Decades at sea, hauling in nets and battling through storms, had worn him out and now came the reluctant acknowledgement that it was time to hand over to the younger generation.

Tom and Bill regrouped then walked a short distance towards the shore for a quick discussion. They let shallow waves curl around the soles of their boots, tumbling small shells and pebbles against them. 'There's a heap of work to do before she's seaworthy,' Tom said, always the voice of reason. 'What do you reckon – five or six weeks?'

'Four if we put our backs into it.' Bill had a wedding coming up and he was keen to have *Annie May* back at sea before then. 'We'll have the old paint stripped off in no time.'

'That's if the Patrol Service doesn't nab us again.' This was a possibility that couldn't be ignored. As members of so-called Harry Tate's Navy, he and Bill might well be conscripted to help maintain the new barrage balloons that were popping up everywhere, up and down the estuary. Or else, God forbid, they might be sent back out to sea on a requisitioned drifter or corvette to perform North Sea minesweeping duties under a Royal Navy skipper.

'Fingers crossed that won't happen. And remember, making *Annie May* seaworthy again could work in our favour – we'd be back under the reserved occupation umbrella for a start.' Bill's enthusiasm couldn't be dented. 'What do you say – are we going to buy this boat or not?'

Tom took a deep breath. They'd saved the money and already bartered with Arthur to get a good price.

For whatever reason, his son Ron wouldn't take her on. 'The lad hasn't got what it takes – and even if he did, he's not shown any interest,' Arthur had informed them in his blunt manner. All that remained on this sunny April morning was to shake hands on the deal.

'Yes, we are,' Tom decided with a nod of his head.

The two men turned and walked back to the *Annie May*.

Arthur eyed them with suspicion. 'I hope you're not going to welch on me.'

Bill offered his hand. 'No, it's a fair price. And now that we've taken a closer look, we're happy to go ahead.'

Arthur and Bill shook on it, then Tom sealed the deal with another handshake.

'You'll look after her?' Arthur asked. '*Annie May* has been good to me over the years.'

'We will,' Tom promised.

'Is that it, then?' Up on deck Ron threw down his saw with a loud clatter and a resentful scowl.

'Aye, lad,' his father confirmed, 'it's up to these boys from now on.'

Ron jumped down from the boat. 'Good luck to you – you'll need it,' he muttered ungraciously as he strode along the beach in the direction of the village.

There was a further discussion about tools. Arthur was prepared to include hammers, saws, chisels and planes in the price, but not new timber, nails and paint. The engine was in good nick apart from worn spark plugs and a small leak in the petrol tank.

As the talk progressed, Connie and Lizzie looked on in growing amazement.

'They kept this quiet,' Lizzie murmured. 'I didn't have a clue.'

'Me neither.' It made sense, though. Connie and Lizzie knew that fishing meant everything to Tom and Bill – ever since they'd left school they'd worked as trawlermen, learning their trade from Bill's dad, before Stan Evans's sudden death from a heart attack when Bill was sixteen. Life at sea suited them both – they were brave, bold and carefree – and without a boat to sail, they'd been at a loose end, filling in their time with ARP duties or helping out at the bakery when needed.

Lizzie approached the flaking hull. 'It'll be a heck of a job to put it right.'

'Rubbish – a lick of paint is all it needs.' Connie was fooling no one, herself included. She sighed then spoke her true thoughts. 'You're right, Liz. There's a lot to do.'

Unaware of Tom and Bill approaching from behind, the girls exchanged doubtful looks.

'Well?' Bill demanded, wearing the broad grin of a man who had just had a major win on the Football Pools.

'What do you think?' Tom sidled up to Connie.

'It's . . . it's . . .' the girls stammered in unison.

'We'll be up and running in no time,' Bill assured them.

'Back at sea, where we belong,' Tom added.

And how could Lizzie and Connie resist? They gazed up at the flaking hull of the old-fashioned trawler lying like a stranded whale in the narrow cove.

'It's smashing!' Lizzie said. She loved this man and his hopes and dreams. She believed in him.

'Hand me that saw and let's get started.' Connie nimbly climbed a ladder on to the deck. 'Watch out, *Annie May*, there's no stopping us Harrison girls once we get stuck in.'

CHAPTER FOUR

The band played a Benny Goodman tune – 'Let's Dance' – to get the evening off to a lively start. It was a lindy hop – a mixture of jazz, tap and charleston.

Pamela stood apart from the throng, reluctant to attempt the energetic American craze. Connie and Lizzie managed it perfectly – kicking, turning, jumping and swinging with the best of them. They'd invited Pamela along at the last minute and she'd scarcely had time to get ready, let alone tell Fred where she was going. She'd left a message with her mother – 'Tell him I'll be at the Harbourmaster's with Lizzie and Connie if he fancies joining us' – then dashed on along the prom to meet the Harrison sisters in the queue outside the large modern pub designed to attract day trippers from Leeds and Sheffield in the decade leading up to the war. The lines of the white stucco building were reminiscent of the *Queen Mary* – sleek and curved, with large, metal-framed windows. The flat roof was even bordered by a low steel railing, which added to the ocean-going effect.

Excitement had been in the air since the moment the girls had stepped through the doors. They'd found that all the tables and chairs had been removed from the large main bar and the carpet taken up to reveal a polished wooden floor – ideal for dancing. A three-piece band, consisting of piano, clarinet and saxophone, had set up on a small platform at the far end of the room. Connie had headed straight for the bar to order drinks while Lizzie and Pamela had deposited their handbags on a window sill and waited eagerly for the music to start.

As the first notes had struck up, two local lads had rushed over to invite Connie and Lizzie to dance. Pamela had turned down the invitation from a third with a shy, 'I'll sit this one out, thanks.' She was regretting it now, feeling that she stuck out like a sore thumb: the only girl not entering into the spirit of things.

But what a daring dance it was! She watched Lizzie's partner lift her clean off her feet then quickly bend forward and roll her over the back of his hips, catching her as she landed. Then they joined hands and rocked back and forth – step to the side, feet together, step to the side once more, then walk, walk, walk before high-kicking and beginning all over again.

Across the floor, Connie was in her element. She kicked the highest and her skirt flared out the most as she twirled. Pamela caught a glimpse of her friend's stocking tops amid a blur of red and white polka dots and a flouncy, white lace petticoat.

At the end of the dance, Lizzie and Connie returned to base, their faces flushed and foreheads damp with sweat.

'Why didn't you join in?' Connie wanted to know.

'I've never learned the lindy hop,' Pamela confessed.

Connie took a sip of her pale ale. 'There's nothing to it – you just relax and let yourself be swung around, that's all.'

'You've done the jitterbug, haven't you?' Lizzie enquired. 'This is easier – there are fewer steps to learn.'

So when the band struck up the next tune – another swing number, this time 'Boogie Woogie Bugle Boy' by the Andrews Sisters – Pamela said yes to a small, dapper man with a dark moustache.

'I'm Reggie,' he announced as he swept her on to the floor.

'Pamela,' she replied.

'"He was a famous trumpet man from out Chicago way."' A girl singer had taken to the stage, her hair curled under and in a side parting like Vera Lynn. Her sleek, silver lamé dress glittered under the overhead lights.

'I had a bet with my pal Sid that I could get you to dance. I said it wasn't right for a stunner like you to stand on the sidelines.'

Feeling the pressure of the stranger's hand against the small of her back, Pamela blushed and smiled.

Reggie led his partner through a series of bouncing steps, ending in a low kick. Then he spun her around and rocked her back and forth. 'See – easy as pie.'

Relaxing into the rhythm, Pamela started to enjoy herself. She smiled at Lizzie as she swirled by with her partner: a tall, serious-looking fellow in a dark blue blazer and open-necked white shirt.

'That's my pal Sid that I mentioned,' Reggie told Pamela. 'We're new in town.'

'Ah, you're in charge of the LZs,' she said, putting faces to the names that Fred had mentioned.

The tempo quickened and Reggie swung her more energetically. 'News gets around,' he said with a wink.

The pace of the dance took Pamela's breath away and when the number ended Reggie drew her into a quick clinch before boldly planting a kiss on her left cheek.

'Ta very much,' she said as she broke away and rushed back to her corner.

'Goodness!' Lizzie joined her. 'I don't know about you, but I need a breather.'

Lizzie refused her next invitation, but Pamela was led on to the floor by Arthur Dixon, owner of the builders' merchant next to the Gas Street sector post. The woman in the silver gown crooned the words to 'In The Mood' – ' "Baby, won't you swing it with me?" ' Smooth words, smooth steps, tight embraces. Girls flashed lipstick smiles while men held the women's perfumed bodies close and forgot their wartime worries.

As soon as the dance was over, Connie, Lizzie and Pamela reconvened in the girls' corner – Connie fresh from an encounter with Sid. 'Boy, where did those RAF erks learn to dance?' she said as a more sedate number began and the floor emptied, leaving only established couples to show off their skills. The crowd at the bar jostled and called out their orders.

'Time to powder our noses?' Lizzie suggested, picking up her handbag and leading the way.

Inside the ladies' cloakroom the three friends

inspected their reflections in the long mirror above the washbasins. Connie reapplied her lipstick – bright red to match her dress – while Lizzie ran a comb through her hair. Pamela frowned at her flushed cheeks.

'Here.' Lizzie dipped into her bag and handed over her compact.

'Ta.' Pamela patted cool powder on to her face.

'This dance is just what the doctor ordered.' Eager to rejoin the fray, Connie was the first to exit the cloakroom, while Lizzie brought Pamela up to date with the day's main event.

'You'll never guess what – Bill and Tom have bought a fishing boat,' she said. 'It needs a lot doing to it, but they hope to have it shipshape before the wedding.'

'That's marvellous news.' Pamela held the door open for her friend and they emerged to admiring glances from the gang of men gathered by the main entrance – Lizzie in her pale blue halter-neck dress that skimmed her knees, Pamela in a short-sleeved lilac one that was nipped in at the waist and flared out into a gored skirt.

Trim figures, good legs, hips that sway as they walk; the whole package – the men enjoyed watching Pamela and Lizzie re-enter the bar.

Holding her head high and making a point of ignoring them, Lizzie was surprised to feel a light tap on her shoulder. She turned to see Reggie grinning at her and inviting her to dance the jitterbug with him.

'Come on,' he cajoled as he wrapped his arm around her waist. 'You know you want to.'

Sid was close on Reggie's heels and he corralled Pamela without even asking whether or not she wanted to dance. 'The night is young,' he insisted in his sing-song Midlands accent. 'And so are we.'

As the dance began, Lizzie found there was no holding Reggie at a decent distance. He had arms like an octopus's tentacles, pulling her close then swinging her out and drawing her back in again, tight against his body.

'You're a proper little Ginger Rogers.' The compliments flowed as the tempo increased. 'Light on your feet and with a sparkle in those lovely brown eyes. It beats me why you haven't been snapped up already.'

'Actually, I have,' Lizzie retorted, quick as a flash. 'Been snapped up, that is.' Lifting her left hand, she waved it ostentatiously across Reggie's line of vision to show off her sparkling engagement ring.

'Fair enough.' Reggie didn't miss a beat. 'Plenty more fish in the sea, eh?'

'That's a nice dress you're wearing,' Sid told Pamela meanwhile, during one of their energetic clinches. His right hand gripped hers as he swung her out to arm's length. 'I bet you have boys swarming around you like bees around honey.'

The cheesy comparison brought a blush to her face. She glanced around the crowded floor, planning a quick getaway at the end of the number.

The music stopped and the pianist announced a pause in proceedings – a short interval would give the musicians time to slake their thirst.

'How about a drink?' Sid asked Pamela in his

overfamiliar way. His height, together with his deep-set eyes and long, square jaw, somehow gave the impression that he was used to getting his own way. Before she knew it, Pamela was swept along towards the bar.

Across the room, Lizzie had managed to escape from Reggie, who instead made a beeline for Connie and offered to buy her a drink.

'I've just been given the brush-off by the little girl in blue.' Reggie gestured towards Lizzie. 'She doesn't know what she's missing.'

'That little girl in blue happens to be my sister.' Connie looked him in the eye. He was a cocky sort, to be sure. 'Her fiancé will be here any minute. Look – here he is now.'

'Bill! Tom!' Lizzie spotted them across the crowded room – how could you miss them? They were both tall and they lit the place up with their open smiles and easy way of threading their way towards the bar, exchanging greetings with everyone they knew.

'Sorry,' Connie told Reggie as she left him in the lurch, 'that drink will have to wait.'

A buzz of excited voices filled the silence. Dozens of flushed faces, perspiring brows and aching feet retreated into quiet corners or sought chairs for a brief sit-down. Lizzie, Connie, Bill and Tom gathered at the bar while Pamela did her best to keep Sid at bay.

'What do you do for a living, Pamela?' The cheeky junior aircraftman thrust a Dubonnet and lemonade at her, then took a deep swig from his pint glass. 'Let me guess – you work in a hairdressing salon. Isn't that the posh word for them?'

'Wrong,' she countered, aware that the thin fabric of her dress clung to her thighs due to a combination of heat and energetic movement.

'All right, then – you don't have to work at anything. Your daddy's rich enough to look after his little girl in the style to which she's accustomed.'

'Do you mind!' At this latest guess, Pamela felt her hackles rise. 'I work as a secretary, if you must know.'

'Keep your hair on, I'm only kidding.' Sid laughed then drank again. Reggie joined them and the two men compared notes – the local shindig was better than expected: pretty lively, music not bad, girls you wouldn't chuck out of bed.

Pamela took a deep breath then placed her glass on the bar. 'Please excuse me.' She sounded stiff and snooty – just like her mother, for heaven's sake! 'If you don't mind, I'll leave you two to talk.'

'You haven't finished your drink,' a disappointed Sid called after her.

'Very tasty.' Reggie appraised Pamela's back view. 'Could do with a bit more meat on her bones, but classy and far too good for you, Spot.'

'Give me strength!' Pamela was still annoyed when she joined her friends.

Lizzie smiled at her exasperation. 'Take no notice. They're not worth getting worked up about.'

'Who? What? When? Where?' Bill wanted to know.

'She means Sid and Reggie, the two new erks who are billeted with Fred at Sunrise,' Connie explained.

'A pair of terrible flirts,' Lizzie added. 'Especially the smaller one – he really gets on my nerves.'

The music struck up again and, within seconds, Arthur Dixon's son Alan had asked Pamela to dance the cakewalk with him.

'You're in safe hands there,' Connie reassured her as a large circle formed around the perimeter of the dance floor. Each pair paraded arm in arm to a jazz number led by the clarinet player, backed by saxophone and piano.

'Do you fancy it?' Tom asked Connie, who naturally leaped at the chance to join in the rapid, prancing performance.

'Yes?' Bill offered Lizzie his hand and they too joined the procession.

The dance was an opportunity to hop and kick, wave and stamp; the more swaggering the better. Dancers unapologetically bumped into nearby couples and trod on each other's toes. When the song finished, the trio onstage slid seamlessly into a foxtrot – slow, slow, quick, quick, slow. The circle disintegrated and couples turned to face each other – Tom smiling warmly and embracing Connie, Bill happy to get into hold with Lizzie. Shy, fifteen-year-old Alan Dixon mumbled his excuses and left Pamela stranded in the middle of the floor.

'We can't have that, can we?' As if by magic, Reggie was there, offering to take the boy's place. Before Pamela knew it, he had his arm wrapped around her waist and was guiding her smoothly across the floor. 'I'm sorry if I overstepped the mark earlier. I never meant to upset you.'

'I wasn't upset.' Pamela fell short of the airy insouciance she was aiming for. Her blushing cheeks betrayed her yet again.

'Anyhow, I came on too strong and I apologize.'

'Apology accepted.' Pamela did her best to keep up with her partner, who was surprisingly light on his feet.

Reggie foxtrotted her around a knot of couples in the centre of the floor. 'I know I can go at things like a bull in a china shop – it happens when I'm nervous.'

'You – nervous?' Her rising intonation conveyed disbelief.

'Yes, a bag of nerves – that's me.' His serious expression cracked into a broad grin. 'OK, I'm kidding.'

'I was about to say!' Pamela's skirt swung out as they rapidly changed direction to find more space. Her partner was an infuriating tease, but he was funny too – she was forced to admit that his quick-fire energy held a certain attraction.

Reggie drew her closer. 'Between you and me, it's a relief to be stationed up here in Kelthorpe for a while. My squadron's lost four pilots in the last month – two over Essen and two over Lübeck. The youngest was only nineteen, for Christ's sake.'

'Yes, I can see why you'd rather be here.'

'Looking after barrage balloons is a doddle in comparison.' He briefly released her hand to tap his forehead – touch wood. Then he seized it again and put in a couple of complicated turns. 'That's right, twinkletoes – let's show 'em how it's done.'

Not far away, Connie was tripping the light fantastic with Tom. Aware that they made a handsome couple – he with his height and strength, she in her bright dress and with her glossy, dark hair pinned up – they brimmed with confidence. Connie waved at Lizzie and Bill as they passed by. Despite his quiet, steady nature, Tom came alive on the dance floor. Connie had always known that he was musical and had a singing voice second to none. But once she'd discovered that he could dance as well as he could sing, she'd seized the opportunity for them to waltz and foxtrot, swing, samba and jitterbug their way around every dance hall in town. 'Lizzie looks like she's having a good time,' Connie remarked as Tom whirled her around.

'Bill too. He's on top of the world because we're due to start proper work on *Annie May* tomorrow. Be warned, we'll be up to our eyes in wood shavings and sawdust for the next few weeks.'

'You don't think you've bitten off more than you can chew?' Since setting eyes on the dilapidated trawler, Connie had had plenty of time to think things through.

'Let's hope not.' Privately, Tom had his doubts about Bill's timescale – making the old boat seaworthy before the wedding seemed ambitious, but then again, where there was a will there was a way. 'Don't get me wrong – I'm as keen as he is to be out casting our nets again.'

'Lizzie and I will give you a hand whenever we can,' Connie promised as the foxtrot ended and couples drifted from the floor. 'I'll be the dogsbody, fetching and carrying, hammering or screwing down anything that moves. Lizzie's more use than me – she knows about engines.'

Tom smiled as he drew her towards the bar. 'You'll

both be busy in the bakery,' he pointed out. 'And you work for the ARP three or four nights a week.'

'We'll fit it in.' Connie beckoned for Lizzie and Bill to join them at the bar.

On another part of the floor, Pamela tried to extricate herself from Reggie's grasp. 'Thanks very much,' she said. 'I enjoyed that.'

As the music started up again, Reggie held on to her hand. 'One more,' he pleaded. 'Come on – don't be mean.'

Pamela pulled away. 'I'm all in,' she protested. 'I could do with a breather.'

'This is a good one – listen!' Reggie mouthed the words to the Judy Garland song that the band was playing. '"You made me love you . . ."'

'No, really—'

'"I didn't want to do it."' Reggie grinned away.

Pamela feared that if she carried on resisting there would be a scene. Anyway, what would be the harm? So, she gave in and was once more swept away in her partner's arms.

Holding her close, Reggie turned and turned until Pamela grew dizzy. If he let go of her, she was sure she would fall down, so she clung on.

'"Give me, give me, give me what I cry for . . ."' Reggie crooned the words into her ear.

The lights began to spin and the floor to tilt beneath her feet.

'"You know you got the brand of kisses that I'd die for . . ."'

Fred entered the room at the moment when the music reached a crescendo. He saw Pamela in someone else's arms, and that someone was Reggie Nolan, damn it. What the hell was the airman up to, spinning her around like that? Feeling a sharp stab of jealousy in the pit of his stomach, Fred took a quick intake of breath.

Connie rushed to greet Pamela's sweetheart, then shoved him forward. 'Quick, Fred. It's time for you to ride up on your white charger.'

He jerked into action. Bloody hell, Nolan was the limit, grinning like an idiot as he held Pamela upright and led her off the floor!

'Someone could do with a nice refreshing drink,' Reggie murmured in Pamela's ear before feeling a heavy hand on his shoulder.

'I'll take it from here, thank you.' Fred was grimly formal – taller than Reggie, he was able to look down on the other man as he slipped his hand into Pamela's.

She took a deep breath and willed the lights to stop spinning.

'Oh, will you now?' Reggie adopted the air of a prize fighter. He didn't quite put up his fists and challenge the interfering bastard who'd stepped in between him and his girl for the evening, but that was the impression he conveyed. 'Says who?'

'Fred Miller – you remember me?' Fred's gaze was steady, though he had to clench his teeth in an attempt to bite back his irritation.

Pamela took another deep breath and had just enough time to regain her balance as Reggie looked quickly from one to the other, read the situation, then backed off.

'Right you are.' Reggie held up his hands in surrender. 'No offence, I hope?'

'None taken.' Clipped in his speech, precise in his movements, Fred put his hand around Pamela's waist and led her away.

'You win some, you lose some,' Reggie told Sid later as they walked back to Sunrise together. 'Not that I'm giving up without a fight, mind you. There's no ring on this one's finger so she's still fair game as far as I'm concerned.'

CHAPTER FIVE

'We had a lone nuisance raider stooging around earlier this afternoon,' Norman Riley reported to Connie when they crossed paths at the corner of Park Road.

Norman had just finished a daytime stint as warden at the North Street sector post when he came across her chatting with Lizzie and Pamela ten minutes before the start of their own shifts.

'Any damage done?' Connie asked.

He shook his head. 'No, but it was a close shave. Fritz came in fast and low in broad daylight, aiming for Wilfred Freeman's grain yard. Luckily, he missed his target. The bombs were jettisoned half a mile out to sea.'

'I didn't hear any sirens.' Lizzie had spent the day helping to rebuild her father's allotment shed, assisted by her young cousin Arnold and a couple of his Boy Scout pals. They'd used the existing concrete base, a metal window frame and a door salvaged from the *Gazette* building's bombsite on College Road, plus odd boards and lengths of timber scrounged from Anderson's to construct a Heath

Robinson affair that would nevertheless be secure enough to store Bert's gardening tools.

'No, the cheeky blighter came in under the radar and was gone again before we knew it.'

'You look worn out,' Pamela commented. Their fellow volunteer was no spring chicken – probably in his sixties, in fact. Norman slotted in his ARP shifts between working as a maths teacher at St Joseph's School. Today was Sunday and he was returning home to piles of ink-stained exercise books waiting to be marked. He was the scholarly type: thin and stooping, with thick horn-rimmed glasses and a chalky, creased look about him even in his dark blue Civil Defence uniform.

'Aren't we all?' he commented as he walked on. 'Still, we carry on as best we can.'

'Is Tom on duty with you tonight?' Lizzie asked Connie before they went their separate ways – she to her ambulance depot and Pamela and Connie to the Gas Street post.

Connie nodded. 'I'll ask him to do a few hours on the roof at Anderson's. We need someone up there to keep a lookout for more tip-and-run raiders, given what Norman has just told us.' The night was clear and calm: ideal weather for a follow-up attack. 'We'd best get a move on. Oh, and don't expect me back at Elliot Street later – I've arranged to stay over at Tom's again.'

'All right, I'll see you first thing tomorrow.' Lizzie set off for King Edward Street at a brisk pace. 'Don't be late!' she called over her shoulder.

'Pot . . . kettle!' Connie retaliated with a light laugh. Whenever Lizzie stayed at Bill's harbour-side cottage she would pull up outside the bakery next morning with a squeal of van brakes and the look of having thrown on her clothes, without taking time even to brush her hair. Connie would already be elbow deep in flour and yeast, mixing the first batch of dough.

Pamela kept pace with Connie as they made their way to Gas Street. She envied the sisters' ease and their relaxed references to sleeping with their sweethearts: a step that she and Fred had yet to take. Not for lack of wanting to – that much was obvious to both of them – but out of a mixture of propriety, circumstance, shyness, lack of confidence; call it what you will. *Perhaps one day soon*, she thought to herself as she gave a wistful sigh.

'I'll get you and Simon to patrol the docks,' Connie decided as they came to the familiar sandbagged entrance of the sector post. 'You can check that the stirrup pumps and Redhill containers are in working order on your way there.'

'Right you are.'

The Union Jack above the entrance hung limply as they entered the gloom of the old cobblers' shop to a lingering smell of leather, boot polish and dust. Connie went straight to the pile of paperwork stacked on the counter and got stuck in, while Pamela made a beeline for the storeroom. Gloves, boots, whistle, emergency first-aid supplies, duty-respirator – one by one she reached for the equipment she would need for her shift.

Lizzie looked forward to hearing from Bill about the progress he and Tom had made on their first full day of working on the *Annie May*. Approaching the

71

ambulance depot from the top of King Edward Street, she let her mind stray to wedding matters. Replies to invitations were coming in thick and fast and the headcount was now up to forty – already too many in Bill's view. Pamela and Connie had started sewing their dresses – they were ahead of Lizzie in that respect. *I must get on with it*, she told herself. *At this rate I'll be walking down the aisle in my petticoat!* She thought of the yards of crumpled silk still waiting to be transformed into her wedding gown. As for a veil – well, she would adapt the one her mother had worn all those years ago. The precious article, wrapped in tissue paper and kept in a bottom drawer in her father's bedroom, would be her 'something old'.

'Watch out!'

A loud yell interrupted Lizzie's train of thought. An ambulance had emerged cautiously from the depot and almost collided with a man on a bicycle speeding recklessly down the steep hill. Without any attempt to apply his brakes, the cyclist swerved off the road, crashed into a dustbin and ended up spread-eagled on the pavement. His cap flew off, his jacket fell open and for a few heart-stopping moments he lay motionless.

Lizzie saw Sam Billington jump down from the ambulance and sprint to the man's aid. But instead of accepting help, the reckless rider leaped to his feet and swung his fists, landing several punches by the time she joined them.

'Bloody idiot!' Despite his slight build, the angry man – dark-haired and with a wiry build – forced Sam back against a garden wall. 'Why don't you look where you're going?'

Stronger by far, Sam was able to fight him off. 'Steady on, Ronnie. I'm sorry – OK?'

'You're bleeding.' Lizzie saw blood pouring from a gash in the man's forehead. She gave a small start of realization; this was Arthur Butcher's son, Ron, who had stormed off when his father had sold *Annie May*.

Ron wiped away the blood with the back of his hand. The sight of it seemed to enrage him further and he swore before lashing out again.

Dodging the blow, Sam picked up the bike and held it in front of him as a shield, but Ron wrenched it from him and flung it to the ground, shattering the headlamp and buckling the front wheel.

'Stop that.' Lizzie tried in vain to intervene. She smelled alcohol on Ron's breath and recalled that he'd made no attempt to brake when he'd seen the ambulance edge out of the yard. In fact, she wondered if he'd been on a kamikaze mission to crash into it head-on, only swerving at the very last second.

Ignoring her plea, Ron used his elbow to shove her away. Blood still poured from the gash on his forehead and now he rushed at Sam, caught him off balance and wrestled him to the ground, so that the two men were caught up in a tangle of twisted handlebars and spinning wheels.

Concerned about the amount of blood, Lizzie ran to the ambulance to fetch a first-aid kit. If Ron was indeed drunk, it would be impossible to talk sense into him – somehow Sam would have to subdue him and Lizzie would be standing by, ready to stem the flow.

'Calm down, Ronnie!' Sam extricated himself from the bicycle and managed to pin down his man. 'I'm going to count to ten – OK? One, two, three . . .'

'Get off me!' Ron kicked and squirmed but Sam held him fast.

'Four, five, six . . .'

'Sam bloody Billington, I'll get you for this!'

The childish threat brought a grim smile to Lizzie's lips. Blood streamed down the enraged man's face and neck, staining the front of his shirt bright scarlet.

'Seven, eight, nine, ten. Right, that's it!' Sam dragged his adversary into a sitting position then shoved him back against the wall, expelling all the air in Ron's lungs with a loud oof! 'Are you ready to see sense?'

'Bloody let go of me, you bugger!' Ron raised his knee sharply and caught Sam in the groin. Sam keeled over sideways, leaving his opponent free to haul himself to his feet and stagger away. Ron lurched unseeing towards the brick archway leading into the brewery yard and straight into Bill's arms.

Bill caught him before he collapsed. He'd heard the disturbance from inside the annexe, where he'd signed on for the start of his shift – the clash of what had sounded like a dustbin being tipped over then raised voices – and he'd rushed out to investigate.

'Ring 999 and fetch the police,' he told Sam as he supported the injured man. 'Tell them to meet us at the hospital.'

Still bent double, Sam managed to do what Bill had asked.

'It's Ron Butcher,' Lizzie pointed out.

'So it is.' Lowering the semi-conscious man to the ground and placing him on his side, Bill told her to fetch a stretcher so they could carry him into the ambulance double quick. 'It looks like concussion and he's lost a lot of blood besides. You'll have to step on it, Lizzie, and drive like the devil up to the Queen Alexandra. I'll stay in the back and do what I can for the daft so-and-so.'

No sooner said than Butcher was stretchered into the ambulance and driven away. His bike was damaged beyond repair, lying among the scattered contents of the dustbin – yesterday's newspaper, potato peelings, a smashed wireless. One bicycle wheel spun silently in the encroaching dusk and Ron's cap lay some distance away in a pool of his blood.

It was a Dornier Do 17 that did the damage – the 'flying pencil' – a light, fast German bomber identifiable by its twin tail fins and engines mounted on the shoulders of the streamlined aircraft. It had outpaced the two outdated Hawker Hurricanes that had pursued it up the north-east coast as far as Kelthorpe. Its pilot jettisoned the last of his bombs on the dockside area, just as Connie had feared.

This time Freeman's took a direct hit, which made her think that the main objective of the lone raider earlier in the day had been reconnaissance. His information had been passed on to a Luftwaffe command unit and the second raid had taken place in the dead of night. The same tactic as before, coming in low and fast and this time achieving its objective: the main silo in the grain storage yard went up in flames.

Pamela and Simon were at the scene within minutes and took stock of the damage. Simon sprinted back to the sector post to ask Connie to phone in a report to the control centre. Connie established the need for a team of AFS firefighters but held back a request for a rescue team – with luck the yard would have been deserted at the time of the attack. 'Stand by until further notice,' she told the switchboard operator who took her call.

At the scene itself, Pamela witnessed the AFS men arrive in their protective gear. Their helmets were covered with oilskin hoods; they wore waterproof leggings and wielded rubber-handled axes as a protection against electrocution. The team of six men pumped thousands of gallons of water out of the estuary to fight the fierce blaze. Not for nothing had Churchill called them 'heroes with grimy faces', Pamela thought when she saw them silhouetted against towering orange flames, engulfed at times by the thick black smoke that billowed from the stricken grain store.

It was only when the fire was quenched and Pamela arrived back at Gas Street at the end of her shift that she heard the full story from Connie.

'The Dornier pilot didn't make it back to base, if that makes you feel any better,' she told an exhausted Pamela and Simon. 'Our boys on the beach scored a direct hit with their anti-aircraft guns and brought him down in flames. Fritz parachuted out and got caught up in the cables of one of the blimps guarding the estuary. Our RNPS boys found him dangling like a puppet on a string.'

The Patrol Service had played their part by cutting down the enemy pilot and carting him off to a POW camp in Lincolnshire.

'That's the end of his war, then,' Simon commented as he signed out.

Pamela waited outside while Connie handed over to the next head warden. It was past midnight and low clouds had blown in off the sea, bringing a cold mist that reduced visibility to a hundred yards. She heard the approach of a car engine before making out the shape of a Bedford van that pulled up at the kerb. Lizzie stepped down from the passenger seat, waved off the ambulance, then joined Pamela as Connie emerged from the post.

'What a night!' Lizzie sighed. 'I've spent most of it at the Queen Alexandra, helping to patch up Ron Butcher.'

In pitch darkness, the three girls made their weary way along Gas Street until they reached the bottom of King Edward Street: the parting of their ways. Longing for her bed, Pamela said a swift goodnight while Connie and Lizzie lingered.

'What happened to Arthur's son?' Connie asked.

'Ron started a fight with Sam Billington and ended up concussed. There was blood everywhere. Bill and I drove him to hospital, then the police got involved. I had to give a witness statement. The police have charged Ron with being drunk and disorderly.'

'Drunk?' Connie echoed. She had a vivid recollection of Ron Butcher ripping up rotten planks from the deck of *Annie May* with his back turned and his dark head lowered, refusing to acknowledge them.

Lizzie nodded. 'Sam lives in Raby so he's known Ron from way back. Apparently Ron went off the rails a few months back. No one knows why. This isn't the first fight he's been involved in – not by a long chalk.'

'What went wrong, I wonder?'

77

Lizzie shrugged. 'I don't know and, to be honest, I don't care.'

She was worn out – it was past midnight and she and Connie had to be at work in the bakery before six o'clock.

'What does Bill think?' Connie looked at her watch and stifled a yawn.

'You know Bill – nothing bothers him. By morning he'll have forgotten all about it.'

'Then so should we.' Connie decided that life was complicated enough without taking on board other people's problems. 'We've got enough on our plates without worrying about Ron Butcher and that's a fact.'

At Sunrise, Fred came downstairs early the following morning to a frosty exchange between Edith and Sid. He heard the tail end of an explanation as to why Edith couldn't buy extra butter unless Sid produced his food coupons, and a sharp retort from the RAF man that he'd left his ration book behind at his base in Norfolk and was he expected to eat dry toast until it arrived in the post?

'It's like eating bloody cardboard,' he complained as Fred entered the breakfast room and Edith hurried off in what could only be described as a huff: her brows were knitted, and the tilt of her head expressed distaste.

'I'm sure Mrs Carr was only trying to help.' Fred spooned tea leaves out of the caddy into the brown pot.

'Help, my backside!' Reggie cut in. 'Old sour face won't lift a finger on our behalf – she looks down her nose at us, full stop. Here, Sid, have some of my butter.' He offered the scrapings from his plate, ostentatiously pushing it across the table. They were both in Hairy Mary battledress, as they called their heavy woollen outfits, and neither minded their manners as they tore into the toast that Edith had made for them.

Frowning, Fred thought it best to change the subject. 'Are your airships up and running?' he enquired, though he already knew the answer since he'd watched a team of RAF engineers inflating the giant balloons on the headland the previous day.

Sid nodded as he scraped the last of Reggie's butter on to his second slice of toast. 'Today we have to check the winches by flying the blimps up to a hundred feet then lowering them again.'

'Then what?'

'Then we sit around twiddling our thumbs,' Reggie shot back. 'Until such time as we get an Alert Yellow.'

'Then we make 'em ready just in case,' Sid said, looking bored. 'If we get an Alert Red we fly 'em up to three or four thousand feet until we get the Alert White when we bed 'em down again.'

'We could go days without getting an alert,' Reggie added smugly.

'Which leaves us at a loose end – fine by me.'

'And me.'

'We'll still be getting paid, eh, Reg?'

'For lounging about and getting into mischief.' Reggie gave Fred a sly wink. 'You catch my meaning?'

Fred made no comment as he stirred the pot. He didn't regard himself as a snob, but Sid and Reggie's distinct lack of table manners – eating with their mouths open, slurping their tea – and their lack of respect for Edith got on his nerves, not to mention the memory of the way Reggie had manhandled Pamela on the dance floor on Saturday night. Deciding to skip breakfast, he rapidly swallowed down his tea. 'I'd best be off,' he told them when he heard Hugh's footsteps in the corridor. 'If I get a move on I'll be able to get a lift in.'

'Fancy that,' Reggie commented as Fred closed the door behind him. Through the window, he watched as Hugh got into his Daimler and started the engine. 'Our friend is in the boss's good books.'

Sid saw Fred exchange warm greetings with their landlord before taking his place in the passenger seat. 'We'd better watch our p's and q's,' he added sarcastically.

'Sod that,' Reggie sneered. 'Personally, I can't see the attraction of a chap who talks as if he's got a poker up his arse. "I'm sure Mrs Carr was only trying to help" – nim, nim, nim!'

'But he's pulled the wool over our landlord's eyes, that's for sure.'

'So what?' Reggie scraped back his chair and brushed crumbs from his uniform on to the floor before standing up. 'I reckon we could still have some fun at Fred's expense.'

Sid grinned. 'The fun wouldn't involve the little green-eyed girl in the lilac dress, by any chance?'

'Maybe.' Reggie's casual response disguised a plan that had been slowly forming since the weekend. It involved putting himself in the right place at the right time combined with lashings of flattery and a soupçon of subterfuge.

'I bet you a quid she won't,' Sid challenged.

'Won't what?'

'Jump into bed with you.'

Reggie laughed then spat on his palm and offered to shake hands. 'You're on!'

'I've put in an order for a new Imperial Model 50,' Pamela informed Sally Hopkins as she showed the junior secretary round the office at the start of her first day at work. She tapped the ancient typewriter on Sally's desk. 'You won't have to put up with this old thing for very long. And here is where we keep the carbon paper. There's a hole punch, a stapler and a stash of paper clips in the top right-hand drawer of your desk. Envelopes on the left. Files containing unpaid invoices are stored in alphabetical order on the shelf behind you.'

Sally's eyes followed Pamela's pointing finger. *Carbon paper, hole punch, stapler, paper clips.* A tiny slip of a thing with bright red hair and freckles, she soaked up the information like a sponge.

'I'm not going too fast for you, am I?' Remembering her own painful introduction to the office, Pamela took care not to replicate Betty Holroyd's supercilious manner. 'I know there's an awful lot to take in.'

Envelopes, files containing invoices. Yes, Sally had felt nervous that morning as she'd got dressed in her smartest clothes – a pale green blouse and straight black skirt with a little kick-pleat at the back. She'd tied back her thick curls with a dark green ribbon and sighed over her recently resoled shoes. Her father's homespun repair wasn't up to the standards of a proper cobbler, but Sally had no choice – this was her only pair of black court shoes so they would have to do. She'd covered the short walk from the pub along the dockside to reach the timber yard with a bad case of butterflies in her stomach. Looking lost, she'd been scooped up by foreman Keith Nelson, who had shown her how to register her arrival. Keith was a gruff type with a squat, muscular physique; never one to waste words, he'd jerked a thumb towards the clocking-in machine outside the office building then ambled across the yard, past stacks of imported timber towards the enormous cutting shed.

Pamela had been waiting for Sally in a small reception area on the ground floor of the office block.

Sally's first impression of her new boss was favourable. Pamela was smiley and smart in a dark blue dress; what's more she was doing her best to make Sally feel welcome. Tall and slim, with her short hair styled by a proper hairdresser, shapely legs and lovely, soft leather shoes, she seemed confident and poised – everything that Sally wasn't.

Sally had taken in her surroundings as Pamela led her upstairs and along a corridor past Hugh Anderson's private office to the small room where the two of them would work. It was Sally's first job as a secretary and a big step up from serving behind the bar at the Anchor: the pub that her father had run since the year dot. She was the eldest of five, and despite her diminutive size, she'd been mother hen to a brood of siblings in the absence of their mother, who had died shortly after giving birth to the youngest, Rita.

'So, as I say, your typewriter should be here by the end of the week.' Pamela had taken to the new junior straight away. She liked Sally's eagerness and the way she simply nodded her head and got on with things. 'I'll set you off with some simple filing work – checking receipts then stamping the files before moving them from the unpaid to the paid section. We break mid-morning for elevenses. Dinner is at half twelve – if you like I'll take you over to the canteen and show you what's what.'

'Yes please.' Sally's chest swelled with pride to think how far she'd come. Those night classes in typing had paid off handsomely; squeezed in as they were between a dozen other demands on her time and in the face of some scepticism from her dad.

'I don't see the point,' Frank Hopkins had said. 'What good will learning to type be once you're wed?'

'I'm not going to get married, Dad,' Sally had replied firmly. 'Not after what I've just been through.' *Once bitten, twice shy.*

'You say that now,' Frank had grumbled, 'but you never know what's around the corner.'

His eldest girl had always been a quick learner and had scored top marks in her typing class. She'd just signed up for a shorthand course when she'd spotted the advert in the *Gazette*: 'Junior typist wanted at Anderson's timber yard. No experience necessary.' She'd applied for the job and hey presto: here she was with her foot on the first rung of the ladder.

Pamela saw that Sally would need a cushion on her chair to bring her up to a comfortable level at her desk. She was amazed by the energy that came off such a little sparrow; the way she darted looks here and there, lifted thick files, flipped them open and firmly stamped them. When it came to half past ten, it was Sally who offered to make the tea and take it through to Hugh's office, which she did speedily and smoothly. Come half twelve she'd replaced the last file on its shelf and was ready when the klaxon sounded for dinner, waiting for Pamela to show her to the canteen, as promised.

The two girls reached the reception area, where Fred and Harold joined them. They crossed the yard together then tagged on to the end of the queue at the entrance to the canteen, where dozens of men in overalls stood chatting. A couple of crane operators eyed Sally through clouds of cigarette smoke and, recognizing her as the barmaid at their local, invited her to join them in the queue.

'How's it going?' Harold whispered to Pamela with a nod in Sally's direction.

'Very well.'

'She doesn't seem old enough to be doing this job. Mind you, everyone looks young to me these days.'

'She may not look it but she's nineteen.'

'And you like her?'

'I do.' Pamela turned from her father to Fred. 'You're quiet,' she said with a touch of concern. 'Is everything all right?'

'Yes – don't mind me.' Fred shuffled forward in the queue. Was it the weather that had affected his mood? he wondered. It was a typically grey, cold April day, with a thick mist coming in off the sea and a hint of drizzle in the air. Or was it the muddle that he was currently trying to sort out with Keith

Nelson – a discrepancy in the order book that the foreman was being deliberately obtuse about?

No, it was neither of those things. If Fred was honest, it was Reggie Nolan and Sid Donne that had got under his skin – a pair of lazy slackers who were too big for their boots; Reggie, in particular. Resentment of their presence at Sunrise had settled heavily on Fred's shoulders. It had wormed its way into each task he'd undertaken that morning as he'd tried to balance the books. What was it exactly? Had the RAF men put Fred's nose out of joint simply by being there? No, again; it was more than that. *Ah!* Fred had sat with his pencil poised over a column of figures. *It all comes down to the way the damned fellow was with Pamela.*

'Are you sure there's nothing wrong?' she asked as they edged towards the counter and the smell of mince and onion stew mingled with overcooked cabbage.

Eifersucht. Jealousy – sharp as a knife in the guts. 'I'm fine,' Fred grunted. 'But I'm not hungry. I think I'll give dinner a miss for once.'

CHAPTER SIX

'Which king burned the cakes?' Bert frowned at a batch of Victoria sponges that he'd just taken out of the oven. The tops were slightly overdone but Lizzie decided it was nothing a dusting of icing sugar wouldn't hide.

'Alfred the Great.' She remembered the story that all school children learned: how the king was on the run from the Vikings and had taken refuge in the home of a peasant woman when he was asked to keep an eye on her cakes – which were actually small loaves of bread, to be precise – these details mattered if your family ran a bakery. Distracted by affairs of state, daft Alfred had ruined the cakes and earned the wrath of his protector. Great he might have been in matters of government, but the warrior king was no shakes as a baker.

Bert shook his head and sighed as he transferred the sponges to a cooling tray. 'I don't know what's up with me – I can't seem to get anything right these days.'

'These things happen – don't be too hard on yourself.' Lizzie quickly changed the subject. 'I was helping Bill with *Annie May* last night – dismantling the head gasket and checking the innards of the engine.'

'In the dark?' Bert queried over the sound of the shop bell tinkling out front and the arrival of the first customers of the day.

'No – we stopped work once we lost the light, then came back to Kelthorpe and adjourned to the Anchor.' Lizzie tapped the bottom of a couple of loaves that had come out of the oven five minutes earlier. The hollow sound told her that they were baked to perfection.

Out in the shop Connie served her cousin Arnold with a Hovis loaf and two teacakes.

'And be quick about it – I haven't got all day,' he told her in his cheeky, chirpy way. At twelve, he was still a whippersnapper: skinny, fidgety and an undoubted show-off. Despite his youth, he and his pal Colin Strong intended to train as stretcher bearers for the ARP and in the meantime the two of them strutted the streets after blackout as if capable of defeating Hitler single-handedly.

'Get on with you.' Slipping a sly extra teacake into the bag, Connie slid Arnold's purchases over the counter then took his money. 'Tell your mum I'll pop in later for a chat about the flowers for Lizzie's wedding.'

He was out of the door before she'd finished her sentence.

'One white tin and a cottage loaf, please, Connie,' said her next customer – a middle-aged woman with work-worn hands and a brown felt hat that had seen better days – with a slight shake of her head at Arnold's lack of manners. 'Oh and I'll have one of those Eccles cakes while you're at it.'

Lizzie emerged from the back room with a tray of warm loaves. She carried them out to the van and was returning to the shop when Bill rode up on his motorbike. Glancing down at her flour-covered apron, she quickly patted her hair into place and prayed that she didn't look as much of a sight as she feared.

Bill parked the bike and approached her, removing his gauntlets and unzipping his leather pilot's jacket, recently acquired from the army surplus store on Gladstone Square. Its sheepskin collar was turned up, giving him a rakish air that sent thrills through Lizzie every time she saw him wearing it. 'I'm glad I caught you,' he told her as he leaned in to kiss her cheek before leading her a short way down the street. They stopped in the doorway of Cynthia's hair salon, forced to raise their voices to compete with the ceaseless trundle of buses, cars and lorries and the occasional clip-clop of a horse-drawn cart.

Lizzie warned him that she couldn't stop for long. 'I'm about to set out on my delivery round.'

'Yes, but I want you to be the first to know.' Bill pushed a lock of dark hair from his forehead. 'The RNPS has been in touch with me and Tom.'

'And?' Lizzie felt a flicker of anxiety in her stomach. Contact from the Patrol Service could mean only one thing – Tom and Bill had been called upon to carry out another important defence activity.

'Don't worry – they only want us to help maintain the blimps out in the estuary,' he reassured her. 'All we have to do is learn the drill then stand by for whenever we're needed.'

'They're not thinking of sending you out on patrol

again?' Lizzie didn't think her nerves would stand it if they did – the days and endless nights of knowing that Bill was sailing those dangerous waters, sweeping for German mines or else using sonar equipment to track U-boats, running the risk of another deadly torpedo attack. Her blood ran cold as she remembered the last patrol, which had ended in the disastrous sinking of *Sea Knight*.

'Not so far as I know,' he assured her. 'We're doing a training course to learn the drill – how to use the Scammell winches, and so on. Like I say, there's no reason to worry.'

A frown remained on Lizzie's usually smooth forehead. 'Shall I let Connie know?'

'No, better let Tom tell her. And can you pass on a message? He's agreed at the last minute to swap shifts with Eddie Fraser.'

'So Tom won't be on duty tonight?'

'That's right – he plans to work with me on *Annie May* instead.'

'Right you are.' Lizzie gave Bill a brittle smile and they went their separate ways. She delivered the message then set off on her round with a heavy heart. True, maintaining the blimps didn't put Bill and Tom in direct danger, but she feared it was the thin end of the wedge. The next thing they knew, the Patrol Service would be making further demands, as they had every right to do.

Since the sinking of their trawler, Bill and Tom were no longer classed as men in reserved occupations. If the Royal Navy didn't conscript them then the army or the RAF were standing by, ready to sweep young and fit men like them off to regiments in Italy, North Africa, Singapore or – God forbid – to enlist them into Bomber Command. *Take one day at a time*, Lizzie told herself as she rounded the headland then dropped off her first delivery at the Harbour-master's. *Try not to think too far ahead.*

Back at the shop, Connie was run off her feet. Her regular customers came and went in quick succession – 'One cottage loaf and three sultana scones, please, love.' 'Have you any of those small custard tarts?' 'A large white, two sausage rolls and one of those teacakes.' Then in sauntered one of the new RAF erks, hands in pockets and whistling as he entered. Connie recognized Reggie at once and was on her guard, resting both hands on the glass counter while she awaited his order.

'Well, look who it isn't!' Reggie perked up at the sight of Connie. 'It's the lindy hop lady in red.'

Connie returned a no-nonsense stare. 'How can I help?'

'You can give me a smile, for a start.' He took out a cigarette then decided against lighting up. The cigarette dangled from his lips as he examined the display of cakes and pastries. 'And I'll have two of those round iced buns with the cherries on the top. They make a nice handful, eh?' A suggestive wink accompanied his order.

Honestly! The bloke couldn't help himself. Connie put the sticky buns into a bag and slid them across the counter minus the smile. 'Anything else?'

'It depends what you're offering.' Ignoring the sound of the shop bell and the entrance of two new customers, Reggie set about breaking down Connie's defences. 'Come on, I'm only kidding. By the way, I think I came across your other half – the lanky bloke you were with last Saturday. Tom Rose, if I remember rightly.'

Connie cocked her head to one side and frowned. 'Whereabouts?'

'On one of the river barges in the estuary. Harry Tate's Navy called us in to teach a group of volunteers how to storm-bed the blimps.'

The common nickname for the Royal Navy Patrol Service was sometimes used disparagingly and Connie's frown deepened. It carried a suggestion that RNPS vessels were old and dropping to bits and the men who sailed them were as decrepit as the boats.

'No need to look like that,' he cajoled. 'I'm only having a bit of fun.'

The customer behind gave him a friendly tap on the shoulder. 'Is that a Scouse accent by any chance? The skipper on my old man's merchant ship comes from Liverpool – his convoy was hit off Malta.'

'Scouser born and bred,' Reggie confirmed, turning back to Connie with his broad smile and bristling moustache to ask how much he owed her.

'That'll be sixpence please.'

'And cheap at half the price.' Delving into his pocket, he handed over the small silver coin, pressing it firmly into her palm and winking as he did so. 'That Tom of yours is sharp as a tack. He already knows all there is to know about wind directions and underwater currents around here. We got chatting – he told me about the trawler he and Bill have set about restoring.'

The unexpected change of tone eased Connie's

frown, though she couldn't rid herself of the suspicion that Reggie might have an ulterior motive for complimenting Tom; namely to soften her up. 'There's a lot to do before she's seaworthy,' she conceded.

'It'll keep your boys out of mischief.' Reggie lit the cigarette that had been dangling all this time. The match flared, the tobacco tip glowed red and he inhaled deeply. 'I'll get out of your hair then,' he told Connie as he made for the door, the ping of the bell marking his exit.

'Nice chap,' the next customer remarked, her gaze following Reggie up the street. 'And not bad-looking either, come to think of it.'

'How can I help?' Connie's tone was thoughtful. Even from the back, Reggie's swagger was unmistakable. Shoulders back, head up and breathing out plumes of blue smoke, he strode along College Road as if he owned it – calling hello to the owner of Benson's music shop, pausing to flirt with Cynthia Leigh outside her hairdressing salon, then on again with his two iced buns stuffed into his jacket pocket and thoughts of how best to fill his spare time circling like hawks over his head.

Sally's third day in the office saw the arrival of her brand-new typewriter. She and Pamela lifted the shiny Imperial out of its cardboard box, remarking on its small size and light weight before poring over the instructions. Pamela then inserted a ribbon and typed 'the quick brown fox jumps over the lazy dog'.

'Perfect!' she declared.

Sally sat at her desk and experimented with the space bar and a series of capital letters. Peck-peck-

peck with the keys; 'SALLY HOPKINS'. She tried the numbers – '12345678910'.

'Happy?' Pamela hardly needed to ask – Sally's smile was broad enough to split her freckled face in two.

'I can't wait to get cracking.' Sally sorted through the pile of letters awaiting reply. 'What do I say to this one?' She showed Pamela the letter of complaint they'd received from Dixon's yard. 'It says we got their last order wrong.'

Pamela read the letter and took in the details. 'This is one for main office to sort out. I'll go while you get on with the rest.'

She left Sally perched on her plump new cushion, happily typing away, and hurried through to the office at the front of the building – a long, narrow room overlooking the yard, lined with shelves supporting thick ledgers and containing two large desks where her father and Fred spent their days checking columns of figures.

'Look who it isn't!' Harold looked up at his daughter and smiled. 'To what do we owe the pleasure?'

Fred glanced up briefly then carried on with his calculations.

'Can you check Dixon's last order for me please?' Handing over the letter of complaint to her father, she sidled over to Fred's desk and peered over his shoulder, willing him to break off from his work. He wore a white shirt with the sleeves rolled up, revealing a wristwatch with a brown leather strap and strong forearms covered in fine, dark hairs.

He completed a column then looked up with a distracted frown. 'What's wrong with the order?'

'Nothing, I expect. Arthur Dixon likes to try it on once in a while, to get out of paying what he owes us.' Pamela held Fred's gaze. 'Will I see you in the canteen later?'

'Probably.' Fred shuffled papers around his desk.

Since skipping dinner on Monday, he had opted out of an arrangement to meet Pamela for a drink after work on the Tuesday, pleading a last-minute shift at the control centre. He'd been behaving differently somehow, as if an invisible barrier had come between them, though he'd denied that anything was wrong. Now, again, he seemed to be intent on keeping her at arm's length. 'Is everything all right?' she murmured as her father left his desk to check a ledger at the far end of the room.

'Yes.' Fred made himself snap out of the gloom that had descended over him since the weekend. He fixed a smile on his face. 'Everything's fine. I'll see you at dinner time.'

'Good.' She breathed a sigh of relief. And yet, and yet – the smile seemed forced. Fred put his head down and made it clear that he wanted to get on. The small signals couldn't be ignored.

Harold returned with the ledger and an air of satisfaction. 'Here's the Dixon order dated March the tenth – just over a month ago. It was signed for on delivery. Everything in order, nothing about any missing items.'

Retrieving the letter, Pamela retreated to her own office where she found Sally typing furiously. Her slim fingers flew over the keys and she bent forward with an air of concentration until Pamela reminded her that it was time for elevenses.

They made tea together in a corner of their office. Sally moved quickly and deftly, setting out Hugh's tray with cup and saucer, milk jug and a plate for biscuits.

Pamela boiled the new-fangled electric kettle and made the tea. 'We make a good team,' she commented.

'I'm glad you think so.' The nerves that Sally had experienced on day one had soon settled, and Pamela's kindness had allowed her to quickly overcome her sense of inferiority. She'd left home that morning with a jaunty spring in her step, waving to little Rita who watched her from the doorstep while their father took a delivery of beer and spirits. Sally's choice of outfit reflected her increasing confidence: an emerald-green dress with a wrap-over bodice and a skirt that swung as she walked. Her vibrant red hair was swept up to add height to her neat, small figure.

'I do,' Pamela insisted. 'I couldn't have hoped for a more willing and capable assistant.'

'I can't tell you how thrilled I was to get the job,' Sally admitted as they waited for the tea to brew. 'If only to prove the naysayers wrong.'

'Which naysayers?'

'My dad, for a start. He thinks my place is at home behind the bar. Then there was my fiancé . . .' Sally's voice trailed off and she took a sharp breath. 'We got engaged while I was going to night classes.'

'Engaged?' Pamela prompted.

'Yes, the wedding was set for November but it fell through at the last minute.'

Tact prevented Pamela from prying further. Instead, she put the teapot on the tray, ready for Sally to carry it through to Hugh.

'He jilted me,' Sally added as she picked up the tray with a rueful smile. 'He changed his mind and that was that.'

'But why?' Pamela held the door open, unable to resist a follow-up question. 'Did he give you any reason?'

Sally shook her head. 'It came out of the blue. At the time I was heartbroken, I can tell you. But I got over it.' She swallowed hard then proceeded along the corridor, tapping on Hugh's door before entering with the tray.

A wave of sympathy swept over Pamela. What a rotten thing for this fiancé chap to have done. Yet Sally had remained determined to better herself – she'd picked up the pieces and carried on at night school. She'd applied for a job. That took courage and will-power. Admiration overrode her sympathy. All in all, Sally Hopkins was quite a girl.

'What was his name?' Connie asked when Pamela related Sally's sad story later that evening. They were starting their shift at Gas Street, hoping as usual for a night without incident and glad of the cold yellow fog that had drifted up the estuary, hiding the usual targets from view. It had crept stealthily along the docks, twisting itself around tall cranes and between warehouses, deadening all sounds and blocking from view the air balloons securely anchored to their moorings on land and sea.

Pamela shrugged as she strapped on her helmet. 'I don't know – Sally didn't mention it.'

'Let me take a wild guess – it was Ron Butcher.' Connie hadn't plucked the name out of the ether.

'Lizzie has been keeping her ears open – according to Sam Billington, Ron went off the rails late last year, round about the time he lost his job on the docks. Since then he's been seen hanging around outside the Anchor. Anyhow, he looks the type to jilt a girl at the altar.'

'That date would fit in with him breaking off the engagement to Sally.'

'I'll get Liz to find out from Sam if Ron was the culprit.'

'Poor girl. I felt so sorry for her when she told me.' The account had chimed with a fear that was germinating deep within Pamela that Fred was cooling in his affections for her. 'Apparently there was no explanation for jilting her, but Sally picked herself up and got on with things. It seems that nothing knocks her off her perch for long.'

'That's the impression I get too.' Connie had known of Sally Hopkins for a long time. All of Kelthorpe had admired the way she'd taken up the family reins and cared for her younger brothers and sisters. The little whirlwind was to be seen hanging out washing in the backyard of the Anchor or haggling over the price of fish in the market, running, never walking, serving pints with a cheerful smile. 'I can't say I know her well, though.'

'She's promised to lend a hand with my bridesmaid's dress.'

'Has she now?' Was there no end to Sally's energy? Connie picked up the telephone to tick off the first thing on her list. 'Hello, operator – get me Kelthorpe 726, please.'

'I didn't have to ask her – she volunteered.' Ready

to depart for the Leisure Gardens, Pamela called these last words over her shoulder as she stepped out on to the street where, by chance, Reggie Nolan and Sid Donne had turned off Park Road and were coming towards her. *Drat!* Both were in civvies: smartly dressed in blazers and trilby hats.

When Reggie spotted her, he gave an admiring whistle. 'Why, it's the poster girl for the ARP!' he called from the other side of the road. 'And if she isn't, she damn well ought to be!'

Determined to go about her ARP business, Pamela ignored his flattery. After a quick exchange, Sid carried on walking, while Reggie crossed the street to follow her. 'What time do you finish your shift?' he pestered. 'Because I was thinking we might have time to squeeze in a quick drink.'

'No, thank you.' Pamela didn't wish to be rude, but really Reggie was getting to be a proper nuisance.

'Come on – just one little drink. Where's the harm?' *Keep it casual, don't scare the horses.* 'I'm new to town. I thought you could show me the sights.'

'I'm afraid not.' Connie would have known how to handle this. She would've given Reggie the brush-off and no mistake. Pamela's face was flushed with embarrassment as she pressed on towards Park Road.

He persisted. 'Tomorrow maybe?'

'No, thanks.'

'If you're bothered about how it looks, we could invite Sid along to keep us company.'

We? Angered by Reggie's cheeky presumption, Pamela stopped short of the entrance to the Leisure Gardens. 'I'm not bothered about how it looks,' she insisted, 'I just don't want to go out for a drink with you.'

'Ouch!' He raised his hands in surrender but there was mockery in his voice. 'You can't blame me for trying, though. That's another compliment, by the way.'

'Why is it?' Frustration reached boiling point. Pamela ought to have walked away, not flung this challenge at him.

'Because I'm saying you're a hard girl for a bloke to resist, that's why.' Suddenly serious, he lowered his voice. 'If you change your mind you know where to find me.'

'I won't,' she said quietly. Out of habit she almost added a polite 'thank you' but she resisted and strode on.

'Message received.' Reggie resumed his mocking tone and gave her back view a sly salute. 'Over and out.'

CHAPTER SEVEN

'From baking bread to boat repair!' It was early Saturday afternoon – half-day closing had come round fast – and Lizzie had scarcely had time to catch her breath.

'Yes, where's the week gone?' Connie, too, had been rushed off her feet. They quickly removed the skirts and blouses that they'd worn for work in the bakery and changed into trousers and jumpers in their cramped shared bedroom on Elliot Street. The girls had ten minutes to snatch a bite to eat before Bill and Tom roared up to carry them off to Wren's Cove for a spot of paint-stripping and tinkering with *Annie May*'s engine parts.

'What's the big rush?' their father grumbled as his daughters clattered downstairs and set about making a flask of tea before slapping margarine and blackberry jam on to slices of bread. He sat at the kitchen table hunched over his *Daily Express*, reading about a plan to award the George Cross to the people of Malta for their bravery under siege – a move he was fully behind. 'We think we've had it bad,' he said with a jab of his finger towards the headline, 'but those poor beggars have had it ten times worse.'

'Bill and Tom are picking us up,' Connie said with her mouth full and one eye on the clock. She'd flung a few items into her haversack and was ready for the off. 'They'll be here any minute.'

'Will you go to the allotment?' Lizzie checked with her father.

Bert nodded and put his newspaper to one side. 'Don't worry, I won't overdo it,' he assured her.

Lizzie kissed him lightly on the top of his head. 'You read my mind.'

The sound of motorbike engines drew Connie to the front room, from where she had a clear view of traffic trundling along the street. 'Here they are. Get a move on, Liz – time to go.'

The girls grabbed their belongings and ran from the house, banging the door behind them.

'Hop up,' Tom invited Connie, patting her leg as she climbed aboard.

Lizzie and Bill followed suit and soon they were off, winding through the narrow streets of terraced houses and only picking up speed once they were clear of the town. Glorious, long-distance views raised their spirits and they felt on top of the world.

The sea! Lizzie drank in the sight of the flat horizon beneath banks of fluffy white cloud. She caught occasional glimpses of waves crashing against rocks below, and there was space; glorious, infinite space. Her heart soared as they rounded the final bend and came to a stop in the lay-by overlooking the cove.

Bill pulled in behind Tom. Soon all four were taking the cliff path down to the beach, battling a strong breeze that chased the clouds over Kelthorpe's distant headland, leaving the sky a pure blue. Eager to get stuck in again, they leaped the last few feet on to the sand, then ran on towards the hidden cove where they found *Annie May* in the same sorry state as before: tilted to starboard, leaky and rotten, crying out for rescue.

Seeing her, Connie took a deep breath. 'Where do you want me to start?'

Tom took charge. 'Why don't you tackle the deck with me?' He climbed the rickety ladder propped against the hull, then went to fetch the metal tool-box stored under the bridge. 'That's rum,' he muttered. The box wasn't where they'd left it.

'Here it is.' Bill lugged it along the deck. He'd found it near the prow, half covered by a tarpaulin. 'But look – the lock's been forced.'

'Who by?' Tom scratched his head.

Still down on the beach, Lizzie and Connie discovered that someone had set fire to their pile of rotten planks. All that remained was a heap of grey ash and a trail of scuffed footprints leading to and from the village. Connie called up to Tom. 'Some idiot has lit a bonfire.'

Bill leaned over the guard rail. 'It must have been kids,' he decided. One hammer seemed to be missing from the toolbox but nothing else, so he wasn't overly concerned.

Connie gave a doubtful frown before pointing out the size of the footprints. 'What kid do you know who has size-ten clodhoppers?'

Tom joined Bill at the rail. 'Are you two girls coming up to give us a hand or are you planning to stand around all day playing at Miss Marple?'

Laughing, the girls pushed the mystery to one

side. Before long, they'd climbed the ladder and were hard at work with saw and chisel, accompanied by the sound of splintering wood and the soft thud of more rotten planks landing in the sand. After an hour, they'd made a worryingly large hole in the deck – ten feet square and worse than they'd originally thought. Even Bill's optimism was dented.

'The beams underneath are rotten as well,' he said with a sigh. 'We'll need to buy extra timber.'

'Where there's a will . . .' Lizzie reminded him.

Connie drew the flask of tea out of her haversack and the foursome took refuge from a strengthening wind under the bridge. The sea had turned choppy and the waves breaking on the shoreline sent up plumes of white spray. Lizzie nestled close to Bill to sip her drink, happily aware of the way their bodies seemed to fit together – he shielded her from the worst of the wind and they were so close that she could feel the warmth of his body through his shirt. Connie and Tom sat a small distance away, his arm around her shoulder and hers around his waist, both gazing out to sea. No words broke the contented silence.

'What next?' Connie asked at last.

'I'll fit that new distributor cap.' Lizzie jumped to her feet.

'I'll start on the second hatch.' Tom intended to replace all the frames to make them watertight.

'The winches,' Bill said. He wanted to deal with the rust that caked the ancient mechanisms.

Connie offered to tackle the back-breaking job of stripping paint from the hull. 'I know my place,' she commented wryly as she descended the ladder armed with scraper and sandpaper, then began to hum a tuneless version of 'When You Wish Upon A Star'.

Her humming was no better than her singing – a fact that Lizzie wasn't slow to point out. 'Give it a rest, Con,' she called from the deck, spanner in hand. 'Do us a favour and stick to dancing. Leave the Walt Disney warbling to Tom.'

The coast road from Kelthorpe to Raby consisted of many twists and turns. The hills were steep and Pamela's legs and lungs had to work hard to keep up with Fred, who cycled ahead as they approached the cove. 'Wait for me,' she called.

He stopped at the top of the final gradient, his heart beating rapidly as he caught his breath and surveyed the scene. There was nothing to beat an English spring, he decided. Wayside flowers were coming into bloom – wild daffodils glowed jewel-like among blades of fresh green grass. At the sight of them, Fred felt his worries melt away. It was as if the spirit of the season had entered his veins and he experienced a sensation of weightlessness, of floating free of the earth while he waited for Pamela to catch up.

She arrived with windswept hair and flushed cheeks, as natural as could be. Her lips were slightly parted as she stopped to draw breath, her eyes wide and shining.

'I'm sorry.' Fred's simple words held a wealth of meaning. Feelings that he'd bottled up for days rose to the surface and he felt unnerved by them, hardly trusting himself to speak.

'Whatever for?' Pamela asked between gasps. They'd set off later than planned and at this rate they wouldn't make it to Wren's Cove in time to help with the restoration of *Annie May* as promised. She was about to set off on the downward slope when he reached out and grasped her handlebars.

'For everything. For how I've behaved recently. I'm an idiot.' Would she forgive him, and did he deserve it if she did? Fred's pulse raced as he studied her reaction.

Their eyes met and she saw that Fred's recently erected barriers had come down and his direct, penetrating gaze was back. The apology was deep and heartfelt.

Her relieved smile drew out a longer confession. 'I mean it,' Fred said. 'I've let Reggie Nolan get under my skin and I shouldn't have. It was just the sight of you and him dancing together – I panicked.'

'What for, exactly?' Pamela was incredulous.

'Like I said – I've been stupid.' That's what jealousy did – it took away every last shred of reason, magnifying the smallest problem and allowing it to gain a stranglehold against all the odds.

'Reggie's the stupid one, not you.' Letting the bike fall on to the verge, she embraced Fred. 'He's not even my type.'

Of course not – perfectly idiotic of me. He held her close. 'So you have a type?' he murmured. *Soft, sweet and gentle; my Pamela.*

'Yes. My type has to be over six feet tall, for a start. He must have thick dark hair and no moustache. There must be a neat side parting. What else?' She ran her fingers down Fred's cheek. 'Smooth skin, clear grey eyes and a certain way of looking at me that makes me go weak at the knees.'

'Stop!' He kissed her lips. 'I don't deserve you, Pamela Carr. I really don't.'

'That's true,' she teased as she drew back. 'Now, are we going to lend a hand with *Annie May* or not?'

They picked up their bikes and cycled on, coasting down the hill until they reached the lay-by described by Connie. It took them a while to discover the overgrown path down to the beach, then to negotiate the perils of the little-used descent, where the steps had crumbled in places. By the time they arrived on the beach and made their way to the narrow inlet named after Daniel Wren, a swashbuckling smuggler from times gone by, they found that the cove was deserted.

'Where is everyone?' Fred made a full circuit of the old trawler.

Pamela climbed the ladder on to *Annie May*'s deck to investigate further. 'We've left it too late,' she lamented. 'And look, the tide's coming in fast.'

True; waves broke on the shingle with furious force then raced up the smooth beach towards the secluded inlet where they stood. The way back was already underwater, with currents swirling around the foot of the cliff and spray rising into the cold, clear air.

'It's almost high tide.' This must be why the others had already left; Fred realized he and Pamela would have to head towards Raby village rather than retrace their steps. 'We'd better get a move on unless we want to stay here overnight?' His sentence ended with an upward intonation – the romantic notion of being trapped by the tide and forced to take refuge in the dark, dry cave where Wren and his piratical band had once stashed their contraband goods had its appeal. A night with Pamela, holding her close leading to heaven knew what . . . For a moment Fred enjoyed the fantasy.

'No.' Pamela kept her feet firmly on the ground. 'We'd freeze to death. Everyone would be out of their minds with worry. No, definitely not.'

'All right – you win,' he conceded.

With the roar of breaking waves and the rush of receding shingle in their ears, Pamela and Fred emerged from the inlet only to find that their way to the village was blocked by another jagged outcrop of rock rising even more steeply from the beach. 'Good Lord!' Realizing that their options were narrowing by the second, Fred anxiously scanned the cliff face. 'Could we climb up?'

'Or swim for it?' Pamela saw that the tide threatened to cut them off in every direction. Mighty waves swelled then broke with great force. White water swirled in foaming eddies before another wave crashed against the rocks.

'Too risky,' Fred decided. 'We'll have to climb.'

So, with their hearts in their mouths, they started to scale the cliff. Pamela went ahead, searching for footholds and feeling her way with her fingertips. She told herself not to look down at the treacherous water below. Fred followed. When loose rocks were dislodged and came rattling down, he pressed himself against the dark cliff face, gritting his teeth as earth and stones peppered his hands and face. 'No damage done,' he called up to her. 'Keep going.'

Pamela breathed hard. She felt a tight knot in her stomach as she inched her way up the cliff but she was determined to get to the top. *Don't look down*, she repeated to herself. *Down is danger. Up is safety. Almost there*.

Both were young and agile. They stretched and reached, clambered and heaved. Though the wind tore at their clothes and the waves thundered below, they climbed on until they reached the top.

Once there, they flopped down on the coarse grass. Two curious sheep approached, then skittered away. A solitary grey van drove along the narrow road towards Raby.

Fred exhaled. 'That was too close for comfort.'

'But we did it.' Lying flat on her back and breathing hard, Pamela gazed up at the sky. 'It'll teach us to check the tides in future.' She got to her feet then pulled him up. They shared an embrace without kissing, holding each other close and letting relief flood their bodies. Then they set off on the short walk to the lay-by where they'd left their bikes, planning their evening as they went.

'I'm on duty at Gas Street tonight, worse luck.' She brushed a streak of dirt from Fred's forehead then kissed his cheek.

'Me too – at the town hall.'

'I finish at eleven.'

'I could meet you afterwards.'

'You could.'

'We could walk to Sunrise?'

Pamela shook her head at his tentative question. 'Not tonight – not at that late hour.'

'Your parents?'

She nodded. 'They wouldn't approve.'

'So we could go to your house?' The bold suggestion

sprang from nowhere. He thought that she was bound to say no.

Pamela paused, then nodded again. 'If you like.'

Yes; she had agreed! 'Eleven o'clock it is, then.'

They reached the lay-by in a whirl of fresh emotions. Much had been left unsaid, but an important commitment had been made.

'Our bikes have been moved,' Fred pointed out. They'd left them carefully propped against a boulder, out of sight from the road. Now the bicycles were clearly visible and lying flat on the ground.

Pamela picked hers up with a confused frown. 'Look, my front tyre is flat.'

'Mine too – flat as a pancake.' It was sabotage; clear as anything. Fred's mind jumped to old suspicions – someone who knew his enemy alien status and who bore a grudge had seized the chance to make life difficult by letting down their tyres and leaving them stranded. It was a petty act but nonetheless it filled Fred with a familiar dread. Who had seen them cycle this way? he wondered.

'Are you thinking what I'm thinking?' Two flat tyres was no accident. Pamela noticed that the tiny screw-on black cap that covered the valve was missing on both wheels.

'Yes. It's deliberate.' Fred scanned the area for clues but found nothing unusual – no cigarette butts or tyre marks.

'Perhaps it was kids larking about.' With a mounting sense of dread, Pamela sought a more innocent explanation. *Not again!* a small voice inside her head whispered. Not more threats, not more vile notes accusing Fred of being a fifth columnist and her of being a collaborator; not more men with twisted notions of patriotism ganging up and lurking in dark corners, waiting to pounce.

'Yes – kids,' Fred said without conviction. He grabbed hold of Pamela's pump, connected it to the valve and began to inflate her tyre. 'Yes,' he said more firmly as the air went in. It was a silly prank carried out by boys from the village; nothing more.

Before the war, no one would have dreamed that patrolling the streets during blackout would become the accepted routine. 'A responsible job for responsible men!' shouted the early posters calling for ARP volunteers. Initially, people had responded with scorn. 'What, me – join that bunch of busybodies?' Families had also refused to use the flimsy Morrison shelters that the government had foisted on them, seeing them as death traps if a bomb should happen to fall. And, in truth, how likely was that? Only after the phoney war had ended and night-time raids became common had Civil Defence been taken seriously. The handful of paid wardens who had been recruited from the beginning were no longer dubbed 'three-quid-a-week army dodgers'. Wardens' posts had sprung up on every street corner and the cry of 'Put that light out!' had become the norm. Silver ARP badges were now pinned to coat lapels with pride.

'Here we go again,' Connie said wearily at the start of her Saturday-night shift. She'd split off from Lizzie at the bottom of King Edward Street and now stood with Pamela outside the sector post, leaning on the sandbag barrier and putting off the moment when she must enter. 'Roll on eleven o'clock.'

Pamela was only half listening. 'Something odd happened earlier today,' she confided. 'You know that Fred and I arrived too late to help with *Annie May*? Well, when we were ready to cycle home we found that someone had let down our tyres.'

'On purpose?' Connie quizzed. 'That is strange. We had a similar thing down in Wren's Cove. Some blighter had forced the lock on the set of tools we keep on board. They hadn't taken much, but they'd set fire to a pile of rotten timber nearby. If the wind had been in the wrong direction and the flames had spread to the boat, we'd have been in big trouble.'

'Kids?' Pamela offered hopefully.

'That's what we thought.' Glancing at her watch, Connie saw that it was time to take over from Brian Bellamy. 'I'll get a flea in my ear if I hang around out here much longer,' she muttered as she went in.

'Here's a copy of amendments to the blackout regulations,' Bellamy growled at her without looking up. He pushed a pamphlet across the counter then licked the end of his pencil and ticked an item off his list. 'We're running low on M3 forms and duty-respirators. You need to order a new batch of each.' Lick and tick. 'Inter-service training is to be stepped up so we're expecting extra manuals to be delivered.' A third lick and a third tick. He glanced up at last. 'Have you got all that?'

'Yes, ta,' Connie replied through gritted teeth. Oh, to be a junior warden again – out on the street or patrolling the dockside and breathing in salty air. Instead, she would be cooped up all evening in a stuffy shoe-mender's shop, filling in forms and talking on the telephone to central report and control.

'I'm bored stiff,' she whispered to Pamela once Brian was out of earshot. 'Give me a Redhill container and a stirrup pump over a pile of rotten paperwork any day of the week.'

'Arnold Kershaw, behave yourself,' Lizzie barked at her young cousin, who was larking around with fellow Boy Scout Colin Strong. 'This is a serious training exercise.'

The Saturday-evening task for the ambulance and first-aid crew based at the King Edward Street depot was to mock up a typical situation following an air raid. The boys had volunteered to act as casualties, enticed by the knowledge that it would involve pints of fake blood and the use of make-up to simulate gruesome wounds. On arrival, Arnold had promptly stripped off his jersey and vest then smeared lashings of bright red paint across his skinny chest. Now he was staggering around the brewery yard, clinging to Colin and crying out for his mother in the most pathetic manner imaginable.

Bill seized Arnold by the waistband of his shorts. 'Come with me,' he ordered sternly as he dragged the lad to a dark, damp corner then propped him against a broken drainpipe. 'Stay there. Close your eyes. Don't say a word. Colin, you as well. You two have to play dead until I send someone to put you on a stretcher and carry you into an ambulance. Is that clear?'

Lizzie took in the scene. Eight volunteer casualties were now deployed across the area. One elderly man had created two convincing black eyes and a head wound for himself and now lay groaning on the dirty cobbles, while Dorothy Parsons, the mild-mannered telephonist from report and control, cowered behind a broken cartwheel. Lizzie's role was to follow procedures outlined in the latest training booklet. The instructions went like this: approach the casualty and check for vital signs. If the victim is conscious and compos mentis, ask the following series of questions before you even think about moving him or her on to a stretcher, et cetera.

At a signal from Bill, Lizzie and two other members of her first-aid team sprang into action. Lizzie's job was to deal with Dorothy, but the telephonist took her role more seriously than expected. At Lizzie's approach, she screamed and resisted all attempts to pacify her.

Taken aback, Lizzie hardly knew how to proceed. She tried hard to remember what it said in the booklet. Was there even a section on dealing with hysteria?

'Help, somebody help!' Screaming, wailing, flinging her arms around in distress, Dorothy displayed a talent no one would have expected.

God in heaven, she deserves an Oscar! was Lizzie's first thought. She remembered that manhandling was one method recommended by the powers that be. They called it 'restraint' and suggested that at least two first-aiders should be present. Lizzie preferred a more rational approach.

Slowly but surely, she advanced towards Dorothy and placed a hand on her shoulder. 'Calm down,' she urged. 'Let's get you to the shelter.'

Lizzie's gentle tone soothed Dorothy and she allowed herself to be led across the yard.

Lizzie called for Bill to join them. 'All's well,' she reported. 'Dorothy needs treatment for shock, that's all.'

'Right you are.' Bill played out the scenario by taking charge of Dorothy. 'I'll manage from here. You can help Walter to stretcher one of the injured boys into the ambulance. Apply a splint to his right leg and a bandage to his chest to stem the bleeding.'

No sooner said than Lizzie sprinted across the yard to the spot where Arnold lay groaning, milking it for all he was worth. 'Ouch – ouch!' he yelped, then 'Agh!' at the top of his voice as Walter and Lizzie eased him on to a stretcher.

'Lie still,' Lizzie commanded sharply. Lord, was she glad that this wasn't the real thing!

'He's heavier than he looks,' Walter grumbled when they lifted their badly injured casualty and carried him to an ambulance.

'Agh-oh-ooh-ouch-aagh!'

'Quiet.' Enough was enough for one training session. Lizzie did what it definitely didn't tell you to do in the instruction booklet and growled at her patient through gritted teeth. 'Pipe down, Arnold, or I'll give you a thick ear.'

The real thing, when it happened, caught Pamela and Simon Fraser off guard.

Connie had sent the pair on patrol to the base of the headland then up Musgrave Street to the top of the hill, where a fire watcher was stationed close to the two newly installed kite balloons. They'd stopped to chat – Roger Calvert had introduced himself as an area officer sent over from Easby for the night. Simon had admired the fire watcher's high-domed Zucker-man helmet, designed to withstand strong impact, and had noted that he wore his armband over a civvy overcoat to keep out the night-time chill. Calvert had been cupping his hands and blowing into them for warmth when searchlights on the beach below were suddenly switched on; the sky went from pitch dark to blinding white light in a split second. Beams raked across the night sky. Red alert sounded – there was no yellow warning period.

'Tip-and-run!' Pamela exclaimed. A lone Jerry bomber was caught in the criss-crossing beams, heading east to west, straight off the sea. Another Dornier: this time a more recent and even more deadly Do 217 – the throaty drone of the heavy twin-engine *schnellbomber* was unmistakable. Then, within seconds, dozens of incendiaries fell to earth. They lit up the black night, making a sound like dried leaves rustling along pavements as they fell before explod-ing in flashes of silver light as they landed on the headland.

'Duck!' Roger Calvert's cry ripped through the air. Jerry flew in low, all guns blazing. Machine-gun bul-lets ricocheted off rocks, sending fragments of limestone flying in every direction. Meanwhile, dozens of fires broke out, setting alight the heather and gorse that covered the headland. Wind fanned the flames, driving them ever closer to the newly installed dirigibles.

Pamela, Roger and Simon flung themselves to the ground, face down, then covered their heads with their arms. An incendiary rustled down, landing within six feet of them and remaining ominously quiet – it continued to hiss but as yet there was no explosion. The threat built with every passing second.

The first to react, Roger sprang to his feet. There were rows of red fire buckets filled with sand ranged along the base of the two concrete blocks that anchored the balloons to the ground. He seized two of the buckets and threw the contents over the unexploded bomb, rendering it harmless. One fewer threat – but there was no time to rest on their laurels.

Simon and Pamela grabbed buckets then ran across the moorland to extinguish other fires with the sand. By now, Jerry had released all his bombs, so he gained height and turned for home. Ack-ack fire from the beach missed its target; mission accomplished, the Dornier pilot escaped scot-free.

Seizing more buckets, the two young wardens and the fire watcher continued to sprint along the ridge to fight the flames. Pamela's face ran with sweat and her throat and lungs ached through inhaling hot, black smoke. Still she fought on until all the buckets were emptied.

'What now?' Simon appealed to Roger. Half a dozen small outbreaks were yet to be dealt with; fingers of flame were licking at the low heather and creeping ever closer to the LZs.

Overhead, the two balloons strained at their metal cables, twisting this way and that in the wind, their silver shells reflecting vivid orange flames.

Roger quickly took off his overcoat and proceeded to beat out the nearest fire. 'Use your helmets,' he ordered. 'Scrape up loose earth then dump it on the flames.'

Once more, Pamela and Simon followed orders,

sick in the knowledge that by staying they ran a huge risk. If the flickering flames were to reach the hydrogen balloons there would be a massive explosion and a conflagration from which there would be no escape.

Pamela heaved at clumps of heather and pulled them out by the roots to expose small patches of soil. She dug frantically with the rim of her helmet, scooping up loose earth, which she flung on to the flames. She repeated the exercise, once, twice, three times, until she ceased counting.

Then, as the exhausted trio paused to drag air into their smoke-filled lungs, an AFS lorry came roaring up Musgrave Street with hoses and water tank at the ready. Half a dozen firefighters leaped out, unreeled their hoses and directed strong jets at the remaining flames. Thank God: water quenched them. They flickered lower, flared in one last act of defiance, then gave a final hiss before expiring. Steam rose from the blackened earth. Darkness swallowed the headland and moonlight reflected off the smooth silver surface of the giant balloons.

'It was nothing – all in a night's work.' Pamela made light of the evening's close shave when Fred came to meet her at the sector post as arranged.

He kept his thoughts to himself. Her face and hands were blackened by smoke. She might have died. He could have lost her and lived the rest of his life with a broken heart. 'The Dornier slipped in under the radar just like the last one,' he admitted. 'I filed the damage report after the event and forwarded it to Home Security – too late to be of much use, I'm afraid.'

They walked hand in hand along Gas Street then across the market square to the bottom of King Edward Street.

'Are you tired? Is it too late?' he asked tentatively.

'For you to come home with me?' She shook her head and they carried on up the steep hill together. When they reached her shabby lodging house, she searched the pockets of her battledress for her key.

Fred's courteousness was at odds with his deep desire to be close to his sweetheart; closer than they'd ever been. 'Really, you must say if you'd rather not.'

She turned the key in the lock. 'Come in,' she insisted gently.

He followed her along a dingy corridor then up the stairs. The dark brown carpet was threadbare, with several brass stair rods loose or missing, but once they reached Pamela's room on the first floor all was spotless. The walls were freshly decorated with a rose-patterned wallpaper and a new green rug covered the cracked lino. There were two table lamps: one on the window sill and one on a bedside cabinet. The eiderdown on the bed was primrose yellow to match the roses on the wall.

Pamela crossed the room to pull down the black-out blind before turning on the lamps. Her heart raced. The moment that she'd dreamed of had arrived at last, yet she felt shy and unsure.

'Your face.' Fred stepped towards her.

'What's wrong with my face?'

'There's a black mark – here.' He brushed her cheek with his thumb. 'Your face is beautiful, by the way.' Extraordinary – truly unique; a perfect pale oval, unmarked by time or tragedy. He loved her

118

startling grey-green eyes, her full, soft mouth. 'Everything about you is beautiful.'

'I love you,' she murmured as she felt his arms enclose her and she leaned her head against his shoulder. 'More than anything in the world.'

The simple, trusting, almost childlike declaration broke down all remaining barriers. 'I love you too,' Fred said, 'and I'd never do anything to hurt you.'

She looked up into his face. 'I know that.'

'I'll keep you safe.'

'I've never—' she began.

'Hush.' He kissed her softly on the lips.

'I don't know what—'

He kissed her again. 'If you're sure?' he breathed.

One by one, Pamela felt the strong ties of convention loosen then slip away. *Good girls don't . . . It's not respectable without a ring on your finger . . . Tongues will wag.* 'Yes,' she whispered. The world and its myriad troubles ceased to exist. All that mattered was Fred's voice, his hands, his lips.

'Take off your jacket.' He helped her with the buttons. She let it drop to the floor. Slowly they undressed. Slowly he led her to the bed, where they lay side by side, staring at the ceiling as they each absorbed what was about to happen. Then Fred turned towards her. 'There will never be anyone else,' he promised. *Niemand anders.*

His lips were against her cheek; she could feel his warm breath. 'Don't say never – you can't be sure.'

'It's true – there never will be.' Through all his years of struggle, Fred had coped alone – in London after his mother and father had died in the arson attack, in Kelthorpe where he'd tried in vain to escape his past. Only Pamela had believed in him and trusted him and shown him her love. 'If you want me to, I'll stay with you for ever. Nothing will tear us apart.'

His words gave Pamela certainty in the midst of chaos. Bombs would rain down, houses would collapse, the streets of Kelthorpe would lie in ruins, but Fred would still be there. She folded herself into him, slipping her arm around his neck and drawing him close. Peace. Silence. Only cool skin tingling as they touched, and then their rapid breathing.

In the first light of day they rose and pulled up the blind. Contentment filled the room. There was no hurry as they got dressed; only a slow ease of movement. Their bodies were familiar now and no less beautiful. Making love had been everything they'd hoped for, dreamed of, yet at the same time feared. Together, they left the house and walked without worry or shame to Sunrise, where they would share breakfast with Edith, Harold and Hugh, unembarrassed and ready to face the world.

CHAPTER EIGHT

'"Though April showers may come your way, they bring the flowers that bloom in May."' Connie sat at her sewing machine and croaked her way through the chorus of a popular Al Jolson song. As usual, she was completely out of tune.

Lizzie dropped her pinking scissors and clapped her hands over her ears. 'You did that on purpose to put me off.' Turning to Pamela and Sally, she advised them to ignore Connie's caterwauling. 'She's like the Duchess's baby in *Alice in Wonderland* – she only does it to annoy.'

Connie grinned. So far, she liked what she'd seen of Pamela's new friend; a little red-haired dynamo who fitted in well with the small group of eager seamstresses.

'I've come to lend a hand with Pamela's bridesmaid's dress,' she'd announced when she'd arrived at the door of number 12, her sewing box tucked under her arm. 'I arranged to meet her here.'

Connie and Lizzie had welcomed Sally in, and Pamela had arrived five minutes later.

'What happened to you?' Lizzie had demanded as she'd shown her into the front room.

'Nothing. Why – what do you mean?' Pamela had been conscious that her blushes gave her away as usual.

'Come off it – you're positively glowing.' Connie had guessed instantly what was what – Pamela and Fred's relationship had finally taken a major step forward. *Yes, and about time too!*

Soon the foursome had settled down to work. Connie whirred away at the machine, attaching her matron of honour's bodice to its flared skirt, then sewing in the zip. Lizzie removed pieces of her bride's dress from the paper pattern before tacking interfacing to the neckline and arm holes. Starting from scratch, Sally knelt on the floor with Pamela to lay pattern pieces on to forget-me-not-blue satin.

'So, Sally – how on earth do you find time to fit everything in?' Lizzie enquired as her needle flew through the fine fabric. 'What with the new job at Anderson's on top of working behind the bar and looking after your brood of little ones.'

'Not so little any more,' Sally pointed out. 'Rita started school last September, bless her.'

'Yes, but you still have all those mouths to feed and clothes to wash and iron. I don't know how you do it.'

'Dotty's not much help in that regard,' Sally admitted. 'She may be eleven but she's a proper dreamer. She'd go out wearing odd socks and with her hair like a bird's nest if I let her.' Chatting easily, she showed Pamela how to fit pattern pieces on to the material with the least possible waste. 'Eric does his best, but have you ever tried to teach a lad how to iron a shirt? It's a lost cause, believe me.'

'And the other boy?' The name had escaped Pamela.

'George. He's not happy unless he's climbing a

tree or else out at the end of the jetty fishing for cod. I reckon that's what George will do when he leaves school – sign up as a trawlerman on any boat that will take him.'

'What about the length?' Connie tried her dress on the mannequin by the window. 'To the knees, or a bit higher?'

'Higher,' Lizzie decided. 'With legs as good as yours it'd be a shame not to show them off.'

Happy with the reply, Connie set about measuring the length of her skirt. 'Sally, what's it like having Pamela as your boss?'

'It's a nightmare!' Sally's freckled face assumed an exaggerated expression of disgust. 'Do this, do that, don't do it that way, do it like this.'

'Uh-oh, I like this girl!' Connie whisked the dress off the mannequin. 'Why not volunteer for the ARP and liven things up a bit? We could do with some new blood over at Gas Street.'

'Much as I'd love to . . .' Sally said with a mischievous wink at Pamela.

'She's busy at the Anchor most evenings,' Pamela reminded Connie. 'Have you finished with the machine? Can I make a start on this bodice?'

Connie gave way to Pamela with good grace, then there was more whirring, more snipping and pinning. Two hours passed before they knew it; nine o'clock arrived and it was time to pack up.

Lizzie was happy with their progress. 'Two more sessions ought to do it,' she remarked as Sally and Pamela prepared to leave. Then she thanked Sally for lending a hand. 'It's made all the difference,' she assured her as they said their goodbyes.

Pamela and Sally's way home took them to the edge of the market square. Not a single shaft of light escaped from any of the cottages, or from the pub where Sally lived, but the night air was alive with the sound of waves crashing against the stone jetty and the sense that soldiers from the 39th Battalion were hunkered down as usual inside the pillboxes ranged along the beach. 'This is where I love you and leave you,' Pamela remarked easily.

But Sally's mood had grown more sombre during their walk home. 'Before you go, do you mind if I get something off my chest?' she said.

'No – what is it?' Pamela envisaged a small problem at work – sometimes the crane drivers and men who worked in the cutting shed under Keith Nelson could make remarks that were a little off-colour.

'It's the man I was engaged to,' Sally confessed. 'He won't leave me alone.'

Pamela was confused. 'But I thought . . .'

'Yes, Ron was the one who broke it off.' Sally bit her bottom lip. 'But it hasn't stopped him bothering me ever since.'

'Your fiancé was Ron Butcher?' Pamela had heard this on the grapevine so showed no surprise.

Sally sighed and nodded.

'Why – what does he do exactly?'

'He hangs around outside the pub most evenings. He doesn't come in, though.'

'No, I expect your father would send him packing if he did.'

'And he's followed me to work most mornings. Sometimes he's still drunk from the night before.'

'Follows you but doesn't say anything?' Pamela was worried by this.

Sally nodded. 'So what does he want?' she pleaded, with a mixture of exasperation and fear. 'If Ron's got something to say to me, why not just come out with it?'

'Perhaps he wants to make up?'

This time the response was a vehement shake of the head. 'You weren't there when we broke up. You didn't hear what he said.'

There was a long pause while Pamela waited for Sally to continue.

'He said he hated me and he hated all women. We tell lies and we can't be trusted. There was worse than that, too.' Tears welled up and she brushed them away. 'I tried to tell him how much I loved him, but he told me he'd never loved me right from the start, that I was a silly little fool if I thought he hadn't noticed me carrying on behind his back. I wasn't, I swear!'

'Of course not.' Pamela felt a surge of anger on her new friend's behalf. How awful it must be to hear those insults spoken by the man you were engaged to.

'I'm not that kind of girl.'

'But in that case, why is he still bothering you? And how much does it scare you?'

Sally hesitated. 'I'm more worried than scared. Ron has a cut on his forehead – a bad one. He's let it get infected.'

'I heard that he crashed his bike when he was drunk and got into a fight with Sam.' Pamela had a clear memory of Lizzie's account.

'That explains the cut.' Taking a deep breath, Sally started to apologize. 'I shouldn't have said anything to you – it's up to me to sort it out.'

'I only wish I could be of more use.'

'That's just it – you can't. No one can.' With a helpless shrug of her shoulders, Sally backed away across the empty square towards the Anchor.

'Maybe he'll lose interest and stop following you,' Pamela said without conviction.

'Maybe,' Sally echoed uncertainly. 'I'll see you first thing tomorrow.'

'Eight thirty on the dot,' Pamela agreed. There would be the usual letters to type, receipts to file, telephone orders to write down – a busy life to lead despite the broken heart.

Pamela watched Sally cross the square with a sinking feeling. Who knew what a man like Ron Butcher would do next? The thought struck her that he might also be hanging around Wren's Cove. Could he be the one who had set fire to the debris on the beach, then let out the air in her and Fred's tyres? *I'll talk to Connie and Lizzie about it*, she decided as she turned for home.

'Fred's not here,' Edith informed her daughter. It was Tuesday evening and Pamela had called in at Sunrise on the spur of the moment, hoping to surprise her sweetheart. 'He's gone with Hugh and Harold to look at some new equipment for the cutting shed. Hugh said he would value their opinion.'

'Fred never mentioned it.' Pamela was disappointed. Since their Saturday night together he'd seldom been out of her thoughts and they'd spent every possible moment in each other's company, not attempting to hide their new intimacy from her parents and uncle. They'd held hands and openly exchanged kisses over Sunday breakfast and dinner. If Edith thought it unseemly, she had hidden her disapproval – after all, in her eyes Fred could do no wrong. Hugh had smiled in avuncular fashion at the billing and cooing as he called it. Harold, on the other hand, had clung to a more traditional role. Pamela was his daughter and it was his duty to look out for her. Ought he to pull Fred to one side and caution him against taking things too far too quickly? Then again, how could Harold possibly risk putting a dent in Pamela's blissful smile?

'Stay and have a cup of tea,' Edith insisted. She invited Pamela into the lounge, where her baby grand took pride of place in the bay window. Every surface was polished, every cushion plumped and every china ornament arranged on the low mantelpiece in perfect relationship to each other – the shepherd lad with fleecy lamb tucked under his arm smiled at his shepherd lass in panniered skirt and beribboned bonnet, while the Doulton cockerel raised his splendid iridescent head and crowed.

Tea. Ginger biscuits – home-made and presented on a plate with a paper doily. Pleasant chatter led by Edith. Her new musical scores had finally arrived, thank heavens. She'd started giving piano lessons to Reverend Greene's daughter, Millicent. Unfortunately the girl was tone deaf. Pamela listened and nodded sympathetically. She looked at her watch and wondered if it was worth waiting for Fred to return, then realized that her shift at Gas Street was due to start in just over an hour. She put her cup and saucer back on the tray and speedily took her leave. 'Tell Fred . . . tomorrow night, all being well. Thanks for the tea and bye-bye.'

Edith walked to the gate and watched Pamela hurry off along the promenade. It was true what they said about young lovers walking on air – her daughter's feet hardly touched the ground as she disappeared into the shadow of the headland. Edith sighed. Once upon a time she'd been that girl, falling head over heels for Harold Carr. She'd felt the same butterflies in her stomach and the overwhelming yearning in her heart that had made her throw aside convention and marry the lowly junior clerk in her father's office. Once upon a time.

Pamela had taken the lonely footpath that rounded the headland and was approaching the harbour when she ran into, of all the people she didn't want to meet, Sid and Reggie. They were dressed in uniform and lounging on a bench overlooking the jetty, but the moment they spied her, they sprang up and intercepted her; one on either side, jostling with their elbows and behaving with their usual over-familiarity.

'Look what the wind blew in,' Sid began cheerily.

'Yes – just what the doctor ordered.' Reggie's patter was accompanied by a wink.

'We promise, Nurse, we'll take our medicine like good little boys.'

'As long as you read us a bedtime story.'

The rapid-fire remarks were whipped away by the wind coming straight off the sea, which tugged at

Pamela's silk scarf. Who did the pair of clowns think they were; Abbott and Costello?

'Come and have a drink with us.' Reggie took hold of her elbow and steered her towards the Anchor.

'No, thank you – I've told you before – I've no wish to have a drink with you. Either of you,' she added with a cool glance at Sid. ('Be firm,' Connie had instructed when Pamela had broached the subject the previous day. 'They're a pair of pests,' Lizzie had agreed. 'If it happens again, don't stand any nonsense.')

'Reggie's paying,' Sid assured Pamela, before sidestepping a pile of lobster pots and two fishermen hanging up their nets. As Reggie and Pamela continued in a straight line towards the pub door, Sid lost interest and instead of following them into the Anchor decided to pass the time of day with the gang of trawlermen gathered by the jetty. He took out a packet of Woodbines and offered them round.

'Really, I wish you'd stop bothering me.' Pamela wrenched her arm free, only to find that Reggie had managed to slip his hand around her waist and was intent on whisking her onwards. *I'm being as firm as I can*, she told herself, *and it doesn't make a blind bit of difference.*

'Just this morning I was telling young Fred what a lucky beggar he was. Two like you don't come along very often and that's a fact.' On Reggie went, unabashed and with a steely determination beneath his jokes. 'Fred's a bit on the quiet, bookish side, if you don't mind me saying. What you really need is a man of the world.'

'What I really need is for you to leave me alone.'

Pamela dug in her heels. What did it take to get rid of a man like Reggie Nolan? Was he so caught up in himself, in his belief that he was irresistible to all women, that he missed the signals she was giving him? 'Seriously, I object to your discussing me behind my back as if I were a bus or a train – and with Fred of all people.'

'Watch out, love.' A thirsty customer in a frayed tweed jacket and a well-worn cap pushed past her as he made his way to the bar.

'I'm winding you up.' Reggie laughed and spread his hands, palms upwards. 'As a matter of fact, your name never came up in conversation with Herr Müller or whatever his name is.'

Not that again! The spectre of Fred's past reared up and a knot formed in the pit of Pamela's stomach.

'Joking again,' Reggie said with that maddening grin. His moustache hid his thin top lip but a set of bottom teeth showed white and even, with a speck of spittle on his clean-shaven chin. 'I don't give a monkey's about where Fred was born or what he got up to after he left Germany. Let sleeping dogs lie, I reckon.'

Knowledge was power – Pamela might be naive but she knew this much. And she didn't trust Reggie not to misuse this vital piece of information about Fred's background. Hesitating, she allowed herself to be ushered into the dimly lit snug.

'There, that's more like it. Dubonnet for the lady and a pint of pale ale for me,' Reggie called to Sally behind the bar.

Sally, help! Pamela's silent appeal came with a meaningful stare and a small shake of her head.

'Hang on a minute.' Sally had picked up Pamela's panicky signal and stood with both hands placed firmly on the top of the bar. 'For one thing, we're clean out of Dubonnet. For another, I know for a fact that "the lady" you refer to is due to start a shift at Gas Street in half an hour.'

'Make it a sweet sherry, then.' Reggie ignored the second part of Sally's rejoinder.

'Pamela doesn't drink sherry.' Sally's challenging gaze was strong enough to take the wind out of even Reggie's sails. Arms braced against the bar, eyes fixed on his face and mouth set firm, she made no move to serve him.

'That's right – I don't.' Seizing her chance, Pamela broke free from her unwelcome suitor and headed for the door. Thirty minutes to get home and then change into her uniform before taking the short cut to the sector post – she could just about make it if she ran every step of the way. 'I can't stand the taste, and even if I could, I've already spelled it out – I want you to stop pestering me, full stop.'

'Hear that?' Sally told the big-headed erk. Her hand reached for the pump and she began to pull him a pint of pale ale. 'You're out of your league there, love. And the sooner you get that into your thick skull the better.'

'Sam reckons that Ron went off the rails when his dad started talking about selling *Annie May*,' Lizzie told Connie as they shut up shop late on Friday afternoon. Connie was sweeping the floor while Lizzie finished tidying up in the bakery.

'Come again?' Connie was expecting Tom to pick

her up on his motorbike, so she opened the door and looked anxiously up and down the busy street.

'Sam puts Ron's queer behaviour down to his dad deciding to sell *Annie May*,' Lizzie repeated. 'Apparently, Ron called Tom and Bill all the names under the sun when the hospital doctors were trying to treat his injuries. He said they were swindlers who had robbed his dad blind. Sam and Ron used to be pals. He says Ron was always a bit of a loner, but he and Sam got on well enough.'

Men were at work on the *Gazette* building opposite the bakery, clearing rubble and erecting a barbed-wire barrier around the site. They'd put up a 'No Looting' sign for good measure.

'According to his dad, Ron wasn't capable of taking over, and anyway he wasn't interested.' Connie recalled the exact phrase that Tom had relayed to her – 'The lad hasn't got what it takes.' She continued, 'Come to think of it, Sam could be on to something – having *Annie May* snatched from under his nose can't have been easy.'

'You might be right,' Lizzie acknowledged. 'Anyway, I can see you're itching to get away.'

'Tom's due any minute.' Connie took off her apron and folded it neatly. She seemed distracted as she went to the door once more.

'You've got ants in your pants,' Lizzie commented. 'You haven't been listening to a word I've said.'

'That's not true,' Connie protested weakly.

'You've been like it all day.' Lizzie had noticed Connie make small mistakes over the change she'd handed to customers – definitely not like her – and she'd been unusually short with their Aunty Vera,

132

who had dropped by to discuss more wedding arrangements.

'I take it you've organized a new suit for Bert?' their aunt had asked Connie just as Lizzie had been heading off with a delivery. 'If not, would you like me to take him to Burton's to get measured up?'

Two new customers had followed Vera into the shop and Connie had given her short shrift. 'I don't have time for that now,' she'd snapped. 'Not everything revolves around Lizzie and Bill's big day, you know.'

Taken aback, Vera had retreated with a flea in her ear.

Now Connie sighed and offered a quiet apology. 'Don't mind me,' she muttered. 'I'm feeling a bit off-colour. Nothing that a good night's sleep won't cure.'

Arranging to catch up with her later, Lizzie left the shop just as Tom purred up on his motorbike. She gave him a cheery wave then headed off in the van for her own rendezvous with Bill. Tom parked the bike and went inside. He took off his gauntlets and goggles while Connie pulled down the blind.

'What do you say to a quick ride out to Wren's Cove?' Tom suggested. 'I haven't been out there for a couple of days. Bill's done more work on the deck – we can see how he's been getting on.'

'Fine.' She went to fetch her coat and hat.

Tom followed her. 'Don't I get a kiss?'

'Sorry.' Connie brushed his cold cheek with her lips. 'What have you been up to today?'

'I was on one of the river barges, learning more about winches and so on from Sid Donne. There's not much to it really.' He flapped his gauntlets

against his thigh as if giving himself a quick repri-
mand. 'Anyway, you don't want to hear about my
boring day. How about you?'

Sensing that he was keeping something from her,
Connie buttoned her coat as she stepped back into
the shop. 'Don't give me that, Tom Rose. What else
has happened?'

'Nothing.' He gave another flap of the gauntlets.
'Ready?'

The choppy conversation had put them both on
edge. 'Do you mind if I say no to Wren's Cove?' Connie asked. 'The truth is I need an early night.'

Tom winced as if he'd nicked his finger with a
sharp blade. 'Rightio – I'll give you a lift home.'

'If you like.' She advanced towards the door.

'The Patrol Service wants to transfer us from airship maintenance to minesweeping duties,' he
blurted out. He'd meant to keep it a secret for now,
darn it, but Connie's terse replies had thrown him
off balance.

'You and Bill?' She took a sharp breath and felt
the blood drain from her face. Feeling suddenly
light-headed, she grasped the door handle.

'Yes, both of us.'

'Does Lizzie know?'

'Not yet. They informed us today but they haven't
given us a date for when we start. Bill's hoping it
won't be until after the wedding.'

'But how can you go minesweeping if you don't
have a boat?' It made no sense; surely for Tom and
Bill to go after the deadly North Sea mines again
they would need a vessel that was seaworthy.

'They intend to conscript us on to a Royal Navy

corvette. They're better equipped than your average trawler – electrical sweeps, bigger guns, more modern sonar. They go after U-boats as well as mines.' Sounding weary, Tom made no attempt to soften his explanation. 'It's better if you don't tell Lizzie,' he warned. 'Let Bill pick his moment.'

Connie closed her eyes and steadied herself. 'What about *Annie May*?' she whispered.

'We'll carry on with the restoration for the time being. Who's to say exactly when the RNPS will give us the nod? It could be months off.'

She nodded; yes, look on the bright side. Why would the navy go to the trouble of teaching Tom and Bill about river barges and barrage balloons unless it planned to put their training to good use in the estuary? Minesweeping duty was surely a long way off – weeks, months, even years – and by then the war might be over.

'I didn't mean to tell you. I knew you'd worry.' A gulf had opened up between them, with Connie on the far side of a rapidly widening chasm, leaving Tom confused and helpless.

'Of course I'm worried! Who wouldn't be?' Feeling hot tears well up, she fiercely wiped them away with the back of her hand. As if things weren't bad enough!

'Connie?' He moved towards her, only for her to step sideways. 'What's up, love? This isn't like you.'

She turned her back, searching for a handkerchief in her coat pocket. 'I've been doing too much,' she told him. 'I'm worn out, that's all.'

'That's not it, though, is it?' Her head was bowed and she trembled. 'Has something happened?' Perhaps her dad's health had taken a turn for the worse – it was the only thing Tom could think of that would cause Connie to act this way.

The words wouldn't come. She had spent the day rehearsing this moment, framing what she would say. But now it came to it – she and Tom together with the blind down, traffic rumbling along the road outside and no earthly reason why she shouldn't deliver her news in a grown-up, calm and practical way – there was a constriction in her throat as if a hand was pressed against it, trying to strangle her.

'Connie?' he said with mounting trepidation.

'It's my time of the month, but I'm late.' Had she imagined speaking or had she actually come out with the dreaded words?

'What?' The gulf widened. She sounded far, far away. The glass counter gleamed and a low sun filtered in through the blind.

She forced herself to turn and face him.

Tom stared at her, dumbstruck, disbelieving and desperate.

'I think I might be pregnant.'

Six simple words shattered Connie and Tom's harmonious world as surely as any Hefty Hermann or anything else Jerry could throw at them. This was a disaster, pure and simple.

CHAPTER NINE

Silence. Tom couldn't speak. He swayed slightly, turning his head towards the door as if contemplating escape.

'Say something,' Connie pleaded.

He swallowed hard and overcame the urge to bolt. 'How late?'

'A week, maybe more.'

'But we've been careful.'

'I know.'

'How then?'

'I don't know.' Misery descended like a wet shroud, clinging to her face and making it difficult for her to breathe, let alone articulate her words.

'How sure are you?'

'Not a hundred per cent. But as a rule, I'm regular as clockwork.'

'A week,' he repeated with a shake of his head.

'There's a test.' She'd looked into it; a sample of her urine would be injected into a mouse or a frog. The mere thought caused a shameful, disgusted shudder to run through her.

'Is there?' Tom shot her a look, grasping at the straw she offered.

'But it's expensive and you have to wait a few days for the result, and anyway, I'm not sure I'd trust the result.' She imagined going to Dr McKay's surgery and admitting that she was in a fix. McKay would look down his narrow nose, peering over the top of his steel-rimmed glasses as he tut-tutted and sent her off to see the nurse.

'Good God in heaven,' Tom muttered, holding back the volley of choice swear words on the tip of his tongue.

Connie tried and failed to read his expression. He no longer looked like the reliable, solid Tom she knew – his gaze was unsteady, flickering from ceiling to floor to door; anywhere to avoid looking at her face. There were frown lines between his eyes and his jaw was clenched tight. She felt her heart race as she battled the fear that had taken root in the pit of her stomach. 'Don't worry – it could be a false alarm.'

'Yes.' *But probably not; not if she's more than a week late. Bloody hell. Bloody, buggering hell!*

Probably not. Aware that she'd been irritable for days, Connie had fretted and waited. She'd felt off-colour, not her usual self. Still, she'd hoped against hope. 'I wish I hadn't said anything until I was sure.'

Tom pictured reaching out to embrace her but somehow his body remained frozen. 'What shall we do?'

'Best not to mention it to anyone – not yet.'

'Right.' Tom shoved his hands deep into his pockets, his frown deepening.

If only he would hold her and assure her that everything would be all right. But no, he stood there and frowned. 'We'll carry on as normal,' she said. 'I'll be working in the shop until half twelve tomorrow then you and I both have an evening shift at Gas Street.'

'Right – if that's what you want.' He couldn't work out what was going on under the surface. Was Connie as cool as she seemed, or was the calm, collected manner simply an act? Whether fake or genuine, it succeeded in keeping Tom at arm's length. 'What do you want, Con – really?'

'Really and truly?' Closing her eyes, she drew a long, jagged breath. Having a baby had never entered their heads. They'd done what everyone else did these days and tumbled headlong into bed. It wasn't as if it had been the first time for either of them – Connie had been married to John Bailey for three years and Tom, though less experienced, had made no long-term promises. They'd simply lived and loved for the moment and been happy together. 'It doesn't matter what I want,' she murmured. 'However it turns out, I'll just have to cope.'

'I'll help.' His offer hovered over the chasm between them while all the loving exchanges they'd ever made seemed to flutter into its dark depths like autumn leaves.

Suddenly Connie felt weary to the bone. She wanted to be left alone, to put her head on her pillow, close her eyes and sleep.

'I will, I'll help,' Tom promised desperately. He had no idea what that meant. And how was he supposed to do it? The decent thing would be to stand by the woman he loved, and be with her every inch of the way. Of course it would. But right now he felt too shaky to make that promise. And from the way

Connie was acting, he wasn't sure that she wanted him to.

'Yes,' she said under her breath. 'But for now, all I want to do is to go home and rest.'

Pamela and Fred were caught out by a heavy shower as they walked on the headland on Saturday afternoon. There was no shelter on the open moorland and they were soon soaked through.

'I wish I'd worn my mackintosh.' Pamela clutched the neck of her lightweight jacket to prevent the cold raindrops from trickling down her neck. Luckily, her corduroy trousers and stout walking boots offered some protection.

They strode along the ridge towards the two LZs stationed at the cliff edge, feeling that they'd reached the end of the earth and all that remained was wild wind, rain, mist and sea for ever more. Waves broke on the rocks below and added to their unease as, heads down, they stumbled on.

'The weathermen didn't forecast rain.' Fred was put out by the Met boys' mistake. 'If they had, we wouldn't have chanced it.'

'Never mind. A little rain doesn't hurt.'

'A little!' he echoed. Raising his head, he spotted a dark blue lorry parked close to the balloons and two men hard at work, cranking the winches to reduce the length of the cables and safely bed down the blimps for the duration of the storm. When Fred recognized them, he suppressed a groan.

A strong gust of wind practically whipped Pamela's feet from under her. She grabbed Fred's arm to stay upright.

'Do you see what I see?' he muttered. Though the men were swathed in oilskin capes and wore helmets that obscured the upper halves of their faces, there was no mistaking Sid and Reggie.

Pamela recognized them too. 'Quick – let's turn around!'

But it was too late; the smaller of the two figures left off winding his winch to beckon them across. 'Bloody hell, you two. Are you out of your tiny minds?'

Blast! 'Hello, Reggie.' Making the best of a bad job, Fred steered Pamela towards the two erks. 'Do you mind if we take shelter in your truck for a few minutes?'

'Feel free.' Reggie opened the back doors then made a point of gallantly offering Pamela a helping hand. 'You need your heads looking at, setting out for a walk in weather like this.'

'It wasn't raining when we left the house.' Realizing that he sounded peevish, Fred clambered in after Pamela. 'Thanks,' he added grudgingly.

'Wait there,' Reggie told them. 'We'll be done in two ticks then we'll give you a lift back to Sunrise.'

Huddled inside the Ford, they watched him finish winding in his kite, helped by Sid, who had already anchored his. When they'd completed their strenuous task, the tightly moored airships tugged at their short cables but stayed in position, facing directly into the wind.

'My, but they're enormous,' Pamela said with a sigh. With their fins, they resembled giant silver fishes set against a bruised purple sky. Sid and Reggie looked tiny in comparison. 'It must be hard work, winding those winches. Let's hope it's worth it.'

'Mr Churchill places a lot of faith in his barrage balloons,' Fred said, doing his best to be positive. 'Remember *The Lion Has Wings*?'

Pamela nodded enthusiastically. 'Yes, it was a good film. Ralph Richardson was great in it. It was airships that did the trick there, wasn't it?'

Sid caught the tail end of their conversation as he removed his cape then climbed into the cab. 'Says who?' he argued. 'That film is a load of old codswallop, if you really want to know.'

'How come?' Fred asked.

'Once you get high-level bombers on the job – the latest Messerschmitts and such like – they come in at twenty thousand feet, well clear of our kites, and do the business without any trouble.'

'Oh.' Sid's depressing explanation silenced Pamela. So what on earth was the point of placing dozens of airships along the Kell estuary? Sitting close to Fred she watched Reggie take up position behind the wheel then turn on the engine.

'Sid's right,' Reggie continued. 'Every blighter with even half a brain could see we're wasting our time here if they stopped to think about it.'

'No need to sound so cheerful about it.' As usual, Reggie's lack of respect for authority needled Fred. As the lorry jolted over rough ground towards the road, his mood plummeted again.

'But don't you worry your pretty little head.' Reggie glanced over his shoulder at Pamela. 'Our boys are currently giving Essen and Hamburg what for and it won't be long before President Roosevelt sends over more troops. The whole country will be swarming with GIs before you know it.'

'Better watch out,' Sid warned Fred. 'You know what they say about the Yanks.'

'Cover your ears,' Reggie advised Pamela.

'That they're oversexed, overpaid and over here,' Sid guffawed.

'Yes, and for that matter, the Yanks say that our lads are *under*paid, *under*sexed and under Eisenhower.' Reggie found the joke uproarious. 'I agree with the underpaid and under Eisenhower parts.'

Oh for God's sake! Staring at the floor, Fred wished with all his heart that he and Pamela hadn't accepted the lift.

'But I bet you wouldn't say no to a nice pair of nylons or a bar of chocolate, eh, Pamela, especially if they came from a Gary Cooper lookalike?' Despite the rain and with the windscreen wipers working overtime, Reggie kept his foot off the brake and let the lorry career downhill. 'No girl worth her salt would, eh, Fred? We fall short of the mark in that department. You wouldn't happen to know where I could put my hands on a buckshee bar of Dairy Milk, by any chance?'

Fred couldn't hold back a churlish retort. 'No, and I wouldn't tell you if I did,' he snapped.

The Ford rattled over a cattle grid and partly drowned out Fred's reply.

'What was that?' Reggie knew perfectly well what Fred had said. 'Bloody hell, Freddie boy, I'm only joking. No need to get so worked up.'

'I'm not worked up.'

'Is he always this touchy?' Reggie turned to Pamela with a conspiratorial wink.

'Stop the lorry!' Jumping to his feet, Fred almost

overbalanced as Reggie slammed on the brakes. 'I mean it – I'd rather walk the rest of the way.'

'In this rain?' Reggie feigned disbelief.

'No – Fred, please.' Pamela put out a hand to restrain him.

He pulled free. 'You stay where you are,' he told her. 'There's no point us both getting soaked to the skin twice in one day.'

'Hold on there – you'll need me to open the door from the outside.' Quick to oblige, Sid jumped down from the cab then nipped around the back.

'See you later, alligator.' Reggie didn't let up, even as Fred splashed into a puddle and Sid slammed the door shut. 'Touchy, touchy,' he repeated, waiting for Sid to return before easing away in second gear.

Pamela's cheeks grew flushed. Why hadn't she insisted on getting out with Fred? It had all happened in such a rush. Now here she was, hanging on for dear life again as the lorry rattled over another grid. And through the small back window she glimpsed Fred standing on the grass verge with his cap rammed over his forehead and the rain lashing down. Full of remorse, she made up her mind to apologize as soon as he reached Sunrise.

Stranded in the downpour, Fred hunched his shoulders. Pamela had stayed put in the lorry. She was driving off with the two erks. *True, I suggested it, but she could easily have said no.* However, deep down he knew it was his fault – he could kick himself for having behaved so childishly again. And it was what Reggie had intended all along – to get under Fred's skin and drive a wedge between him and Pamela.

It's only a small thing, Pamela told herself as Fred's figure receded. *We won't argue over it, surely?*

'All right back there?' Reggie glanced round and grinned, thinking that this had worked out very well, thank you. 'We'll get you back to our digs and make you a nice cup of tea. Sid will put the kettle on for us, won't you, Sid?'

'Something's definitely up with Connie,' Lizzie confided as she and Bill sawed and hammered.

The sun had refused to come out from behind a bank of white clouds settled on the horizon but the previous day's wind and rain had cleared, leaving them free to ride out to Wren's Cove to continue work on *Annie May*.

'How do you mean?' Bill measured an oak plank, made a mark with his carpenter's pencil then got to work with his saw.

'She's been in an odd mood these past few days – making silly mistakes in the shop and generally drifting off into a world of her own. She even said no to the tea dance at Raby village hall this afternoon. She bit my head off when I asked if she and Tom were going.'

'Tom's been a bit off as well.' The blade of Bill's saw cut through the wood, sprinkling sawdust on to the deck. He had his own theory – Tom must have dropped the bombshell news about the Patrol Service call-up and Connie had reacted badly. There'd been a row and now she was giving him the silent treatment – hence Tom's moodiness. Just as well that Bill had decided to keep the sensitive information to

145

himself; otherwise he and Lizzie would be at logger-heads too in the build-up to the wedding. 'Don't worry,' he told her. 'It'll all come out in the wash.'

'You know what Connie's like – she never says no to a dance,' Lizzie went on. She remembered arriving home on Friday night to find Connie curled up under a blanket, apparently asleep. Lizzie had suspected her of pretending – Connie's eyes had been shut but her breathing hadn't been right. 'Con?' she'd whispered as she'd turned on the lamp. No reply. 'Con, are you awake?'

'Leave me alone.' Underneath the blanket, Connie had turned towards the wall.

'What's up? Have you been crying?'

'No. Leave me alone – I'm trying to get some sleep.'

And that had been it. It had been the same all day yesterday and again this morning – Connie had faked sleep while Lizzie had crept around the room getting dressed.

'What's up with your sister?' Bert had asked when she'd gone downstairs for breakfast. 'She's been going around with a face like a wet weekend.'

'Don't ask me.' Lizzie had no answers, only questions.

Connie still hadn't put in an appearance by the time Lizzie and Bert left for the allotment, where they'd worked companionably all morning. From there, Lizzie had come straight to Wren's Cove with Bill and her father had gone on to visit Vera.

'What about you?' Bill interrupted Lizzie's train of thought. 'Didn't you fancy tripping the light fantastic?'

She drove a nail home with her hammer. 'Not really, no.'

'The foxtrot isn't your cup of tea any more?' Bill stopped sawing to wink and smile. 'It's all jitterbug and jive with you girls now, isn't it?'

That lopsided grin, that twinkle! 'If you say so.' She returned his smile, but then Bill's face turned serious and he jerked his thumb towards the entrance to the cave.

'What was that?'

'What?'

'Didn't you hear it – a noise coming from in there?'

'What kind of noise?' Lizzie had heard nothing except Bill's teasing voice and the sound of the sea.

'I thought somebody was hollering for help. Better take a look.' No sooner said than Bill descended the ladder and jogged up the beach to the cave's entrance. He stood and listened.

'Anything?' Lizzie called.

Bill disappeared into the dark interior without replying, leaving Lizzie wondering.

She waited for what felt like a reasonable amount of time before she heard a rumbling noise. Startled, she followed Bill, sinking into the soft, dry sand, not knowing what she would find beyond the mouth of the cave.

The entrance was high enough for Lizzie to enter without ducking her head, but the rock walls and roof soon closed in. There was a scattering of white shells and strands of olive-brown bladderwrack beneath her feet, and the sound of water trickled from above. Several sets of scuffed footprints and a cigarette butt told her that Bill wasn't the first person to have entered the cave recently. She peered into the darkness. 'Bill, where are you?'

There was an echo but no answer. She considered returning to the boat for the torch but then thought better of it. How far back did the cave go? she wondered. 'Bill?'

Fat drops of cold water splashed down on to her face and hands. As her eyes grew accustomed to the gloom, she made out the glistening surfaces of rocks all around. A light scraping sound directed her attention to a low ledge a couple of paces to her right. A match flared and she caught sight of Bill's face and cupped hand.

'Rockfall,' he muttered in a shaky voice. 'Not someone shouting for help after all.'

'Did you take a good look around?'

He nodded. 'I must have been mistaken.'

By the light of the match, Lizzie saw sizeable fragments of rock balanced precariously on the ledge and strewn across the floor of the cave.

When the match was spent, Bill lit a second. He pointed to the largest jagged lump of limestone on the ground nearby. 'That one missed my head by inches.'

'But what set it off?' Lizzie stared into the impenetrable gloom with a strange, tingling sensation that they weren't alone. A flashback to the scuffed footprints and cigarette butt backed up the notion as the second match flared then died.

'Who knows? Just one of those coincidences,' Bill said, brushing aside his narrow escape and setting off towards the daylight. 'Come on, let's go back. We've got work to do.'

Lizzie hesitated. Was the rockfall really an accident? What about the voice Bill thought he'd heard? The sense that she was being observed lingered, but darkness pressed down on her and she couldn't see a darned thing. Swallowing hard, she shook off her doubts.

'Lizzie?' Bill's figure was silhouetted at the mouth of the cave – tall and strong and beckoning for her to join him.

'Coming,' she called, turning her back on her suspicions and striding towards the light.

Connie was living on her nerves. How she'd got through the previous day, she would never know. Her morning routine serving in the shop had helped stave off her fears but the free afternoon had dragged. She'd had to force herself to put on her uniform and turn up for duty at Gas Street, steeling herself to act as if nothing was wrong and dreading the moment when she must come face to face with Tom. Luckily, she'd been able to avoid that – he'd evidently made arrangements to swap his shift and she'd immersed herself in paperwork and phone calls instead. It had been a quiet night, and at the end of her shift, she'd slid out of the sector post without talking to anyone. She'd hurried home to Elliot Street and been in bed before Lizzie had shown up.

But this morning, alone in the house where she'd lived for most of her life, number 12 had never seemed so cramped and claustrophobic. Connie paced the floor of the bedroom until she was sure the house was empty, then she went downstairs and paced again, from living room to kitchen and back again. Every photograph on the mantelpiece brought a pinprick of fresh shame. Her mother in her old-fashioned bridal gown and veil smiled sweetly for the camera. A much younger Lizzie and Connie posed for a studio portrait in white ankle socks with cropped hair and straight, thick fringes. Bert in shirtsleeves with his trousers rolled up relaxed in a deckchair on Blackpool beach – black-and-white snapshots of a perfect life. Who would have thought that the eight-year-old girl with the fringe would find herself in such a fix?

Connie went outside to the privy and sat staring at the peeling limewash on the brick walls. This time would be different; the toilet paper would provide the evidence that she longed to see. It would lift the wicked spell. But no – nothing. She trailed back inside.

Her tumultuous thoughts didn't let up for a second as she washed cups and rearranged shelves. Why hadn't she kept quiet? Why blurt it out, only to see the panic in Tom's eyes? She could have spared him that. This was women's business. Men couldn't be expected to deal with it. No wonder he'd swapped shifts to avoid her. And suppose she was pregnant, as seemed more and more likely? There were midwives (so-called) to go to, things that could be done. An empty jar dropped from Connie's trembling hands and shattered on the floor.

It was Pamela's first visit to Sally's living quarters and she couldn't get over the fact that so many people lived in such a tiny space – six in all, counting Sally and her father Frank. The family had one living

150

room above the pub, with doors leading off to a galley kitchen and two small bedrooms. Sally, Dotty and Rita shared a room, while the two boys went in with their father.

'George pulled my hair!' Rita bleated at Sally, who sat with Pamela by a small mullioned window overlooking the sea. It was Sunday afternoon and Sally had invited Pamela to the Anchor to put the finishing touches to her bridesmaid's dress. They'd retreated to the window seat in an effort to ignore the mayhem around them.

'Didn't!' George aimed and fired a toy pistol at Rita; bang-bang.

'Did!'

'Didn't!'

'George, go and play outside, there's a good boy,' Sally instructed without looking up from the hem she was sewing. 'And, Rita, ask Dotty where your teddy bears are or, better still, ask Eric to read you a story.'

'I don't want a story. I want a biscuit.' Rita tugged at the collar of her cherry-red dress and pushed out her bottom lip.

Pamela noted the smallest Hopkins child's impressive pout. Dotty the dreamer sat at a small, gate-leg table drawing pictures of horses' heads, while Eric perched opposite, elbows on the table and eyes glued to the pages of a book about buccaneers and buried gold.

The living room was low-ceilinged with heavy oak beams and uneven, sloping floorboards. Pictures and photographs hung cock-eyed on rough stone walls, while a toy box in one corner overflowed with colourful spinning tops, wooden building bricks and various dolls with shabby dresses and missing limbs. Yet somehow, in the midst of it all, Sally retained an air of calm.

'You must ask Daddy if you're allowed to have a biscuit. Remember to say please.'

To Pamela's surprise, curly-haired Rita trotted off obediently in search of her father, leaving Dotty and Eric to their own devices and giving Sally and Pamela the chance to chat as they worked.

With nimble fingers, Pamela sewed pearl beads on to the waistband of the dress. 'I didn't mind when Tom asked me to swap shifts with him last night,' she confessed. The request had come out of the blue – a knock on the door at King Edward Street and a shout up the stairs from one of her fellow lodgers had brought Pamela out from her room to see Tom hovering in the hallway downstairs. He seemed unsettled. Would Pamela mind? he'd stammered. Something unexpected had come up. He hoped she wasn't busy. Pamela had thought it odd, knowing that Connie was on duty tonight and assuming that Tom would want to spend precious time with his sweetheart. But she'd agreed to the swap – she had nothing special to do so wouldn't mind at all.

'I've always had a soft spot for Tom Rose,' Sally admitted.

Pamela paused, her needle in mid-air, and raised an eyebrow.

'Oh no, not in that way – though he is above average as far as looks go. But Tom's too old for me. Then again, I suppose there are advantages to walking out with an older man who's settled and who's had the chance to save up for a deposit on a house. But anyway, he's taken.'

'Shall I hand you a spade so you can dig yourself a deeper hole?' Pamela asked with a grin.

Sally blushed. 'When I say soft spot, I mean that Tom Rose strikes me as the type of man you can rely on.'

'That's true,' Pamela agreed cautiously. Natural delicacy held her back from gossiping about her friends' love lives.

'Not like some I could mention.' A thick lock of wavy hair hid Sally's suddenly serious expression.

'But can you, though?' Pamela went off on a tangent of her own.

'Can you what?'

'Can you rely on any man?' Letting the dress rest in her lap, Pamela stared out of the window at the watery horizon. 'I'm starting to wonder.' Take her and Fred; they'd finally taken the step that they'd both longed for. They'd lain in each other's arms and sworn eternal love. Everlasting. Timeless. Without beginning or end. Unchanged.

So why did small irritants still throw them off balance? Reggie Nolan, for instance. She'd been sure that she and Fred had cleared the air as far as the annoying erk was concerned, so how come Fred had reacted so touchily to the RAF engineer's crass sense of humour? 'I'm sorry,' she'd said when Fred had joined her and the two new lodgers in the kitchen at Sunrise after his thorough soaking on the headland. 'Reggie drove off before I could gather my wits.'

'No matter,' Fred had assured her.

153

Just that; two short words and a refusal to meet her gaze.

'It beats me why you decided to walk in the first place.' Reggie had played the innocent, adding hot water to the pot then pouring Fred a cup of weak tea. He'd plonked himself down at the head of the table and told his off-colour jokes and handed out cigarettes. 'No hard feelings, Freddie boy?' he'd said in a casual, conspiratorial undertone – slippery as an eel, escaping Fred's grasp.

Pamela hadn't seen Fred since.

'A penny for them.' Sally brought Pamela back to the present with a jolt.

Pamela shook her head and returned to her sewing.

'Where's Rita got to?' Sally wondered. 'Eric, run downstairs and see.'

The boy was still deep in the throes of piratical plunder.

'I'll go,' Pamela offered when he didn't look up from his book. 'It'll do me good to stretch my legs.'

She hurried downstairs and through the empty bar, which smelled of stale beer and cigarette smoke. The front door was ajar, allowing a glimpse of the empty market square. Pamela opened it wider and called Rita's name. Stepping outside, she glanced to the right then left. Two figures standing at the end of the jetty hand in hand caught her attention – a thin, dark-haired man and a small girl in a red dress with a mop of curly hair.

Pamela's heart skipped a beat. She knew immediately that something was not right. 'Sally – come quickly!'

154

'Whatever's wrong?' Sally flew down the stairs.

'Over there on the jetty – who's that with Rita?'

'Ron!' With a cry of dismay, Sally set off at a run towards the jetty.

Pamela followed. Ron Butcher had his back turned and he crouched to point something out to Rita. They were dangerously close to the edge and there was no railing to stop them from falling.

'Leave her alone!' Sally's high-pitched, frantic yell pierced the still air.

Keeping his back turned, Ron picked Rita up. Beyond them the sea was unusually calm. Two tugs towed a freighter out of the harbour, the low throb of their engines providing a soundtrack to the events on the jetty.

Sally raced ahead. 'Put her down. Ron, do you hear me?'

Slowly he turned with Rita in his arms. Her chubby fingers clutched his jacket lapels as he cocked his head to one side.

'Sally, wait!' Pamela's plea went unheeded.

'Put her down – what for?' Ron's heels rested at the very edge of the pier. There was a drop of ten feet into the swirling brown water below. 'I'm not harming her.'

Pamela caught up with Sally, who had stopped just short of where Ron stood with the girl. Sally's eyes were wide with fear and she fought for breath. 'Wait,' Pamela repeated quietly.

'We're pals,' Ron insisted in the same eerily even tone. 'You like me, don't you, Rita?'

Pamela studied his fleshless, unshaven face. There were dark shadows under his eyes, deep furrows across his forehead and lines etched from his nose to the corners of his mouth that spoke of a troubled soul. His friendly tone was at odds with the circumstance.

Picking up on Sally's distress, Rita started to squirm and reach out, but Ron kept firm hold.

'Look – now you've upset her,' he complained, his heels still teetering on the brink. 'I only brought her here to show her the big boat leaving the harbour, didn't I, love?'

'I want to go home now.' Rita squirmed in his arms.

Pamela took a step forward, knowing that it was vital to appear confident. 'Shall I take Rita from you?' she asked with forced casualness.

The tugs sounded their horns. Wake from the freighter splashed against the jetty, sending up cold spray. Rita wriggled and started to whine.

'She's peckish – she was asking for a biscuit,' Pamela explained as she held out her hand.

Ron closed his eyes and screwed up his features as if taking his time to reach a decision. They stayed closed as he set Rita down. She darted towards Pamela, who scooped her up and slowly backed away.

Ron opened his eyes defiantly. 'I wouldn't have done anything,' he snarled at Sally, who was retreating towards the square with Rita and Pamela. They went one slow step at a time. 'I've got nothing against the kid. It's you I can't stand – I wanted to give you a scare, that's all.'

Pamela walked with the precision of a tightrope walker, knowing that one false move could bring disaster. She prayed that Sally wouldn't retaliate.

'You know the reason.' Ron raised his voice, malice oozing from every pore. 'You and that Sam Billington – you make me sick.' His top lip curled as he spoke and his eyes were narrowed in disgust. 'Don't try to deny it. Anyhow, I told Sam he's welcome to my leftovers. Feel free, I said. Do what you want with her – I couldn't care less.'

'Take no notice,' Pamela whispered. 'Keep on walking.'

'You're nothing to me,' Ron jeered, as wave after wave sent up white spray. 'You can go to hell, the lot of you – you, my dad and the two bastards who tricked him into selling *Annie May*. I know you're ganging up against me, talking behind my back, doing the dirty. And you're the worst, Sally Hopkins. You're a little tart – you'd do it with anyone, you would!'

'Walk!' Pamela urged through gritted teeth. Rita's weight made her arms ache as they reached the stack of lobster pots at the edge of the square.

Still in a state of shock, Sally managed to stagger the final few steps towards the pub. Pamela followed with Rita. She slammed the door shut then settled the child on a bench near the fireplace. Sally sank down next to her, trembling and heaving up strangled sobs.

At the sound of the door slamming, Dotty and Eric ran downstairs. They took in the scene – Rita perched on the bench and still whining for a biscuit, Pamela pressed against the door, head back and eyes closed, and Sally sitting with her hands over her face.

'Are you laughing or crying?' Dotty approached Sally warily.

'She's upset, you idiot.' Eric kept his distance; he'd rarely seen his eldest sister cry.

'No.' With a supreme effort, Sally raised her head and pushed her hair back from her wet face. 'I'm not upset – I'm fine.'

'Oh, good.' Dotty gave a relieved sigh. 'I just remembered – Dad went out fishing for crabs. He told me to look after Rita. I forgot.'

'Biscuit?' Rita looked hopefully from Dotty to Sally.

'On top of the kitchen cupboard.' Sally had battled through her fright and was back in charge. 'Dotty, fetch the tin. It's the square one with a picture of a Scottie dog on the front.'

CHAPTER TEN

Lizzie had several scraps of news for Connie as she returned to Elliot Street to change into her uniform in preparation for her evening shift at the ambulance depot. She dashed into the kitchen before poking her head around the living-room door, then, finding both rooms empty, she rushed upstairs.

'Guess what! The verger at St Joseph's has had a stroke and been carted off to hospital, poor man. I heard about it at the allotment this morning. The vicar has found a replacement. Oh, and the city of Bath took a pounding last night. It was in this morning's *Sunday Express*.'

Connie sat on the edge of the bed, still in rumpled clothes from the day before.

Lizzie stopped dead in her tracks. 'Are you poorly? Do you need to see the doctor?'

'It's Sunday – the surgery's closed,' Connie replied in a flat voice. She felt dull and weary but not sick. 'Anyway, I'm fine.'

'Says you.' Pulling down the blind, then turning on the lamp, Lizzie saw that Connie was far from fine – her face was pale, her eyelids heavy and her movements listless. 'Bill and I worked on *Annie May* this afternoon. We're making headway at last.'

Connie acknowledged the information with a nod.

'A word of warning – take care if you ever venture inside the cave. There was a fall of loose rock while Bill was in there this afternoon. He could have been knocked out, or worse.' Lizzie changed her clothes as she talked. 'We wondered where you and Tom had got to.'

Connie cut her short. 'I haven't seen Tom lately.'

'I see.' Lizzie buttoned the waistband of her trousers. In that case, something was seriously amiss.

'What do you see?' Connie snapped back. 'Trust you to read a drama into it. All I'm saying is that we've both been busy.'

'Busy – yes.' Lizzie straightened up from tying her shoelaces. This situation must be tackled head-on. 'Listen, Con, I'm worried about you. It's not like you to mope around or to keep secrets from me. We share everything, you and I.'

'What secrets do you imagine I'm keeping, pray?' Connie made an attempt to shore up her crumbling defences with a dose of scorn.

'I'm guessing that you and Tom have had an argument.' Sitting on her own bed, Lizzie faced Connie across the narrow gap.

'And what if we have?' Connie stood up jerkily and walked to the door. 'Just because you and Bill float around on cloud nine doesn't mean life is plain sailing for the rest of us.'

'Ouch.'

'I'm sorry, that was a cheap shot.' Connie's hand rested on the edge of the door. 'If you must know,

Tom and I did have a row. He's keeping his distance for the time being and that's all right by me.' The biggest lie of all; every waking minute Connie had expected Tom to walk back into the house with a plan for their future. He would tell her that he'd had time to get over the shock and she wasn't in this alone. He would wrap his arms around her. Together they would work things out.

'You don't look as if it's fine. What was the row about?' As Lizzie edged Connie towards a confession, the seed of an idea was planted in her brain. It quickly took root, developed green shoots and grew into a flourishing certainty. When it came to it, Lizzie could imagine only one event that could have thrown vibrant, fun-loving Connie so far out of kilter.

'Nothing much.' Connie grasped the door more tightly. 'Honestly, don't worry.' Why, oh why hadn't Tom shown up? The yawning disappointment was worst at night, when she lay in the dark and remembered.

'I think I can guess,' Lizzie whispered, her heart thumping against the wall of her chest. It was more than shrewd supposition – she felt sure.

Without warning, Connie slumped against the door and started to weep.

Lizzie leaned back and closed her eyes. 'You're expecting a baby.'

'I'm over a week late.' The words were out. There was no denying them. 'How did you know?' Connie sobbed.

'I'm your sister, Con. We can practically read each other's minds.' Lizzie supported Connie back to her bed. 'Here, sit down. Take your time.'

'I told Tom, more fool me.'

'No, you were right to do that.' Fresh thoughts flew furiously in and out of Lizzie's head. Connie ought to see a doctor; Tom would turn up when he was ready; they should keep it from their father at least until the pregnancy was confirmed.

'He's vanished,' Connie cried. 'He walked out on me, Liz!'

Lizzie held her tight and let her weep. 'Tom wouldn't do that,' she murmured.

'But he has.' Sobs tore through Connie. 'He stared at me open mouthed when I gave him the news. You should've seen him. The look on his face told me it was the end of the world as far as he was concerned.'

'He must have said something.'

'Hardly anything. He asked how it could have happened – we'd been careful.' Connie recalled that rabbit-caught-in-the-headlights look and the frown as the truth slowly dawned. 'He asked what we should do.'

Lizzie held her tight. All Connie's strength and energy seemed to have drained away. 'He said "we"?' she coaxed.

Connie nodded. 'He offered to help.'

'Good.' Lizzie pressed her lips against Connie's hair. 'That's something.'

'But then he left. I wanted him to stay but he didn't. He walked out on me.' Shock, dismay, sickening disappointment – these were the feelings that had distorted Connie's view of events. Tom had abandoned her, full stop!

'It must have been the shock. Give him time.' Despite the soothing words, Lizzie couldn't help but feel angry at her sister's sweetheart – she would have expected better. It wasn't fair to leave Connie in this state, shock or no shock. 'Shall I get Bill to talk to him?' she suggested tentatively.

Connie's pride reasserted itself and she drew herself upright. 'No. It's bad enough already. I don't want Bill to know – or anyone else, for that matter. Besides, if Tom has to be talked into doing the decent thing instead of doing it of his own accord, I'd rather he stayed away.'

'I see that,' Lizzie conceded. 'So we'll leave Tom to stew while we take this forward one step at a time. First, we make the appointment with Dr McKay. Second, it's important for you to take it easy from now on. I could ask Aunty Vera to step in at the bakery for a while – what do you say?'

'No need.' Connie dried her eyes. 'Even if I am expecting, I intend to carry on as normal – in the bakery by day, at Gas Street in the evenings.'

'No, it's too much,' Lizzie argued.

'I can't just drop everything – what would people think?'

'Does it matter?' The most important thing in Lizzie's mind was for Connie to look after herself. 'And won't you at least consider giving up the head warden's job? That would allow you to cut back on your shifts – down to two nights a week out on patrol instead of three or four chained to a desk with all that responsibility.'

'No.' Connie dug in her heels. 'I might moan about being cooped up in the sector post from time to time, but deep down I take pride in being head warden. Anyway, there would be all sorts of tittle-tattle. Why

163

has Connie Bailey taken a step back from the role she loves? Surprise – she and Tom Rose have gone their separate ways! And have you noticed? Connie's definitely putting on weight.'

'Stop – you're letting your imagination run away with you.' Lizzie was fearful that Connie would rush headlong into actions she would later regret.

Connie nodded. 'You're right about seeing a doctor, but not at our local surgery. I'll go somewhere else – preferably out of town. To Easby, perhaps.'

'When?'

'Tomorrow – I'll make a few phone calls.'

Lizzie realized that this would have to do for now. 'Promise me?'

'I promise.'

'And you must let me take the brunt of the work in the bakery. Why don't we switch? You can come in later and drive out with the deliveries while I do the baking. I can get started an hour earlier so as to be ready to open the shop on time.'

'No, that's not fair on you. I want to do my share.' Connie struggled against the despair that threatened to envelop her. 'Let me do it my way, Liz, please.'

'Very well.' A glance at her watch told Lizzie that she had less than thirty minutes to get to the depot.

'What time is it?'

'Time I wasn't here.' Lizzie grasped Connie's hand and squeezed it. 'Will you be all right?'

'Good Lord!' Reading the time on Lizzie's watch, Connie sprang to her feet and began to rummage in the chest of drawers. 'I'm due at Gas Street at half past. I have to get dressed!'

'Surely not?' The change from apathy to frenzied activity alarmed Lizzie.

'Yes – why not? My name will be mud with Brian if I don't turn up, and quite right too.' Fresh underwear and clean socks, trousers, white shirt, battledress jacket – Connie scrambled for the items she needed.

Lizzie saw that it was useless to argue. 'I'll walk part of the way with you,' she offered.

'Right you are.' Connie ran a comb through her hair before jamming her ski cap on to her head. 'Ready!'

They set off together along Elliot Street, sidestepping three girls playing hopscotch on the pavement and on past the barbed-wire fence protecting the corporation baths building that had taken a direct hit during a bombing raid the previous year. They heard mothers calling their children in for tea and wirelesses playing faintly in the background as they reached the end of Gas Street.

'Are you expecting to see Tom tonight?' Lizzie wanted to know.

Connie braced herself before replying. 'Who knows? He may have swapped his shift again. Though let's face it – I'll have to see him sooner or later.'

'I'm sure it'll work out.' *Please let it be true – please let Tom step up to the mark!* Lizzie crossed her fingers behind her back.

'It doesn't matter either way.' At last, after seemingly endless hours and days of agony, Connie had her rebellious emotions under control. 'I've come to a decision – I'll write Tom a letter.'

'Saying what exactly?' In the early-evening light,

the tall, terraced houses on either side of the street gave off a depressing air. Two female wardens at the end of Valley Road exchanged information about their shifts. No alerts, no emergencies, all quiet, thank God.

'I've decided to put him out of his misery,' Connie declared. 'I'll write and say he's off the hook as far as the baby is concerned.'

'Wait!' Lizzie begged. The train was running off its tracks. Derailment beckoned. 'Don't make any decision until you two have talked it through.'

Connie was defiant. 'What's the point? It's clear Tom Rose wants nothing more to do with me, and the feeling is mutual. Whatever I thought we had during our time together has gone up in smoke. Puff – the fling is over, Lizzie.' *Finished. Kaput.*

Perhaps it would have been better if Pamela and Fred had argued following their stormy walk – cleared the air. As it was, the distance between them remained throughout the following week. All was perfectly civil and apparently unchanged when they were at work but during their evenings together it was as if they'd taken several steps backwards in their relationship. There were still kisses on the cheek and walks hand in hand along the promenade, but their conversations were stilted and limited to recent events – damage reports that Fred had collated at the control centre or the new machinery that Hugh had installed in the cutting shed at the timber yard – and nothing was said about the disastrous end to Saturday's walk in the rain.

Pamela fretted in silence. A kiss on the cheek was a poor substitute for tender endearments and passionate embraces, skin against skin, but perhaps this was normal? She had never been in love before and so had nothing in real life with which to compare her affair with Fred. Of course, she'd read books where ardour cooled after those first heady days or where intense highs and lows settled into an affectionate pattern of compromise and cooperation. Jane Austen's *Sense and Sensibility* came to mind; sensible Elinor Dashwood was the picture of restraint and reason, while younger sister Marianne's emotions ran riot with predictably disastrous results.

In any case, Pamela felt she ought to be thankful for small mercies when she considered what had happened between Tom and Connie. Though nothing had been said, Pamela was increasingly convinced that they'd run into difficulties – they'd been avoiding each other for days and Connie had been acting like a bear with a sore head: first, ordering Eddie Fraser to polish his ARP badge and spruce up his uniform, then complaining about the untidy state of the rest room above the shop where the wardens drank tea, played cards and smoked. Pamela had taken Lizzie to one side and questioned her about Connie's black moods. Lizzie had reluctantly confirmed that there was indeed trouble between Connie and Tom; leave it at that. As for Sally and Ron, Pamela shuddered at their current situation. And to think that in the early stages of their affair Sally had been genuinely in love with the man – she'd confessed as much – having no inkling of what Ron was capable of. This in itself was alarming, since Pamela saw Sally as a girl with her head screwed on, not as someone who could be easily fooled.

Her admiration for her new friend increased by the day. At work, Sally had picked things up so quickly that Pamela now left most of the typing to her while she followed up queries over accounts and kept track of deliveries. She enjoyed listening to the repetitive tap-tap-tap of Sally's typewriter keys as she delved into reasons behind a delay or else processed invoices and transferred them to the Paid files. Their chats during breaks for elevenses were as animated and free as ever. Sally quizzed Pamela about Fred; what were his hobbies and did they have plans for the fast approaching weekend? He liked reading and rambling on the moor and no, they had no special plans, Pamela replied with a rueful smile.

'I envy you those walks.' It was Friday afternoon and the weather looked set fair. 'I used to go hiking with Ron when we could find the time.'

Her casual mention of Ron's name left the door open for Pamela to pursue the subject. 'I take it you haven't seen him since . . . you know when?'

'Since Sunday?' Sally's fingers hovered over the keys. 'I haven't talked to him, but he still hangs around the square, worse luck. I warned Rita not to have anything to do with him, poor mite.'

'It's a shame.' Pamela picked up several typed letters from Sally's desk. 'I'll take these through for signatures,' she offered.

She found Hugh talking on the telephone while Fred waited patiently by the window overlooking the yard.

'I could come back later,' she whispered, but Hugh motioned for her to sit down. Fred gave Pamela an awkward smile. His jacket was unbuttoned and he'd loosened his tie and undone the top button of his shirt but still somehow managed to look serious and businesslike as Hugh put down the phone.

'Yes, Fred, what can I do for you?' Hugh asked.

'I've brought the balance sheets that you asked me for.' Coming forward to place them on his boss's desk, Fred avoided eye contact with Pamela. 'Our profits have improved week by week since we cut down on overheads and eliminated waste in the catering department.'

'Yes, yes, most satisfactory. That was a good suggestion of yours.' Hugh scanned the paperwork. 'Thank you, Fred – that's all for now.'

Fred retrieved the papers then departed.

Hugh gave Pamela a quizzical look before dropping office formalities. 'Now then, Pamela – trouble at t'mill?' The colloquialism, intended to put her at her ease, sat oddly on his lips.

'What do you mean?' She blushed furiously.

'Come on, do you think I haven't noticed that something is up between you two love birds? It used to be that you could hardly keep away from Sunrise. Now we barely see you.'

'I've been busy,' she stammered.

'And Fred – he takes extra shifts at the control centre as if my house is the last place on earth he wants to be. Anyone would think that he's avoiding me.'

'Oh, I'm sure he's not.'

Hugh sniffed sceptically and twitched his trim white moustache. 'It's either me or those two RAF chaps we have billeted with us.'

'That's more likely,' Pamela admitted before pushing the letters across his desk. 'Could you sign these please so Sally can catch the last collection?' As her uncle's pen nib scratched away, she ventured further into non-office territory. 'May I ask you a question, Uncle Hugh?'

'Fire away.'

'If you had a friend you cared about and you thought that friend might be in danger from someone she once walked out with, what would you do?'

Hugh blotted the last of his signatures then looked directly at her. 'What kind of danger?'

'For instance, the man might pester her, even though they're no longer sweethearts. He's the type who drinks then gets into trouble – serious fights and accidents. He ends up in hospital and the police are involved.'

'I see.' Hugh looked relieved. 'Forgive me – I thought . . .'

'No, I wasn't referring to me and Fred,' Pamela said firmly. 'Say the man in question is likely to turn violent when he drinks – ought my friend to report him?'

'To the police?' Hugh gave the question serious thought. 'That depends . . . You say he pesters her, but has he committed an actual crime?'

'Not as far as I know, unless you count lying in wait for my friend and calling her names that I couldn't possibly repeat.' *Go to hell . . . little tart.* Sally had described each insult that Ron had flung at her as being like a punch to the stomach.

'Unpleasant,' Hugh agreed. 'But no, unfortunately I don't believe that constitutes sufficient grounds to report him. My advice would be for your friend to sit tight.'

'And hope that the man leaves her alone eventually?' But her uncle hadn't seen the angry light in Ron Butcher's eyes or sensed his low cunning or heard the hatred in his voice.

Hugh nodded. 'These things – affairs of the heart – usually die down in the end. And while we're talking frankly, my dear – ought I to give Reginald Nolan and Sidney Donne their marching orders? I will if you think it's affecting Fred.'

Within seconds Pamela had thought of half a dozen reasons to say yes and an equal number to the contrary. 'But where would they go? What reason could you give?'

'There are plenty of spare rooms in hotels along the seafront. Provision could easily be made. I'd inform their squadron leader that it was no longer convenient.'

Caught between two difficult alternatives, Pamela hesitated. 'They'd be upset. Sunrise is so handy for them. Sid might not mind, and anyway he's not the main culprit, but Reggie would be livid. I know what he's like – he could easily look for ways to get his own back, the worst of which would be attacking Fred for his family's German origins. No, Uncle Hugh. I think it's best for them to stay put.' She gathered the letters, then stood up. 'But please don't mention our conversation to Fred.'

'Not a word,' he promised as he watched her retreat. 'And, Pamela . . .'

'Yes?'

Hugh screwed the top on to his Parker pen. 'Fred is a decent chap. I'm fond of him.'

'Yes – and so am I.'

Tap-tap with the end of his pen on the white blotting pad. 'He's been through a lot.'

'I know.' Wishing for the ground to swallow her, Pamela opened the door and stepped out into the corridor when Hugh delivered his parting shot.

He clipped his pen securely in his top pocket. 'So be a good girl and sort out the difficulties between you, whatever they are.'

Tom had filled his week with non-stop activity. By Thursday evening the paint on *Annie May*'s hull had been stripped bare and the hatches made watertight. On Friday, he and Bill underwent another training day with the Patrol Service, visiting several of the river barges to learn how to operate various winches in addition to inspecting two new LZs that had been sited on Kelthorpe FC's grounds and on a playing field on the outskirts of town. Mike Scott, a crisp, plain-speaking Royal Navy sub lieutenant whom they knew from earlier minesweeping duties, had made a point of seeking them out and informing them that several corvettes were due into dock for refits and that trawlermen up and down the north-east coast were expected to volunteer for anti-submarine duties once the work was complete. 'There'll be no excuse, lads,' Scott had told them in no uncertain terms. 'In my book, maintaining blimps isn't top priority. The Patrol Service will need every pair of skilled hands they can find on board those minesweepers, so you two had better stand by your beds.'

'Bloody hell, do me a favour,' Bill had grumbled. 'I'm getting married in a fortnight.'

'Yes and Göring's going to call off his dogs of war

until after you're spliced, is he?' Scott had turned on his heel and marched away without further comment.

That evening, Tom returned to his digs on North Street to find an envelope on the doormat. His name was written on the front but there was no stamp so he knew it had been hand-delivered. The writing was unmistakably Connie's.

Tom took the stairs two at a time and threw the unopened letter on to his bed. Reminders of Connie were strewn around the room: a comb and some Kirby grips on the window sill, her red jacket hanging from a hook on the back of the door, a lily of the valley perfume bottle on his bedside table. He'd moved nothing.

The white envelope demanded to be opened. But before he did so, Tom attempted to collect his thoughts. The whole week had been an agony of hurt and confusion. First, Connie's news – a baby, for Christ's sake! Not set in stone but pretty bloody likely. Then his own complete and utter failure to deal with it. Idiot that he was, he'd just stood there with his mouth hanging open, unable to find words to express how he felt. How *did* he feel? Stunned, obviously. It wasn't meant to happen – he'd always done the right thing and taken precautions. This happened to other couples, not to him and Connie. There'd be a scandal, unless they got spliced in double-quick time – in which case they could bluff their way through. No one would know for sure whether it had been a shotgun wedding or not. But marriage? They'd never discussed it, though the thought had crossed his mind when Bill and Lizzie announced their engagement. He'd looked for signs that Connie was considering it too, but she'd breezed on, dancing the night away, having fun, laughing at life even when sirens sounded and bombs dropped all around.

Tom paced the room. He was due at Gas Street shortly. The blackout was already underway.

Why had he stood there like an idiot when Connie had delivered her news? Talk about the cat getting his tongue. At first, she'd fended him off with excuses – I'm tired, I'm worn out. Then, when she'd dropped the bombshell, she'd seemed too calm, too much in control. What the hell had she been thinking, feeling, expecting? He hadn't been able to fathom it – they were so far apart that they might as well have been standing on different continents.

Later, after he'd left the bakery, he'd walked for miles in the dark. Instead of coming home, he'd hiked all the way up to Raynard's Folly then back by the cliff path, scarcely caring whether he lost his footing and tumbled to his death. Strong winds, wild thoughts, clouds covering the moon. Tom had made a determined effort to stride his way out of confusion back into clarity. He'd considered going to Elliot Street and hammering on Connie's door to swear that he would stand by her, whatever happened. But then the whole world would find out – Lizzie and Bert, and soon afterwards all the neighbours. Connie would never forgive him. So Tom had crept back into the shell of his lodgings: a nondescript room in the new part of town, close to the bus station. Connie's stuff was everywhere. He was filled with dread that she might never want to see him ever again.

The secret of the pregnancy had wormed its way

into his skull and become an obsession. He hadn't slept or eaten for days and he'd thought about it endlessly. Best to keep out of Connie's way until she was ready to talk to him. Tom had yearned to see her but the urge to knock on her door had faded. He'd even rearranged a couple of his shifts so as to stay out of her way – whether out of cowardice or consideration, it was hard to tell. She hadn't got in touch.

So instead, he'd sawed and hammered, stripped wood, scraped and sandpapered and sealed hatches. Bill had had a go at him, demanding to know what was up. Had Connie given him a hard time because Tom, silly fool, had spilled the beans about the Patrol Service call-up? They'd both been on edge: Bill about the wedding and Tom for reasons he refused to share. Their friendship was under strain. The whole bloody world was going to pot.

And now the envelope. It stared at Tom, blindingly white on the dark blue bedcover. Forcing himself to get it over and done with, he tore it open and read.

Dear Tom,

I hope this letter doesn't come as too much of a shock. I asked Lizzie to hand-deliver it for me because I wanted to make sure that you received it. Lizzie knows. No one else does.

I saw a doctor in Easby on Tuesday who confirmed what we were both afraid of. I'm pregnant – there's no doubt about it. No one is to blame. It's just one of those things.

There is plenty of time for me to decide what to do. This letter is simply to let you know how things stand. I understand that you don't want to be involved and that is fine by me. You are under no obligation.

I'm sorry that things have turned out this way and will remember the happy times we had, as I hope you will too.

I hope also that we will be able to work together as wardens and that there will be no hard feelings between us. Please keep this matter private and tell no one.

That's all. I close with best wishes – Connie

CHAPTER ELEVEN

The first incendiary crashed through the roof of the Harbourmaster's less than thirty seconds after the town hall control centre received warning of an attack. There was no time for a yellow alert. Friday 1 May was a clear, cold night with a stiff breeze blowing and the favourable conditions made it easy for fifteen high-level German bombers – Junkers and Dorniers flying at top speed towards Kelthorpe with an ear-splitting howl – to detect then hit their targets with deadly precision.

The initial firebomb exploded on impact and the blaze spread quickly. The pub was soon engulfed by flames, its plate-glass windows shattering in an instant. Soon, hundreds more incendiaries rained down on, among other things, the bus station, a secretarial college and a Methodist chapel. Fire gained the upper hand, raging through buildings on the north side of town like a giant blowtorch. Sizzling white flames erupted from roofs and roadways, exploding petrol tanks in cars parked along the promenade. Fire watchers armed with a few sandbags and hand-operated stirrup pumps were overwhelmed by the sheer number of fizzing fire sticks that exploded in their faces with a blinding light. The wind gusted golden showers of sparks along narrow, blacked-out streets, setting light to a tobacconist's shop, a butcher's and a newsagent's. The roar of flames filled the night sky. Panic-stricken families fled their houses and took refuge on the beach, cowering against the sea wall as Tommies from the 39th Brigade aimed their ack-ack guns into the sky and fired in vain.

Over in Gas Street, Pamela was on duty with Connie and the Fraser boys. They were coming to the end of their shift and heard Jerry before they saw him – the whine of his approaching engines gave them a brief warning before the call came through from the control centre to sound an immediate red alert. The wail of sirens was accompanied by the first bright flash as an incendiary hit its target on the far side of the headland, followed by more fire sticks raining down, whistling through the air before they landed and set Kelthorpe New Town ablaze. Mission accomplished in little more than the blink of an eye, the triumphant enemy pilots executed a synchronized victory roll then headed for home.

'All wardens attend the scene immediately.' Connie snapped out of the exhaustion she had been feeling after a long stint behind the desk. 'Simon, take stock and report back to me pronto. Eddie and Pamela, link up with the wardens from North Street; assist in whatever way you can. I'll send back-up ambulances from King Edward Street.'

There was no panic. Deciding that cycling around the headland would the quickest option, Simon commandeered three bikes from residents of Gas Street while Pamela and Eddie stuffed goggles and gauntlets

into their haversacks. Mounting the bikes, they ped-
alled frantically towards the scene of the latest attack.

They arrived just as one of the hydrogen balloons
exploded over the estuary.

'There goes one of the blimps,' Eddie muttered
through gritted teeth.

There was a massive boom before the blazing
shreds plummeted. Then, it was as if the water itself
was on fire. Worse was to come. Pamela, Simon and
Eddie found the Harbourmaster's ablaze and several
lodging houses along the promenade flattened by
bombs. An elderly man covered in grey dust tore at
the rubble with his bare hands while close by the first
rescue squad to respond to the alert dug frantically
for survivors. Two dead bodies were laid out side by
side on the promenade.

'Go back to Gas Street and tell Connie to send more
rescue squads.' Pamela's quick decision sent Eddie
cycling back the way they'd come. 'And we'll need as
many emergency ambulances as she can find – and
stretcher parties too,' she shouted after him.

'God in heaven!' Through dense clouds of black
smoke Simon spotted a third body being carried on
to the prom. He flung his bike to the ground then
rushed to join the rescue team, ducking to avoid the
icy blast from a hose manned by men from the AFS.
The fire service team pumped gallon after gallon of
water into the gutted lodging houses until one of the
rescuers suddenly called a halt.

'Listen – there are people in this cellar!' he warned.
'Switch off your hoses.'

Reacting without a thought for their own safety,
Pamela and Simon entered the hissing shell of the

building. They waded towards the entrance to the cellar. Together, they wrenched open the door to cries of help from below. Again without thinking, Pamela switched on her torch then followed Simon down the stone steps, dreading what they might find.

'Help us!' a woman's voice pleaded.

Pamela swung her torch around the windowless cellar that was already four feet deep in filthy water. Her yellow beam rested on the woman and the child that she clutched to her chest. Both were drenched and immobilized by panic. Water swirled everywhere and was rising rapidly.

'Take the kid,' Simon instructed Pamela as he waded towards the woman, holding out his hands for her to grab them. But she was frightened to death and refused to move. Her toddler son clung to her, his head buried against her shoulder.

Pamela's torch beam wavered as she fought the force of the rising water. It flashed over the low ceiling, revealing a row of large meat hooks, and then darted towards the stone steps where water still cascaded down from the ground floor, carrying kitchen debris with it – pans, smashed plates and part of a broken chair. She knew they didn't have long before the water level reached the ceiling. 'It's all right, we'll get you out,' she promised as she fixed the beam on the terrified mother.

'Help me – I can't swim,' the woman gasped, her eyes starting out of her head as the water rose to chest level.

'Take Simon's hand. Give me the boy.' Pamela's instructions were calm and simple. There was a gap of some fifteen feet between them and the cellar steps.

'Do as the warden says,' Simon urged.

With a cry of desperation, the mother surrendered her son to Pamela, then threw herself at Simon, who swayed violently before regaining his balance. He hooked his hands under the woman's armpits to tow her towards the steps. Pamela, meanwhile, staggered under the limp weight of the boy in her arms. She drew on every last ounce of energy to enable her to carry the drenched child, struggling to hold him clear and keeping her lips firmly closed as foul water splashed against her face. They had only moments to make their exit.

At the bottom of the steps, Simon gathered up the woman, taking her full weight as he carried her out of the flooded cellar. Pamela felt the boy's arms tighten around her neck. Water continued to pour down but she fought on – up one, two and then three steps. A heavy object – the door of a kitchen cupboard carried by the torrent – slammed against Simon as he reached ground level, almost knocking him off his feet. He steadied himself and bore the woman through the shell of the smoking building on to the prom. Pamela followed close behind with the boy. They emerged to a low cheer from the firefighters and rescue party, who were standing by.

Blankets were fetched, the shivering woman and child were led away. Close by, the white-haired man who had been searching through the rubble sat on the pavement with his head in his hands.

Further along the promenade, an ambulance screeched to a halt and Lizzie jumped out. She surveyed the scene – mountains of bricks and burning timber, fire engines with ladders extended towards

the upper floors of buildings that remained standing, walls that leaned and threatened to topple,
smoke billowing, water gushing through the ruins,
men digging, bodies laid out on the promenade. Bill
flung open the back doors of the ambulance and
emerged with a first-aid haversack slung over one
shoulder – but how far did bandages and rubber
gloves get you when faced with a disaster of this pro-
portion? Lizzie spread her hands in a gesture of
helplessness.

'Over here!' A member of the rescue squad called
for them. He pointed to a partially uncovered victim
lying among the rubble. 'This one's alive. See what
you can do for him.'

The man was face upwards. The lower half of his
body was trapped by a charred beam that Bill and
Lizzie would have to lift before they could offer
assistance.

'Gauntlets,' Bill muttered.

Lizzie sprinted back to the ambulance. She found
two pairs of leather gauntlets stored under the
driver's seat and quickly ran back. By the time she
arrived, Bill had brushed dirt from the man's mouth
and was offering him water. He put the metal bottle
aside and pulled on the gloves.

'Ready?' Lizzie asked.

Together they took hold of the blackened, smouldering beam and carefully raised it. The man
groaned and begged for more water. Kneeling beside
him, Lizzie soaked a pad of cotton wool then gently
wiped his lips before pouring cool liquid into his
mouth. 'What's your name?' she asked.

'Sid.' The croaked reply was almost inaudible.

Alarm bells sounded in Lizzie's head – she wasn't certain because of the dark conditions, but this could be one of the erks she'd danced with at the Harbourmaster's. 'Listen, Sid – we're fetching a stretcher. We need to get you to hospital.'

He raised his head and looked around wildly. 'I was with my pal. We were drinking at the Harbourmaster's. Reggie told me to scarper when Jerry dropped his first bomb then I lost sight of him.'

Yes, she'd thought as much; Sid Donne had copped it along with his fellow engineer. 'Don't worry about that now.' Lizzie tried to calm him and waited for Bill to clear slabs of concrete and brick from Sid's lower half. She could tell from Bill's expression that the injuries were serious.

'Wait here. I'll fetch that stretcher.' It was Bill's turn to run to the ambulance. Meanwhile, as Lizzie loosened the patient's collar, she noticed that he wore a gold cross around his neck.

'I can't move,' he moaned, letting his head fall back and fumbling for the cross. She guided his hand towards it.

'Take it easy.' Bill had returned and was in the process of enclosing the victim's legs in temporary splints. 'We're going to lift you on the count of three – one, two, three!'

As they raised him, Lizzie averted her gaze from his lower half. She glimpsed charred fabric and caught the awful smell of burned flesh. Sid emitted a series of low moans, letting his head loll to one side as they carried him swiftly to the ambulance.

'Drive – as fast as you can,' Bill told Lizzie as he strapped the patient into a King's harness. Bad burns to the legs and Lord knew what else; it was touch-and-go for the poor beggar.

With pounding heart and dry mouth, Lizzie set off for the Queen Alexandra. She threaded through streets clogged with dense black smoke, past burst water pipes and fractured gas mains along roads that had been torn up during the raid. Craters yawned and progress was painfully slow. In the back of the ambulance, Bill did his best to keep the patient conscious by talking to him and reassuring him. 'They'll put you right in next to no time, pal. Just hang on until we get you to the hospital. Here – drink this.'

Sid's head lolled and his eyelids flickered shut. Water trickled from the corner of his mouth.

Bill grasped his hand. 'We'll be there in five minutes – you hear me? The docs can perform miracles these days.'

Sid clutched his cross. The ambulance swayed around a corner. Sounds faded and all was silent.

Back at Gas Street, Connie handed over to Norman Riley, who had been called in to provide extra cover. The immediate crisis was over – Jerry had done his job and flown back to base. All available rescue teams were deployed. Reports of casualties were grim: five people killed and more than a dozen wounded.

'A bad business,' Norman concluded as he sifted through her reports. 'I pity the poor beggars who live on that side of town.'

'Yes, it doesn't bear thinking about.' Connie gathered her belongings – gas mask and haversack – then made for the door. An orange glow lit up the sky to the north and she saw a fire engine speeding along the street towards the inferno beyond the headland. 'They'll be working all night to put out those fires,' she predicted wearily. After that, it would be up to the rescue boys to salvage what they could. Depending on the extent of the damage, the foremen and their parties of volunteer plumbers, builders and electricians would be on site for days with their jacks and cutting equipment, their cranes and searchlights.

'You look as if you need some sleep,' Norman remarked with a sympathetic smile.

'Yes – I'm off.' Connie set off for Elliot Street, dragging her feet as she went. She breathed in the smoke that drifted over the headland and only picked up her pace when she thought of her father, who had been at home by himself during the attack. Perhaps Bert would have had time to go up the street to his sister Vera's house to seek shelter in her newly kitted-out cellar rather than sit it out at home on his own. Sure enough, Connie found that Bert wasn't at number 12. But when she knocked on Vera's door he wasn't there either.

'You know what he's like.' Vera stood on her doorstep in her dressing-gown and slippers. Her hair was in rollers beneath a thick hairnet and her lined features gave her a permanently worn-out look. 'He probably nipped along to the shelter on College Road to see if he could lend a hand.'

'Against doctor's orders,' Connie muttered. 'Thanks anyway, Aunty Vera.'

From Elliot Street she took a short cut through an alley on to the main road lined with shops and office buildings. The smoke was thicker in the centre of town and she felt her chest tighten as she approached the communal shelter. *Trust Dad not to do as he's told*, she thought.

With her mind focused on getting her father safely home to bed, she paid little attention to the warden standing at the entrance to the underground toilets. It was only when Tom stepped in front of her that she registered who it was. For a moment, her heart came to a sudden, thumping halt.

'Connie,' he said in a flat voice. *The letter!* Her terse, emotionless words had burned themselves into his consciousness. *No one is to blame. There is plenty of time for me to decide what to do. No obligation.*

'Tom,' she breathed.

'What are you doing here?' She looked exhausted – there were shadows under her eyes and none of that clear, laughing sparkle that he loved.

'Is Dad here?' She wasn't prepared. Her guard was down. And God, Tom looked dreadful: drained and hopeless, a shell of his former self. Guilt dealt her a hammer blow to the chest.

Tom nodded. 'He's down there checking names off against the household register. Don't worry – he's safe.'

Shock robbed Connie of her voice. What did you say to a man whose heart you'd broken?

'I offered to do a shift on North Street.' He felt he ought to explain his presence.

'I didn't know that.'

'We brought a few families over. They'd escaped from their houses on to the beach – it wasn't safe for them there.'

He stood, tall and gaunt, a stranger in his uniform,

searching her face for answers that she couldn't give. 'I'd better go down and fetch Dad,' she said.

Tom stepped aside, but as Connie eased past, he spoke again. 'What did you mean, there's plenty of time for you to decide what to do?'

Her heart lurched again. A shield of defiance replaced the guilt. 'I don't know – it's early days.'

'Connie, don't brush me off.' He reached for her hand. 'I deserve a proper answer.'

She didn't pull away but she lowered her head to avoid his gaze. 'I know you do, but you have to let me get used to the idea of being pregnant first. I have to weigh up my options.'

'What does that mean?' She wasn't being fair; she ought not to cut him out entirely. Tom experienced a sudden, unexpected spurt of anger.

'There are ways forward,' Connie murmured, withdrawing her hand.

'But you'll keep it?' Surely he had a say too.

'I don't know – anyway, it's my decision.' She narrowed her eyes, determined to press on.

'No – the baby is mine too. You can't just cut me out. It's not fair.'

'Hush!' Connie's eyes widened again. Enough; she must find her father and take him home. 'Nothing's fair, Tom. You should know that by now.'

'But I want to be involved. Why won't you let me?'

Really? He said this now, when it was too late! Scorn burned like acid in Connie's throat. 'How involved were you all last week?' she taunted. 'I'm asking you, Tom – where were you when I needed you?'

*

187

'"From Hull, Hell and Halifax may the Lord preserve us."' Bill quoted an old saying as he sat at Lizzie's kitchen table nursing a cup of tea. 'They should include Kelthorpe in that list.'

'Poor old Kelthorpe.' It was the afternoon following the raid and rumours were flying in all directions. The death count was up to fifteen, the number of injured to thirty-three. Raby had been hit as well – true to form, Jerry had committed one final random act of destruction by ditching the last of his bombs over the small fishing village.

'Why us?' Lizzie was in a gloomy mood, partly thanks to another cold shoulder she'd received from Connie after her return to Elliot Street at two in the morning. It seemed they were back to square one – arriving home to an empty house, Lizzie had collapsed on to her bed and sobbed out of sheer exhaustion. Despite their best efforts, she and Bill had been unable to save Sid Donne, who had been pronounced dead on arrival at the Queen Alexandra. They'd driven back to North Street and ferried three more victims to hospital before being ordered home. Later, when Connie had at last returned with their father, she'd undressed in the dark and rebuffed any attempt at conversation. It had been the same this morning when they'd gone into work: bread had been baked and orders delivered in deafening silence.

'Why not us?' Bill replied to Lizzie's forlorn question. 'We ship out arms and munitions to our Russian allies, don't we? The fact is, we're as vital to the supply chain as Hull these days. We even sent food to the Red Army in Kharkov.'

'Which makes us a number-one target.' Lizzie

rinsed out the teapot and cups and saucers. When she felt Bill's arms encircle her waist from behind, she leaned back against him. 'Have you come to whisk me off somewhere nice?'

'To Wren's Cove,' he told her. 'I'm your Prince Charming, in case you didn't know.'

She turned to embrace him with a smile. 'What's the dress code – ball gown or overalls?'

Their delicious kiss lasted a long time. Bill was the one to break away and tell her to wrap up warm. 'We won't stop long. I just want to give *Annie May* the once-over, check that she's still in one piece. After that we can ride on up the coast and have tea in White Sands Bay.'

'I like the sound of that.' Lizzie ditched her apron and was soon ready for action. Before long, she was riding pillion as Bill steered carefully through Saturday-afternoon traffic until they were clear of the town, where he upped the revs and headed for the hills. A bird's-eye view showed a pall of smoke set-tled over Kelthorpe with little wind to clear it, but beyond that the shoreline curved into the far distance, and there were no clouds clinging to the headlands. In spite of everything, Lizzie saw hope reflected in the sparkling sea, freedom in the azure sky.

Bill pulled into the lay-by above Wren's Cove, close to the familiar cliff path leading to the beach. A glance in the direction of Raby was enough to prove that the village had indeed been hit; the evidence was there in thin threads of smoke rising from the ruined remains of a row of terraced houses overlook-ing the small harbour. 'You see that?' He jerked a thumb towards the smoke.

Lizzie acknowledged the question with a dip of her head then went ahead of Bill down the steep path. She picked her way carefully, concentrating on where she placed her feet. It was only when she reached the beach that she looked towards the cove and stopped dead, scarcely able to believe her eyes.

Bill jumped the last few feet to join her. What he saw rooted him to the spot. An outcrop of rock partly hid *Annie May* from view but he could see enough. 'Jesus Christ!' He shook his head as if to rid himself of the image.

Lizzie walked ahead around the outcrop. All that remained of *Annie May* was the charred skeleton of her hull – the stout curved framework and the bulwarks that had strengthened it. Her carefully restored oak deck was no more and the metal winches, the rudder and what was left of her restored keel had caved in completely. 'All that work down the drain!' she cried.

Bill followed her. *All those dreams!* He gawped, open-mouthed. It was hopeless – *Annie May* was damaged beyond repair. His and Tom's future had gone up in smoke.

Lizzie walked slowly around the burnt-out shell. What had been the point of Jerry jettisoning a bomb on such a target? But then again, that was just it – there was no point! All that remained were ashes and broken dreams. She went back to where Bill stood. 'What now?'

'I'll have to tell Tom.' This much he knew: it didn't matter how young and strong you were, or how much you believed in yourself, disaster could strike without warning. And when it did, it robbed you of all that strength and optimism.

'I'll come with you.' She would stand at her beloved's side and they would come through this together.

'Knowing Tom, he won't say much but he'll take it hard.'

Lizzie slipped her hand into Bill's. 'You can always buy another boat.'

'What with? We've used up all our savings.' It was like a house of cards tumbling down around him. 'I wanted to be back at sea before the wedding. I was depending on it. What will we do for money if I'm not fishing?'

'We'll manage with what I earn at the bakery.' She knew as she spoke that she'd delivered a blow to Bill's pride.

'No, that wouldn't be right.' He stared beyond the wreckage at the dark entrance to the cave, his handsome face a picture of misery. 'We might have to shelve getting married until I get a job and I start earning again.' A bitter taste came into his mouth. First the loss of *Sea Knight* and now *Annie May*, not to mention the prospect of the Patrol Service packing him off on minesweeping duties – everything was stacked against the wedding going ahead as planned.

Lizzie let her hand drop to her side. A wave of dismay swept over her, and another wave and another, like the relentless sea. 'It doesn't matter,' she whispered against the sound of breakers crashing against the rocks. 'I don't care whether you have a job or not.'

'But I do, Liz. I can't marry you if I can't provide for you.' Forcing himself to look at her, Bill saw that her eyes were full of tears. 'Because I love you,' he added, drawing her to him and resting his chin on the top of her head. 'We'll only have to wait a few months, until I'm back on my feet.'

A May wedding; spring blossom, a white dress with bridesmaids in forget-me-not blue – it was her dream. To have a ring on her finger. To walk down the aisle and be Mrs Bill Evans. All vanished in a puff of smoke.

'By autumn,' he promised. 'Give me until then.'

'Your mother got through it but only just.' Harold talked Pamela through the previous night's events. 'I managed to get her into the Anderson shelter in the nick of time. Hugh joined us there.' He wouldn't admit it to his daughter, but the latest raid had thoroughly shaken him up too. It had been too close for comfort, with firebombs falling within a hundred yards of Sunrise. The flames had heated up the corrugated roof of their shelter and made it too hot to touch. 'You know Fred was on duty at the control centre. He's back there again today, writing up his reports.'

Pamela sat in the lounge of her parents' bungalow, refusing to go into detail about her experiences during the raid. For a start, the shock of seeing the dead bodies had left her drained, and even though she and Simon had succeeded in getting the mother and son out of the flooded cellar, she'd witnessed other harrowing events that she was reluctant to share. 'Thank the Lord you did,' she told her father. 'Some other poor souls weren't so lucky.'

'Including poor Sid Donne,' Harold reported.

Pamela looked at him with a mixture of surprise and alarm.

'You didn't know?'

'No – it's the first I've heard.'

'Apparently he and Reggie were drinking in the Harbourmaster's. Sid was trapped by flying debris. He died before they could get him to hospital.'

'What about Reggie?' Pamela's heart battered at her ribs.

'There's been no news as yet. The last your mother and I heard he was listed as missing.'

'Poor Sid – that's dreadful news.' She wouldn't have wished his fate on her worst enemy. As for Reggie, it was best not to think too far ahead.

Edith began to fuss with the tea tray, apologizing for the absence of biscuits and sugar. 'I know you won't want to hear this, dear – but please won't you consider handing back your uniform and standing down from your warden duties?' she asked Pamela as they sipped their tea.

'No, Mother, I won't.' Pamela dragged her attention away from the ill-fated engineers. 'I'm proud of that uniform. I wouldn't dream of handing it back.'

'There – that's telling you.' Harold patted his wife's hand.

Edith heaved a sigh. 'You can't blame me for trying.' Last night, cowering in the shelter as the bombs fell, she'd tried to block out any picture of her precious Pamela out on patrol. Time had dragged and even though the raid had been brief, the noisy aftermath had lasted through the night – ambulances speeding along the prom, fire engines passing the house with bells clanging and, worst of all, the sound of men yelling and women sobbing. 'I wasn't the only one. Your uncle was at his wits' end too.'

'Well, as you see, I came through without a scratch.' Pamela finished her tea.

'I'm sorry Fred isn't here, love,' Harold said. 'He left for the town hall ten minutes before you arrived. He said how sorry he was to miss you.'

Pamela attempted a smile. 'No matter. I'll pop across to the main house and have a quick word with Uncle Hugh before I go.'

'Right you are.' Harold gathered the cups and saucers and stacked them neatly on the tray. 'Your mother and I will take a stroll around the headland.'

Edith dabbed her lips with her napkin. 'Yes, we'll stay well away from the prom for the time being. It's heartbreaking to see what's happened there.'

'Chin up.' Pamela gave her a peck on the cheek. At times like this her mother seemed especially fragile, like an autumn leaf blown hither and thither in the wind. 'The war can't go on for ever – there has to be an end to it sooner or later.'

'Tell your uncle he's welcome to come and have supper with us later on.' Harold showed her to the door then waved her across the lawn.

She entered the big house by the side porch, noticing Hugh's collection of umbrellas and walking canes in the rack beside two pairs of RAF-issue boots and two heavy canvas rucksacks. As she walked along the corridor past a row of servants' bells she called her uncle's name.

'He's gone out,' a voice replied in a harsh monotone. Reggie came up the two steps from the kitchen covered in black dust and dressed in torn jacket and slacks. His face was pale and haggard, scarcely recognizable under the grime, with his hair hanging lank over his forehead and his shoulders sagging. 'You just missed him.'

'Good Lord, Reggie!' Pamela took a step back and tried to gather her thoughts.

'What's up? You look as if you've seen a ghost.'

'Reggie, it's not funny!'

'No, and I'm not laughing.'

She recovered her wits enough to understand that he'd evidently escaped from the previous night's inferno more or less unscathed. 'Dad said you were reported missing. He told me about Sid. I'm so sorry—'

Reggie raised a hand to interrupt her. 'Not half as sorry as I am.'

'Yes, I realize that. You were lucky to get out alive. Please tell Uncle Hugh I called.' She spoke jerkily then continued along the corridor towards the front hallway. The sun's rays slanted through a stained-glass panel, casting red and green light across the tiled floor.

'Is that all?' Reggie said in the same flat tone.

Relenting, Pamela turned back. 'No, I can stay a while if you like.'

Reggie retreated into the kitchen and she followed him. 'It was my fault. Sid was all for leaving when the landlord called time but I made him stay for a lock-in. If I hadn't, he wouldn't . . .' He lapsed into a silence punctuated by the regular tick of the wall clock above his head.

'I see.' She pulled out a chair from under the table and made Reggie sit. 'You can't blame yourself. You weren't to know.'

'The fact remains.' Resting his elbows on the table, Reggie buried his head in his hands, which were square, with dirt embedded under the nails. 'I got out with a simple knock to the head and not another scratch on me. He didn't, poor beggar. I had to spend a night at the hospital before they found a doctor to give me the once-over. And abracadabra . . . !' He sat up straight and spread his palms towards the ceiling.

'You were lucky. I was there – I saw how bad it was.'

Reggie went on as if she hadn't spoken. 'Sid was a good pal. One of the best. Drove his car like a maniac, mind you. Quite the daredevil was Sid.'

'Is that so?' Pamela sat down opposite. 'How long had you known him?'

'We joined the RAF on the same day and got sent to a training camp in East Anglia. We've shared a billet ever since.'

'What about his family?'

'Two brothers – younger than him. His dad's a mechanic in Wolverhampton – that's how come Sid knew so much about engines. He went as an apprentice to the same firm as his dad.'

Pamela stared at her hands, regretting that it had taken the man's death for her to learn more about him. 'I didn't know any of that.'

'Why should you?' Reggie laid his hands flat on the table. 'Sid never gave much away. We came up north soon after we'd lost three of our lads in a single raid over Hamburg, hoping to escape the worst of it. And now look.'

'I really am very sorry.' Reggie looked and sounded broken. Gone were the jokes and cheeky chat. In fact, he seemed close to tears. Pamela reached across the table and grasped his hand.

'Sid ran one way when the bombs dropped and I ran the other. I ended up on the beach with half a dozen others from the lock-in. A whole house fell on top of Sid – he never stood a chance. After they discharged me from the hospital I went straight to the morgue to identify him.'

Lost for words, Pamela felt Reggie's grip tighten over her hand.

He looked up at her with tear-stained cheeks. 'Thank you for listening to me bleating on,' he murmured with a catch in his voice. 'It means a heck of a lot, believe you me.'

CHAPTER TWELVE

Lizzie stooped to firm broad bean seedlings into the earth. The potatoes they'd planted in early spring had already sent up healthy green shoots but there was as yet no sign of life from the lettuce and carrot seeds that she'd put in a week before.

'Let's take a breather.' Pamela's suggestion was welcomed by both Lizzie and Connie. The three girls had been working on Bert's plot for two hours solid, hoeing and planting alongside half a dozen other keen allotmenteers, all eager to make up for time lost due to April's Hefty Hermann.

Pamela set out a flask of tea and three tin mugs on the bench beside the new shed. 'You say your dad is having a lie-in?' she asked as she filled the mugs and handed them out.

'He needed it,' Connie said. 'He didn't get to bed until two o'clock the night before last – that was when I had to drag him out of the shelter on College Road and march him home.'

'Bless him,' Lizzie added. 'He won't admit that he doesn't have the same get-up-and-go since his heart attack.' The tea tasted good, the morning was fine and she felt reassured by the methodical digging and planting going on around them. War couldn't disrupt nature's rhythms, however hard it tried.

'I ran into Tom at the shelter,' Connie mentioned, as if in passing. 'He'd read my letter.'

'What letter?' Pamela demanded, sensing an unmistakable frisson.

'I broke off with him, that's all.' Connie shot Lizzie a warning look. *Don't say a word!*

'But why?' In spite of her brief conversation with Lizzie, Pamela had supposed that Tom and Connie would get over their difficulties. After all, they were perfectly matched: Connie with her larger-than-life enthusiasm and lovely, kind Tom acting as a quiet, steadying counterbalance.

'No special reason.' Connie put down her mug and picked up her trowel. 'And it's fine – Tom and I will still work together down at Gas Street.'

Pamela was confused. 'But I don't understand. You two had so much going for you.'

Connie shrugged. 'These things happen.'

'And Tom is so easy-going—'

'Appearances can be deceptive,' Connie shot back. 'Lizzie, where's that packet of radish seeds?'

'In the shed.' Feeling awkward, Lizzie issued a stiff thanks to Pamela for the tea. 'While we're on the subject of bad news, I'm afraid I have some of my own – two things, to be precise.'

'You know what they say – troubles come in threes,' Connie commented drily as she emerged from the shed with the packet of seeds and went back to work. *Not single spies but in battalions* – it was strange how well-worn Shakespearian phrases from her school days stuck with her.

'*Annie Rose* took a direct hit on Friday night. There's nothing left of her – just a heap of ash and burned beams.'

'Oh Lord – what will Bill and Tom do now?' Pamela wanted to know.

'That's just it – they have no idea. All their money was tied up in *Annie May*. Which brings me to the next difficulty . . . Bill has decided that we can't get married on the sixteenth.'

'Bill has done what? You mean the wedding is off!' Pamela's eyes widened in pure dismay. There was to be no walk down the aisle in her bridesmaid's dress after all.

'Not for good.' Lizzie had had time to paper over the cracks of her own disappointment. 'We have to wait until he's back on his feet, that's all.'

'But you've planned everything – the church, the reception, the dresses . . .'

'I know.' A heavy sigh slipped out. 'But I told Bill that I understood and I do. Honestly, I do.'

'Of course.' Pamela admired Lizzie's attempt at putting on a brave face. 'And I'm sure it will happen in the end – just not as soon as you'd hoped.'

'Yes – I keep telling myself that there are a lot of people worse off than me. And as long as we're all alive and kicking – you and Fred, me and Bill, Connie . . . Dad and all our nearest and dearest – then we really have no reason to be too down in the dumps.'

Pamela spotted Lizzie's hesitation and the gap in her list of names. She glanced across the allotment to where Connie's back was turned as she crouched to create a shallow drill for the radish seeds.

200

Convinced that she'd been left out of something important, Pamela recalled the uncomfortable but familiar feeling of being excluded by gangs of girls in the school playground. 'Are you sure Connie's all right?' she asked Lizzie, who rolled her eyes but stayed silent.

There was nothing for it but to get back to banking up earth around the potato shoots while Connie planted and Lizzie hoed. But there was something missing between the three of them. Pamela couldn't put her finger on it until they were putting the tools away and preparing to leave. Then, as Connie locked the shed door, it came to Pamela with a small jolt of surprise: for the first time during the trio's close-knit friendship, it was honesty that had gone absent without leave.

Connie hated having time on her hands. Ever since learning that she was pregnant, she'd preferred the weekdays when she was able to stay busy – at the bakery and at Gas Street – and it had been possible to ward off black thoughts. So when she returned to Elliot Street after her morning on the allotment, she wandered restlessly from kitchen to living room, desperate to find something to occupy her. Eventually, she picked up a soft cloth and dusted the ornaments, then she took down the net curtains from the front window, intending to wash them in warm, soapy water. She was back in the kitchen, up to her elbows in suds, when there was a knock at the door.

'I'll get that.' Bert stood up from the table where he'd been reading his *Express*, then shuffled along the corridor to open the door. 'Hello, Tom lad. Come in.'

Connie froze at the sound of Tom's name. If she'd had her wits about her, she would have slipped out of the back door into the yard and from there down the alley past the area where the communal bins were kept. Instead, she dithered and was still drying her hands on a towel when he followed her dad into the kitchen.

'Look who it isn't,' Bert commented drily.

Tom stood by the door, clutching his leather gauntlets, with his checked scarf tied loosely and his short brown hair ruffled by the wind.

'I didn't hear your bike pull up outside,' Connie said without turning her head.

'Is this a bad time?' Tom had changed his mind a dozen times. Yes, he would call in to have it out with Connie; no, he would steer clear until the dust had fully settled. He'd replayed phrases from her letter – *what we were both afraid of . . . there's no doubt about it . . . you are under no obligation* – over and over like a scratched record. She'd claimed there were no hard feelings, but when they'd run into each other outside the underground shelter, they'd both realized that this was untrue. Then hadn't been the right time or place for lengthy explanations, but perhaps now would be, when they could talk privately and clear the air?

'I'll leave you two to it.' Sensing a chill in the atmosphere, Bert made himself scarce.

Connie waited until she heard the front door shut behind him. 'What do you want, Tom?' She turned slowly to face him.

'To talk.'

'What about? We've said all there is to say.'

'No,' he argued, without budging from the doorway. 'It takes more than a letter to get rid of me.'

The way he phrased it made her bristle. 'I offered you a way out, that's all.'

'And what if I don't want a way out – have you thought of that?' Damn it, he hadn't meant to lock horns, but that was the way it had come out: as a challenge.

'What was I meant to think?' Connie retorted. 'I didn't see hide or hair of you for days. You even swapped shifts to avoid me.'

'Yes, and for that I'm sorry. It was a big mistake.' As Tom came forward to put his gloves on the table, he noticed that she retreated towards the back door. 'Please don't run away from me.'

'I'm not running away.' How dare he suggest that? She stood her ground, hands on hips. 'Say what you have to say and be quick about it.'

Ouch! He paused before replying. Everything he said was coming out wrong. 'Listen, Connie – all I want to tell you is that I'm sorry.'

'Is that it?' Her stomach churned. Here he was, standing with his feet wide apart, his voice low and quiet, his gaze steady and direct like the Tom of old.

'No. It was the shock – I stayed away because I didn't know what else to do.'

'*You* were shocked!' she echoed. 'What about me?'

'I know – I got it wrong.'

'I ought never to have told you – I knew it would alter everything.' She relived the panic, the heartbreak – her racing pulse and fluttering heart when she'd broken the news, and the fear in his eyes. 'Listen, I appreciate you coming to apologize, but what I said in my letter still stands,' she insisted. 'We can't go back to the way we were, not after this.'

'Why not?'

'Because!' Because being sorry wasn't enough. Because she interpreted the look in Tom's eyes and his words as pity, not love.

'Please,' he stammered.

'Please what?'

'Let me help.'

She shook her head. 'I don't want your help. It's over between us.'

'How can it be, after everything we said, all the promises we made?' A long, drawn-out sigh followed Tom's question.

'There were never any promises. We lived for the moment and now the moment has passed.'

Tom blinked and when he opened his eyes he felt he was looking at a stranger. 'I've been a fool,' he murmured. A naive idiot, imagining that Connie Bailey – a beautiful woman of the world who had been married and widowed, who loved to dance and to gaily lead where others followed – would settle for an ordinary, common-or-garden bloke like him.

'There's no going back.' A cold shiver ran through her as she looked ahead and came to terms with what she must do.

'If that's the way you feel.' He picked up his gauntlets and backed away.

'It is.'

'Then I won't bother you any more.'

He went. She heard the slam of the door and the sound of his bike engine starting up. He'd gone without looking back.

Connie left the house soon after, clutching an address – number 127a North Street. She walked in the direction of the headland without noticing whether the day was fine or cloudy or if the rescue parties had finished their work in the north part of town. She remained unaware when she got there of the spirals of smoke rising from the Harbourmaster's and of a gang of men working hard to repair a damaged gas main.

There were few people on the prom and none on the beach as she turned into North Street without seeing anyone she knew. 123, 125, 127 – Connie read the house numbers and saw that the one she was looking for was part of a tall Victorian terrace with a neat front garden and three steps leading up to a blue-painted door. A sign to 127a indicated that she must follow some narrow steps to a basement flat. Glancing quickly up and down the street, she descended below street level and knocked on a second blue door.

A woman in her forties answered the knock. She was small and primly dressed in a dark green blouse with white collar and cuffs, a tailored tweed skirt and brown court shoes. Her short hair was greying at the temples. 'Mrs Bailey?' the woman enquired, noticing the absence of a wedding ring on Connie's finger.

'Yes, I telephoned you yesterday evening. You must be Mrs Coulson?'

'Indeed you did and indeed I am. But please call me Mavis.' She opened the door wide and Connie followed her through a dark vestibule into a clean, tidy living room with armchairs either side of a small fireplace complete with polished brass fender and coal scuttle. A small amount of daylight filtered in from pavement level, supplemented by a circle of yellow light from a standard lamp in the corner. 'Please sit.' Mavis Coulson indicated the chair to the right of the fire before sitting to face Connie, resting her hands in her lap and waiting patiently for her to begin.

'Thank you for seeing me so promptly.' Neither the room nor the woman was what Connie had expected. She'd imagined somewhere dingier, perhaps facing on to a dark, weed-choked courtyard, and someone much older with a hard, businesslike expression.

Mavis smiled. 'People generally like to see me as early as possible.'

'I was given your name by a . . . friend.' In fact, Connie had combed the back pages of the *Kelthorpe Gazette* until she'd found a smattering of adverts for so-called handywomen skilled in the preparation of tonics and remedies including juniper and black hellebore as well as the more modern Beecham's Pills, aloe and ginger – a thinly disguised code for those who dealt with unwanted pregnancies. Mabel's name had been among them.

'Quite. There's no need to go into details.'

'I'm ashamed to admit that I've got myself into a fix.'

'Quite.' Why else would Connie be here? 'Relax. You've come to the right place.'

'Only my sister knows that I'm pregnant – no one else.' It seemed important to establish this.

'Except for the father, perhaps?'

Father! The word made Connie hold tight to the arms of her chair. 'Yes, he knows,' she confirmed reluctantly. 'We're not married.'

'I see.'

Mavis Coulson's expression remained serene and Connie didn't feel judged. 'It was an accident, pure and simple. I was just getting back on my feet after my husband died when this happened.'

'There really is no need to explain. If you've made your decision then my job is to make it happen, no questions asked.'

'Yes – thank you.' Connie's gaze strayed to a doorway through which she caught a glimpse of what must be a bathroom with shiny, cream-painted walls and furnished with a narrow metal table on wheels – the sort to be found in operating theatres. She winced at the sight and held her breath.

'We don't do anything in a rush,' Mavis assured her. 'You must think of this as a preliminary visit, allowing me to learn your details. You're not far on, I take it?'

'Around seven weeks.'

'Good. And is this your first pregnancy?'

Connie nodded. 'I'm in full-time work, and I'm a member of the ARP besides. People rely on me.'

'No need to explain,' Mavis reminded her with a dismissive wave of her hand.

'Sorry,' Connie mumbled.

'Try not to worry – I've been doing this for many years. Girls as young as fourteen come to me, as well as wives well into their forties who find themselves with too many mouths to feed, and every circumstance in between. Women who have been forced into doing something that they didn't want to do. Women whose men have run off and left them in the lurch – I find that's very common these days.'

'He didn't run off,' Connie responded, a touch too quickly. 'He's offered to help but I don't want him to. I prefer to do this alone.'

'As I said before, there's no need to rush into anything.'

All it took was a specially equipped bathroom with a narrow table and no doubt a shelf with gleaming steel instruments set out. It would be over quickly and life would return to normal. 'Do I have to make an appointment?'

'Not right this minute. Now that you've taken the first step, the best thing is for you to telephone me again when you feel absolutely ready.' Mavis stood up and waited for Connie to follow suit. They shook hands and went out into the vestibule together. 'A word to the wise,' Mavis said gently as Connie prepared to mount the steps. 'I say this to all my ladies, no matter what.'

Dazed by the prospect of what lay ahead at some point in the coming weeks, Connie held her breath and listened.

'Think it through. Talk to your sister and to the man involved, if that helps.' Mavis's advice was clear and unhurried. 'Take your time, Mrs Bailey. Take all the time you need.'

Bill and Tom stood on the shoreline and stared at what was left of *Annie May*. Behind them, the ebbing tide had left rock pools that glinted in the evening sun.

'That's it, then.' Tom had come to Wren's Cove at Bill's suggestion and the worst of his fears had been confirmed. There was nothing to be done; their dream of owning their own trawler was over.

Bill walked up the beach and kicked at the charred remains of the toolbox that they'd left on board. 'Not even the bloody tools . . .' he muttered savagely. 'Nothing.'

Tom felt heavy and hopeless as he followed Bill then raked his foot through the ashes. 'It couldn't have come at a worse time,' he admitted. 'The Patrol Service has already marked our cards, and now with the boat gone we've no chance of playing the reserved occupation card.'

'Damn it, I'm thinking we should volunteer our services for minesweeping and get it over and done with.' Bill's frustration was mounting with every passing second.

'You mean, not wait for them to give us a date?' Tom jammed his hands deep into his trouser pockets and stared out to sea.

'Yes, why not? They'll nab us soon enough so why wait? The last time I took a walk along St Stephen's dock I noticed that they'd finished the refit work on the corvettes that Mike Scott mentioned.'

'Minesweeping is no picnic.' Tom didn't need to remind him; memories of the sinking of *Sea Knight* remained vivid in both their minds. 'Besides, have you even mentioned it to Lizzie?'

'Not yet.'

'Maybe you should.'

'And maybe you should keep your nose out.' Bill strode towards the mouth of the cave then wheeled around. 'Sorry,' he mumbled sheepishly as he came back.

'No, you're right; it's none of my business.'

'It's bad enough that I had to tell her that the

209

wedding's off for now,' Bill explained. 'But I didn't have any choice, did I? How could I let it go ahead with no money coming in?'

Tom had no ready reply. On the one hand, he understood that Bill's self-respect was at stake, but on the other, he knew how important the wedding must be to Lizzie – to all the girls, in fact. 'Don't ask me – I'm no expert.' Look at what had just taken place between him and Connie. 'I never know what women are thinking.'

'Me neither. But I explained my reasons and she took it well, considering.'

'Yes, you can talk to Lizzie. She's not the type to fly off the handle.'

'Unlike her sister?'

It was Tom's turn to glower then stride away.

'Sorry – sore point,' Bill called after him. He knew only the bare bones of Tom's split from Connie; that it had been her decision, written in a letter that had left his best friend reeling. 'I'm fond of Connie but there's no denying that she and Lizzie are chalk and cheese.'

'Let's drop the subject, shall we?' With a forlorn expression Tom wandered back and continued to poke at the debris. 'You know what? I would've expected to find bomb parts among this lot.'

'True.' This hadn't occurred to Bill. 'If *Annie May* took a direct hit, where's the evidence?'

For a while, they searched in silence for telltale metal fragments, observed only by two herring gulls perched on a ledge above the cave entrance. Further doubts crept in as Tom and Bill sifted through the ashes.

'Did Jerry really do this?' Bill asked. 'Or could it have been something or someone else?'

Tom frowned deeply. 'Someone who intended to lead us up the garden path.'

'Ron Butcher,' Bill and Tom said as one.

Then thoughts tumbled out in quick succession. 'For all we know, he could have done this.' Bill set the ball rolling. 'Who's to say it was definitely a bomb?'

'We just supposed . . .'

'But there's not a scrap of evidence.'

'He's mad as a hatter, by all accounts.'

'God knows, he might have done it to spite us.'

'Hold on.' Tom paused for breath. 'How can we be sure?'

Bill charged on. 'That rockfall inside the cave – what if it wasn't really a coincidence and Ron Butcher was behind it? I told Lizzie I'd heard a cry for help but when I followed it up there was no one there.'

'You're saying it was him, trying to trick you?'

Bill nodded. 'Picture it – Ron bears a grudge because we bought *Annie May* from under his nose. He's already ditched his fiancée and gone off the rails and now he's dead set on getting his own back. How does he do it? First, as a kind of threat he sets fire to the rotten planks we've ripped up, then for good measure he lets down the tyres on Fred and Pamela's bikes. After that he decides to scare the living daylights out of me by lying in wait, ready to tip a load of rocks on my head.'

'Why us, though? Why not blame his dad for selling the boat in the first place?'

'I don't know. Maybe he did. Then Ron gets to thinking – if I can't have *Annie May* then no one will.'

'So he chooses his time and sets fire to her during an air raid, hoping Jerry will get the blame.' Tom followed his friend's logic. 'You might be on to something,' he conceded. 'But how the hell do we prove it?'

'I haven't thought it through that far, other than having it out with the bastard, face to face.'

'No, that's not a good idea. Ron Butcher would deny it and fly off the handle. Someone might get hurt.'

'It'd be two against one, though.' He and Tom were fit and strong, easily a match for their opponent.

Tom came up with a more sure-footed way forward. 'Why not check our facts first?'

'How?'

'By finding out where Ron was when the raid happened.' If it turned out that he had an alibi then they would have to drop all charges, so to speak.

'Right you are.' There was no time to lose. Bill made a beeline for the cliff steps with Tom hard on his heels. They quickly reached the lay-by where their bikes were parked and seconds later they were riding side by side along the road towards Raby.

'Where are we going, exactly?' Tom yelled above the sound of their engines.

'To Raby – to pay Arthur Butcher a visit,' Bill replied. 'Let's find out if the old man knows what his layabout son was up to on Friday night.' With that, he opened the throttle and roared on.

The Leisure Gardens at the end of Valley Road was a peaceful haven as yet unspoiled by the war. The sun colonnade built a decade before added a modern touch and ran the length of the park, which contained a paddling pool, tennis courts and a children's playground. A wide stream ran through it, home to ducks and moorhens and bordered by tall plants with giant, umbrella-shaped leaves.

'Gunnera,' Pamela responded to Fred's query as they took an early-evening stroll.

Children's voices reached them from the pool that lay behind an ornate, octagonal bandstand.

Fred's gaze strayed up a hill towards the colonnade, which was bedecked with sprawling clematis, yet to flower. The slope, which in normal times would have been laid to smooth green lawn, was currently ploughed into neat furrows and planted with potatoes. 'There are pictures in the town hall of this place during Victorian times – ladies in crinolines and bonnets, gentlemen in top hats and tailcoats.'

'Those days are long gone. Back then these gardens were full of invalids in bath chairs who came to take the sulphur waters.' Pamela held her nose. 'I don't know if you've ever smelled it, but it stinks to high heaven.'

'Let's hope it cured their ailments then.' Fred drew Pamela to one side as two boys on roller-skates sped recklessly by. 'Did you play here as a child?'

'Occasionally on a Sunday – after Mummy had finished playing the organ at St Joseph's.' Edith had been a fussy, anxious mother, reluctant to let her only daughter play with other children. 'As long as I didn't get my best clothes dirty she didn't seem to mind.'

'You were lucky. We had nothing like this in Berlin.' Fred's early memories were of bustling city streets and of parents too busy in their jewellery business to take him to the park. Similarly, after his family had fled from the Nazis and ended up in

Hatton Garden, there had been little opportunity to seek out green spaces and relax. Instead, he'd worked hard to learn English and succeed in lessons across the board – especially in mathematics, for which he had a talent. There'd been some bullying, of course. Cockney boys had mocked his accent and called him Fritz, while girls had whispered in corners of the playground about the strange Jewish boy who always had his head buried in a book.

'Did you ever go roller-skating?' Pamela felt a touch of envy for the boys racing on towards the park gates, whooping as they wove between parents pushing prams and Darby-and-Joan couples tottering along arm in arm.

'No, but I was the proud owner of a pair of ice-skates.' Fred smiled at the memory. 'Unfortunately, I had to leave them behind when we left Germany.'

'The pond here freezes sometimes. I've seen people skating on it, but I've never tried it.' Sharing these details felt like petals opening one by one to uncover the centre of the flower. 'I'm glad we made time for this,' she said with a sigh.

He squeezed her hand. 'Just you and me – it feels good.'

'Especially after these last few days,' she agreed. 'Here's hoping that the Luftwaffe will leave us alone, for a little while at least.'

'Don't count on it.' Fred was not at liberty to divulge information recently received by control centre operatives warning of another imminent attack.

'Why – what have you heard?' A cool breeze shook the petals of the newly opened flower.

'I'm afraid I can't say.' Reaching the wrought-iron

gates, he stopped to ask her what she wished to do. 'Shall we take another turn around the park or is it time to wend our way home?'

'"Wend our way"!' she echoed with a delighted smile. 'That's one of the reasons why I love you, Fred Miller.'

'Because of the way I speak?'

'So correct and old-fashioned – it's lovely.' She turned to retrace their steps.

He shrugged. 'I'm happy that it makes you happy.'

'It's not the only reason.'

'What else?' Lately he'd been unsure of his ground; bland conversations and demure kisses had left him with frayed nerves, wondering if Pamela was undergoing a change of heart. Then there was the whole Reggie Nolan issue that they'd failed to get to the bottom of, which chafed at his brain and made him sullen and uneasy where once he'd been open and honest.

Pamela nudged him with her elbow. 'Are you fishing for compliments, by any chance?'

'Perhaps.' Suddenly serious, Fred walked her as far as the paddling pool, where they found a bench to sit on while they watched children play with their model yachts. The tiny boats bobbed bravely in ripples caused by the breeze. 'No, it's not compliments that I'm after, but I would like to hear the truth.'

'What about?' An arrow of alarm shot through her.

Fred's answer was slow and deliberate. 'About us – you and me.'

So here it was: the moment she'd secretly dreaded, when Fred would turn a searchlight on their romance and she would be forced to examine in detail what was happening between them. 'Explain what you mean,' she said faintly.

'Reggie and Sid – ever since they moved into Sunrise I've sensed a shift in your feelings towards me.'

'There have been a few problems,' she admitted. 'Reggie can be a nuisance and so could Sid, though I shouldn't speak ill of the dead. Even Uncle Hugh has noticed it. But my feelings haven't altered.'

'Honestly?'

'Yes – why would you suppose otherwise?'

'So I'm imagining things?' Unanswered questions flew back and forth. 'As far as you're concerned nothing has changed?'

Instead of replying, Pamela turned the tables. 'What about you – why have you been avoiding me?' There; she'd said it! 'You spent the whole of yesterday in the library when we could have been walking on the moors or cycling to Wren's Cove? Why? Why choose extra shifts at the control centre? Why let Reggie upset you so much that you prefer to get soaked to the skin rather than accept a lift home?' Pamela's hands shook as she questioned him.

'How can you ask me that?' Fred raised his voice against her. 'A nuisance, you say? Reggie Nolan is more than that – he's an ignoramus, a clown, a buffoon! He doesn't just dance with you. No, he paws you and holds you too damned close. And you – you do nothing to stop him.'

'That's not fair.'

'Isn't it? You let him act as if I don't exist, offering to buy you drinks and no doubt passing rude comments behind my back. And now!' Red-faced with exasperation, Fred spluttered to a halt.

216

'Now, what?' She knew there was more to come. 'Don't stop there – better to have it out in the open.'

'Now that he's lost his pal – for which I'm sincerely sorry – you put yourself forward as a shoulder for him to cry on. Yes, he told me all about it last night – how you came to the house and sought him out with the express purpose of comforting him, holding his hand while he cried his eyes out, telling him how much you wanted to help, that he could always rely on you, day or night.'

'No,' Pamela objected. 'I didn't seek him out, but yes, I comforted him, because who wouldn't in the circumstances? But Reggie's exaggerating – I never said he could rely on me or anything of that sort.'

A tousle-haired boy in a striped sailor's jersey and blue serge shorts waded knee-deep into the middle of the pond to retrieve his becalmed boat while his shrill mother warned him not to get his trousers wet. A black-and-white dog jumped for a ball and flipped sideways into the water – boy and dog were wet through. Dog jumped out and shook himself, mother fetched boy a clip around the ear. These things went on in the background as Fred and Pamela continued to argue.

'Why must I defend myself?' she demanded. 'Look at your own behaviour towards me – the snubs at work, the excuses not to meet. Have you forgotten our time together?' *That precious night, the murmured endearments, the promises that you made.* 'There will never be anyone else.' It was too painful to put into words.

'I haven't forgotten anything,' he muttered ungraciously. 'That's why it's so hard to see the way you are with Reggie.'

'Stop. The man has lost his best friend. He deserves sympathy, not blame.' How could Fred not see this? Until now, he'd been perfect in her eyes – she'd put him on a pedestal and adored him. But it was like worshipping a beautiful statue only to find that the marble it was fashioned from was flawed. A fault line ran through it that couldn't be overlooked.

Fred leaned forward, clasping his hands together and letting his head drop. 'The worst of it is – I know you're right.'

The sudden reversal silenced her.

'It's unworthy of me. I detest myself for it.' The effort of keeping up appearances – of being polite at all times and maintaining the veneer of good manners – had proved too much. Underneath it all, this wretched, acidic jealousy was eating away at him from the inside.

'Please don't say that.' Pamela resisted an urge to move closer and slide her arm around his shoulder. 'You're right about one thing – I should have tried harder to get my message across to Reggie. I wish I'd been more no-nonsense, like Connie would've been. But also – and this is hard for me to say – you ought to have trusted me more.'

Fred glanced at her face, then stared fixedly ahead. 'I might have, if only Reggie Nolan hadn't got on my nerves the way he does . . .'

'Why would that have made any difference?'

'I could most likely have kept a level head through all of this and I'd have expressed some sympathy for him after Friday's events.'

'But?' she prompted, glad that they seemed to be

getting rid of all pretences and games. At last, Fred was speaking from the heart.

'But, tragedy or not, the man's a complete and utter fool.' Bitterness soured Fred's expression as he turned his head once more. 'He never misses an opportunity to make snide remarks about MI5 arresting more German spies, then he gloats about them being lined up against a wall and shot.'

Pamela was shocked but not surprised. 'When did he say that?'

'Every chance he gets. He also reckons that enemy aliens should be shipped off to Newfoundland for the duration of the war. Oh, and he spouts Churchill's "Collar the lot!" nonsense for good measure.'

The setting sun had disappeared behind a stand of beech trees that bordered the park, leaving a chill in the air. Families packed up their picnics and prepared to depart. A toy boat with limp sails had been abandoned in the middle of the pond. 'Does Reggie know the full story?' Pamela whispered in a sudden, rising panic.

'Without a doubt,' Fred confirmed. 'He called me by my German name on one occasion. Another time he demanded to see my tribunal card to prove my Category C status. He kept at me until I showed it to him.'

'You should have told me about this,' she breathed.

'What good would it have done?' Weary to the core, Fred let his head hang lower still. 'You know better than most that men like Reggie think what they want to think and nothing I say will make any difference. According to him, I shouldn't be allowed anywhere near work connected with the war effort.'

'Ridiculous!' Such unfounded accusations had happened before and the exact wording of Fred's tribunal card was etched in her brain.

'Müller is of Jewish race. His father was deprived of his business as a diamond importer in Berlin by the Nazis. His mother was English, his father German. Both his parents are dead. He is currently employed as a clerk at Anderson's Timber Company and works as a volunteer in the ARP Report and Control Centre in Kelthorpe, North Yorkshire. The committee regards this alien as a genuine racial refugee whose being at liberty in no way constitutes a danger to the State.'

But try telling that to Reggie Nolan.

With a terrible sense of déjà vu, Pamela sat with Fred as dusk fell. 'Time to go,' she murmured at last. She slipped her hand into his and they walked together through the gloom.

CHAPTER THIRTEEN

A sad sight greeted Bill and Tom as they coasted down the hill towards Raby's ancient harbour. A cluster of cottages lay in ruins; their red-tiled roofs were caved in and their walls reduced to rubble by Friday's raid. It was dusk and men in thick sweaters and wellington boots and women wearing shawls and headscarves had gathered by the jetty, attempting to come to terms with their loss.

One of the men stepped forward to challenge the new arrivals. He was old-school, a fisherman with grey beard and heavily lined face whose boat had been blown to bits along with the house that his family had owned for two hundred years. 'If you've come to gawp like all the other nosy so-and-sos, you can turn right around and go back the way you came,' he spat at them.

Other suspicious villagers murmured their support until a young, sprightly woman in a tight-fitting scarlet sweater and black slacks broke free from the group and approached Tom and Bill. 'It's all right – I know these two,' she informed the old-timer, who lost interest and backed off.

'Molly Chambers?' Tom did a double-take. The

last time he'd come across Molly, she'd worn her hair in pigtails. Now she was tall and shapely and her hair, cropped short in a modern style, was a lighter shade of blonde than it had been when she was at school.

'Yes, it's me. What brings you here, Tom Rose? I hope it's not to take snaps of the mess that Jerry made.' Molly gestured towards the ruined dwellings. 'We've had a bellyful of that type of visitor, thank you very much: newspapermen from the *Gazette* – and from further afield, too.'

'No, nothing like that,' Tom assured her.

They were joined by a thickset man in his early twenties with dark hair and strong features. 'Bob Waterhouse,' he reminded Bill curtly.

Bill recognized him at once. It was none other than Lizzie's ex-fiancé, damn it. Still, it was best to rise above old rivalries. 'How are you, Bob? Are you still working for Hugh Anderson?'

'No, I got laid off. I'm driving a crane for Alf Mason now.' Bob folded his arms and rocked back on his heels. 'I didn't expect you to show your face round here.'

Molly raised her eyebrows at Tom. 'No love lost there,' she said to no one in particular. Then louder, 'I was sorry to hear about *Annie May* – she was burned to a cinder, by all accounts.'

'That's why we're here,' Tom admitted. 'We were hoping for a word with Arthur Butcher.'

'You'll be lucky.' Finding sly satisfaction in Bill's discomfort, Bob gave a grim barking laugh. 'That's his house, right over there.'

Following his pointing finger, Tom and Bill's gaze

rested on the nearest roofless cottage. Little was left of the building except a stone chimney stack and a side gable that had been sheltered from the blast by an overhanging rock. Its fire-damaged contents were heaped by the roadside – the remains of an iron bedstead, a scorched mattress, a dented tin bath and a washing mangle.

'What happened to Arthur?' Tom asked Molly.

'He got out in the nick of time. Bob here is an air raid warden – he led the old man to one of the tunnels that smugglers used to use. There's a network of them running under these houses. Thank the Lord for smugglers, eh?'

'Yes, thank God.' Bill was forced to see fellow ARP man Bob Waterhouse in a more favourable light. 'Fritz was on us before we knew it. Good for you for getting Arthur out in time.'

Bob acknowledged the praise with a grunt. 'Luckily we had a few minutes longer than your lot did to get ourselves organized. We ended up with minor injuries, that's all.'

'And where's Arthur staying now?' Once more Tom turned to Molly for an answer.

'He's with Nancy Lennox on King George's Close – thanks to Bob again.'

'Nancy is a decent sort and I knew she had a spare room.' Bob shrugged off his good deed.

'So that's where we'll head now.' Tom was eager to be on his way. 'You don't happen to know if his son Ron has taken up lodgings there as well?'

Molly shook her head. 'Search me. Ron's nickname round here is The Scarlet Pimpernel. "They seek him here, they seek him there . . ." He could be lying dead under that heap of stones for all I know and care.' Jerking her thumb towards the remains of Arthur's cottage, Molly then brushed her palms together in a gesture of dismissal. Definitely no love lost there either.

'Let's find out, shall we?' Like Tom, Bill was keen to move on.

'How's Lizzie?' Bob's quiet question dropped like a pebble into a smooth millpond, causing ripples of curiosity amongst the onlookers. Molly's tweezered eyebrows shot up in anticipation.

'She's fine, thanks.' Bill jammed the peak of his cap further down his forehead then made for his bike.

'Tell her I was asking after her.'

Not bloody likely! 'Will do,' Bill lied as he slung one leg over the saddle then kicked the starter pedal, marvelling at how the past came up and bit you on the backside when you least expected it.

'What about you, Tom?' Molly laid a hand on his arm and batted her thick, dark lashes at him. 'Are you engaged to the merry widow yet?'

Tom's cheeks blazed red and a tumult of emotion swept over him. 'No,' he replied as he followed hard on Bill's heels. *Not engaged and never likely to be. End of story.*

Following a good deal of persuasion, Nancy Lennox let Bill and Tom into her house. She warned the visitors that her new lodger was in no fit state to be badgered or bullied.

'Arthur might not show it, but this latest business has knocked the stuffing out of him,' she told them before withdrawing.

224

Arthur Butcher looked a beaten man. At the age of sixty-five, he'd lost both his occupation and the roof over his head, landing on the scrapheap with scarcely a possession to his name. Shock had cut deep into his ravaged features, hollowing his cheeks and emphasizing his sharp cheekbones and prominent nose.

'What do you want?' Sitting poker-stiff and defiant in Nancy's kitchen, he glared at the visitors. 'If you're after your money back for *Annie May*, you're wasting your time.'

'We're not,' Bill assured him.

'We're as cut up about losing *Annie May* as you must be,' Tom told Arthur. 'We put everything we had into that boat.'

The old man sniffed and took a second or two to regain control of his emotions. 'Aye, I was relying on you two to look after her. She was a good old girl. There wasn't a better trawler for miles around.'

'You can say that again.' As Bill hovered by the door, he noticed a row of Kilner jars on a high shelf, placed in descending order, large to small, and each neatly labelled: raspberry jam, orange marmalade, pickled onions, pickled eggs, and so on. There was an earthenware crock on a lower shelf next to some well-used bread tins and a pot containing wooden spoons and other cooking implements. Arthur seemed sadly at odds with his tame, orderly surroundings – diminished and ill at ease.

'Sit yourselves down.' He pointed to two wheel-back chairs positioned either side of an old-fashioned cooking range. 'I took the odd walk over to Wren's Cove at low tide to see how you were getting on. You were doing a grand job, the pair of you. But it just goes to show . . .' Instead of finishing his sentence, the old trawlerman spread his gnarled hands palms upwards on the scrubbed deal table.

'You can never bank on anything these days,' Tom acknowledged.

'Aye, worse luck. Though God only knows what made Jerry take a detour to the cove to drop the last of his bombs on my poor old girl. What harm could she do to Herr Hitler and his pals?'

Tom flashed Bill a warning look not to charge in. 'It doesn't make sense,' he agreed. 'At any rate, we're glad you made it through all right and I take it Ron did likewise?'

Arthur pursed his thin lips. 'How should I know?'

'So he wasn't at home with you on Friday night?'

'No and I hadn't clapped eyes on the daft beggar for weeks before that. We fell out over me selling *Annie May* and my lad's not the sort to forgive and forget.'

Tom pushed a little harder. 'But we thought you said Ron wasn't interested in taking her on?'

'I might have bent the truth a bit there.' Arthur cleared his throat before continuing. 'Think back – I did say he didn't have what it took as well. He was interested, but I doubted he could make a proper go of it.'

Bill sat forward in his seat. 'In what way?'

'Ron's been a problem as far back as I can remember – bright enough when he was at school and with one heck of a photographic memory, but moody with it. Over the years that lad of mine has lost more jobs than I've had hot dinners. He never

226

lasted more than a few months at any of them before he'd let his temper get the better of him. It would be over summat or nowt. Either he would storm off or else he'd get the sack, then he would drink himself stupid and get into even more bother.'

Tom absorbed the implications of what they'd been told before scraping back his chair and nodding towards the door. 'We'd best be making a move,' he said to Bill.

'Hang on a minute. Does Ron even know what's happened to you and your cottage?' Bill asked Arthur.

'No and even if he did he wouldn't give a damn.' The latest rift was too deep to mend. 'For all I know he's buggered off for good this time.'

'Where to?'

'You tell me. He doesn't have many choices left. The navy won't have him, I know that for a fact – and neither will the army. You have to pass tests before they put you in uniform and Ron failed all of them. Summat to do with the way his mind works. I don't recall the jargon.'

Seeing that the old man was growing agitated, Tom gave Bill's sleeve a sharp tug. 'Thanks, Arthur – we're glad you're all right. We'll see ourselves out.'

Nancy Lennox – she of the neatly labelled Kilner jars and home-baked bread – appeared as if by magic. 'This way,' she told the visitors, before leading them through the living room and out into the gloomy yard. 'You see how badly Arthur has taken things,' she muttered darkly. 'You oughtn't to have mentioned that son of his – it always upsets him.'

'I'm sorry – we didn't realize.' Bill's apology was sincere.

'That's why you came in the first place, isn't it?' Nancy was more perceptive than she appeared in her flowered pinny and woollen carpet slippers. 'It's Ron you're after, and you supposed his dad would know where he was.'

'That's true,' Tom acknowledged.

Nancy looked them up and down and, against her expectations, liked what she saw. 'I won't ask any questions and you won't mention my name?' she checked.

'No – hand on heart,' Bill promised.

'If you really want to track Ron Butcher down you could try Fletcher's Yard behind the Kelthorpe gasworks.'

'Why? What would he be doing there?' Tom made no attempt to disguise his surprise.

'That's where Edna Shaw lives – or did, the last I heard.'

'Edna Shaw?' The name appeared on the household register that Tom carried with him when out on patrol, but he couldn't put a face to the name.

'Edna Butcher as was,' Nancy explained carefully. 'She ditched Arthur and went to live at number six when she got married to Ernest Shaw. Edna is Ron's mother, in case you didn't know.'

Pamela's long legs had to work hard to keep up with Sally, who was a good three inches shorter but still full of energy even after a long day at her typewriter. 'Slow down,' she pleaded as they made their way past the warehouses lining St Stephen's dock towards the market square.

Sally obliged by stopping and allowing Pamela to

catch her breath. 'Dad says I'm like a runaway train,' she apologized. 'I tell him it's because I have so much to cram into my day. Someone's always hungry when I get home or has fallen over and needs an Elastoplast, or else wants help with their homework. You name it . . .'

'You're a marvel.' Pamela meant it – capable and unflappable, Sally gave no sign that she was under strain. And she looked so fresh and dainty in the crisp blouses that she wore to work, with her flaming red hair pinned back from her freckled face. 'I honestly don't know how you do it.'

'I'm used to it, I suppose.' Sally adjusted the leather handbag that was slung satchel-style over her shoulder, ready to march across the market square. 'The little ones drive me round the twist, but I wouldn't be without them for a single minute.'

As she spoke, the door to the Anchor opened and young George bounced out in shirtsleeves and bright red braces, jauntily carrying a fishing rod over his shoulder. He was followed by Rita, who scampered after him along the jetty.

'Uh-oh – I'd better keep an eye on her.' Sally set off across the cobbles but hadn't got far before her father came out of the pub. Frank rolled an empty barrel clear of the door and had his back turned when a figure emerged from the shadows cast by the terraced houses at the bottom of Tennyson Street.

'Sally, wait!' Pamela recognized Ron Butcher even before he accosted Frank Hopkins. Ron bawled the landlord's name to attract his attention and the two men immediately started to argue – tempers flared, and voices were raised.

As Sally hesitated, Pamela ran to join her. 'What on earth's going on?' she asked.

Sally swallowed hard. 'Dad warned Ron not to show his face round here ever again – last weekend, after he caught him lurking in the square at closing time. It must have been Saturday, the night after the last air raid.'

The argument grew louder still as Ron tipped over the barrel and sent it rolling towards the jetty. 'You've no right to order me about,' he snarled. 'I can go where I bloody well like.'

Ignoring the stray barrel and the gathering onlookers, Frank stood his ground. Although balding and approaching fifty, he'd kept in good shape thanks to the heavy lifting that his job involved, so thought nothing of clenching his fists and squaring up to a man half his age.

Ron, by contrast, was slightly built and the worse for wear, having drunk steadily all through the day. He was without his jacket and the back of his shirt had come untucked. 'You hear me? I can go where I like and talk to who I damn well please!' His slurred voice rang out across the square.

Frank didn't flinch. 'Not to my daughter, you can't. When will you get it into your thick head that my Sally wants nothing more to do with you? If I catch you bothering her again, I warn you – I'll knock your block off.'

'You and whose army?' Ron reeled sideways and fell against a second barrel.

'Try me.' Frank grabbed the front of Ron's shirt and pulled him upright. Ron clasped him in a bear hug and wrestled him to the ground. Locked together, they rolled over in a grim embrace.

'Oh, Lord!' Sally ran forward to intervene, along with Pamela and two of the onlookers. 'Dad – Ron, stop it, please!'

Frank pulled free and sprang to his feet, raising his fists ready for action. Ron hauled himself up more slowly then promptly swayed forward and lost his balance, crashing to the ground again and staying there, allowing time for the two spectators to take him by the elbows and drag him away, face down and horizontal, with his head hanging and the toe-caps of his boots scuffing the cobbles.

'Stand clear,' one of the men warned Sally.

It was a pitiable sight – Ron was so drunk he scarcely knew what was happening. Several people jeered as he was carted off along Tennyson Street.

'Good riddance to bad rubbish.' Frank turned away in disgust. He retrieved the stray barrel and set it upright by the door, all the while assuring Sally that he was none the worse for wear. 'Stark-staring bonkers,' was his final comment on Ron Butcher as he stomped inside.

'Now will you call the police?' Pamela demanded.

Batting the question away, Sally hurried towards the jetty, where she called for George and Rita to come quickly.

'Will you?' Pamela repeated.

The children dawdled towards them. 'Hurry up!' Sally shouted. 'What can the police do?' she asked Pamela with an air of exasperation.

This was the conclusion her Uncle Hugh had

reached too – unless Ron had committed an actual crime, there was little to be done. Then again, this latest drunken brawl in broad daylight and without provocation surely constituted a breach of the peace. 'Get them to issue a warning,' Pamela insisted. 'Perhaps Ron would pay more attention if it came from them.'

'I doubt it.' Sally sighed. 'He didn't take any notice the last time they prosecuted him for being drunk and disorderly, did he? And honestly, Pamela – you don't know what he's like.'

'I think I'm beginning to get a pretty good idea.' Drunken, quick to anger, out for revenge to the point where he was willing to risk a small child's safety – this much was certain. 'Really, Sally, I don't like to think of you and your family having to put up with this.'

'And thank you for that – I'm grateful.' Sally waited for Rita to reach her then took her firmly by the hand. 'But we'll cope without the police. From now on, Dad won't stand any nonsense – he'll spread the word among our customers that Ron is banned from the Anchor and before long the whole of Kelthorpe will know.'

'If you're sure . . .' Pamela took a step backwards and was about to turn and make her way towards Sunrise for a pre-arranged meeting with Fred when she recognized a familiar face in the small crowd of interested observers. Her heart sank.

'Hello, Pamela.' Reggie broke away from the gossips and quickly approached. He was in Hairy Mary uniform, minus his cap – an indication that he'd finished his shift and headed straight for the pub. 'Fancy meeting you here.'

'I'll leave you to it,' Sally muttered, leading Rita away. 'Good luck,' she called over her shoulder.

'Reggie.' Pamela's face gave nothing away. 'How are you?'

'Not bad, considering. How about you?'

'Tired,' she admitted. 'I'm on my way to see Fred, actually.'

'Champion – I was heading that way myself.'

As they walked together towards the narrow foot-path that would take them round the headland, Pamela was careful to keep her distance and stick to safe topics – the weather forecast for the next day, the clean-up operation that was still ongoing after Friday's raid.

The path narrowed to single file as they approached the shadow of an overhanging rock. 'After you.' Reggie stepped to one side with exaggerated gallantry. He walked behind Pamela – his favourite view of her – until they were clear of the rock and the path opened out again to give them a clear sight of the bay and of the cranes and lorries of the rescue squads busy clearing rubble and filling in craters in the roads. Low, pink clouds resting on the flat horizon absorbed the last rays of the setting sun. 'Sid's brother is coming from Wolverhampton to pick up his belongings tomorrow,' Reggie told her with a sudden, calculated shift into more serious matters. 'He said I can choose a keepsake – a tiepin or cuff-links, maybe. Sid wasn't big on cufflinks, though.'

'That's nice of Sid's brother.' She waited for her companion to come alongside.

'I've packed his stuff into a suitcase, ready for col-lection.' Reggie filled a pause with a heavy sigh designed to make Pamela feel sorry for him. 'A tie-pin's not a lot to remember a bloke by, is it? A life snuffed out at the age of twenty-three, just like that – it makes you think.'

'It does.'

'They'll send a replacement for Sid up from Norfolk before the end of the week – another aircraftman first class. It won't be the same, though.'

'I suppose not.' Pamela resisted the appeal for sympathy. She'd learned that if she gave Reggie an inch he would take a mile, whatever the circumstance. To maintain her resolve and keep him at a distance, she must concentrate on Fred and on how badly Reggie had treated him.

'What's up?' Reggie strode ahead then swung around to block her way and challenge her, craning his head forward and staring directly into her eyes. 'Have I done something wrong?'

'No, nothing.' She stepped to the side then kept on walking.

'Hang on – I never meant to upset you. It's just the Sid business – it's preying on my mind.'

'Look.' Pamela stopped to clear the air once and for all. 'I'm sorry about Sid – I really am. I know how much you'll miss him. But you must find another shoulder to cry on, not mine. It's not good for either of us to go on like this.'

'Uh-oh!' Reggie's expression changed and a glint of malice appeared in his eyes. 'I thought so – Fred's been having a go behind my back. What's he been telling you?'

'"Collar the lot!"' she quoted. 'Does that ring a

bell? Or ship them off to Australia, or line them up and shoot them?'

'And what's wrong with that?' Reggie was obliged to hurry to keep pace with Pamela as she continued walking along the wide, empty prom towards Sunrise. 'We're talking about spies, aren't we?'

She picked up even more speed. 'Fred is not a spy and you know it.'

Reggie began to see that his bridges were burned as far as Miss Pamela was concerned – the pursuit was over. A pity; a sweet, sexy girl like her would have been a real feather in his cap. Besides, he'd developed an unexpected soft spot for her after she'd held his hand and listened to his woes, so this rejection hurt more than he'd expected. 'Do I know that?' he countered. 'It's not what people round here are saying. They downright hate Fred Miller and anyone who has anything to do with him. I've had to stick up for you more than once in the Harbourmaster's and other watering holes – I've told them you're not to blame if the bloke you're walking out with turns out to be a secret Nazi spy. Some of them aren't convinced.'

'Stop!' Furious, she swung her handbag at him and caught him in the chest. 'Enough, enough! Have you any idea what it's like to be hounded and threatened every single day of your life for ten whole years? That's what happened to the man I love. Then after it got too bad in Berlin, he had to build a new life in a different country. He was forced to forget who he was, to start all over again with a new name, only for liars and bigots – Mosley's men – to drive him and his family out again, smashing their windows and setting fire to their house, killing Fred's parents while they were at it.' She paused for breath but hadn't finished yet. 'You call yourself a patriot, Reggie Nolan, and you fly the Union Jack in everyone's faces, but you're a vicious thug like the rest of them. Yes, a thug! There, I've said it. And now step aside and don't bother me again.'

He popped his lips and exhaled loudly – an angry, deflating sound that showed he'd accepted defeat. 'So much for my master plan,' he quipped. 'I thought for a while I was getting somewhere.'

The cheek, the nerve – the sheer crassness of the man – made Pamela catch her breath. Him and his well-oiled hair and bristling moustache, his puffed-out chest and military strut – loathing overwhelmed her.

'I knew you were wet behind the ears,' he informed her with an insulting grin. 'I must admit that was part of the appeal. But I didn't think you were this simple.'

Pamela stormed ahead through the gate into the grounds of Sunrise. 'Get out of my way,' she told him as he tried to overtake her. 'And don't ever – *ever* – speak to me again!'

The mystery of how *Annie May* had met her end continued to eat away at Bill and Tom, but further training work on the blimps kept them fully occupied until the Tuesday evening following their visit to Raby. In the meantime, Tom had stuck to his painful decision to stay away from Connie, and Bill had dug in his heels over his decision to postpone his and Lizzie's wedding.

'I tried to convince her the time will fly by,' he said to Tom when they met at the corner of Gas Street and Valley Road an hour before their ARP shifts were due to start. The huge round gasometer dominated the skyline and a strong smell of coal gas filled their nostrils as they approached. 'Her dad agrees it's for the best. We've cancelled the flowers and the rest. Lizzie's looking on the bright side, saying it'll give us more time to save up food coupons for the reception.'

'Have you told her—'

'About the Patrol Service call-up for minesweeping?' a red-faced Bill interrupted.

'You haven't,' Tom guessed. 'I'd do it sooner rather than later if I were you. The first thing I look for when I go downstairs in the morning to pick up the post is the official envelope giving me my starting date. It'll land any day now.'

'I know – I just haven't got round to it.' The truth was, Bill was still hoping that it would never happen, despite the evidence of the refitted corvettes anchored in the estuary and Mike Scott's conviction that they were only days away from call-up. He stopped short of the entrance to the gasworks beside an alley leading to Fletcher's Yard. 'I wouldn't fancy living here,' he commented. 'Not with that smell hanging around. Give me a view of the open sea and a blast of fresh air any day.'

They ventured down the narrow passage and found themselves in a dark courtyard littered with bits of machinery – parts of an oily car engine and a broken bicycle frame among them – and with untidy dustbins that were full to overflowing. Straggly weeds grew between the cobbles and the doorsteps of the terraced houses huddled in the shadow of the huge green gasometer were worn and covered in moss.

'Number six,' Tom said quietly.

They approached a faded green door with an iron knocker. Rat-a-tat-tat; Bill announced their arrival then waited. A thin grey cat jumped down from one of the dustbins then shot down the alley out of sight.

'Yes?' A respectable-looking woman answered the door and her eyes locked on to Bill and Tom's uniforms. 'If it's about the household register, I'm up to date. My name is Mrs Edna Shaw. My husband, Ernest Shaw, is listed as missing at sea. No one lives here now except me.'

'We haven't come about that,' Tom assured her. 'We just wondered if we could have a quick word.'

'What about?' Arthur's ex-wife viewed them with growing suspicion. Blocking the doorway with her tall, solid frame, she made it plain that she didn't welcome strangers knocking on her door at this time in the evening. 'It can't be my blackout blinds either. I'm particular about that.'

Bill supposed that Edna Shaw was particular about everything. She was a well-turned-out woman, from her carefully permed grey hair to her light brown twinset and skirt and polished shoes. There were even signs of her attempts to smarten up number 6 with fresh net curtains and a donkey-stoned top doorstep. 'We've come about Ron,' he explained.

With an angry gasp Edna took a quick step back and slammed the door in their faces.

'Blimey.' Tom sucked his teeth. 'I wasn't expecting that.'

'Me neither.' Bill knocked – once, twice, three times.

An elderly neighbour with her head wrapped in a checked woollen scarf opened a window and poked out her head. 'You'll be lucky,' she said. 'She doesn't like visitors, that one.'

The head disappeared and the window slid shut. Tom and Bill stepped back and stared up at Edna's house. 'Try one last time?' Tom suggested.

But as Bill raised the knocker for a fourth time, the door flew open. 'Ron isn't here,' Edna told them loud and clear. 'Whatever you want with him, I can't help you. And if he owes you money, I can't pay and that's that.'

'He doesn't owe us anything,' Bill tried to explain. The nosy neighbour had reopened her window and was peering out.

'Noreen Cartwright, keep your nose out of other people's business,' Edna snapped before changing her mind about her ARP visitors. 'You'd better come in if you don't want the old witch to hear every word we say.'

Tom and Bill stepped into a living room that was shabby but clean. A worn sofa was covered by a crimson chenille throw, and there were two framed pictures above the fireplace depicting roses in cut-glass vases. An array of shiny ornaments sat on the mantelpiece and the grate was neatly swept and re-laid with kindling and coal, ready for lighting.

'What's Ron done this time?' Edna demanded once they were out of the neighbour's earshot.

'We're not sure that he's done anything.' Tom trod carefully as usual.

'So what might he have done?' She folded her arms with a long-suffering expression and a wide-legged stance that said nothing they could say would surprise her.

Bill was more direct. 'It's about our boat, *Annie May*.'

'Don't you mean Arthur's boat?'

'No – we bought her from him.'

'Did you now? Ron wouldn't like that,' his mother said in the same sharp tone.

'She went up in flames last Friday,' Tom informed her. 'We've had to write her off as a dead loss.'

'Ah!' The arms stayed folded but the expression altered – Edna could be surprised after all. 'You think Ron did it?'

Talk about direct and to the point! Bill glanced at Tom before proceeding. 'We don't know. At the moment it's just a theory.'

'He's capable of anything, is that one.' With no hint of maternal loyalty, Ron's mother rushed to have her say. 'He's been a handful from the word go – since before he could walk – and no amount of smacking and shutting him in his room made the slightest bit of difference. Always in a world of his own, dragging rubbish into the house. Broken shells, fossils, bits of dead birds – whatever he could scavenge. He never had any friends to speak of. As soon as he started school, he got into fights; his father used to give him the belt but that didn't work either. The boy had a terrible temper on him – it would flare up, and woe betide anyone who got in his way. In the end, when Ron reached eleven and he grew strong enough to get the better of me, I'd had enough. I said to his father, he's your son – you deal with him from now on.'

Tom raised his hands to interrupt the flow of words. 'We're only interested in finding out where Ron was last Friday night.'

But it was as if a dam had burst. 'I walked out of that cottage in Raby and never went back. I came to Kelthorpe and married Ernest Shaw, who didn't want anything to do with Ron either. And that was that. I'd hear of him from time to time – how he'd had a scrap with this one or that, or else he'd broken someone's windows. And then he started drinking and, lo and behold, things went from bad to worse. Then blow me down, he managed to get together with the little red-headed girl from the Anchor – don't ask me how because I never bothered to find out. Of course, it didn't last long. And if you're asking me whether I know what Ron was up to last Friday, you know what my answer is going to be – it's a flat no!'

The torrent dried up at last. At the finish, both Bill and Tom felt drained. Tom offered Edna a faint thanks before backing towards the door.

'He did come knocking a week before that, asking me for money.' Edna's afterthought stopped them in their tracks. 'If you must know, I hardly recognized my own son. You should've seen the state of him. He looked as if he hadn't washed or shaved for a week and his clothes hung off him like a scarecrow. I told him no, I didn't have a penny to give him, and sent him packing straight away.'

'Thank you, Mrs Shaw,' Bill said, taking his opportunity to escape into the yard with Tom close behind. 'We're sorry to have troubled you.'

241

Edna peered down at them from her top step. 'If you find him, be sure and tell him not to come bothering me again. I can't be doing with it.'

'Right.' They set off towards the alley without a backward glance. Coal gas fumes filled their nostrils, but it wasn't this that brought a bad taste to their mouths; it was the whole sorry state of affairs that Ron Butcher's parents had created, and the feeling that the poor lad hadn't stood a chance from the off.

CHAPTER FOURTEEN

There was nothing else for it – Reggie Nolan had to go.

All during the evening and through the night, Pamela had stewed over the situation and by morning she'd reached a decision: she would speak to her uncle and ask him to send Reggie packing.

If not, she'd reasoned, *I'll be forced to stop visiting Fred at home. I won't even be able to call at the bungalow to see my own mother and father for fear of running into the wretched man. I must stick by what I said and avoid him at all costs. I can't trust myself to remain civil, not after our last conversation.* Full of a mixture of anger and dogged determination, Pamela had risen early. She couldn't shake the exact wording of Reggie's swaggering boasts. 'Master plan'? Then there was 'getting somewhere' and the insult that she was 'wet behind the ears'. Pamela dressed with mounting fury, then vigorously ran a brush through her hair. And the sneers that had accompanied the boasts and the viciousness of his lies! She brushed again until static crackled through her hair. Her mind was made up – she would seek out her uncle the moment she arrived at the timber yard.

'Something's the matter,' Fred had observed when

he and Pamela had got together the evening before. He'd noticed that she seemed upset and had heard raised voices on the driveway. Was Reggie causing trouble yet again?

'No,' Pamela had insisted. 'Nothing's the matter.' This was an action she was determined to take without involving Fred. She owed him this at least.

If only I hadn't been so naive. I ought to have stood my ground and not carried on dancing with Reggie in the first place. Why, oh why didn't I take a leaf out of Connie's book? In this defiant mood, she marched down the stairs, buttoning her coat as she stepped out on to King Edward Street, to the cacophonous roar of buses, bikes and cars. She found herself carried along by the throng setting out on foot for shops and docks, offices and warehouses. It was a cold morning for May, with a touch of frost in the air, so everyone was muffled up in heavy coats, scarves and hats, walking head down and with hands in pockets, shoulders hunched and shuffling like snails to school and work.

Pamela crossed the market square with a glance in the direction of the Anchor – there was no sign of Sally. She continued along the harbour-side towards St Stephen's dock, where she caught up with two girls who worked in Anderson's canteen. Deirdre Howard and Marjorie Dean were chatting with Lionel Simmons, who worked in the cutting shed.

'We just keep rolling along, eh?' Lionel winked at Pamela as he quoted lines from the famous American slave song. He was known at the timber yard as a loudmouth who tried too hard to impress the girls, and Pamela remembered him as the troublesome bully who, along with his father, had caused problems during the Hefty Hermann evacuation of St Joseph's church. 'You and me, we sweat and strain, eh, Deirdre?'

'Horses sweat,' the canteen worker reminded him with a dig of her elbow.

'Perspire then.' Lionel nudged Pamela and winked again.

'No – we glow.' Marjorie put in her cheeky two penn'orth.

Pamela tuned out from the conversation long before they reached the machine that stamped their cards. She stood apart and focused on what she planned to say to her uncle – how she would phrase her request and the reasons she would give. She would keep it short and to the point. Hugh would understand and agree that Reggie's departure was for the best.

When, having stamped her card, Pamela made her way to the cloakroom, she ran into Sally, who told her that she'd seen Mr Anderson leave the yard minutes earlier. He'd been driving through the gates as Sally had arrived and the gateman had told her that the boss had a meeting with a wholesaler in York and wouldn't be back until midday.

'Dash it.' Pamela's plan was put on hold. 'I wanted to speak to him urgently.'

'What about?' Sally and Pamela went upstairs together.

'Promise you won't tell?'

'Cross my heart.'

'I want to ask Uncle Hugh to get rid of Reggie Nolan,' Pamela confided. 'I can't bear the man or what he stands for. It turns out he's one of those bigots baying for the blood of all German Jewish refugees.'

'Of which Fred is one.' Settling down behind her typewriter, Sally understood immediately. Fred's background was common knowledge, as were the vicious attacks that had taken place the previous year. 'I thought that nonsense was over and done with.'

'I only wish it were.' Pamela remained fired up by the unfairness of it all. 'The truth is, there will always be these groups – men and women who follow Oswald Mosley and his Blackshirts, even though Mosley is safely behind bars these days. Reggie makes no secret of his views, so I don't see why Uncle Hugh should carry on providing a roof over his head.'

'He doesn't know about Reggie's political leanings?' Sally had listened carefully without expressing an opinion.

'Not yet. But I intend to tell him.' Pamela shuffled papers in her in-tray, arranging them in date order. 'Keep it under your hat,' she reminded Sally. 'If Reggie found out that it was me who got him turfed out of his billet, Lord knows what he might do to get his own back.'

She was on tenterhooks all morning, constantly looking out of the window for Hugh's car as the hours ticked by. When at last it appeared, sleek and shiny as it pulled into the yard, it coincided with the sound of the klaxon signalling the dinner break.

'Here he is!' Pamela ran to the window to check the busy scene. She made out her uncle in his smart overcoat and trilby hat among the crowd of men in overalls all making a beeline for the canteen.

Sally joined her and peered down at the yard.

'Maybe it would be best to wait a while,' she suggested uneasily.

Ignoring her advice, Pamela hurried out of the room and dashed downstairs. She found Hugh talking to her father by the canteen door, catching snatches of their conversation as she picked her way between workers. Apparently mines had been discovered in the estuary and St Stephen's dock faced a fresh threat. Supplies from the Baltic were likely to be held up as a result.

Should she interrupt? Frowning, she decided to hang back until the two men had finished their talk. There was a tap on her shoulder and she turned to see the squat, square figure of Lionel Simmons grinning at her and offering her a place beside him in the queue.

'No thanks – I'm waiting to talk to Mr Anderson.'

'Please yourself.' Lionel shrugged and pulled out a packet of cigarettes, lighting up as the queue moved at snail's pace towards the door.

'Yes, Pamela?' Seeing her hovering, Hugh muttered a quick goodbye to Harold then advanced towards her. 'What can I do for you?'

A deep breath. Keep it brief. 'Reggie Nolan,' she began in a low voice.

'Is he still bothering you?' Hugh had weightier matters on his mind so he got straight to the point. 'You'd like me to ask him to leave Sunrise after all?'

'Yes,' Pamela breathed, blushing furiously and aware that her uncle had spoken too loudly. It hadn't even been necessary for her to mention Reggie's unpalatable views on Jewish refugees. 'Please,' she added.

'Consider it done. Nolan will be gone by the end of the week.'

And that was it – Hugh turned towards the office block and the queue parted to allow his passage across the yard.

'The princess speaks, and lo, her wish is granted!' Lionel's cynical remark, issued through a cloud of blue cigarette smoke, caused smirks up and down the line. 'If we speak nicely to Pamela, maybe she can persuade her kind uncle to give us a wage rise. How about it, m'lady? Tell him an extra shilling a week would do nicely, ta very much.'

Thank God for the ARP. The act of changing into her battledress then arriving bang on time for the start of her shift sharpened Connie's focus and for a few valuable hours she hoped to concentrate on placing roof spotters on tall buildings along College Road before taking action against a junior warden caught asleep at his post. She checked that five rescue and repair squads were in place on North Street for tonight, Wednesday 6 May. A demolition gang had at last finished work on the Harbourmaster's; now it was the turn of a decontamination party to check for gas leaks and other noxious substances. Leafing through the paperwork at the Gas Street post, she was able to pretend that life went on as normal.

'Would you mind distributing these new safety leaflets after your tea break?' Connie called upstairs to Pamela. 'And while you're at it, please can you update any changes to the household register? I know for a fact that Ben Simmons at number eight Valley Road has recently taken in a new lodger.'

'Right you are.' Pamela washed out her mug at the sink, secretly hoping to avoid Ben's son Lionel during her visit. 'I'm on my way.'

'No hurry – take your time.' Connie turned her attention to an updated training pamphlet issued by the local authority – there were to be further small changes to blackout regulations and a venue must be arranged for a training lecture on the eighth that new volunteer wardens should attend. Where would Connie get hold of a 16-millimetre projector and a white screen at such short notice?

Ah yes; she knew just the man! Picking up the telephone to liaise with Ronald Atkinson at the town hall, she was aware of Pamela setting off with the leaflets. At the same time, the Fraser brothers returned from Tennyson Street: they'd been manning a new IIP – an Incident Inquiry Post – set up in a greengrocer's shop for the purpose of reassuring the anxious public. The boys went upstairs for their break and their relaxed chatter drifted downstairs as Connie finished her call.

What next? It was important to keep busy. But instead of flying on to the next task, she faltered and in that split second of indecision she plummeted to earth. It was all a pretence. Nothing was normal. She was expecting a baby.

'Connie, shall I make you a cuppa?' Simon called down the stairs.

She was pregnant and scared, drowning in uncertainty after her weekend visit to Mavis Coulson's house. It was all very well being told to take her time and consult with the other party involved; had Mavis any idea how hard that was to hear? Had she been through this torment herself? If not, how could she dish out advice to others? As for the physical side, Connie had become alert to every small change in her body. Obviously it was too soon for the pregnancy to show, but she might expect morning sickness to kick in at any time and she dreaded this. It would have to be explained away, and Lizzie would have to cover for her with their father, as she had when they'd switched roles in the bakery, giving Connie the extra hour in bed. But the pressure to reach a decision was growing to the point where Connie felt she would explode. True, Mavis's door stood open – a calm, clean end to the problem lay behind it. But Connie shuddered whenever she considered it. A life was at stake; the fact that a baby was growing inside her had become undeniable.

There must be another way. Women in her situation were known to continue with their everyday lives until they went away and had the infant in secret before handing it over for adoption. Such things could be arranged; there were Christian hostels for unmarried mothers where few questions were asked and childless couples queued up to adopt a baby. Again, she shuddered.

'You didn't answer my question,' Simon commented as he brought a mug of tea downstairs and placed it on the counter. 'I made you one anyway.'

Connie drifted towards the door and stared out into the darkness.

'I'll leave it here.' Puzzled, Simon went back upstairs. 'I don't know what's got into Connie lately,' he told his brother. 'She acts like she's carrying the weight of the world on her shoulders.'

Outside on the street, Tom approached the Union Jack that fluttered in the breeze above the entrance to the post. His eyes were accustomed to the dark and he saw Connie standing at the door before she saw him, so he had time to prepare himself. 'I've just come from North Street,' he informed her.

'Good Lord, you made me jump,' she gasped.

He cleared his throat, then went on. 'The road's been closed because of a new water leak outside the bus station. I'll log it then be on my way.'

'But you're not on duty.'

Her lame objection felt like a slap in the face. 'No – I happened to bump into Norman Riley – I said I'd pass on the message.'

'You knew I was here?'

'Yes,' he admitted awkwardly, then went on in an undertone. 'I'm doing what we agreed – trying to carry on as if nothing is wrong.' *Bloody impossible* – just looking at Connie now made Tom's heart thump like mad against his chest. 'Shall I go ahead and log it?'

'If you like.' She stood aside to let him pass, watched him take off his gloves, pick up a pencil and start to write.

The letters seemed to float across the page – *21.00 hours. North Street; burst water main. Road closure until further notice.* His usually neat writing was an untidy scrawl.

Connie observed how Tom's familiar physical presence filled the small room – his shoulders were broader than ever in his overcoat and his back was long and straight. She drew a deep breath, waiting for him to finish.

'Have you heard anything of Ron Butcher lately?'

He turned as casually as he could and steered the conversation away from the seemingly bottomless void that had opened up between them.

'No – why?' she answered cautiously.

'We – Bill and I – suspect that he set fire to *Annie May* out of spite. But now he's done a vanishing act.'

'Wait – Pamela did mention something when she reported for duty. Apparently, Ron started a fight with Frank Hopkins and was dragged off up Tennyson Street in a drunken stupor.' The details were unclear – Connie hadn't been concentrating.

'When was that?'

'Last night, I think.'

'Why Tennyson Street? Is that where he's holed up?'

'Pamela didn't say. She was there, though – she saw the fight with her own eyes. She's worried about what Ron might do to Sally but Sally refuses to go to the police. It's a proper mess.'

'Tell Pamela not to worry about her friend – we'll track Ron down sooner rather than later.' Squeezing past Connie as he made his way to the door, Tom sensed that she had more to add.

There was a pause, filled by sounds of the Fraser brothers clearing away their tea things in the room above.

'What?' Tom prompted. They were so close he could smell the soap she'd used to launder the cotton blouse that she wore under her uniform.

'If – *when* – you find him, remember he's a ticking time bomb. He could easily blow up in your faces,' she said softly.

'I'll remember.' Hope stirred. Did this mean Connie still cared?

She put a hand on his arm, then quickly removed it, her tone changing from gentle to brisk. 'I don't want my sister's fiancé to end up in hospital over the loss of *Annie May*, so watch your step, both of you.'

How flat life felt for Lizzie now that there was no wedding to look forward to.

She worked alone in the bakery, following a routine she'd known for most of her life. It had still been pitch black when she'd left Elliot Street and driven the van through the mostly deserted streets, following a route that had taken her past St Joseph's Church and the school next to it. At the end of College Road, a newspaper delivery boy had appeared in her dimmed headlights. She'd swerved to avoid him then overtaken a milk float parked outside Benson's music shop, hearing the clink of bottles and the cheery whistle of the milkman as she'd passed by.

Now, inside her warm, brightly lit workspace, she measured flour, yeast, a pinch of salt and warm water into the pancheon, mixing the ingredients well before kneading the dough then leaving it to prove. Next, she turned to a batch that was ready for the oven. She checked that it had reached the right temperature, slid in the trays and set the timer.

Normally, sealed inside this sweet cocoon, Lizzie would have taken pleasure in the familiar work – but not today. Worries niggled at her: would her father remember his doctor's appointment, and would Connie hang the washing out to dry as Lizzie had requested? Her sister was impossible to talk to these days, and Lizzie understood why. A massive decision

253

hung over Connie's head and every passing day seemed to make matters worse.

'Don't ask,' Connie had said the previous evening when she'd returned home after her shift and mentioned to Lizzie that Tom had turned up unexpectedly at Gas Street. 'Like a bad penny,' she'd muttered as she'd flung off her clothes and slid into bed.

'I only wanted to know how you dealt with seeing him,' Lizzie had objected. 'And how Tom acted towards you. Did you talk about . . . it?'

'It' – that was as close as Lizzie dared come to mentioning the unmentionable. 'No,' Connie had snapped, turning off the bedside light. End of subject.

As Lizzie weighed ingredients for the next batch of loaves, her mind strayed inevitably towards Bill. He popped into her thoughts at all times: in the middle of brushing her teeth this morning, or passing the ambulance depot at the old brewery on King Edward Street on her way here, or glancing up at the two blimps on the headland, shining silver in the moonlight. In fact, there wasn't a moment of her day when she wasn't aware of her sweetheart and what he might be doing, thinking or saying. As her fists pummelled and kneaded dough and clouds of white flour rose from the wooden board, Lizzie recalled the look of devastation on Bill's face when he saw the burnt-out wreck of *Annie May*. His dream was shattered and hers with it. Now they stepped carefully through the fragments of that dream, afraid that the jagged pieces would cut through the tender bonds of love that united them.

'I'll find something,' Bill had promised the previous

evening. 'Even if I have to go as far as Hull to find work, I'll do it. The big trawlers there need experienced men. I'll get a job in no time.'

Hull wouldn't be the same as Kelthorpe – he would have to leave his cottage and instead of stepping straight out into the harbour and on to *Annie May* he would have to travel at least thirty miles on his motorbike, which meant that Lizzie would scarcely see him. Also, she knew that those large trawlers were at sea for days on end. She'd voiced none of these fears, merely nodding her head and continuing to hide her own disappointments as best she could.

No spring wedding – that was the sharpest, most cruel cut that she was forced to endure. She, Connie, Sally and Pamela had finished sewing the dresses. She'd bought white satin shoes. She'd chosen flowers to decorate the church and picked hymns for the choir to sing.

Not this coming Saturday but the one after would have been their big day, organ music filling the church and the rustle of blue satin and the smooth feel of white silk against her skin as she and her bridesmaids processed down the aisle. Now none of that would happen. The day of May the sixteenth would be empty, the horizon flat and featureless as far as the eye could see.

Sighing, Lizzie opened the oven door to a blast of intense heat that forced her to concentrate on the task in hand. She donned a pair of thick oven mitts, then tapped the bottom of each tin before tipping the freshly baked loaf on to a wire tray. Hearing the muffled tinkle of the shop bell, she stopped what she was doing.

'Lizzie, are you there?' a familiar voice called.

'Bill?' Alarmed, Lizzie hurried into the shop. 'What brings you here?'

He stood in his second-hand airman's jacket, holding a letter and frowning deeply. He was unshaven and his hair was uncombed. 'I got this in the post,' he said with a tremor in his voice.

Lizzie took off the mitts with a rising sense of dread. 'What is it? What's wrong?'

'Those corvettes – the ones in dry dock that they've been refitting . . .' The words stuck in his throat.

'What about them?'

'They're ready for relaunch.' He should've warned her earlier, as Tom had nagged him to. But Bill had been guilty of putting his head in the sand, of believing that the call-up papers would never arrive; that he'd jump straight into a job on a Hull trawler and be back on the list of reserved occupations.

'So what does that have to do with you?' Lizzie clutched the bib of her apron with both hands. Her question hung in the air but she already knew the answer.

'Those minesweepers need experienced crew – sailors who know these waters, men like Tom and me.' Bill hung his head. 'You know the drill.'

All too well! Lizzie felt every drop of colour drain from her cheeks. 'When?' she whispered.

'Here, see for yourself.' Bill thrust the letter at her.

She took it with trembling hands.

'Go on, read it.'

Scanning the RNPS letter head, Lizzie's eyes fixed on the short paragraph below.

William Evans of 6 Harbourside Cottages, Kelthorpe, is hereby transferred from voluntary maintenance work to full-time minesweeping duties on board *HMS Northern Lights* commencing Monday 18 May 1942. Report for duty at St Stephen's dock at 0.600 hours.

Averting his gaze, Bill heard Lizzie gasp and imagined her look of dismay. 'I'm sorry, I should've warned you.'

Lizzie shook her head. 'No, it was bound to happen. I just couldn't bear to think about it.'

'You and me both.' He clenched his jaw and tried to put his arms around her. 'We'll cope with this,' he promised. 'We've done it before and we'll do it again.'

No! Every atom of her being wanted to protest at this latest news. She pushed him away and held him at arm's length. 'I don't know if I can get through more days of waiting for news or the sleepless nights not knowing if you're alive or dead. You don't realize how hard that is.' Lizzie knew that Jerry wasn't the only enemy; it was the sea itself – the restless, angry sea.

'Best not to think about it.' Bill drew her close and this time met no resistance. He hugged his Lizzie tight. 'That's what I try to do – I stuff those dark thoughts into a bottle and jam the cork in tight. That way, I get on with doing what I have to do. It's the same when you drive your ambulance, acting as if nothing can touch you, as if you're invincible. Otherwise you'd never be able to do it.'

She rested her head against the fleecy collar of his jacket. 'You're right,' she murmured. 'We all do that – Connie, Pamela and me.'

'You three girls have come through a lot together.' Bill kissed the top of her head. 'I'm proud of you, Lizzie Harrison.'

'And I'm proud of you too, Bill Evans.' She gazed up at him and felt the touch of his lips on her forehead, cheeks and mouth. They would keep the bottle tightly corked, honour King and country and do their best to take one day at a time.

CHAPTER FIFTEEN

'It's definitely happening,' Pamela reported to Sally, bringing her up to date on the Reggie Nolan affair. Their tea break gave them a chance to catch up with the latest events. 'Uncle Hugh has ordered Reggie to pack his bags and move out by the end of tomorrow.'

'Good for you.' Perched on a stool in the corner of their office where the tea things were stored, Sally was nevertheless muted in her approval. 'I'm worried, though. Like we said, there's no telling what Reggie will do if he finds out that you were behind it.'

'I'll cross that bridge when I come to it.' Pamela took her tea to the window and looked down on the busy scene. A new consignment of uncut timber had arrived and two cranes stationed at the dockside were transferring it from freighter to yard, guided by men who waved their arms and yelled loud instructions. She frowned when she spotted Lionel Simmons enjoying a furtive smoke by the side of the cutting shed. 'Some people!' she exclaimed.

Sally slid from her stool and came to see what had made Pamela angry. 'Lazy so-and-so,' she agreed. 'Lionel needs to watch out. One of these days he'll get caught.'

'He's the limit.' Pamela saw the offender glance up. He spotted them at the window and grinned from ear to ear. *Idiot!* Dismissing her scruples, she decided to tell Sally about the visit she'd paid to the Simmons household, following Connie's instructions. 'I called at his father's house on Valley Road last night. I was there to update the register and it was just my luck to run into Lionel. He answered the door, then insisted on me going into the house to meet their new lodger in the flesh – a chap named Howard Enright – the aircraftman who's been sent to take Sid Donne's place.'

'Let's hope this one is better behaved than Sid.' Sally watched Lionel throw down his cigarette and stamp on it. 'I know it's wrong to criticize, but there you are, I just did.'

'Or better behaved than Lionel, for that matter.' Pamela's impression of the cutting shed worker hadn't improved since the visit. 'Guess what I saw on the dining-room table at Valley Road.'

'I haven't a clue.' Taking Pamela's empty cup, Sally washed it at the sink.

Pamela raised her voice above the sound of the running tap. 'Copies of *Action* – you know, the old British Union newspaper that was banned a little while back.'

'Never heard of it. But go ahead – I'm all ears.'

'*Action* was banned by the government for being against the Jews and siding with Hitler, no less. Mr Churchill called members of the British Union fifth columnists and put their leader in prison. And yet, there the magazines were, displayed on Ben and

Lionel's table, clear as day. It made my blood boil to see them.'

'Ah yes, I can see why you were bothered by that.'

'I was never keen on Lionel or his father anyway. Now I know that they're a pair of rotten Jew haters I like them even less. I can just imagine them dressed up in their black uniforms marching down the street, flying their lousy fascist flag. As for Howard Enright, luckily he seems nothing like Reggie. He's a new recruit and his uniform was on the big side – he looked a bit lost and out of his depth, to tell you the truth.'

'Did you warn him about Reggie?' Sally was back at her desk, sorting through the letters in her in-tray.

Pamela, who had stayed where she was and still looked ruffled, shook her head. 'He'll find out soon enough.'

'What else?' Sally prompted. 'Come on, I know you.'

'Nothing.' Pamela sighed as she continued to gaze out of the window. 'Well, if you must know, I caught a glimpse of Ron as I was coming back through the Leisure Gardens.'

Sally gasped and stopped what she was doing. 'Where exactly?'

'He was sitting on a bench by the paddling pool – you know where I mean? The second he spotted me he took off for the woods behind the pool. It was all over in seconds.'

Sally's hands hovered over the pile of unopened letters. 'But it must have been dark. Are you sure it was Ron?'

Pamela nodded. 'It was him all right.' There had been no mistaking the slight build and hollow features or the way he'd staggered and swayed as he ran. 'I'm sorry, Sally – I hate to be the bearer of bad tidings but Ron had had too much to drink again.'

'What in the world was he doing in the Leisure Gardens of all places?'

'Maybe he's been sleeping rough. I noticed empty beer bottles under the bench and a pile of old newspapers that he might use to keep warm at night.'

Sally closed her eyes and breathed in deeply. 'Did you tell anyone that you saw him?'

'Just Connie. I mentioned it when I went back to the post with the register. Why – did I do wrong?'

'Connie,' Sally echoed quietly. Word would inevitably get around – it wouldn't be long before Tom and Bill found out. She pictured the two angry men making a thorough search of the park and its surroundings. If Ron had taken refuge in the bandstand, for instance, or found an alcove in the sun colonnade where he could lay his head, they would be sure to track him down.

The truth hit suddenly; whether or not Ron had set fire to *Annie May*, and however badly he'd behaved towards Sally and her family, this was the man she'd once had fond feelings towards, despite his faults, and the last thing she wanted was for him to be found. Trapped, Ron would lash out. There would be a fight and someone would get hurt. 'Oh, Pamela,' she whispered. 'I wish you hadn't told Connie. Lord knows what will happen now.'

*

'Your sister looks like death warmed up.' Bert's opinion was blunt and to the point as he and Lizzie finished off the morning's baking and Connie tidied up the shop. He stacked big wooden trays against the side of the oven and kept his growling voice low. 'Is it because her and Tom have parted company? Is she pining for him, or what?'

'Who's she, the cat's mother?' Connie had overheard. She barged into the bakery and cast a warning glance in Lizzie's direction. 'I'm feeling a bit under the weather, if you must know. It's nothing that a few early nights won't put right.'

'She thinks I was born yesterday,' Bert went on, grumbling to Lizzie as if Connie weren't there. 'But I wasn't. She's been stewing over summat for a couple of weeks and I reckon you're in on it too.'

'Where are the keys for the van?' Connie's stubborn expression suggested gathering storm clouds.

But Lizzie felt that their father deserved an explanation of sorts. 'It must be because Tom and Bill have received their start date for minesweeping from the Patrol Service,' she declared nervously. Still drained by the shock of receiving the news from Bill, she waited anxiously for her sister's reaction.

'The actual date?' Connie took a step backwards. 'When did you find out?'

'Early this morning. Bill told me.' Lizzie studied her sister's guarded expression. 'I take it you've known it was on the cards?'

Connie nodded. 'I promised Tom I'd keep it to myself.'

'Connie – we're not supposed to have secrets, you and I!' Disappointment flowed through Lizzie's

263

body, producing hot tears of exasperation. 'It never used to be like this. What's happening to us?'

Bert observed the altercation with a troubled frown.

'If you don't like secrets, try this one for size.' Connie found the keys hanging on a hook behind the door. 'Pamela caught sight of Ron Butcher in the Leisure Gardens last night – there, how's that?'

Lizzie used her apron to wipe away the tears. 'And how long were you intending to keep that one quiet?'

Connie swung the keys in front of her face. 'Honestly, I don't have time for this – I have bread to deliver.'

'Calm down, girls.' Bert decided it was time to intervene. 'This isn't like you. Take a deep breath – think about it. For one thing, even though you're upset, the news about the call-up hasn't come out of the blue – it was bound to happen sooner or later. For another, if Arthur Butcher's son has been spotted, Tom and Bill need to be told.' He turned to Lizzie. 'That'll be your job, since Connie and Tom aren't on speaking terms.'

'What's the betting Sally won't want anyone to follow it up?' Connie began to regret her outburst.

'You mean Frank Hopkins's girl? What's she got to do with anything?' Failing to keep up, Bert sat down heavily on the nearest stool.

'Dad, we'll explain later.' Lizzie patted his shoulder. 'You mean she might be scared that it'll end up in a fight?' she asked Connie.

'Bullseye.' Gritting her teeth, Connie made a beeline for the door. But before she made her exit, she hesitated. 'I take the point – it would end in tears,' she said quietly. 'And none of us wants that.'

'So, we keep quiet?' Lizzie was pulled this way and that. 'What do you think, Dad?'

Bert's verdict was prompt and left Lizzie and Connie in no doubt. 'Tom and Bill deserve to know what really happened to their boat, and if the only way to find out is by tackling Ron Butcher head-on, then that's what they should do.'

'Even if someone gets hurt?' Connie asked. 'Someone' meaning Tom, she realized with a sharp jolt.

'Even so.' Bert stood up and reached for his cap and jacket. 'And if you girls don't tell them then I will.'

Another difficult week was approaching its end, but relief was on the horizon for Fred: Reggie Nolan was leaving Sunrise.

'He'll be out of your hair by the weekend,' Hugh promised as the two men drove home from work on the Thursday evening. 'Then you and Pamela can resume normal service. She'll be able to visit you again without fear of you locking horns with our least favourite leading aircraftman.'

'Thank you, I appreciate it.' Respectful as ever, Fred stared out of the window at the towering headland, which was in deep shadow with a veil of mist obscuring the barrage balloons stationed on the ridge. 'I'm sorry that you've lost your lodger, though.'

'Don't think twice about it. I'll be glad to see the back of Nolan; I've a good mind to write to his squadron leader and tell him so.'

'Oh no, sir, don't do that.' Fred wished to avoid

more trouble. 'As you say, let's get back to normal and forget all about it.' This is what Pamela and he had vowed to do after their last heart-to-heart, and for them it was working well. He'd taken to visiting her at her lodgings and, joy of joys, had even stayed the night there on one occasion. Reggie Nolan's name hadn't been mentioned in all the time they'd spent together, and Fred had regarded it as a happy coincidence that Hugh had decided off his own bat that Nolan's time was up.

'He never was my cup of tea.' The airman's lack of manners had rubbed Hugh up the wrong way from the start. 'I ought to have listened to Edith – she's a good judge of character.' Turning off the promenade into his drive, Hugh gave Fred a reassuring smile. 'Stay out of his way in the meantime, eh?'

'I'll do my best.' Fred made his way towards the side door into the house. 'And thank you again.'

The two men parted – Hugh to his sitting room, where he closeted himself with his copy of the *Radio Times*, and Fred upstairs to his first-floor bedroom, where he sat at the window gazing down at the promenade and the grey expanse of sea. A sudden knock at the front door roused him from his reverie and he rushed to answer it. 'Don't worry – I'll get it,' he called to Hugh, taking the stairs two at a time.

Opening the door, he was surprised to see Lionel Simmons, still in his work overalls, with a trademark half-smoked cigarette tucked behind his ear.

'What's up – cat got your tongue?' Lionel's nicotine-stained fingers brushed his forehead in mock salute. 'Reggie asked me to call.'

Hearing the thud of Reggie's footsteps down two

flights of stairs, Fred recovered quickly and stepped to one side. 'Please come in,' he said hastily, hoping to be off the scene before Reggie arrived.

But it wasn't to be; Reggie appeared, a carrier bag in one hand and a canvas kitbag in the other, and collared Fred as he crossed the hall. 'Where are you sneaking off to?' he demanded, dropping his bags to the floor. 'Don't you want to bid me a fond farewell?'

'Goodbye,' Fred muttered, heading on towards the kitchen.

But Reggie blocked his way. 'Don't you mean *auf wiedersehen*, Herr Müller?'

Irritated, Fred jabbed at him with his elbow, only to be shoved back against the wall.

'You see, Lionel – our friend here can't wait to see the back of me. Well, the feeling's mutual.'

'What's he doing here?' Fred pulled free and jerked his thumb towards Lionel.

'If you must know, I'm moving to his dad's place on Valley Road to be with Sid's replacement. Not so handy for work, granted – but the atmosphere there will suit me far better. We're a like-minded bunch, aren't we, Lionel?'

'You can say that again.' The visitor had enjoyed the sight of Fred pinned against the wall and had made no attempt to intervene. Instead, he'd flipped the mis-shapen cigarette from behind his ear and taken out his lighter. 'None of us likes having a spy in our midst, except a certain person who fancies herself as Clau-dette Colbert. You know – green eyes, kiss curls and the rest.' Lionel outlined the shape of an hourglass with his hands.

Fred clenched his fists in an effort not to react.

Reggie smirked. 'She's the one who snitched on me to Uncle Hugh, in case you didn't know.'

The snide claim hit its mark. Fred abandoned his resolution to stay calm and launched himself at Reggie, seizing him by the lapels and almost lifting him off his feet. 'Take that back – Pamela had nothing to do with this!'

'Oh yes she did.' Lionel tapped Fred's shoulder. 'She asked the boss to get rid of Reggie – I heard her with my own ears and so did half a dozen others in the queue for the canteen. That's when I stepped in and offered him a room at Valley Road.'

Letting go of Reggie, Fred exhaled and sagged forward. Although Pamela hadn't said a word about this, he believed what Lionel had told him. It hurt that she'd gone behind his back, but he defended her, nonetheless. 'Leave Pamela out of it, for God's sake. It's me that you have to deal with, not her.'

'No, you two are yoked together like a – I don't know, like a horse and plough.' By this time, Lionel was thoroughly enjoying himself.

'In a way, you're right about Little Miss Perfect being a sideshow.' Reggie straightened his jacket with his customary sneer. 'You're the main target, Jew-boy. Don't try to deny it – I saw it on your tribunal card, remember.'

'So what?' Regretting that he'd been dragged down to Lionel and Reggie's level, Fred made an effort to regain some dignity. 'You saw from the card that Mr Anderson has vouched for me and the committee regards me as a genuine refugee.'

'You certainly pulled the wool over their eyes – I'll

give you that. But you don't fool me, Mr Clever-clogs.'

'Nor me neither,' Lionel added. 'Be warned – this isn't over, not by a long chalk. In fact, your name appears at the top of our list.'

'What list?' Fred demanded. Reggie's mockery and Lionel's sneers made him see red.

'Shall I tell him, or will you?' Lionel asked.

'Our list of enemy aliens who we want to see the back of. Good riddance to Friedrich Müller is what we say. And the same applies to your fancy woman!'

'I've told you once already, leave Pamela out of this!' Fred launched himself at Reggie, but Lionel came between them and pushed Fred back.

'She's got it coming to her,' Lionel insisted with increasing nastiness.

'Got what coming? What exactly are you planning to do?'

'Oh, perhaps Lionel can have a quiet little word with her in an out-of-the-way corner of the timber yard,' Reggie suggested. 'He can choose his moment to scare the living daylights out of your precious sweetheart – then we'll see whether or not she's willing to risk her film-star looks for the likes of you.'

The sour taste of bile rose in Fred's mouth. The pair's fascist views were bad enough, but now the direct threat against Pamela took things to a new level. Again, he clenched his fists, ready to make a second rush towards Reggie.

Luckily, at that moment Hugh provided a distraction by opening his sitting-room door. 'I thought I heard voices. Lionel Simmons, what brings you here?' he demanded sternly.

Lionel nipped out the burning tip of his cigarette then lodged it behind his ear before adopting a humble tone. 'I'm helping Reggie with his stuff,' he mumbled. 'Don't worry, sir – we'll be out of your hair before you know it.'

'Good – make it quick.' Hugh glanced from Lionel to Fred then to Reggie, who was gathering up his bags. 'It seems he can manage perfectly well without your help,' he commented.

'Is that all you've got?' Lionel checked.

'Yes – travel light is my motto.' Reggie breezed across the hall. 'You can open the door for me, though.'

Lionel quickly obliged, allowing Reggie to step outside without a backward glance. In an instant, the door closed firmly behind them with a rattle of its stained-glass panel.

'And there's an end to it,' Hugh declared, turning to Fred. 'Are you all right, my boy? You look rather pale.'

'I'm fine, thank you. I'm relieved that he's gone.'

'Onward and upward,' Hugh said. 'Forget about Reggie Nolan and his like. Remember, Fred – you're worth two of him put together. Now, what do you say we retire to my sitting room and partake of a small whisky before dinner?'

Pamela looked anxiously at her watch. Sally was late for work and there had been no message to say that she was ill. Five minutes earlier, Hugh had put his head briefly around the office door. 'No Miss Hopkins?' he'd enquired. 'Do we know what's held her up?'

'I'm afraid not.'

Her uncle's disapproving grunt had said it all – Sally had blotted her perfect copybook.

Unable to concentrate on her work, Pamela ran through various options. Perhaps one of the little ones was poorly and Sally had been forced to stay at home to look after them. Or else she'd been held up en route to work by a fresh road closure – a regular occurrence since the last disastrous air raid. Neither seemed likely, though; if it was an illness in the family Sally would have sent Eric with a message. If the latter, she would soon have chosen a different route and arrived breathless and apologetic.

The door opened again and Pamela looked up expectantly.

'Only me.' Fred appeared with a sheaf of papers for filing. He placed them on Pamela's desk. 'No Sally?' he enquired as he looked around the room.

'Not yet.' Pamela went to the window to check the dwindling queue at the clocking-in machine.

'That's handy.' He hovered by the door. 'It gives me the chance to get something off my chest. You know we have this new rule of complete honesty?'

'Yes?' she said uncertainly. Fred wore his serious expression: a slight frown and an intense stare that always made her heart flutter. *What now?*

'But you kept something from me, something important.'

She knew straight away what he meant. 'Reggie,' she murmured.

'Yes – Reggie. You asked Hugh to give him his marching orders without telling me.'

'I did,' she confessed. 'Are you angry with me?'

'No, not angry.'

'Disappointed, then?'

'A little,' he confessed.

This was worse than angry. Pursing her lips in an effort to hide her distress, Pamela fell silent.

'You went behind my back – perhaps to protect me. But I don't need protecting from Reggie Nolan and his like. I can stand up for myself.'

'I'm sorry – truly I am.'

'Why did you do it?' Fred's unwavering stare was still trained on her face.

'I thought it was for the best.' Pamela answered from the heart. 'I did it because I was angry with him and with myself for not acting sooner. Reggie is vile, Fred. I had to do something.'

'Stop.' He moved swiftly to join her at the window. 'You're not telling me anything I didn't already know, but I still wish you'd confided in me. A secret between us is like a piece of grit in a shoe – it chafes until it gets sore and can't be ignored. You don't want us to limp along as we did when Reggie first showed up, do you?'

'No, I don't want that,' she said miserably. *I want loving caresses, murmured words, more passionate nights together.*

'As I say, I already know the worst there is to know about Nolan,' Fred insisted. 'Last night, before he left Sunrise, he and Lionel left me in no doubt about their affiliation with Mosley. I'm afraid you're in their firing line, too – they're aware that it was you who asked Hugh to send Reggie packing.'

'No!' Pamela had nursed a forlorn hope that Lionel would keep his mouth shut but Sally's prediction had come true. In fact, Sally's advice had been spot on: she ought to have waited. Now she'd made matters worse and her neat plan lay in ruins at her feet.

'You were overheard.' Fred squeezed her hand and spoke tenderly. 'What's done is done and at least we're in no doubt as to what we're dealing with.'

'We never were,' Pamela whispered. 'We always knew that Reggie was dangerous.'

'He's joined a nest of vipers based at six Valley Road – Ben Simmons and his son live there, and now Nolan has joined them.'

She gasped at this surprise news. 'Is that his new billet? But do you know that the Simmons have copies of banned material there? I saw it for myself. This is serious. What shall we do?' Her first thought was that they should report it to the authorities.

'We wait,' Fred insisted, letting go of her hand as light footsteps hurried along the corridor. 'Until we work it out.'

'Together,' Pamela promised.

'Together,' he agreed, rushing across the room and opening the door for Sally, who entered the office in a rush, flustered and dishevelled. She was red in the face and still wearing her coat and hat.

'Oh Lord, how late am I?' As Fred closed the door behind him, Sally took off her coat and brushed dirt from the sleeve. She didn't remove her beret as she sat at her desk and tried to catch her breath.

'Thirty minutes. What kept you?' Pamela too sat down, fingers poised over her typewriter.

'Ron is what kept me.' Sally fanned her face with a large envelope. 'He waylaid me on my doorstep. I was on time up until that point. There, now you know.'

Pamela leaned back in her chair. 'I might have guessed Ron Butcher would be behind it. What did he want this time?'

273

'To talk to me, as per usual. I tried to tell him I was in a hurry, but he wouldn't listen. He was sober for once.'

Sally's bright tone belied the fear she'd felt when Ron had accosted her. He'd stepped out from the alley beside the pub, looking worse than ever. His hair was long and lank, his unshaven cheeks more hollow and his eyes sunken. He'd grabbed her by the arm and used his superior strength to march her all the way to Gas Street and down a short passage into Fletcher's Yard.

Sally had struggled and demanded that he let her go. 'Please – I'll be late for work.' She'd already dirtied her coat against the alley's grimy walls and had been taken aback by the stench of coal gas and the filthy state of her surroundings. 'What do you want with me? Tell me – and be quick about it.'

'See that house?' Ron had pointed across the yard. 'The one with the net curtains – that's where my mother lived with her new husband until he went missing. You didn't know that, did you?'

She'd shaken her head but otherwise kept very still, sensing that one false move could push Ron over the edge. 'You've never mentioned it.'

'She's still there now. Edna Shaw is her name.' Livid spots had appeared in Ron's pale cheeks. He'd spat out the words and tightened his grip on Sally's arms. 'Recognize it?'

Sally was shocked. Edna was respected locally as a member of the WVS; she provided blankets and other provisions for families who had been made homeless. 'Yes, I know who she is, but not that she's your mother.'

'I thought it was time you learned the truth.'

The grip of iron had intensified and she'd struggled again, turning over on her ankle and losing a shoe in the effort to escape. It had been no use. The curtain in the window of Edna's house had twitched but no one had come out to assist her.

'If you're looking for help in that quarter, think again.' Ron had bared his teeth in a mirthless grin.

Sally had grown desperate. 'Why on earth have you dragged me here?'

'Just listen – all right? My mother walked out on me when I was a kid. Turned her back and never got in touch, acted like I didn't exist. I used to dream that she'd come home one day and say she was sorry. But that never happened, did it? She's there now, spying on us, not giving a damn, like all women.'

Sally had twisted and pulled to finally wrench free but instead of taking flight she'd been drawn further in. 'You compare me with her?' she'd said in astonishment.

'You're all the same,' he'd snarled. 'Running off the minute a new bloke catches your eye. Lying little bitches, the lot of you.'

'Who? Who did I run off with?'

'Sam Billington, for a start. And you flirted with every Tom, Dick and Harry who crossed the threshold of that pub. Don't deny it – I saw it with my own eyes.'

'I've told you before – I wouldn't. I didn't.' She'd known it was hopeless to protest.

'Don't waste your breath. Keith Nelson, Lionel Simmons, Bill Evans, Tom Rose.' The list had run on and on. 'Those last two are the bastards who stole

Annie May from under my nose. And that new friend of yours – the one you work with who wears the warden's uniform and goes out on patrol, lording it over people – now she's after me, spying on me and no doubt dropping me in it by telling everyone where I am and what I'm up to.'

Ron's wild, rambling accusations and his mention of Pamela had made Sally shudder. It had only been when Edna's curtain had ceased to twitch and the door of her house had been flung open that Ron had stopped ranting and turned his anger on his mother. 'What do you want, you nosy cow?' He'd rushed towards Edna, giving Sally the chance to escape.

She'd picked up her shoe and run – down the alley out on to the street, on towards the harbour and the dock beyond and finally to the safety of the timber yard.

Now, as Sally took off her beret, Pamela saw that her knuckles were badly scraped. 'Did he hurt you?' she asked quietly.

'It's nothing.' Sally brushed her injury to one side. 'He said he wanted to show me where his mother lived.'

'And did he frighten you? Don't lie.'

'Yes,' Sally admitted.

'He frightens me too,' Pamela told her. 'Ron is building up to something really bad. I feel it in my bones, and to be perfectly honest, it scares me to death.'

CHAPTER SIXTEEN

Connie had made her decision.

'Where are you off to in such a rush?' Lizzie demanded after her sister had displayed the closed sign on the bakery door and was preparing to make a quick exit.

'Nowhere.' It was half-day closing and all the jobs were done. The counter was wiped clean, the floor swept and mopped; everything was in apple-pie order. 'I'll leave the van with you. I'm going for a walk.'

'To clear your head?' Lizzie fretted constantly about Connie's stubborn refusal to talk about what Lizzie delicately termed her 'predicament' but, so far, she'd been unable to break through her defences. 'Shall I come with you?'

'No, I'd rather be by myself.' Connie made for the door. 'I'll see you later.'

Lizzie grimaced at the sound of the door slamming shut. Her sister's infuriating behaviour – her recent touchiness and shortness of temper – was beyond anything Lizzie had experienced, and there seemed to be no way of getting through to her. 'She's the limit,' she muttered to herself as she pulled down the blinds, then checked that everything was secure.

Out on the street, Connie took a deep breath before setting off towards the harbour. For some reason, she was more aware than usual of the sights and smells around her. Weary market traders packed up their stalls as she crossed the square to the scrape and clatter of empty vegetable crates being loaded on to carts, and the sight of women in shawls and headscarves expertly gutting the last of their fish to sell cut-price to latecomers. On the harbour-side she noticed Bill tinkering with his motorbike outside his cottage and forced herself to respond to his wave. She didn't stop to chat.

On she went, along the headland path, buffeted by the wind. Gulls flying overhead split the air with their shrieking calls while the unchanging sound of waves breaking against rocks provided an accompaniment to Connie's troubled thoughts.

She'd come to a decision – yes, she had! She couldn't, *wouldn't*, change her mind. Two grey gulls swooped down from the cliff face then rode an air current far out to sea against a backdrop of dark grey clouds. She wouldn't change her mind because there was so much to lose if she went ahead with the pregnancy: her reputation, for a start. There would be enormous shame attached to having this baby and in the end the person who would suffer the most would be her father. Knowing him, Bert would hold up his head and defend his daughter against all comers, but deep down he would be cut to the quick. Connie would be unable to bear the hurt in his eyes. So it was partly for him that she was doing this.

Then there was the prospect of having to relinquish her post at Gas Street. She couldn't – she just couldn't! Volunteering for the ARP team had meant everything; from the day she signed up, she'd been immensely proud of her uniform and of being an air raid girl. It signified that she was vital to the war effort, that she was doing her bit to defeat Hitler. Then, when she'd been promoted to chief warden and been given extra responsibility, she'd been recognized as a leader who could set a good example, who kept her head in a crisis. She'd grown into her job and done it well. Could she relinquish her badge and the yellow chevrons on her sleeve, her battledress and her double-breasted overcoat, her ski cap and the status that went with it? No – it would cost her far too much to give it all up.

People rely on me. That's what Connie had told Mavis Coulson, to whose house she was now headed. Reaching the end of the headland path, she proceeded along the prom, where she noted a flotilla of tiny warships on the horizon, the row of squat concrete pillboxes lining the beach and half a dozen silver barrage balloons strung out across the estuary – familiar sights that served to remind Connie how much her country continued to need her. The bus station was in sight, and before it, the turn into North Street.

When she reached the junction, she hesitated. She must pass Tom's lodgings to reach number 127a. What if she ran into him and was forced to explain her reason for being here? For a few moments, she considered where he was most likely to be at this time on a Saturday afternoon. In previous weeks, he would have been with Bill at Wren's Cove working on *Annie May*, but now his whereabouts were more difficult to pin down. Connie cast her mind back to a recent conversation between Lizzie and Pamela to the effect that Bill and Tom were hot on the trail of Ron Butcher. So that was most likely what the pair were up to right now. Then again, no; hadn't she just seen Bill working on his bike?

The single-minded determination that Connie had felt when she'd set off from the bakery was waning rapidly, and she had to force herself to continue up North Street. Seeing Tom's bike parked by the kerb, she hurried past his house with her head down, holding her breath. *Please don't come out to speak to me!*

A girl with her hair chopped short cycled down the pavement towards her, followed by a small boy. A woman on a doorstep shouted for the boy to come back. 'Alfie, get back here this minute!'

All of life went on around her while Connie set about putting an end to one as yet unformed.

Her heart was in her mouth as she approached 127a.

Mavis would open the door to her basement rooms. The neat handywoman would express no surprise. *Come in. Please be seated.* All would be done in a calm and friendly fashion.

Connie dragged her feet over what she was about to do, held back by the knowledge of how selfish she was being. Yes; selfish and proud. In the end that was what her sense of shame boiled down to. A new thought occurred: if she gave up her warden's role while she had the baby, perhaps she could return afterwards. It would cause a hundred practical problems but there would be ways around them – Aunty Vera, Lizzie, their father could all step in and help with babysitting. And she reminded herself that she, Connie Bailey, could do anything that she set her mind to.

'Connie?' Tom had seen her pass by his house like a woman on a mission; head down, hurrying on, looking nothing like his confident Connie of old. His heart had gone out to her. Never mind that he'd agreed to step back from the big decision she had to make, he hadn't been able to stop himself from rushing out to speak with her.

She turned at the sound of his voice. He hurried towards her with his long stride; jacketless, with his waistcoat hanging open. 'Tom.'

'Are you all right?'

'Yes. Why shouldn't I be?'

'You don't look it.' This time there was no sharp retort, no defiance. 'What's the matter?'

'Everything,' she confessed in a dazed voice, suddenly sagging under the effort of holding herself upright. Tom had caught her at her weakest, most vulnerable moment.

'Come with me to my house.' Taking her hand and turning back down the street, he felt her resist.

'No – I'd rather walk.'

'Where to?'

Connie pointed towards a footpath that led to the headland.

It was a steep climb but at least they would have the wind behind them. 'Are you sure you can make it that far?'

'Yes, I may be pregnant but I'm not an invalid.'

There she was: the old Connie. Tom nodded, and they walked together past 127a until they reached the stile that would take them across open country towards the two kite balloons and beyond that to Raynard's Folly. 'I won't risk offending you by offering you a hand,' he said with a wry grin.

She hopped over the stile, then set off ahead of him along the rough path that cut through the heather and fresh green ferns. This wasn't meant to happen. She ought this minute to be knocking on Mavis Coulson's door. As they gained height, the wind strengthened and propelled them forward in silence until they reached the twin concrete storm beds that held the new blimps in place. Here they stopped and looked down on the town they'd left behind – at the bay with its curve of pale sand fringed by white breakers. Tom waited for Connie to speak first.

'I don't want to give up my warden's work,' she said with tears in her eyes. 'It would mean letting people down.' Strands of dark hair blew across her cheeks and she made no attempt to brush them back.

He stood beside her, gazing at the empty horizon and giving her time and space to speak.

'I know this town like the back of my hand – where to go for builders' materials and breakdown lorries and every inhabitant within half-a-mile radius of the sector post. And I care about each and every one of them.'

'No one's arguing with that.'

'Who would step into my shoes if . . .?'

'If you went ahead with the pregnancy?' There; he'd said it.

'I would miss my warden's role if I had to give it up.' The friendships, the loyalty, the saving of lives.

Connie tried to picture how she would deal with watching Lizzie put on her ambulance driver's uniform and set out on patrol while she stayed at home twiddling her thumbs. Worse than that – she would become one of the residents that Pamela herded into the communal shelter at the sounding of the alert. Connie would hurry to College Road as the drone of bombers grew louder, or else take refuge with her father in their cellar, waiting for the danger to pass.

Tom carried on staring steadily out to sea. 'I thought it was the end of the world when Bill and I lost *Annie May*.'

'So you understand what I'm saying?'

'Yes, but I found a way of carrying on – we both did. We've decided to save up again and buy another boat. Fingers crossed we'll get there in the end.'

'And I could go back after . . .' It was the first time that Connie had tried to express this thought.

'After you'd had the baby?' He turned his head slowly to look at her.

'I could, couldn't I?'

A question for him at last. It was as if a lock-keeper had opened the canal gates and let the water slowly rise, bringing them up to the next level from where they would be able to sail smoothly on. 'Don't ask me – you already know what I think.'

'Do I? You've never told me.'

'Because you wouldn't let me get a word in. Anyway, you know without me saying.'

'Say it anyway.'

The lock gate swung open and the water rose. 'I want to help – I always have. I know I was lousy at showing it. And what I think – no, what I feel – is this: nothing's changed. All that matters is that I love you and I always will.'

'Even after the way I've treated you?' The hydrogen-filled blimps rocked and swayed above their heads and high above them a trio of RAF planes flew east towards the clouds that hugged the watery horizon. 'You weren't alone. Dad and Lizzie have had to put up with a lot from me.'

Tom shrugged but didn't comment. 'Were you on your way to see Mavis Coulson?' He watched the planes disappear into the clouds. 'Don't answer that if you don't want to.'

Connie was astonished that he'd been able to guess her intention across the chasm that she'd created. 'How did you know?'

'I know what Mavis does; it's common knowledge. And I knew she'd be one of the options that you mentioned.'

'Would you have blamed me?'

'No. Who am I to pass judgement?'

'But would you have wanted me to?'

'To go to Mavis? No,' he said forcefully. 'That isn't what I want. But I won't interfere if it's what *you* want.'

'I thought it was. I was almost certain until now.' *A heartbeat, a new life.* And a decision that was hers and hers alone, cemented during this conversation with the man who loved her and was the father of their baby. 'Tom, I believe I can do this after all. I *want* to do it.'

'With me?' At last he'd asked what was, for him, the most important question of all.

Connie nodded slowly. So far, only Lizzie knew their secret but now everyone would hear about it.

There would be no more hesitating, no more agonizing over what to do; Connie Bailey was expecting a baby with Tom Rose and she was happy about it. She would shout it to the world and to heck with the scandalmongers. 'Yes, with you,' she told Tom as they set off along the ridge towards the folly, hand in hand and in perfect step without the need for words.

Pamela thought she knew who her enemies were – Reggie Nolan and Lionel Simmons had made their views quite clear. But the attack, when it came, was from a stranger in broad daylight and in full public view.

She and Fred set out from Sunrise on an errand for Edith, who had run out of embroidery silks.

'I'd like to finish sewing a tray cloth for your Uncle Hugh,' she'd informed Pamela. 'It's a gift for his birthday next week.'

Despite the day being overcast, Pamela and Fred were happy to oblige. They strolled along the prom then around the headland, stopping to chat with acquaintances in the market square before proceeding along College Road, where they would buy the thread from the haberdashery shop opposite Cynthia's hair salon. It was late in the afternoon and stall holders were packing up for the day.

Dorothy Parsons, the drama-loving telephonist at the report and control centre, hailed them from across the square. She hurried to join them and share news about Ronald Atkinson, the ARPO controller at the town hall.

'Have you heard? Ronald's doctor has ordered him to give up his post.' Dorothy was breathless and flustered, tugging at the lead as she ordered her Yorkshire terrier to stop snapping at market traders' heels. 'Things have caught up with him. He's not as young as he was.'

This was news to Fred. Ronald had been in charge of the control centre from the start, coordinating rescue teams and synchronizing the responses to raids. He was built in the mould of Field Marshal Montgomery: small in stature but sharp-speaking and authoritative, with a clipped, nasal voice and a military turn of phrase that brooked no argument. 'Who will take his place?'

'It hasn't been decided yet.' Dorothy gave Pamela a knowing wink. 'Fred is too modest to say so, but I wouldn't be surprised if he were the one. He's already been promoted to executive officer and his damage reports are second to none.'

'Mind your backs!' the last of the fishmongers warned as she approached with her empty barrow.

Fred's face reddened at the telephonist's compliment. He and Pamela gave way to the barrow woman, then said their goodbyes to Dorothy.

'Could that be true?' Pamela asked as they made their way along College Road. 'Might you be promoted again?'

'It's not out of the question,' Fred conceded. 'It depends who else is in the running.'

Traffic was busy along Kelthorpe's main shopping street. Car drivers honked their horns at cyclists who veered across their paths and a bus stopped outside the Red Lion to let passengers step down on to the pavement. There was some jostling and a few complaints from those attempting to board the bus. Fred

286

and Pamela paused briefly in the entrance to a chemist's shop to allow the crowd to thin out before they proceeded.

A bus passenger spied them – heavyset and clean-shaven, dressed in a black trench coat, wearing a trilby hat and thick-rimmed glasses; a man with unremarkable features. He came close to Fred and seemed about to pass by, but instead suddenly leaned in and spat in his face.

Fred was too startled even to raise his hand to wipe away the spittle from his cheek. The man spat again – this time at Pamela. It was over in a moment and he was gone, swallowed by the crowd.

A small group of observers waited to see what Fred and Pamela would do. No one spoke or made any attempt to collar the culprit.

A tremor of disgust ran through Pamela as she searched in her handbag for a handkerchief. *Vile, vile man!* She felt wounded by the sudden violation, then blazingly angry. 'What are you staring at?' she demanded of the small crowd as she wiped her face.

There was no answer but she heard the murmurs. 'German . . . Hitler's spy . . . traitor . . . no, he's Jewish . . . even worse . . . as for her, consorting with the likes of him . . .'

Anonymous faces in the crowd passed cruel judgement, and Fred and Pamela's humiliation was complete.

She grasped his hand. They would not respond to these people; they would rise above it. A second bus arrived and disgorged its passengers. In the ensuing melee, Pamela and Fred managed to melt into the crowd.

They went ahead and made their purchase in the haberdashery. Three skeins of embroidery silk for nine pence; emerald green, crimson and indigo. They heard the ring of the till and Pamela took the threepenny bit change for the shilling she'd tendered. Making their exit from the shop, they returned along College Road, walking with heads high and without looking to right or left. The sound of the assailant spitting and the sensation of the saliva trickling down their skin stayed with them – over and over again, Pamela shuddered and grasped Fred's hand even more tightly.

As soon as they reached the relative quiet of the headland path, Fred spoke for the first time. 'It's never going to stop,' he said with terrible finality.

'They're wrong. We're right,' Pamela said, reminding herself as much as him.

'That's not the point.' How much more of this could they stand? Every morning he woke and wondered what ills the day would hold. There was always a Reggie or a Lionel, or else a hundred nameless men and women who pored over forbidden fascist literature and idolized Oswald Mosley; men who were immune to reason and spat in your face and humiliated you then walked on. 'Perhaps we should leave Kelthorpe after all.'

'Start afresh?' Dismal grey clouds over the sea threatened rain. Pamela pictured being swallowed up by them, then emerging from cold mist into a shaft of bright sunlight.

'Without anyone knowing who we are. It may be the only way.'

He'd said so before but this time felt different. She

and Fred wouldn't be separated – they would be forced out together, leaving behind the town where she was born, walking away from her family and friends. 'Where to?' she breathed, her head spinning.

'Anywhere,' Fred said fiercely. 'A new beginning – perhaps that is what we need.'

'There's been a report of looting on the dockside.' Connie had begun her shift with renewed vigour. It felt as if a great weight had been lifted from her shoulders and she issued brisk instructions to a team that included Simon and Eddie. 'Apparently a bunch of spivs have been using a bombsite to store black market goods – cigarettes, whisky, and such like. A second gang got wind of it and tea-leaved the lot. Now the warehouse owner is worried that what's left of his building will go up in flames because of the rivalry between them.'

'A case of pistols at dawn,' Simon remarked. It hardly seemed worthwhile investigating, given that the warehouse in question was most likely little more than a blackened shell. 'Oughtn't we to concentrate on clamping down on blackout offenders?'

'Let's divide and conquer,' Connie decided. 'Eddie, your job for the night is to patrol along the dock and make sure that the site of Wilson's warehouse is secure. Simon, you can follow up complaints about number twenty-eight Maypole Street not observing the blackout times.'

Having sent them off on their tasks, Connie turned her attention to updating the report book. She noted a shortage of stirrup pumps and fire buckets on Tennyson Road then ordered warrant cards for three new volunteers due to finish their training and start their shifts the following week. Without their Fire Guard cards, they would lack the authority to enter premises. After this was done, she went to the door for a breather and spotted Lizzie's ambulance idling at the corner of the street with the back doors open and her sister leaning against the side of the van. Connie beckoned her over and invited her in for a cup of tea.

'Just a quick one.' Lizzie followed Connie upstairs. 'Nothing much is happening out there at the moment. I'm on duty with Sam Billington for a change. There's a new trainee from the St John Ambulance Brigade. Sam's running through the first-aid drill and the contents of our pouches – the various dressings, rubber gloves, splints, et cetera. The new chap is a quick learner so it shouldn't take long.'

'Stop!' Connie came to a halt at the top of the stairs and seized Lizzie's hands. 'I've got something to tell you.'

'Spit it out.' Lizzie could tell from the excited gleam in her sister's eyes that the 'something' was important.

'You'll need to sit down.' Connie pointed to a chair, then sat opposite. 'Forget the tea. This is about my predicament. It's been complicated but I've made a decision.'

Lizzie frowned. To the outside observer being pregnant presented only two options: either to go ahead and have the baby or not. What was compli-cated about that?

'Don't you want to know?' Connie urged.

'Yes, if you want to tell me.' Lizzie preferred not to dwell on the 'not' side of things that often entailed secretive visits to unregistered midwives, or doctors who had been struck off for malpractice. 'Finally! Put me out of my misery – do it quickly.'

Eager to fill in the background, Connie continued at her own pace. 'Tom and I have had a heart-to-heart – this afternoon, as it happens. It turns out I was too quick to judge. He does care after all. Tom told me that he loves me and he always will.'

'Hallelujah! Connie, dear, that's not news to anyone but you.'

'You may be right but I chose not to see it. I was convinced that my being pregnant would alter things so, typical me, I jumped the gun and pushed him away before he could do it to me. That's what made everything so tangled up – it was my own fault.'

'But now you've cleared the air?' Lizzie knew that they didn't have long – Sam would soon have finished his teaching stint and would be ready to resume their patrol.

'Yes. I said I was sorry and in the end we came to a joint decision, which was the right thing to do and I should have seen that in the first place and saved us both a lot of heartache.'

'Connie!' Lizzie stood up and paced the room. 'Are you going to tell me what you've decided or not?'

'Keep your hair on. Tom and I are back together – aren't you pleased?'

'Thrilled. I mean it. But what about the . . .?'

'Baby?' Connie's voice softened and the look in her eyes was now unmistakable. It was one of pure, unadulterated happiness. 'Oh, Lizzie – I'm going to have it. I'll go out and shout it from the rooftops if necessary. Tom Rose and I will celebrate having this child together. There, what do you say to that?'

'Connie and I are talking again.' Tom's laconic announcement came soon after he and Bill had left the Anchor and set out on Ron's trail. They'd begun with the area around the pub and quayside, where they'd found no trace, and now they were on their way to the Leisure Gardens to follow up Pamela's sighting. 'I won't go into details,' Tom added. 'I'll leave that to her.'

'Just talking?' Bill led the way through the old town. 'Or back together properly?'

'Back together,' Tom confirmed. Again, no details. Talking about Connie's pregnancy on the headland had led to a few hours at his lodgings before she'd had to leave for her evening shift, but what had gone on there was between him and her alone.

'About time too.' Arriving at the entrance to the park, with his brain less than razor-sharp after the three pints they'd consumed at the Anchor, Bill made a confession of his own. 'I don't know about you but I'm not looking forward to the eighteenth – leaving Lizzie for a narrow bunk aboard HMS *Northern Lights* has lost its appeal.'

'It never had much in the first place,' Tom agreed. 'But there's no getting out of it – we're obliged to do our bit.'

'You're right. But before that we have to sort out this problem with Ron.' It was down to business again as they entered the park.

'This is where Pamela caught sight of him,' Bill reminded Tom. 'Mind you, he might have moved on since then.'

'It won't harm to take a good look around.' It was Tom's turn to take the lead. First they searched the bandstand, then the shadowy area behind the paddling pool, treading carefully and feeling their way between the trees with little hope of finding evidence of a man sleeping rough.

'I can barely see the nose in front of my face,' Tom complained as they emerged from the wood and made their way up to the colonnade to continue their search. It had begun to rain heavily, so they stayed undercover until it eased. It was almost midnight and any hope that Tom and Bill had entertained of tracking Ron down had evaporated.

'Shall we call it a day?' Bill suggested.

Tom was happy to agree. 'Yes, let's try again in the daylight.' In any case, he and Bill had yet to think through what their tactics would be once they found Butcher.

'The chances are we'll find him hanging around the Anchor at some point.' Bill turned up his coat collar and stepped out into the open, disturbing two squirrels that promptly shot out of sight up the smooth trunk of a nearby beech tree. 'We can ask Frank to keep his eyes peeled for us. Why not stay at my place tonight? That way you'll be on the spot.'

Tom declined the offer. 'My own bed is calling me, thanks.'

He quickened his pace as he set off around the headland, wrapped up in glad thoughts about himself and Connie. *Such a turnaround!* Tom smiled to himself as he kept on walking, sidestepping a young CD messenger, Arnold Kershaw, who cycled full tilt towards him while yelling a warning about a UXB on the prom. Tom thanked Arnold and carried on. *Not only Connie but a baby, too.* It was a lot to take in. Life was about to change in a big way. Sure, there was a spell of minesweeping duty to get under their belts, and there was no telling how long that would last – most likely their new duties would continue for months if current reports on the wireless were anything to go by. German cities were being knocked down like skittles by the RAF boys, and the Yanks were at the throats of the Japs in the Far East, but the situation in the Med was still dire and Jerry's raids on Kelthorpe and other northern ports showed no sign of abating – the blimps across the estuary were all the proof anyone needed of an ongoing threat.

Even these grim thoughts couldn't wipe the smile off Tom's face. *Me and Connie are back on and that's the main thing*, he told himself, a lone figure emerging on to the dark, damp promenade.

Tom passed the ruins of the old Royal Hotel and approached the bus station. Noticing the barriers erected around the UXB some twenty yards ahead, he turned off up North Street still grinning from ear to ear. Home was in sight, a short way up the hill.

Ron Butcher lay in wait down some external cellar steps. He'd watched Tom and Bill leave the Anchor and stealthily followed them to the Leisure Gardens. Did they think he was an idiot, hanging around in the area where the blasted, busybody warden had spotted him? Yes, he knew his cover had been blown and straightaway he'd made himself scarce – 'vanish without a trace' was the rule that Ron lived by. After they'd sheltered from the rain, then decided to retrace their steps to the harbour, Ron had followed again. He'd heard Tom tell Bill that his own bed was calling him and that had been enough. Ron had sprinted on ahead, thinking that the headland path was the ideal place to launch an attack until a boy riding a pushbike had put paid to that plan. The lad had worn a steel helmet and carried a gas mask: signs that he was a messenger for the Civil Defence busybodies. Seeing Ron, he'd slowed down and issued a warning about a recently discovered UXB at the far end of the promenade. Rescue teams were on their way. Ron had sworn at the lad then broken into a run. Change of plan; the attack would have to wait until Tom Rose was closer to home.

Here he came now; those footsteps belonged to a man with a long stride. Hiding at the bottom of the cellar steps, Ron heard his enemy whistling a jaunty tune.

Tom took his door key from his jacket pocket before mounting the three steps. He'd be glad to get out of his wet things and into his pyjamas. The key was in the lock when Ron struck from behind.

The hammer he'd stolen from *Annie May* was an ideal weapon. You could knock a man out with it then bludgeon him to death – a slower method than a knife but none the worse for that.

Tom felt the blow to his head and staggered back down the steps. Catching sight of a raised hammer as he collapsed to his knees, he managed to roll out of reach as the weapon came down again.

Ron swore savagely and aimed a kick at his victim,

who curled on to his side and raised both arms to protect his head. Ron smashed the hammer down – once, twice, three times more.

Tom ignored the pain in his hand and arm and kicked back. He scythed his legs against his attacker's calves to throw him off balance. It worked – Ron toppled to the ground next to him and they grappled. The hammer flew from Ron's hand and skidded out of reach. The two men writhed and wrestled towards it, hands reaching, sinews straining. It was inches from Tom's grasp when Ron broke free. He seized the hammer, sprang up and lashed out with his feet.

Tom felt the kicks to his ribs. He saw a blurred image of Ron Butcher towering over him, wielding the hammer. After that, nothing.

CHAPTER SEVENTEEN

A weary Connie approached the end of her shift. At the last minute, Arnold had shown up at the sector post out of breath after a cycle sprint around the headland. He flung his gas mask on to the counter and demanded her attention.

'There was this bloke on the path,' he jabbered as Connie completed her report of the evening's unremarkable events.

'Wait.' She finished writing then closed the ledger. 'What are you doing here, Arnold? I thought you'd trained to be a stretcher bearer.'

'I start next week. I'm a messenger until then.' Full of the inflated self-importance of a thirteen-year-old volunteer, he took off his adult-sized helmet to reveal tousled, mousy hair badly in need of a trim. His pale, peaky face was alive with excitement. 'Listen, this bloke—'

'Can't it wait? I'm tired.'

'No, you have to write it down. This bloke – he was a proper bad 'un. He swore at me when I told him about the UXB on the promenade. What was he up to, wandering about all by himself.'

Connie reopened her book with a sigh of resignation. 'I don't suppose you recognized him?'

'No, it was pitch black under that cliff. The geezer was definitely up to no good, though. He swore at me, then he tried to push me off my bike. Nearly knocked me flying.' There had been no shove – as usual, Arnold enjoyed exaggerating the drama of the occasion. 'He had summat in his hand – it looked like a hammer.'

'Roughly what age was he?' Thinking that this might turn out to be a police matter, Connie stood behind the counter with pencil poised. 'How tall? Was there anything out of the ordinary about his appearance? Come on, Sherlock – you must have noticed something useful.'

'Skinny – not much taller than me.' The young witness racked his brains. 'He shoved me hard as he could then ran off. He must've heard Tom Rose coming along the path towards us.'

Connie stopped scribbling and looked up in sudden alarm. 'What does Tom have to do with this?'

'Dunno. I expect he was on his way home. I told him about the UXB but I didn't mention the bloke with the hammer.' Arnold saw a worried look cloud his cousin's expression. 'What's up? Should I have done?'

At that moment the phone rang and Connie picked up the receiver, covering the mouthpiece with her hand to reassure him. 'No, you didn't do anything wrong. Run along home – Aunty Vera will be worried about you.'

Relieved, Arnold put his helmet back on and made a quick exit.

'Head Warden Bailey?' the voice on the phone asked down a crackly line. 'Norman Riley here from the North Street post.'

'Yes, Norman; what can I do for you?' Arnold's mention of Tom walking home alone had sent an icy shiver down Connie's spine – on top of which, 'small and skinny' described Ron Butcher perfectly.

'There's been an incident on North Street,' Norman continued carefully in his well-educated voice. 'A vicious attack. An ambulance was called to the scene. One casualty has been reported. Your sister insisted that I telephone you.'

'Lizzie?' The cold dread had reached Connie's brain and paralysed all capacity for logical thinking.

'It was her ambulance that attended the scene. She and Sam Billington were able to confirm the identity of the victim. Connie, are you still there?'

'Yes,' she said faintly.

'It's bad news, I'm afraid. They've taken Tom Rose to the Queen Alexandra hospital.'

Please God, no! Connie strung three desperate words together. 'How is he?'

'I have no information as far as that goes,' Norman reported stiffly. 'Your sister has advised that you go straight to the hospital and she will meet you there. I'm sorry, Connie – that's all I know.'

Lizzie and Sam waited for Connie outside the hospital entrance. Though it was well past midnight, ambulances came and went continually, sirens wailing. All seemed to take place at a distance and beyond a transparent barrier as Lizzie turned down Sam's offer of a cigarette.

'You're sure you don't want one to calm your nerves?' His own were shot after what they'd just been through, so he fumbled for a match and lit up with trembling fingers.

She shook her head.

'I'd stake my life on this being Ron Butcher's handiwork.' He glanced down at his battledress, which was soaked with Tom's blood. 'I've always said he needed his head looking at, ever since we were kids, and this has his signature written all over it.'

Lizzie raised a hand in warning. 'Let's not talk about it.'

'Don't blame yourself,' Sam advised through a cloud of cigarette smoke. 'You did everything you could.'

'I wish we'd got there sooner, that's all.' She thought back to the moment they'd received the phone call from Norman Riley. She and Sam had been at the depot about to sign off when they learned that a first-aid party had been requested by a member of the public on North Street. The caller's name was Mavis Coulson; she had phoned in to report a neighbour lying unconscious on the pavement outside his house. The injured man's name was Tom Rose. Lizzie had a clear memory of the sequence of events up to this point, after which the whole thing turned into a blur. Jumping into the ambulance with Sam, she'd driven like the devil through the old town, then up Musgrave Street and over the only road that would take them into the new part of town. Vital minutes had passed before they'd reached the promenade, where they'd been stopped by an officious member of an ARP rescue party, who had warned them about a new barrier erected half a mile along the road, just past North Street. Sam had leaned out of the window to assure him that North Street was where they were headed, then Lizzie had slammed her foot on the accelerator pedal and roared away.

'You couldn't have driven any faster,' Sam insisted.

'Yes, but we're dealing with head injuries.' Blood – so much blood on the pavement. 'The sooner they're treated, the better the chances of recovery – we both know that.' Brain damage could result if the injury was severe, and Tom's wounds had looked pretty bad. He'd been unconscious and had remained unresponsive despite Sam's efforts to rouse him. Mavis Coulson had already brought towels to stem the flow. Sam had checked the patient's airway, then put an ear to his chest. He'd detected a faint heart-beat and decided on a neck brace plus splints to stabilize the obvious fracture of Tom's right arm.

Connie – whatever would Lizzie say to her? She dreaded the moment that would bring her sister's bright new world crashing down.

She and Sam had strapped the brace and splints in place then stretchered Tom into the ambulance.

'Will he make it?' As they'd left the scene, Mavis had ventured to ask the unanswerable question and received no reply.

Then Sam and Lizzie had raced back over the headland, through the old town and up the steep hill leading to the hospital. The Queen Alexandra stood on the western edge of town, where buildings gave way to moorland. Lizzie had gritted her teeth at every bump and bend in the road. In the back of the ambulance, Sam had checked Tom's blood pressure and taken his temperature. He'd warned Lizzie that there was a high chance of bleeding inside the skull.

She'd known this already from her first-aid training. Subarachnoid haemorrhage – that's what it was called; a result of severe head trauma. Additionally there would be a risk of blood clots. The hospital would X-ray Tom's head then consider surgery. Craniotomy; it entailed cutting a hole in the skull. And that was if the patient made it as far as the operating table.

'It's not looking good,' Sam had muttered as Lizzie had screeched to a halt outside the hospital entrance and nurses and porters had rushed to take over.

They'd watched helplessly as a middle-aged doctor in a white coat with a stethoscope around his neck had run out to supervise his patient being wheeled into the Accident and Emergency department.

'Not good at all,' Sam had repeated.

Connie, oh, my poor Connie! Dazed and defeated, Lizzie walked by herself to the hospital gates and stared up at a black, starless sky.

So Ron Butcher had taken his revenge; this was the one certainty in Connie's mind as she drove to the hospital. Everything else was up in the air. She had no idea how badly hurt Tom was or whether a weapon had been used. Driving the van through the dark, deserted streets, Connie gripped the steering wheel and held her nerve. She must not panic or let her thoughts run wild – after all, Tom was more than a match for Ron Butcher and would surely have defended himself strongly.

All this because of a second-hand boat! Bill and Tom had bought *Annie May* in good faith, but it had turned out to be a calamitous decision, all because Ron Butcher wasn't right in the head. Everything stemmed from that simple fact. She gripped the wheel to steady herself. The hospital was in sight on the brow of the hill. A figure wearing battledress and carrying a steel helmet waited at the gate.

Lizzie flagged down Connie's van. *At last!*

Connie braked hard and came to a halt, allowing Lizzie to open the passenger door and slide in beside her.

'Park by the main door,' Lizzie instructed.

With her heart in her mouth, Connie drove towards the tall, imposing building with its narrow arched windows and elaborately carved entrance. 'How bad?' she asked.

'We don't know yet. They took Tom straight through to the emergency ward.'

'But you were on the scene. How bad did it look?' Connie parked the van then leaped out. A fresh wave of panic threatened to break over her head, but she resisted it by calling upon her warden's training. How would she act if this were an air raid? She would be calm, she would show no fear. Tom would expect no less.

'Bad,' Lizzie confessed in a shaky voice. 'He's unconscious. Head wounds, probably from a blunt weapon. Loss of blood.'

Sam saw them pause at the entrance to the building. Beckoning them, he guided them silently down

303

a wide corridor. Two nurses came out of the emergency ward in immaculate blue and white uniforms. As the doors swung closed behind them, Lizzie caught sight of two rows of beds, one with green screens around it.

'We're here to see Tom Rose,' Sam informed the nurses.

'You can't go in,' the more senior one answered. She spoke with a cool authority that matched her starched cap and apron. 'You must wait here.'

'But we want to see him,' Lizzie pleaded.

'I'm afraid that's not possible.' The ward sister asked her junior to fetch three chairs. 'You may sit out here until we have news.'

'But you can tell us something, surely?' Lizzie spoke again on Connie's behalf. 'Sam and I are the ones who brought him in.'

The nurse took in their first-aider uniforms then reassessed the situation. 'Your patient is alive but unresponsive. We're doing our best to stabilize him before we take him for X-ray.' Her gaze transferred from Sam and Lizzie to Connie and rested there with an inquisitive expression.

'She's his sweetheart,' Lizzie explained as she took hold of Connie's hand. The act of sisterly kindness caused Connie to close her eyes and sway backwards.

'Ah, I see.' The stern nurse nodded sympathetically. 'Rest assured that the doctors will do everything they can. We must hope for the best.'

Hope – Connie clung to the word. Tom was strong and brave. He had everything to live for. As for her, she would pour every last ounce of her own energy into willing him to live.

'Will they have to operate?' Lizzie eased Connie into one of the chairs then sat down beside her.

'That depends on what the X-rays show.' The sister resumed her businesslike manner. 'If there's a depressed fracture of the skull then, yes, the patient will require surgery to recover fragments of bone. However, in the event of a linear fracture, the bone will heal itself over time and an operation won't be necessary.'

A third nurse emerged from the ward and spoke quietly in the sister's ear before hurrying off along the corridor. Then, as Connie absorbed the latest piece of information, the doors swung open again and two porters wheeled Tom out of the ward. He lay under a pale green sheet with only his head and shoulders visible and his face partly obscured by a mask connected to a tank of oxygen. His bruised forehead and the matted blood on the crown of his head were evidence of the violent attack that had taken place. His eyes were closed and his skin deathly pale.

Connie gripped Lizzie's hand more tightly. 'Where are they taking him?' she cried.

'For his X-rays.' Still brisk, the sister ordered her junior nurse to change the blood-stained sheets on Tom's bed in preparation for his return, then she warned Lizzie and Connie not to expect any update for at least an hour. 'Stay here, by all means,' she told them.

So Connie and Lizzie settled into their vigil while Sam offered to let Bill know what had happened.

'Tell him it's serious and ask him to come straight to the hospital.' Connie shored herself up with a conviction that the people who were closest to Tom could sit at his bedside and communicate their love. The power of positive thinking would will him back to life. 'Bill has to be here,' she murmured to Lizzie as Sam hurried off. 'Tom needs him.'

Lizzie bowed her head and closed her eyes. *Don't let Tom die*, she prayed silently. *He doesn't deserve this and I know for a fact that losing him would break my sister's heart.*

News travelled fast; Tom Rose was at death's door. Wild rumours took over from scant facts and flew from North Street along the prom, around the headland to the quayside and market square. Tom had breathed his last. His head had been bashed in with a hammer and there'd been no hope from the start. Or else a miracle had happened: he was already back on his feet and vowing to track down his attacker. Then there was disaster number two: he'd gone under the knife and the doctors had found irreversible brain damage – Tom would be little better than a vegetable and was destined to end his days in an asylum. Or somewhere in between: the patient had come round but had lost his memory. He knew no one, not even Connie.

Sally stood at the door of the Anchor, doing her best to resist the stories. Her father warned her not to believe everything she heard. People invented things and they should wait until Bill returned to his cottage to learn the truth.

'This is Ron's doing,' Sally said with quiet conviction. 'And he's still on the loose.'

She promptly put on her coat and left Eric in

charge of the little ones. 'Don't let them out of your sight,' she warned him. 'I won't be long but if you see Ron hanging around, be sure to keep everyone inside and lock the door.'

She crossed the square quickly – Tom's neck was broken and he was paralysed from the chest down: this was the latest rumour she picked up as she headed for Pamela's lodgings on King Edward Street. She knocked on the door to learn that Pamela had spent the night with Fred at Sunrise.

'I can pass on a message,' Pamela's obliging fellow lodger offered.

Sally thanked her – but no; it was essential to speak to Pamela face to face – then hurried back the way she'd come. Crossing the market square for a second time she heard the first mention of Ron's name. The coppers should be looking for Butcher. He's the one that did this – with a hammer, no less. The man's a lunatic – they ought to have locked him up and thrown away the key long since.

Pushing their angry accusations to one side, Sally ran swiftly along the headland path: a small, lonely figure dwarfed by the massive black cliff. She disappeared into the deep shadow of the overhang. As she emerged at the far side, the wind strengthened. It blew straight off the open sea and brought with it a fine, cold mist. Clutching her coat collar, she hurried on along the promenade.

Pamela woke up next to Fred, basking in the peaceful silence. For a few blissful seconds, she lived in the precious moment – wind rattling the window pane and daylight seeping through the sides of the blackout curtain, his warm body beside her, eyes closed, face unlined, hair ruffled; perfect.

Fred's room belonged to a bachelor and no mistake. His shaving set and mirror stood on a washstand next to a plain white pitcher and ewer. His suitcase was stowed on top of the wardrobe and a striped towel hung on a wooden towel rack. There was a pile of library books on a mahogany chest of drawers beside a hairbrush and Fred's cufflinks and tiepin.

He stirred and she broke out of her reverie. Drowsily opening his eyes, he reached out and drew her close. 'Why didn't you wake me?' he murmured.

'Because I like watching you sleep.'

They exchanged soft kisses. 'I like that you're here and I don't care if the whole world sees.'

'What have we got to hide? I love you and you love me.'

Since the humiliating event on College Road the day before, Pamela and Fred had talked, walked, talked again and finally gone to speak with Pamela's parents in their bungalow. They'd described exactly what had happened and how no one had stepped up to help.

'We're telling you this because we want to include you in any decision we may make in the near future,' Fred had explained in his usual rational style.

'That dreadful airman threatened you and then you were spat at in the street?' Edith had sat poker-straight in her pearls and twinset, eyes darting from one to the other. Harold, on the other hand, had seemed to quietly resign himself to what he knew was coming. They'd occupied their usual armchairs with their backs to the bay window where Edith's piano partly obscured the view of the sea.

'Even before today we've been living on our nerves,' Pamela had continued. 'We tried to keep it from you, but ever since Fred was set upon by Alf Tomkins and his gang last year, we haven't been able to relax. And more recently we've had Reggie Nolan and Lionel Simmons to deal with.'

'This problem is never going to go away,' Fred had added.

'Please don't continue!' Edith had raised her hand with a look of anguish.

'Hush.' Harold had stepped in with a gentle admonition. 'Edith, my dear, you must let the young ones have their say.'

'Everyone in this town knows my background.' Fred had chosen his words carefully, every now and then looking to Pamela for reassurance. 'They can't un-know it. Most are honest, generous folk who judge me by my actions and not simply by where I came from. But the fact is, the few bad apples who gang up against me and Pamela and wish us harm are capable of making our lives a misery.'

'You wish to leave Kelthorpe?'

Her mother's plaintive cry had brought a rush of tears to Pamela's eyes. 'We don't know yet – we haven't decided. But do we have your blessing if we do? Please say yes – I couldn't bear for you to blame us.'

Harold hadn't hesitated. 'Do whatever keeps you safe. Your mother and I won't stand in your way.'

'But, Fred, you may be in line for promotion at the town hall. And, Hugh – what will he do without you?'

Edith had scrambled for reasons to make them stay. 'And your jobs – how will you find new ones in a place where no one knows you?'

'Uncle Hugh would still have Dad as his right-hand man,' Pamela had pointed out. 'And Sally would take up where I left off in the office. We wouldn't leave him in the lurch if . . .'

'If you decided to go.'

Edith's flat, faint voice had made Pamela's tears fall faster. It would be a mighty wrench to break away from everything she knew.

Fred had laid bare the rest of their concerns. 'Of course, our departure might be seen as a victory for Reggie and company. Pamela and I have given this a good deal of thought.'

'We don't want them to be seen to win,' she'd added fiercely.

'It's this wretched war.' Edith's sudden, vehement declaration had surprised everyone. 'We all live in fear of being blown to bits – it brings out the worst in people.'

'And the best,' Harold had reminded her. 'Most of us do our utmost not to let it get us down and once we emerge from this war – once Hitler is well and truly beaten – then things are bound to be different.'

Edith had grasped at this straw. 'You see – all you two need to do is sit it out. What's the point of your running off into the blue if it will all come right in the end?'

'My dear,' Harold had interrupted again, 'we're not just talking about a matter of weeks. The fighting could go on for much longer than that and the feeling against German refugees might get worse, not better.'

Back and forth they'd gone, talking themselves into the ground, even going over to the main house to draw Hugh into their conversation. At first, Hugh had expressed dismay – he loved his niece, and Fred was dear to him, but then they both knew that. And well, if they felt strongly that the best option was to leave Kelthorpe and start afresh, Hugh wouldn't stand in their way. In fact, he would use his connections in the business world to help set them up somewhere new – in total secrecy, of course.

More tears had flowed. Hugh's whisky bottle had been brought out to ease the pain in the warmth and comfort of his sitting room. The fire had glowed in the hearth and the drink had mellowed them and warmed them through.

Hugh had put his arm around Fred's shoulders. 'My boy, I consider you to be part of our family, as do Edith and Harold. We wish you well.'

Fred remembered these fond words as he gradually came round from sleep with Pamela in his arms. Somehow they made him less afraid. 'Ought we to make firm plans?' he asked softly.

'I don't know – have we made a decision?' Rising from the bed, she went to pull up the blind and let the daylight in. She ignored the click of the gate latch and padded back across the room, intending to slide between the covers once more.

'Have we?' he mused, turning on to his back with his hands behind his head, staring at the ceiling.

A loud knock at the main door altered the slow, soft mood. Pamela jumped up and threw on Fred's

311

dressing-gown, then ran along the landing, calling out to her uncle that she would answer the door.

Sally knocked again. Her friend opened the door to a blast of cold, damp air. 'Sally!'

'Can I come in?'

'Yes – quickly. You look frozen stiff. Let's go into the sitting room.' Pamela led the way and invited the visitor to sit on the chesterfield sofa while she pulled back the curtains and opened the blinds.

'Have you heard about Tom?' Sally began without further ado. Her features were drawn and her breath came in short gasps.

'No.' Here came the real world, roaring and snarling at Pamela, whose defences were temporarily down. She sat beside Sally, feeling the apprehension rise.

'He's in hospital. They say Ron was involved . . . he . . . savage attack . . . he injured Tom badly.' Sally was unable to marshal her thoughts into coherent sentences.

So Pamela's chilling premonition had come true. She took a deep breath and waited for more.

'Bill has joined Connie and Lizzie at his bedside. The whole town is praying for him to pull through.'

'But he might not?' Pamela saw in Sally's eyes that this was the case.

'There's been no definite news. But the reason I'm here is because of something Ron said the last time I spoke to him, when he dragged me off to Fletcher's Yard.'

'You've come to warn me.' Pamela's sixth sense saw where this was leading. The attack on Tom was only the start – Ron's wild anger ranged far and wide, way beyond his bitterness towards the two men who had bought his father's boat. It was all-consuming, indiscriminate and utterly out of control.

'He mentioned you,' Sally admitted without noticing that Fred had entered the room. 'He blamed you for driving him out of the Leisure Gardens and forcing him to find a new place to spend his nights. In his mind, you've become the enemy too, and if I know Ron, he won't let it drop.'

'Why didn't you tell us sooner?' Fred frowned as he took up position with his back to the fireplace, hands clasped behind his back.

'I wish I had. I'm truly sorry. I did fall in love with Ron once upon a time; and until now, I suppose I kept hoping he would come to his senses.' Sally bowed her head, allowing wisps of damp hair to fall forward and hide her face. 'I ought to have known better.'

'It's not your fault,' Pamela reassured her. 'You were terrified – he'd hurt you. And anyway, you've told us now.'

'All the more reason for us to make our move.' Fred's resolution came across loud and clear. 'Pamela, if you're in danger from a mad man on the loose as well as Nolan's bunch of thugs, then we must act more quickly than we might have wished. We should leave Kelthorpe as soon as possible.'

'Fred's right,' Sally agreed. 'You can't afford to wait to find out what Ron does next.'

But Pamela shook her head; it felt too sudden, too hasty. 'What about Connie? How would she feel if I abandoned her now – right this minute when she needs her friends the most? And you too, Sally. I

313

can't leave town until Ron is found – I'd never forgive myself if something were to happen to you.'

'Don't worry about me.' Sally stood up with renewed determination. 'I can look after myself; you two must do what's best for you.'

'You're both right,' Pamela admitted. 'I know you are, but my heart breaks for Connie. It's not fair. She and Tom deserve to be happy.'

'We all do.' Fred put his arms around her, and she rested her head on his shoulder. 'And God willing, we will be.'

He made a valiant attempt to sound more certain than he felt; for what God allowed millions of innocent men, women and children across Europe to be persecuted? And what deity permitted violence to stalk the streets of Kelthorpe and creep into every corner of his adopted land?

CHAPTER EIGHTEEN

'We'll go soon,' Pamela promised. Sally had departed, leaving her and Fred to finalize their plans.

'Today,' Fred insisted. 'Knowing what we now know, why wait?' He imagined them flinging essentials into suitcases then hastily boarding a bus to carry them across the moors to Leeds or York and from there travelling on by train to an as yet unknown destination; it didn't matter where so long as they acted before Reggie or Ron pounced.

'No, not today.' Pamela stood firm. 'Today is Sunday. I feel certain that nothing bad will happen before we go back to work.'

'But it would catch the enemy unawares if we went now.' In the face of a plot that had become all too real, Fred was unwilling to accept delay. 'We could pack, say our goodbyes to your parents and Hugh and be gone before nightfall.'

'I can't.' Pamela was on the verge of tears. 'You heard what Sally said about Tom – I must find out how he is before we leave. I need to talk to Lizzie – she'll put me in the picture. I want to know if there's anything I can do to help.'

'But he's in good hands,' Fred argued. 'The doctors will be doing everything they can.'

'I know they will. But we can't even leave a forwarding address or a telephone number until we get to wherever it is we're going – it would be too risky to create a trail of that kind. And that means Lizzie and Connie would have no way of keeping in touch with us. No, Fred – give me a day or two. We'll leave by Wednesday at the latest.'

'Wednesday?' he repeated. This might work as long as he didn't let Pamela out of his sight for a second of the remaining time, but the mere thought of Ron lying in wait and of Reggie and Lionel carrying out their filthy plan was enough to enrage him. 'If anyone so much as lays a finger on you I'll kill them with my bare hands,' he swore.

'I promise I'll be careful.' She drew him to her.

'I'll be at your side day and night.' Fred's arms encircled her.

'Give me three days to say my goodbyes.'

'Three days,' he agreed. Then they would take their giant leap into the unknown.

Sally hurried around the headland, her mission complete. Now that she had warned Pamela of the threat from Ron, she must get back to the little ones. With her mind overflowing with dreadful possibilities, she broke into a run. Pamela wasn't the only one still in danger from her one-time sweetheart's vengeful nature – he had devious ways of getting at Sally through Rita and the others. God only knew where he was right this minute or what he might do next.

'Watch where you're going!' shouted an elderly

couple taking their Sunday-morning stroll as Sally tried to squeeze past. The path allowed them to walk two abreast but there was no space for her to overtake.

'Sorry – excuse me.' She edged past and ran on. Ron had tried it on with little Rita when he'd led her to the end of the jetty, hand in hand as if he meant no harm but managing to terrify Sally all the same. He could be there now, lying in wait for his next opportunity, aware that the police might be closing in on him after the attack on Tom and realizing that his time was almost up.

Sally's only hope was that he would be arrested before he could do more harm. Yes; arrest him and put him behind bars! There was no shred of affection left in her heart for Ron, not after what he'd done to Tom. She'd been a naive fool ever to hope that he could be saved from himself. Looking back, it had always been a case of her trying to rescue him – as you would if you found a wounded fox in a trap. You could put it in a box lined with straw and keep it warm and feed it as you slowly nursed it back to health, but the ungrateful fox would eventually turn on you; it would bite and claw its way out of the box, leaving behind a trail of destruction. It would revert to nature.

Sally picked up speed. Eric was in charge at the Anchor while their father was busy in the cellar, changing barrels and preparing for the week ahead. Fear fluttered around her heart.

From the clifftop, Ron watched Sally round the headland then emerge on to the quayside. High above his head, the two kite balloons tugged at their long cables, playing a mournful tune in the wind. He climbed on to one of the concrete bases for a better view. Way below, Sally cut a lone figure at the harbour's edge, running for all she was worth.

The cables whistled, whined and strained. Ron Butcher bided his time.

Connie counted the hours. Tom lay with his eyes closed and a needle in the back of his hand connected to a tube that drip-fed blood into his veins. He was breathing normally and the oxygen mask had been removed.

Busy nurses came to check his temperature and blood pressure, then entered the results on a chart. They smiled reassuringly at Connie but said there was no new information. Eventually, the strict sister appeared at Tom's bedside.

'There are two positive signs,' she reported whilst shining a torch into Tom's eyes. 'His pupils are responding normally and his X-rays showed a clear linear fracture to the back of his skull that should heal over time.'

'So no need for an operation?' Connie gasped as if she'd been deep underwater and had only now reached the surface. Her lungs ached as she dragged air into them.

'That's correct – Mr Rose was remarkably lucky. However, the right ulna is fractured in several places. Once the swelling has reduced, we'll put the arm in a plaster of Paris cast to immobilize it.'

'But when will he open his eyes?' Seeing Tom so helpless and unresponsive was hard to bear.

'That's difficult to say.' The sister checked the charts at the end of the bed. 'He's your sweetheart so perhaps you could talk to him – whisper sweet nothings into his ear. That may help.'

Connie took the sister at her word. 'Tom, it's me,' she murmured once they were alone again. 'Did you hear that? The doctors say you're doing well. They hope you'll get better without an operation – it's just a matter of time.'

He lay perfectly still, his eyes closed and his arm in the temporary splint that Bill and Lizzie had applied. A bright light shone on his face, making his skin appear paler than usual and Connie noticed a small vein pulsing in his neck.

'I know you can get through this,' she continued. 'You've been through much worse. An incendiary has blown up in your face and thrown you ten yards down the street. You've run into burning buildings and risked your life time and again for other people. Now you must fight for yourself – and for me and our baby. Do you hear me?'

There was no response – not the faintest flicker of his eyelids or twitch of his mouth; only the small, regular pulse under his ear.

'Connie.' Bill's voice drew her attention. 'A police sergeant is in the corridor wishing to speak to you.'

'Now?'

Bill nodded. 'I'll sit with Tom while you're away.'

She stood up reluctantly.

'Go,' Bill urged. 'And don't worry – I'll be here.'

Connie forced herself to leave the ward. Her head spun and she felt like she was floating as she pushed open the doors and found the policeman standing close by, looking unconcerned and eyeing the young nurses as they hurried by. He was a stout man in his forties with a bushy grey moustache, eyebrows to match and a florid complexion.

'Connie Bailey?' he asked abruptly, all the while taking in the details of her crumpled uniform.

She nodded. An anxious backward glance through the small window in the door told her that Bill had done as he'd promised and taken up position at Tom's bedside.

'I'm Sergeant Walter Newman. I gather you know the victim of this assault better than most?'

'I'm his sweetheart.' Connie nodded again before getting straight to the point. 'Have you found out where Ron Butcher is holed up? He's the man you should be looking for.'

'Hold your horses.' Newman was infuriatingly slow in taking out his notebook and licking the end of his pencil. 'What makes you think Butcher was involved? We're not aware of any witnesses.'

'Of course it was Butcher.' Connie couldn't hide her impatience. 'He held a grudge against Tom, and besides, there *was* a witness – my cousin Arnold Kershaw ran into him just before the attack. Butcher was carrying a hammer. Arnold reported the incident to me at the Gas Street post. His description fitted Butcher perfectly.'

Newman tilted his head to one side. 'But did this Arnold Kershaw actually see what happened?'

'Who else could it be? Tom doesn't have enemies. And you know as well as I do that Butcher has a record of violence.'

'Yes, but unless Kershaw witnessed Ron Butcher carrying out the attack, we can't use him as a witness,' the policeman pointed out bluntly. 'Anything else?'

'What else do you need to know? Butcher burned the boat that Tom and Bill were restoring.'

'Witnesses?' Newman repeated, wrinkling his nose and twitching his moustache, his pencil poised.

'Not as such,' Connie was forced to admit. 'But Ron couldn't stand the fact that his father had sold the boat from right under his nose. He tried to make it look as if a bomb had fallen on *Annie May* during an air raid but really it was him deliberately setting fire to her.'

'No witnesses.' Newman made a brief, definitive note. 'Let me get this straight – your boyfriend was attacked by an unknown assailant. You may have your theories about the whys and wherefores, but until the victim comes round and is able to describe his attacker, there's not a shred of evidence to back them up.'

Connie felt her cheeks flush with anger. 'Won't you even go out looking for Butcher?' she demanded. 'The man is dangerous. Tom is lying unconscious in that bed and God knows what the long-term damage will be.'

The policeman shut his notebook. 'Look, love, I know you're upset and I don't blame you. But we can only act on evidence, and so far there's precious little of that.'

'Won't you even start looking for Butcher?' Connie grew desperate. 'Are you happy to let him roam the streets, waiting to pounce on his next victim?'

'Calm down – his name's in my book. I'll see what I can do.'

Her exasperation broke through in another torrent of words. 'The man I love is lying there at death's door and you'll see what you can do! I'm having his baby and you'll see what you can do! He puts his life on the line for the people of this town and you'll see—'

'What I can do.' Raising his thick eyebrows in disapproval before pocketing his notebook, Newman made it clear that the interview was over. He set off down the corridor at a slow, steady pace, immune to Connie's distress.

Inside the ward, Bill sat and watched. He hated hospitals – their disinfected cleanliness and starched sheets, the sound of nurses' shoes squeaking along corridors, the sight of solemn doctors with their stethoscopes and self-important air. And above all else, he hated to see his best friend lying helpless on a hospital bed.

'We've got to get you out of here,' he muttered. 'You hear me, Tom? This isn't where you belong.' Bill glanced round self-consciously to make sure that no one could overhear the one-way conversation. 'You and I should be out there trawling for cod, hauling up the nets, bringing in the catch. That's what we do.'

Tom's breathing grew faster and the pulse in his neck quickened.

'We know these waters like the back of our hands. We've seen the worst the weather can throw at us – thick fog, gale-force winds, waves as high as a house – and we've lived to tell the tale. We're not about to let Ron Butcher stop us. We can soon get another boat and do it up. We'll call her *Annie May 2*.

Then, once the Patrol Service lets us off the hook, we'll be out there again, the two of us, doing what we've always done.'

Tom's eyelids flickered and the fingers of his undamaged hand flexed.

Connie returned quietly to the bedside in time to hear Bill's final words.

'And if you think I'm doing minesweeping duties all by myself you've got another think coming. You hear that, Tom Rose? I'm not going anywhere without you.'

Tom opened his eyes. A bright light shone above his bed. All was blurred. But it was Bill's voice and the voice of the sea that had called him. He turned his head towards two indistinguishable figures by his bed and tried to open his mouth and speak.

'At last – he's awake!' Connie sank on to the seat next to Bill and craned forward. 'He wants to say something.'

Gradually, the pale oval of a woman's face and her mass of dark, wavy hair came into focus. It took a while for Tom to make it out. His tongue wouldn't work properly; it seemed too big for his mouth, so the best he could manage was an incoherent mumble.

'It's me,' she said softly.

'Connie?' Tom finally got his tongue around the two syllables that meant the world to him. It really was her flawless face, her deep, dark eyes, her full lips – and the soft, low voice was hers too.

'Bill's here with me,' she whispered. 'We've been here all night.'

Bill's face was next to Connie's; both were staring anxiously at him, watching him take each breath. Slowly, Tom emerged from his daze. 'Where am I?'

'In hospital. You're safe. You're going to be all right.' Relief washed over Connie as she rested a hand on his shoulder and let the tears fall.

'You see?' Bill added, his voice breaking with emotion. 'I said we wouldn't let Butcher win.'

'And did I tell you how much I need you?' Connie smiled through her tears. 'If not, then I'm telling you now. *We* need you, Tom – me and this baby. We love you with all our hearts.'

The sun shone brightly and the door to number 12 Elliot Street stood open as Fred and Pamela approached the house. Well-wishers had arrived throughout the day to ask after Tom and learn the latest from the hospital. Arnold had been in attendance, sitting on the front doorstep in his Boy Scout's uniform and fending off questions on his Uncle Bert's and his cousin Lizzie's behalf. 'No news,' he'd told early visitors with boyish relish. 'Tom had his head bashed in. There was masses of blood. He's dead to the world.'

'Go easy on the gory details, young Arnold,' Bert had advised between visitors. 'Things are bad enough without.'

Then, later, 'Brilliant news!' Arnold had delivered the optimistic hospital update with equal enthusiasm. 'Glory hallelujah. Tom's back in the land of the living and he's recognized Connie and Bill! How about that?'

Neighbours had gathered at the street corner. It

was just what everyone needed: a drop of good news for a change. Not that they'd ever doubted the outcome – it would take more than a bump on the head to finish off the likes of Tom Rose.

Eventually Arnold's Sunday dinner of mutton stew and dumplings had beckoned and he'd deserted his post by the time Pamela and Fred arrived, so it was Lizzie who greeted them and welcomed them inside.

'It's such a relief,' she told them as they sat around the kitchen table. 'It seems there's a good chance of Tom making a full recovery.'

'Can he remember what happened?' Pamela asked, her mind abuzz with the plans that she and Fred were making.

'Not yet. The doctor says his memory of events will come back slowly but not to put him under too much pressure until he's ready to talk.'

'And how's Connie bearing up?' Fred sipped at the cup of tea that Bert had supplied before slipping down the road to partake of Vera's stew and dumplings. 'Is she over the shock?'

'You know Connie; she bounces back better than anyone I know.' Lizzie said proudly. 'I took her a change of clothes and brought her uniform home with me. She wants to stay on at the Queen Alexandra until she's sure that Tom is properly on the mend. They'll put a plaster pot on his broken arm tomorrow at the earliest.' Studying her young friend's face more closely, she went off on a new tack. 'Pamela Carr, why do I get the feeling that you're hiding something from me?'

Pamela glanced uncertainly at Fred. 'Shall I tell her?'

'Only if you promise not to say a word,' he warned Lizzie, his face deadly serious.

'I swear.' Lizzie put down her cup with a light rattle.

'Fred and I have decided to leave Kelthorpe.' The announcement came after a deep intake of breath and was blunter than Pamela had intended.

Lizzie gasped. 'Whatever for? No, don't tell me – Fred, you've received more threats. Who is it this time? Can't you go to the police and make them put a stop to it once and for all?'

Pamela and Fred shook their heads. 'Ron Butcher is after her and so are Reggie Nolan and his gang of bigots. Pamela's a prime target for both of them,' Fred explained. 'We have to leave to keep her safe.'

'But it's not right for Pamela to be driven out of Kelthorpe!' Lizzie was incensed. 'This is her home – she's lived here all her life. If she leaves, she'll be saying goodbye to everything she knows – the town, the people, her friends and family, her sector post team.'

Pamela sighed. 'Don't go on, Lizzie. I know it'll be a big wrench, but Fred and I have reached a decision. We leave on Wednesday and that's that.'

'Where will you go? What will you do?'

'Top secret,' Fred replied, tapping the side of his nose with his forefinger.

Pamela was more honest. 'The truth is, we have no idea. All we know is that we must make a completely new start. And now that Tom is on the mend and he and Connie are back together, it's taken a load off my mind.'

Staring into space, Lizzie considered how much

Pamela had changed since they'd first become friends. Back then, she'd been a shy, brainy girl scarcely out of childhood. She'd been unsure of herself and inexperienced in the ways of the world. How much she'd blossomed since that time. Now she was a quietly confident and fiercely loyal, loving woman; what's more she was an excellent member of the ARP team who showed courage and wisdom beyond her years. And Pamela had Fred, whom she loved. 'I'll miss you,' Lizzie confessed with genuine sorrow.

'I'll miss you too,' Pamela whispered back.

Since the vicious attack on Tom, Sally had lived on her nerves. She'd scarcely let the little ones out of her sight. Her father tried to calm her with reassurances that he was ready for whatever Ron might throw at them.

'I'll give him what-for if he tries anything,' Frank insisted over their Sunday dinner, his sleeves rolled back to show muscular forearms. Rita and George gripped their knives and forks and followed the exchange with wide, frightened eyes. 'Don't you worry – I'll beat the living daylights out of him.'

'Stay out of it,' Sally warned as she toyed with the food on her plate. 'Ron's dangerous. His mind doesn't work like yours or mine.'

'It beats me why you had anything to do with him in the first place.' Frank didn't mince his words. 'No one in Kelthorpe has a good word to say about Ron Butcher.'

'I thought I saw a different side to him,' she confessed falteringly. 'He's had a raw deal, what with his mother disowning him when he was young and his father not bothering with him. Ron was left to fend for himself, so was it any wonder he went off the rails?'

'You're too soft by half,' Frank declared; no more to be said.

'Is Ron a bad man?' Rita asked in a quavering voice later that day as Sally tucked her up in bed.

Sally tenderly brushed her young sister's hair back from her round, scrubbed face. 'It's best to keep out of his way,' she murmured. 'If you see him and he tries to talk to you, run straight home and tell me or Daddy.'

Why hadn't she been able to shake off the feeling that she was being watched? The evenings were lengthening enough for Sally to take a stroll along the quay once the children were in bed. But she'd been mistaken if she'd thought the fresh air would do her good. Instead, she kept on looking over her shoulder, imagining that footsteps followed her or that she was being spied on from the top of the headland. She heard Ron's voice on the breeze, whispering new threats and insults that carried over into a vivid nightmare later that night of a sudden wildfire starting in Wren's Cove and of the conflagration spreading down the coast all the way to Kelthorpe, consuming everything in its path – trees, ferns and heather; houses, schools, churches and shops. Flames and black smoke blotted out the sun. Everyone perished.

Only after Sally woke from her disturbed night's sleep and got the children ready for school was she able to settle her mind and concentrate on the day ahead. She dressed for work in a shop-bought frock of jade green that she'd been able to afford after weeks of scrimping and saving. Looking in the mirror after she'd swept up her glorious red hair and pinned it in place, she pinched her cheeks to bring some colour into them, then set out for the timber yard. Ignoring the wolf whistles from Keith Nelson and Lionel Simmons that greeted her at the gate, she skipped a visit to the cloakroom and headed straight upstairs and was at her desk by the time Pamela arrived.

'Someone's an early bird.' Pamela tucked her handbag under her desk then removed the cover to her typewriter. 'Is everything all right?'

'As it can be, while Ron is still at large.'

'You haven't seen him?' Pamela asked uneasily. 'Lizzie tells me that the police are dragging their heels until after they've talked to Tom. Meanwhile, Ron is free to come and go as he pleases.'

'No, I haven't seen him,' Sally confirmed quietly. 'Thank heavens for small mercies,' she added as she fed a sheet of paper into her typewriter. 'How is Tom, by the way?'

'He's come round and is doing well, by all accounts. But so far he doesn't remember much about what happened.'

Tap-tap-tapping of typewriter keys filled the ensuing silence.

'I have an announcement,' Pamela said during a pause.

Sally's eyes widened in expectation. It was unlike Pamela to break off from her work.

'I want to tell you this before it becomes common knowledge,' Pamela explained. 'Lizzie already knows but you must promise not to tell a single soul.'

'Cross my heart,' Sally swore.

'Fred and I are leaving Kelthorpe.'

Suddenly Sally found it hard to breathe. Their departure was what she'd expected and yet now that Pamela had confirmed it, she couldn't bring herself to believe it was really happening. 'No,' she breathed. 'Oh, I wish you didn't have to.'

'I'm afraid we do have to and quickly too. We wrote our official letters of resignation last night, and we intend to hand them in later this morning. But Uncle Hugh – Mr Anderson – already knows. So do my mother and father. Don't look so sad – the timber yard will carry on perfectly well without us. You'll continue in your job here in the office and Daddy will take over the accounts from Fred.'

'I *am* sad!' Sally insisted. Her face was white and she clasped her hands together as she made her way to the window overlooking the yard. 'I still have so much to learn.'

'You can do it.' Pamela assured her she had every confidence in her. The view of the prosaic comings-and-goings – cranes swinging loads of timber from ship to dockside, workers stacking it in the yard, cutting-room men carrying in sections of raw trunk and carrying out planed planks – gave her a jolt. This was the familiar life she was turning her back on. 'No doubt you'll get a pay rise for taking on the extra responsibility.'

'The money will come in handy,' Sally admitted. They noticed Keith taking over from Lionel in the cab of one of the cranes, then watched as Lionel slipped out of sight for a sly, unscheduled break. The telltale spiral of blue cigarette smoke from behind

330

the cutting shed told Pamela and Sally exactly what he was up to.

Pamela grew tight-lipped. 'Come on, it's time we made elevenses. Let's both take the tray through to Mr Anderson's office. You can watch me hand over my official letter.'

Sally cooperated with a heavy heart. Pamela had been her inspiration: the girl whose fashionable dress sense she'd slavishly copied when she took up her secretary's job, who had been patient and kind throughout. And more than that; Pamela had become a loyal friend outside of work, too. So Sally carried the tea tray down the corridor and followed Pamela into the boss's office with a sinking feeling that life was about to take another turn for the worse. 'When?' she asked as Pamela tapped on the door.

'Tomorrow is my last day at work,' Pamela confided. 'Fred and I leave on Wednesday. Remember, don't breathe a word.'

CHAPTER NINETEEN

'Don't think for a minute that I'm not grateful,' Tom told the nurses who fluttered around his hospital bed, administering painkillers, disconnecting tubes and filling in charts, 'but I'm keen to get back home. Have you any idea when that might be?'

'Not yet,' was the brisk response.

Connie made way for the nurse whose job it was to remove the drip. For once her advice erred on the side of caution. 'Try not to run before you can walk,' she told Tom. 'You must give the doctors time to check you over and make sure there's no lasting damage.'

He gave an embarrassed shrug. 'I make a lousy patient, don't I?'

'Why am I not surprised?' she countered fondly.

Tom laughed then winced.

'What hurts?'

'My ribs, my arm, my head – bloody everything.'

'Then lie still and do as you're told.'

Once the nurses had departed, Connie resumed her place at the bedside, laying a gentle hand on Tom's uninjured arm and leaning forward to kiss his cheek.

'Shouldn't you be giving Lizzie a hand at the

bakery?' Tom asked. Events were gradually coming back to him: their walk up on to the moor and the promises that they'd made about their future.

'No – Dad and Bill have stepped into the breach. I can stay here as long as you like.'

'How about for ever?' he joked.

Connie kissed him again. 'Yes, if you swear you'll be good.'

'I swear.' Despite a splitting headache, he felt content. 'And that includes letting sleeping dogs lie as far as Ron Butcher is concerned.'

Mention of the man's name made the hairs on Connie's neck prickle. 'Yes, best not to think about that,' she murmured. Sitting there in the bright and shiny, disinfected atmosphere of the hospital ward made events in the outside world seem distant and unreal.

Making a feeble attempt to sit up but finding that he was in too much pain, Tom fell back on the pillow. 'This is important, I have to warn Bill – he's to steer clear of Butcher until I'm out of here.'

She stroked his cheek. 'I'll tell him to hang fire.'

'Events are still foggy, but some stuff is coming back to me – how I was heading home . . .'

'Yes?' Connie urged him to continue.

'I remember I was looking forward to getting some shut-eye.' Tom shook his head and grew agitated.

'Hush.' She did her best to calm him. 'It's good that you're remembering but there's no need to rush it. Wait until you're feeling stronger.'

'No, listen!' The memories came roaring back in all their terror. 'I was thinking about us and the baby, nothing else. How we'd tackle it together. I rehearsed telling your dad and tried to picture his reaction. I was ready to admit it was my fault.'

'It wasn't anybody's fault,' she interjected softly.

'And I'd say I intended to stand by you and help in any way I could. I loved you and we both wanted the baby. Everything would work out fine.'

'Hush,' she whispered again, her heart full to bursting.

'Then out of the blue, Butcher cracks me on the back of my thick skull. I see stars and the next thing I know we're on the ground, scrapping it out. You should've seen the look in his eyes, Con – like a wild animal. I knew I was fighting for my life.'

Connie interrupted him again. 'You must tell every bit of this to the police – that's the best way to stop him. I'll fetch the sergeant as soon as you're ready.'

'I'm ready now.' Details flashed into Tom's head with frightening clarity. His last memory before he blacked out for good was of Butcher raising the hammer. 'Tell Bill to steer clear,' he repeated.

'I will. You can make your statement, then Sergeant Newman will start a proper search. It won't take them long to track Butcher down.'

'Unless the bugger's already bolted.' Tom closed his eyes and sighed. Weariness overcame him and he felt himself drifting off. 'Tell Bill,' he said for a third time.

Connie sat for a while and watched Tom sleep. An attentive nurse – a stout, older woman with a practical, no-nonsense air – told her that the patient needed to rest and that it would be best for Connie to go home for a while.

'If he wakes up, can you tell him that I'll be back later this afternoon?'

'Of course.'

'I serve as head warden at the Gas Street post – I'm on duty tonight but I can probably get someone to switch shifts with me.'

'No, don't do that.' Advice from the nurse was firm. 'Call in here for an hour or so before you start your shift. That will be enough excitement for one day.'

'It won't look as if I'm abandoning him?' For the first time in her life Connie was torn between duty and love. 'I wouldn't want Tom to think that.'

'He won't.' The nurse bustled and chivvied her out of the ward. 'Let us do our work, there's a good girl. You carry on with what you have to do – patrolling our streets and making sure that everyone is safe from the worst that Herr Hitler can throw at us. Now, shoo!'

Instead of going home to Elliot Street as the well-meaning nurse had suggested, Connie went straight from the hospital to the bakery, where she intended to telephone Sergeant Newman to provide an update on Tom's recovery. She rehearsed her speech in advance: 'Tom's getting his memory back. It's exactly what I've said all along – Ron Butcher is who you should be looking for.'

She arrived to find her father pulling the last batch of bread from the oven and Lizzie using the phone to place the following week's order for sacks of flour. Connie's own phone call would have to wait, but all felt reassuringly familiar: the sweet smell of warm scones, the scrape and rattle of wire trays being stacked and the gleam of the glass-topped counter – all gave the impression that life went on regardless.

'There you are at last. We've been rushed off our feet,' Bert admitted to Connie as he dusted his floury hands on his calico apron. 'We've sent Bill out to deliver the last orders.'

'Here – let me do that.' She snatched a cloth from her father and started to wipe down the surfaces. 'I've been shooed out of Tom's ward by one of the nurses, so I might as well make myself useful.'

'How's the lad doing?'

'Better. They're making him comfortable and glory be; he's remembered what happened on Saturday night.' Buoyed up by the good news, Connie prattled on about X-rays and plaster casts and how Tom was already champing at the bit to be discharged. 'They've told him it might be a while. His injuries were serious and they want to be sure he'll make a full recovery.'

'Champion.' Bert took off his apron and hung it on a hook. 'That's the spirit. It takes more than a knock on the head to keep a good man down.'

Connie paused mid-wipe and her face took on a dreamy quality. 'Tom is a good man, isn't he?'

'The best,' her father agreed phlegmatically. 'It beats me why it took you so long to see it.'

She laughed then held her breath before speaking again. 'I'm pregnant, Dad.'

He cocked his head and looked directly at her. 'Course you are,' was all he said.

'You knew?'

'Course I did – I'm not daft.'

'And you don't mind?'

'Your putting the cart before the horse?' Bert asked. 'No, what would be the point? What's done is done. I'm just glad Tom is on the mend, that's all.' He took off his apron, put on his jacket and cap and made his way through the shop and out on to the street.

Lizzie finished her phone call and joined Connie in the bakery. 'How's the patient?' She held up her crossed fingers for Connie to see.

'*Im*patient,' Connie replied with a quick, characteristic rise of her eyebrows. 'He can't wait to get out.'

'Details, please!' Lizzie's demand was accompanied by the tinkle of the shop bell. 'Later,' she added as she hurried back to the counter.

'Have you any of those fancy butterfly buns left?' The short-sighted customer peered along the shelves. 'If not, I'll have three sultana scones.'

Then the next: 'A small brown tin loaf, please.' And the next: 'I'll take that last cottage loaf off your hands.'

And so it went on, with Connie at last able to telephone the station before snatching a quiet word with her sister.

'Dad knows about the baby,' she whispered.

Lizzie's eyes widened. 'How did he take it?'

'He said, "Course you are."'

'That was it?'

Connie nodded and Lizzie laughed. 'Trust Dad!' they chorused. Then they hugged by way of celebration. *Good old unshockable, devoted Dad.*

'Tom really is on the mend,' Connie reported. 'He's off the drip and having the proper plaster pot put on his arm as we speak.'

'What a relief!' Lizzie gave her another impetuous hug.

'Yes, and he can remember what happened.' Connie altered her tone as the shop bell rang again. 'Listen, Lizzie – he wanted me to warn Bill not to go after Butcher. He says it's too dangerous.'

Bill himself made his way into the bakery carrying two empty wooden trays. 'Should my ears be burning?' he enquired. 'I thought I heard my name.'

'You did.' Lizzie took the trays from him and stacked them beside several others. 'Connie has a message for you from Tom.'

Bill frowned. 'Don't tell me – he's warning me to steer clear of Butcher.'

Connie nodded vigorously. 'Those were his exact words. How did you guess?'

'I can read the daft beggar's mind, that's how.' Apparently unperturbed, Bill rolled down his sleeves and buttoned the cuffs.

'Tom has a point,' Connie argued. 'I've called the station and the sergeant there has promised to pay him a visit. Then hopefully they'll go after Butcher, no holds barred.'

'So we leave it to the boys in blue?' Bill's frown deepened. Inaction was foreign to him – the bold part of his nature longed to be up and at the enemy, however dangerous. 'How long is that likely to take?'

'Who knows? We'll have to wait and see. A few days, maybe.'

Bill shook his head. 'I don't have that long,' he reminded them. 'I start minesweeping duties again next Monday.'

Lizzie felt her throat constrict at the two-fold threat to Bill's well-being. Going after Butcher without

Tom's help was bad enough without being reminded of the deadly dangers he was soon to face at sea.

'Tell him,' Connie instructed Lizzie before answering yet another ring of the shop bell.

'No need,' Bill insisted. 'Butcher's a lunatic – everyone knows that. But what am I supposed to do, sit on my hands while he buggers off out of here? Look at the damage he's already done – first he sets fire to *Annie May*, robs Tom and me of our livelihoods, and gets away with it. And now the lousy so-and-so beats my best mate to within an inch of his life. I can't sit around doing nothing, can I?'

'Yes, you can – for my sake,' Lizzie pleaded. 'Leave it to the police.'

'Damn it, I won't sleep until he's behind bars.' Bill clenched his jaw and clung fast to his point of view.

'If you won't do it for me, do it for Tom.'

Bill turned for the door then in a split second thought better of it. 'I'm sorry,' he mumbled.

'For what?' The deep sorrow in his eyes made her world shift and tilt.

'For everything – for being an idiot and not thinking of you. For believing I was in the right. I mean it – I'm sorry.'

Lizzie trembled as she held his gaze, sensing that there was more to come.

'I'm not talking about Tom.' Bill's stubborn wrongheadedness had struck him like a thunderbolt. 'I mean our wedding – it was me who said we should put it off until I was back on my feet.'

'But now?' Lizzie could scarcely breathe as Bill pulled her towards him. His arms were around her;

they were so close that she felt the beat of his brave, strong heart.

'What the hell – now I think we should go ahead and get married straight away.'

'Why?' she gasped.

'Because the way things are right now, none of us can know what's going to happen tomorrow, let alone next week or next month. So, what do you say, my Lizzie – shall we just do it?'

'When?'

'This coming Saturday, the sixteenth, like we said.'

Dresses, flowers, fresh invites, a new best man! Lizzie's mind was a whirl of last-minute preparations.

'Well?' Bill asked. 'What do you say?'

'I say yes,' Lizzie replied. 'A hundred, a thousand, a million times yes.'

Pamela's resignation was formally accepted – with regret, Hugh said from behind his wide mahogany desk. Fred had already handed over his letter. The deed was done.

'Now there's no going back,' Pamela told Sally during their afternoon break. 'It feels as if Fred and I have jumped off the edge of a cliff into the unknown.'

'I don't know if I could do it – you're braver than I am, the pair of you.'

'It's different for you,' Pamela argued. 'You have the little ones to consider.' She lifted some buff-coloured files from a shelf and showed them to Sally. 'These are unpaid invoices from February and March. You'll have to write final reminders. If there's no reply, write again to say that the matter will now be referred to our solicitors.'

There was a lot of business to get through in the little time that remained and Pamela was determined to leave everything in good order. Fred would do the same, providing Harold with the most up-to-date information about expected shipments – types of timber, dates of arrival and eventual destinations spread across Yorkshire and beyond.

By the end of the afternoon, Sally's brain was brimming over with new facts and figures. 'Can we stop now?' she pleaded.

Pamela relented with a tired smile. 'Yes – we'll save the rest for tomorrow.'

Together they tidied their desks then went to fetch their coats. It was while they were in the cloakroom that Sally turned her thoughts towards the evening ahead. 'I promised Dotty that she could go to Brownies tonight,' she told Pamela. 'But now I'm having second thoughts – I think she should stay at home until . . .'

'Until the police track Ron down.' Pamela guessed the reason behind her friend's hesitation.

'Yes, what do you think?'

'Keep her at home – that's what I would do, at any rate.'

'You're right – better safe than sorry.' As Sally led the way out of the cloakroom into the reception area where Fred waited for Pamela, she came to a sudden, unexpected halt.

Pamela shunted into her from behind. 'What is it? What's the matter?' After they'd both regained their balance, she saw that Sally had turned pale.

'Nothing – don't mind me.'

'It's not nothing,' Pamela insisted as Fred joined

them. 'Something's upset you. Is it still to do with Ron?'

Sally swallowed hard then nodded. 'I suddenly remembered a favourite spot of his – it's where we used to walk on a nice light evening like this.'

'Might he be holed up there now?' Fred quickly picked up on Sally's train of thought.

'Yes – why didn't I think of it earlier?'

He grew alert. 'Never mind that – where is this place?'

'Near Raby village. There's a cave in Wren's Cove . . .'

'We know it!' Pamela exclaimed as she glanced at Fred to check his response.

'Ron used to wait for me outside the pub on my evenings off then we'd hike along the cliff path as far as the cove.'

'It makes sense,' Fred agreed. 'Butcher could well have taken refuge there. The cave is dry and off the beaten track. If he has provisions and is careful to stay out of sight, he could hole up in that cave all summer.'

'The police need to know this.' Pamela was certain that the lead should be followed up immediately. 'We'll go to the station, all three of us – right now this minute.'

'I can't – I have to tell Dotty that she can't go to Brownies.'

'Then Pamela and I will do it,' Fred decided. 'Don't worry, Sally – we have to collect the rest of Pamela's belongings from King Edward Street. We can easily call in at Gladstone Square on the way there and ask them to send a constable to Wren's Cove.'

The plan was hastily made and they hurried along the dockside before parting ways at the market square.

Unable to dismiss Ron from her thoughts, Sally delivered the disappointing news about Brownies to her sister then scraped together a meagre tea of toast spread with beef dripping.

'A penny for them,' her father said as she cleared plates from the table.

'They're not worth it.' A strong urge to investigate Wren's Cove for herself was building within her. Fred and Pamela meant well, but why wait for the police? They no doubt had a dozen crimes to follow up – cases of looting, infringements of the blackout rules, shoplifting and worse – and were slow to act at the best of times. It stood to reason – this had to be followed up now before Ron did more harm. Sally only needed to cycle to the cove and carry out a quick search for signs that he'd been there: a campfire on the beach, say, or recent footprints leading to and from the cave.

After taking Eric to one side and quietly issuing instructions about putting the little ones to bed, she slipped out into the backyard, took her bike from the shed, crossed the square and set off up the steep hill leading to the Raby road.

'I'm in a hurry – can I take the van?' Connie asked Lizzie as they changed into their uniforms. 'I'd like to drop in at the hospital before I start my shift.'

'Keys are on the hook,' Lizzie informed her. *You're in a hurry! What about me? I have a wedding to organize and a thousand and one things to do before Saturday.*

She'd practically shouted her news from the

rooftops – 'Bill and I are getting married on the sixteenth after all! I'll be Mrs Evans and the happiest woman alive!'

'Well, I never,' Bert had growled. 'You girls are full of surprises. I'd best get my suit out of mothballs.'

'Blow me down,' had been Aunty Vera's response. 'That doesn't leave me much time to ice that cake.'

'About time too, you lucky beggar,' Connie had commented before hugging Lizzie and lifting her off her feet.

'Put me down!' Lizzie had protested. 'A woman in your condition shouldn't be lifting heavy objects.'

'A list of jobs,' Connie had proclaimed, grabbing a pencil and a sheet of paper. 'Number one – wedding ring. Has it so much as crossed Bill's mind? Number two – rebook St Joseph's and tell the vicar that we're back on. Number three – food for the reception.'

'All in hand,' Lizzie had assured her. 'First thing tomorrow, I'm going to ask Sally to stand in for Pamela as my bridesmaid.'

'Yes. From what you've told me, Lord knows where in the world Fred and Pamela will end up by the weekend. Sally will be thrilled and she'll do a good job, I'm sure.'

So much still to be done! Lizzie gazed into the mirror as Connie left the bedroom. Her face was flushed, her eyes gleaming with relish at the task ahead. Did all brides-to-be feel this mixture of anticipation and trepidation? Were all their cheeks permanently flushed in the build-up to the big day and were they too excited to eat, sleep or think straight?

Connie dashed downstairs and out of the house, collecting the van keys on the way.

Damn the rush-hour traffic, she thought as she crawled through the centre of town. At this rate, she would have less than an hour to spend with Tom. A bus in front of her stopped without signalling and then a beer delivery wagon pulled out from a side street, forcing her to slam on the brakes. It took her twice as long as usual to reach the bottom of the hill leading to the hospital and when she finally arrived at the gates her heart pounded as if she'd made the journey on foot, running every step of the way.

Finally! Visiting time had begun and finding a parking space had proved difficult. Inside the building at last, the corridors were crowded. Connie was obliged to stand to one side as orderlies wheeled a trolley towards her. The door to Tom's ward stood open, and there he was, with the screens removed, propped against pillows and sitting up, his head turned expectantly.

Entering the ward, Connie discovered that other visitors had pinched all the chairs.

'Don't sit on the bed.' A nurse's barked order made her jump.

A young wife about to leave her husband's bedside took pity on Connie. 'Here, love – have mine. You look as if you need it.'

Connie thanked her and set the chair down at Tom's bedside. There was colour in his cheeks and the red bruises on his forehead had begun to darken to a shade of blue. His arm was in the clean new pot. 'How are you? I'm sorry I'm late. Do I look as though I've been pulled through a hedge backwards?'

He sighed with relief and spoke over her. 'You're here – that's all that matters.'

They laughed self-consciously, aware that eyes were on them – she in her head warden's uniform and he looking much the worse for wear. A handsome couple, nonetheless.

'Really, how are you?' she said again.

'Getting there, slow but sure. The doc gave me another once-over and said not to worry. I'll be out and about before you know it.'

'Lizzie and Bill have decided to get married after all.' The good news burst from Connie like sun coming out from behind clouds. Her face shone with happiness.

'By Jove,' Tom said.

'This coming Saturday – the original date. Do you think you'll be out of hospital by then?'

'Wild horses won't stop me,' he vowed. 'How come Bill changed his mind?'

Connie wasn't sure. 'Most likely a case of seize the day. That's what this war does – sends couples trotting down the aisle regardless.'

Tom nodded and looked thoughtful. 'It's grand to see you,' he murmured. 'You're taking it easy, I hope?'

'I am,' she fibbed.

'Liar. I know you, Connie Bailey – the way you dash around, trying to fit everything in. You'll have to slow down now that you're having our baby.'

'And pigs might fly.' He'd said the baby word again – how bloody frightening and breathtaking and awe-inspiring and downright impossible to get her head around. A baby – their baby!

'Wait till I get out of here, then I'll make sure you do.'

She smiled and drew the chair closer. 'You and whose army?'

'I mean it, Con. I want to look after you.'

'And I don't want to be molly-coddled, baby or no baby,' she insisted.

'Are we about to have an argument?' Ignoring the pain in his ribs, Tom reached for her hand.

'I don't know – do you want to have one?'

'No,' he said softly, his eyes gazing intently into hers. 'What I really want is for us to get married. What do you say?'

CHAPTER TWENTY

Sally's old boneshaker had no gears, so cycling up the hill on to the cliff road was harder work than she'd expected. Buffeted by a strong crosswind and poorly dressed for the occasion in a light sweater, cotton trousers and canvas plimsolls, she cycled on until she reached the top, where she paused to catch her breath. Would there be time to get all the way to Wren's Cove and back again before it grew dark? she wondered. And did she have the energy and will-power to do it?

Giving herself a good shake, Sally carried on with her plan. If her theory about the cove was right and she found evidence that Ron had been there, it would be a big step forward. The police would be forced to take prompt action and, with luck, the nightmare they were all living through would come to an end.

Setting off again, she was able to freewheel down the next stretch and make good progress. Then she reached a more sheltered section of the twisting road, where she was protected by high hawthorn hedges that had recently come into leaf. Emerging from the green tunnel, Sally gained a clear view of the coast, the red-tiled roofs of Raby in the distance, and before that, the narrow inlet where she was headed.

The sight of her destination renewed her determination. On she cycled until she came to a lay-by at the side of the road. Here was where she must abandon the bike and take the steps down to the beach. Time was short – she must hurry.

She found that weather had eroded some of the wooden steps and there was no handrail. Luckily, she had a head for heights. Where necessary, she steadied herself by holding on to clumps of heather or bracken. Loose stones rattled down the steps ahead of her, the noise drowned by the roar of the ebbing tide.

Sally remembered the times when she had walked here with Ron, when the black moods that plagued him would lift for a time and he would seem almost happy. They would stroll hand in hand like regular sweethearts and he might stop to point out a fishing boat returning to harbour with its catch, describing the vessel in great detail – a sixty-four-foot, deep-sea trawler with a high bow to cope with the notorious North Sea storms, crewed by skipper, first mate, second mate, bosun and boy. Steam-powered, which put it at around 1910 – before then it would have been sails only, or a combination of sails and steam. Ron's love of facts and figures had intrigued her and made her smile.

There'd been hope for him then, before his father decided to sell *Annie May*.

Or perhaps Sally had merely fooled herself and there'd never been any hope for a man whose anger was beyond control – quick to catch light and slow to die down – who saw insult in a stranger's casual glance and rejection lurking around every corner.

She jumped from the final two steps on to soft, brown sand. The burned skeleton of *Annie May* was still there, silted up and with three large herring gulls perched on what remained of the stern. Between the trawler and the water's edge there was a smooth, untouched band of dark, wet sand. Behind the boat, where the water seldom reached, Sally made out scuffed footprints leading to the cave.

With a rapidly beating heart, she considered her options: one was to turn around and report recent comings and goings in Wren's Cove to the police. Another was to take a closer look. Gathering her courage, she made her way towards the cave. Some of the footprints were child-sized, an indication that the beach had been visited by young fossil hunters or other groups of adventurers. But some were large enough to belong to a fully grown man, apparently made by the same pair of boots trekking in and out of the cave. Sally followed them, noticing a stack of driftwood close to the entrance and the remains of a small fire nearby. Common sense told her not to venture further – she had no torch, and the interior of the cave would be pitch dark. Yet footprints and fire might still not be enough to convince the police that Ron had been here. She needed better evidence.

Behind her, the three gulls rose with a sharp flap and snap of their wings, screeching as they flew over-head. Directly in front of her, the blackness of the cave's interior sent shudders through Sally's body.

'What am I doing?' she said out loud. *Don't risk it. Turn around*, an inner voice told her.

What if Ron was actually in there, right this moment, lying in wait? Once the possibility had lodged in her brain, Sally found it impossible to shake off. She took a few steps backwards and collided with the driftwood. The stack collapsed in an untidy heap, and she turned tail and ran. The soft sand slowed her and she grew breathless. Her chest was tight, her legs ached. Glancing over her shoulder, she saw only the black entrance to the cave – thank God, no one was following her. The gulls wheeled on an air current, watching her clumsy progress. The thunderous sound of breaking waves drove her on, up the rotting wooden steps, sliding and skidding. She reached the top. There was no bike. She searched frantically until she found it behind a boulder with both tyres slashed and its handlebars bent beyond repair.

Nothing could dent Connie's joy. She walked to Gas Street past piles of rubble that had once been houses, oblivious to the wreckage. Teams of civilians in grimy overalls and caps sorted through piles of brick and splintered wood to salvage whatever they could – a settee with its stuffing hanging out, a cast-iron fire grate, a miraculously preserved baby's cot. They made the most of the long spring evenings, working uncomplainingly to sort scrap metal into one pile, rags into another and paper into a third. A defiant Union Jack had been planted atop the rubble, fluttering in the breeze as Connie passed by.

'I said yes!' she told Pamela the moment she

entered the post, ignoring Brian, who stood at the counter, and seeking out her friend in the storeroom. 'Tom has asked me to marry him and I accepted!'

Pamela was flabbergasted. She stopped counting eye shields and gloves, knocking a wooden rattle off a shelf and hearing it clatter to the ground as she spun round. 'You don't say!'

'I do say!' Connie beamed from ear to ear. 'Out of the blue, he said he wanted to marry me.'

'When?'

'As soon as they let him out of hospital. Are you going to congratulate me, or what?'

'Yes!' Pamela found her voice. 'That's marvellous. I'm so happy for you.'

'And I'm having his baby,' Connie confessed, believing herself to be out of earshot from Brian. 'That's not the reason we're getting married. What's the matter – has the cat got your tongue?'

Only Connie Bailey could have kept this to herself! Pamela demanded more facts as she followed her friend upstairs to the rest room. 'How long have you known? Why on earth didn't you tell me? Is that why you've been acting strangely? Oh, Connie, trust you!'

'I know, I know.' Connie spread her hands apologetically. 'I had to work out how I felt first. And how Tom felt, too. In the end we found we both wanted the same thing. Then he went and got himself bashed on the head by Ron Butcher and I nearly lost him.' The weekend's events had passed in a blur and it was only now that Connie could begin to make sense of them. 'Now that he's on the mend, I want the whole world to know how happy we are.'

Noises from below told Pamela that other wardens had arrived to start their shift. 'Does Lizzie know that Tom proposed?' she asked hastily.

'Not yet. I came straight from the hospital. She's on duty tonight so I'll tell her at the end of our shifts.'

'She'll be thrilled,' Pamela predicted before heaving a sigh. 'My two best friends are getting married and I'll miss both weddings. Fred and I leave the day after tomorrow.'

The reminder that this was to be Pamela's last shift brought Connie back down to earth with a bump. 'Lord, here am I going on and on! I haven't asked you how your mum and dad are coping with the idea of you leaving. There'll be tears all round, I expect.'

'Head Warden Bailey, are you there?' A tetchy Brian shouted up the stairs. 'I haven't got all night!'

'Coming!' she replied. 'Lizzie and I would like to give you a proper send-off, Pamela – tomorrow night, if you have the time.'

'Connie?' Brian yelled.

'Coming! We'll talk about it later,' she promised Pamela as she answered Brian's call.

The Fraser boys stood to attention at the bottom of the stairs, next to Brian. All were smiling broadly as they broke into song. '"Here comes the bride,"' they chanted as Connie descended the stairs. '"Short, fat and wide, slipped down the banister and fell into the Clyde."'

Connie lunged at her fellow head warden. 'Brian Bellamy, I'll crown you!'

Grinning, he fended her off. 'That'll teach you to keep your voice down.'

'Simon, Eddie, just you wait!'

They dodged Connie and continued to chant.

Connie laughed. Everyone laughed. They shook hands and slapped her on the back, congratulated her and joked that poor Tom didn't know what he was letting himself in for.

'I'd have thought once bitten was twice shy for you, Connie Bailey.' Brian was back to his curmudgeonly self as he handed over various reports. 'But then I'm a confirmed bachelor, so what do I know?'

Dusk gathered as Sally walked her broken bike along the winding road to Kelthorpe. Unable to rid herself of the terrifying feeling that she was being spied on, she constantly looked back the way she'd come. Who else but Ron could have damaged the bike? He must have been observing her as she'd descended the steps, studying her movements from the clifftop as she'd crossed the beach.

One driver stopped and leaned out of his window to ask if Sally needed a lift into town. She thanked him and declined – it would mean abandoning the bike and she had hopes that it could be fitted with new tyres and handlebars and be made roadworthy once more. Trudging the final mile along the headland, she planned what she would do when she reached the town.

Ron had seen her return to the lay-by and watched with satisfaction as she'd set off for home: a dejected, frightened, isolated figure. Now, he followed in the shadows. Hiding behind trees, hedges and walls, he revelled in Sally's fear – he could almost touch it; the way she glanced behind her then picked up speed, head thrust forward, hands gripping the misshapen handlebars. It served her right; she'd never been honest with him – in fact, she'd lied about the other men, brazen and bare-faced as you like. She'd gone behind his back and had the gall to deny it, leaving Ron no other choice but to ditch her. The lying little bitch deserved everything she got.

Sally approached Musgrave Street. The sheltered harbour and quayside lay below her like a picture postcard. Fishing boats bobbed in the water, the red sun setting made the sea sparkle and dance. Overhead, the two kite balloons shone pink in its rays.

Ron stopped beside one of the concrete bases and watched Sally arrive in the market square. He had time – plenty of it. He decided to toy with her for another day or two – the thrill of the chase. He perched on the base, crossed his legs and lit a cigarette. Above him, the balloon floated sedately. Sixty-six feet long, thirty feet wide, maximum altitude 1,524 metres, filled with 20,000 cubic feet of hydrogen. As ever, Ron revelled in facts and figures – they never let you down.

All was well at home. Sally checked in on her father and brothers and sisters before making her way to Gas Street in the dark, where she found Pamela and Connie coming to the end of their shift. Lizzie's ambulance was parked outside.

Inside the post, the faces of all three girls were wreathed in smiles.

'Sally – you're the very person!' Lizzie bustled from behind the counter to greet her. 'How do you feel about helping to sew a wedding dress for Connie? Yes, I know – it came as a shock to me, too. But you know Connie – she's always springing surprises. Now, about the wedding dress – we have plenty of white silk but do you perchance have any lace trimming or shiny buttons stashed away in a drawer?'

'Perchance!' Connie scoffed as she closed her report book.

'Ignore her,' Pamela said with a wink. 'I was the one who reminded these two that you're a wizard with a sewing machine. I said I was certain you'd lend a hand.'

'Of course I will.' Sally held back her news – it seemed a shame to spoil the celebratory mood. 'And yes, I have a set of nice pearl buttons.'

'Nothing too fancy,' Connie insisted. 'You know I'm not one for frills and bows.'

'What are you doing here anyway?' Pamela thought to ask. 'Didn't your dad need you behind the bar?'

'Not tonight.' Sally made up her mind; instead of talking through her findings in Wren's Cove with Pamela, Connie and Lizzie as she'd planned, she would go from here straight to the police station. 'Now, Connie, about a pattern for your dress – I have a few that might do. One with long sleeves and a dropped waistline that would definitely suit you.'

It was eleven o'clock precisely. Three stealthy Junkers Ju 88s approached the Yorkshire coast, hugging the waves and flying as low as they dared in order to avoid radar detection. As they sighted their objective – the port of Kelthorpe – they rapidly gained height, ready for the attack to come.

At the Gas Street post, Connie and Pamela signed off for the night while Lizzie and Sally continued their chat about dress patterns on the pavement out-side. Lizzie cocked her head at the sound of the sudden drone of approaching engines. 'Let's hope that's our RAF boys stepping up their night-flying training programme,' she commented uneasily.

Over at King Edward Street ambulance depot, Bill reacted differently. 'Mark my words – that's Jerry!' he exclaimed to Sam. 'Junkers, if I'm not mistaken.'

'Spot on,' Sam agreed.

The two men waited on tenterhooks for the wail of sirens.

At the town hall, Fred sat surrounded by telephon-ists, clerks and messengers as he put the finishing touches to his final damage and situation report that listed blocked roads and broken water mains in the new part of town. He would miss this stuffy, airless smell of dust, old linoleum and wax polish, he thought, not to mention the sound of ping-pong being played in the recreation room next door. He imagined Pamela finishing her last shift at Gas Street.

'Enemy aircraft – Alert Red!' A cry went up from one of the telephonists. 'Warn all sector posts. Three Junkers 88s heading our way.'

The belated wail of sirens woke Kelthorpe from its sleep. At the top of Musgrave Street, Lily Majors at number 52 ran next door to check that her hard-of-hearing, widowed mother, Irene Cawthra, had responded to the alert. She rushed her into the brick shelter between the bungalows to take refuge with Lily's husband Bernard and their three children.

Then the first incendiaries fell. The deadly missiles – the Luftwaffe's favourite – hissed as they plummeted to earth and exploded in blinding flashes of light. A dozen sailors who were passing through the battered port, playing their part in the Murmansk Run that took supplies back to beleaguered Soviet Russia, leaped from their beds in a dozen seedy boarding-house rooms and headed to the communal shelter on College Road. It was bad enough to perish at sea like thousands of their comrades, let alone be burned to a cinder in your bed.

The Junkers circled for a second attack. Half of Tennyson Street was ablaze before the fire guard sprang into action or wardens had time to herd residents into their shelters. Squaddies from the 39th Brigade aimed their ack-ack guns and fired into the starlit sky. A direct hit brought one enemy plane spiralling down into the sea, where it exploded in a spectacular mass of flames and steam.

Late drinkers in the Red Lion on College Road ignored the scalded-cat raid for as long as they could. Let Jerry do his worst; why waste a good pint?

At the ambulance depot, Bill and Sam responded to a call for them to attend an incident on Musgrave Street. A brick shelter between two bungalows had been blown to smithereens. Six residents – three adults and three children – were thought to have been inside.

'Next time, Jerry will aim for the dockside,' Connie predicted amid the flurry of activity at the Gas Street post. There was now no question of anyone returning home at the end of their shift. Kenneth Browning and a new team of volunteers had arrived for their overnight spell of duty, so ARP numbers were doubled. Kenneth deployed Eddie Fraser to the dockside and Simon to stand guard outside the

College Road shelter, then spoke on the phone to the Tennyson Street sector post, promising to send two more wardens to fight the blaze there. Meanwhile, Connie and Pamela commandeered a lorry from Dixon's yard then followed an AFS trailer pump to the headland where the main action was taking place. Grabbing helmets from the store and without a second's hesitation, Sally and Lizzie went with them; the more willing hands the better.

A second round of machine-gun fire from the beach brought down another Junkers before it reached the dockside. Only one remained. Beset by panic, its young pilot flew dangerously low over the headland, continuing to drop incendiaries. The fire-guard team sped to the top of Musgrave Street with Connie close behind, and Lizzie, Pamela and Sally clinging on for dear life. On arrival, they saw that little remained of two bungalows on the brow of the hill. The shelter where the Majors family had taken refuge was a sorry sight – the hot-burning magnesium of an incendiary had transformed it into a smouldering heap of bricks and red-hot sheets of corrugated iron. Connie's heart fell as she warned Pamela, Lizzie and Sally to stay well back.

The surviving Junkers pilot released his last cluster of bombs. He was clearly visible in his cockpit: leather helmet and goggles illuminated by a rapid succession of dazzling white flares from his incendiaries. He flew much too low; the tip of his starboard wing snagged a steel cable that tethered one of the kite balloons and within a split second his Junkers crashed to the ground in flames.

'Jesus Christ!' A member of the fire-guard team

watched in horror as a whirl of red sparks rose, dervish-like, towards the nearest hydrogen-filled balloon.

'Take cover!' another yelled. Men scattered in every direction.

Quick-thinking Connie dragged Lizzie, Pamela and Sally under their truck while the fire team took refuge beneath their trailer. They lay face down, covering their ears and averting their gaze from the blazing Junkers and the rising sparks. Seconds passed – a lifetime – then there was a massive boom and a ball of flame. The world was on fire. Floating shreds of blazing fabric drifted on to the headland, setting light to the heather as far as the eye could see and draping the landscape in a pall of black smoke. Burning fragments of the airship made contact with the second balloon and there was another huge explosion.

'Stay where you are,' Connie ordered, her heart pounding as she recognized the hopelessness of the situation. The heat was too fierce, the flames too widespread for them to emerge from their impro-vised shelter.

And so the fire raged, carried by the wind, travel-ling across the moor away from the town: the sole blessing, as far as the ARP teams were concerned. Dense smoke billowed high above them and death was all around. Three pilots had been killed; a fam-ily was known to be buried beneath the rubble.

At last, as the heat and glare from the two blasts faded, the four girls dared to crawl out from under the truck. The brave fire team was already at work, unreeling hoses and starting to aim their jets towards the smouldering shelter. Another trailer arrived, towed by a taxi, and a second team of three men jumped out, complete with special goggles to combat the intense white light of the incendiaries. They conferred with the first team, yelling above the roar of the conflagration that rapidly ate up the moorland to the west. There was a problem with water supply – the pumps would soon run out.

'There's a hydrant pipe halfway down Musgrave Street.' Connie was able to point one of the men towards a solution. His thick woollen tunic was already wet through and his face smeared with soot. A blast of scorching wind drove sparks into his eyes and ears, partially blinding him as he staggered down the hill to investigate, meeting Bill and Sam's ambulance on its way up.

'Here's our first casualty,' Bill muttered as Sam squealed to a halt. They'd watched in horror from the bottom of Musgrave Street as the two blimps had gone up in flames, only too aware that the outcome would prove fatal for anyone unable to find shelter in time. They'd driven on up the hill with their hearts in their mouths.

But the firefighter waved them on up the hill. 'The family at number fifty-two needs you more than me,' he told them.

Sam drove slowly through clouds of smoke and sparks. 'Not good,' he said repeatedly, bracing himself for the worst.

Bill didn't wait for the ambulance to reach the summit. Instead, he slung his haversack over his shoulder, then opened his door and jumped out, sprinting towards a small group of uniformed figures standing by a lorry. As he drew near, he recognized Lizzie and called her name. She turned and hurried towards him.

'There's no rescue team as yet,' she reported, her voice strained and her eyes full of dread. She pointed towards the ruined shelter. 'We've carried spades in the back of the lorry. Sally and I are about to start digging.'

'All right. Sam and I can help with that.' Privately, Bill feared there would be little point – it was unlikely that anyone had survived. Still, they would try.

Lizzie ran to fetch the spades. 'Connie and Sally reckon they should take a look at what's left of the Junkers, once the fire team gives them the all-clear.'

'What's Sally doing here?' Bill asked.

'She happened to be at the Gas Street post when the news came through from the report centre. She offered to help.'

Lizzie led the first-aiders towards the bungalows. 'I wouldn't bother with the pilot,' Sam grumbled. 'Why take the risk for the bloke who caused this mess in the first place?'

There was no time to think it through, and everything was happening through a thick pall of smoke, occasionally illuminated by late-exploding firebombs suddenly activated by forceful jets of water from the firefighters' hoses.

'Watch where you step,' Lizzie called after Connie and Pamela.

Connie took the lead. Her boots sank deep into squelching mud. 'There's a chance that Jerry bailed out before the Junkers hit the cable,' she said through gritted teeth.

Pamela doubted it but didn't say so. As air raid wardens, they must be seen to be doing their duty, which was to save lives wherever possible, so they pushed on towards the square outlines of the two concrete slabs that had tethered the blimps to the ground.

Fifty yards from the bases, Connie pulled out her torch and aimed the beam at the shards of metal scattered among the blackened heather, finally letting it rest on the twisted frame of the Junkers' cockpit, its Plexiglass shattered into a thousand fragments. Other parts of the fuselage had slammed against the foot of the nearest concrete block – Connie spotted a propeller and part of the control panel.

Meanwhile, Pamela took out her own torch and scanned the ridge. No sign of a parachute – evidently Jerry hadn't had time to bail out. Patches of earth hissed and sent up jets of steam, like a scene from hell. 'It's no good,' she whispered. 'Let's go back.'

Connie's yellow beam raked across the hillside. She heard raised voices from Musgrave Street and the whine of more vehicles straining up the hill. Everything possible was being done to find the poor souls trapped underneath the rubble. 'You're right.' She agreed with Pamela. 'We've done all we can here.'

They were about to turn and retrace their steps, when a man's voice pleaded out of the darkness. 'Help me.' English; not German.

Connie and Pamela froze.

'Help me,' he repeated.

They swung their weak torch beams towards the sound. An incendiary flared some twenty yards from where they stood and its glare lit up the ridge bright as day. Pamela and Connie felt its blast. In the seconds before the explosion, they made out the shape of a man lying close to the concrete slab furthest away from them.

Without a word, they set off again, stumbling against hidden rocks and stepping deep into swampy hollows, straining to keep their balance. The injured man groaned and raised an arm, let it drop, then lay motionless.

'Is it the pilot?' Pamela wondered as they drew near.

'No.' Connie couldn't make out a helmet or sheepskin flying jacket. This man was wearing an overcoat, part of which had burned away to reveal a battledress underneath. His helmet lay nearby. 'It's one of ours.'

'Who?' Pamela held her breath as she ventured nearer. There was another low groan and the man turned his head towards her. Shining her torch directly on his face, she recognized him by his dark moustache. 'Reggie,' she breathed as she crouched beside him.

He stared up at her with unseeing eyes. One arm lay trapped awkwardly beneath him and his body seemed twisted out of shape underneath the RAF overcoat.

Connie came to a halt. She'd spotted a second victim, half hidden behind the slab of concrete. He lay motionless and would be impossible to identify, to judge by the blackened state of the body.

'Reggie, can you hear me?' Pamela asked. The earth hissed and smoke billowed. The fresh flare of yet another exploding firebomb detonated nearby.

'Yes, I can hear you but I can't see you. Help me,' he pleaded for a third time.

Noting that there was nothing to be done for the other man, Connie joined Pamela. 'He looks in a bad way,' she murmured. 'He must have been working the winch to raise the blimp when Jerry snagged the cable. He was lucky to survive.'

'Take me to the hospital, damn it.' In desperation, Reggie reached out and grasped Pamela's wrist – a macabre reminder of the way he'd waltzed her out on to the dance floor the first time they'd met. 'I can't see a bloody thing and I can't move my legs.' His grip tightened and his voice sank to a barely audible croak. 'I'm a dead man unless you get me there fast, whoever you are.'

CHAPTER TWENTY-ONE

'Here – let me.' Connie saw that Pamela was in deep shock as she eased Reggie's fingers from around her friend's wrist. She unscrewed the top of her water bottle and put it to Reggie's lips. 'Drink this,' she told him.

Pamela stared blankly into the dark distance, paralysed by a thought that had struck her like a bolt from the blue. *Leave him to rot.*

'Lie still.' Connie spoke calmly to Nolan as she took over from Pamela. 'A stretcher will be on its way shortly.'

Reggie suffered a short coughing spasm then shot her a desperate question. 'Why can't I move my legs?'

Connie ignored Pamela's shuddering intake of breath. 'I don't know – the doctors will find out,' she promised the man whose fate lay in their hands. *Your dancing days are done*, she concluded as she shone her torch along Reggie's twisted body. Dark saliva trickled from the man's mouth and his trousers were soaked in blood.

I wished him dead! Pamela sank to her knees and buried her head in her hands. *How could I? What kind of person does that make me?*

'Run and tell Lizzie we need her help,' Connie urged. Reggie's breathing had grown shallow and his eyes had flickered shut. 'Do you hear me? We need a first-aider – fast!'

'Don't leave me!' Reggie begged.

'I won't – I'll stay here,' Connie promised.

With a huge effort, Pamela raised herself from the ground. Of course she wouldn't let a man die; even one like Reggie. She would carry out her duty.

'Good girl.' Connie sensed rather than saw that her friend was rallying, which left her free to concentrate on the injured man. She offered him more liquid and was dismayed to see that he was unable to swallow – he gagged and the water trickled down his chin. 'He's losing consciousness,' she muttered. 'Reggie, stay awake. For God's sake, Pamela – fetch Lizzie!'

Pamela was on her feet but her head was swimming. *He mustn't die*. If he did, she would never forgive herself for willing it to happen. *No, Reggie must live!* She shone her torch erratically across rough moorland. *Which direction?* At last she located a group of vehicles and teams hard at work with hoses and spades, and she set off towards them, stumbling, pressing on through the darkness until she reached them.

Bill, Lizzie, Sam and Sally dug feverishly. Drenched by the firefighters' hoses, they worked non-stop, stooping to clear bricks with their bare hands then digging afresh into the sodden heap of mortar, crumpled metal and dirt. Sally and Lizzie freed a sheet of corrugated iron that had formed part of the shelter's roof. It was still warm to the touch as they flung it to one side. The digging continued.

'Lizzie!' Pamela ran blindly towards the rescue team. 'We've found Reggie Nolan up there on the ridge – he's badly hurt.'

Without a word, Bill and Lizzie threw down their spades. They sprinted to the ambulance for a stretcher and first-aid kits while Sally comforted Pamela. She led her away from the action and found a bench that had been upended by one of the blasts. Sally set it on its legs and sat her friend down. 'Take your time,' she soothed. 'Let the others take over from here.'

Lizzie and Bill set off with their equipment. The situation sounded serious, but Pamela hadn't given them much information to go on – the victim could be badly burned, for all they knew. Plus, there was the possibility of major blood loss. Either way, their job was to get him to the Queen Alexandra as soon as humanly possible.

Meanwhile, Sam took charge of the two remaining volunteers – a pair of civilians who had turned up out of the blue to offer their services. 'Careful,' he warned as they tugged at a second sheet of corrugated iron. Their action dislodged several bricks, which collapsed inwards. 'There's a gap under there,' he decided. 'It looks like the shelter has been dug into the hillside.' If so, there was hope for the trapped family.

Flinging aside their spades, the men began to lift the bricks one at a time. Sure enough, there was a cavity. Sam reached in and his fingers came into contact with a smooth, flat surface. 'A door!' he guessed. 'Still upright and in one piece, by the feel of it.' They lifted more bricks from the heap; a part of the green shelter door was exposed. Hands scraped away wet mortar and brick fragments until a muffled voice could be heard.

'Take it easy,' Bernard Majors warned from deep within the shelter. 'Don't bring the roof down on us.'

A voice – a miracle. 'How many are you?' Sam raised his hand to order the others to stop clawing at the heap.

'Six.'

'Anyone hurt?'

'No. Thank God.'

'All right – hang on while we open this door.'

A lorry had been driven close to the shelter entrance and its driver was ordered to redirect its headlights, allowing Sam's team to see what they were doing.

'We're soaking wet in here,' Lily Majors complained. 'Can't you get those idiots to turn off their hoses?'

'Blimey, is that all the thanks we get?' Sam's muttered remark brought smiles to the weary rescuers' lips. The whole of the door was visible and the last of the rubble cleared away. Sam took hold of its metal handle and pulled with all his might. It opened with a loud scrape and muddy water gushed out.

Doughty Lily was the first to emerge, wading ankle deep through the flood and carrying the youngest of the children. Her mother came next, shivering but smiling triumphantly and holding the hands of the older girls, both in sopping-wet dressing-gowns and slippers. Bernard brought up the rear. 'You took your time,' the head of the household grumbled to Sam. 'That water's freezing cold – if you'd left us much longer we'd have caught our deaths.'

'But you didn't.' Sam smiled as he offered them blankets from the WVS van that had just arrived.

'Jammy beggars,' one of the helpers added.

'Hot tea is available,' the WVS woman announced in a hoity-toity voice. 'This way, if you please.'

Back on the ridge, Bill and Lizzie reached the base of the exploded blimp, where they found Connie talking urgently to a semi-conscious Reggie.

'Listen to me.' Connie patted his cheek in an effort to keep him awake. 'You can't give up – you have to hang on. The stretcher's here now and the ambulance is waiting.'

She stepped aside to allow Lizzie and Bill to unroll their stretcher. They worked quickly and smoothly, ignoring Reggie's groans as they moved him gently on to the stretcher.

'Burns to the upper torso,' Lizzie commented. 'Most likely smoke inhalation too. That's the real danger.'

'Multiple fractures,' Bill added. 'Ready? Let's go.'

They carried Reggie away, leaving Connie to check on the body she'd spotted close by. As she'd suspected, there was no sign of life in the poor soul. His clothes were mostly burned away, his features unrecognizable. Connie covered her nose and mouth to block out the stench, then backed away from the horrifying sight. Her first thought was that this was the Junkers pilot who had been flung from his aircraft as it crashed. Her second was that it might be Reggie's junior erk, Howard Enright. 'Bad luck,' she breathed as she started back towards Musgrave Street.

'Too late to do anything.' Connie delivered her grim, truncated account of discovering the body to the rescue teams through a clenched jaw. She felt that she might vomit. 'The second chap bought it good and proper.'

'Ought we to move him?' Sally asked Pamela, who had just watched Reggie being stretchered into Bill and Sam's ambulance then driven away.

'Yes – we can't just leave him there.' Pamela willed herself back into action. 'You're sure there was no way to identify the body?' she checked with Connie.

Connie stepped over a fireman's hose and felt a welcome spray of cold water from its jet drift towards her. The fire team was still hard at work, fighting the fresh flames that flared unexpectedly. 'Honestly, no. But my money is on young Enright – he was probably working alongside Reggie when all hell broke loose.'

'Sally and I will fetch him off the ridge.' Pamela was keen to make up for her earlier lapse by carrying out the grisly task. 'Connie, get someone to contact the team from the morgue – tell them we're bringing in a body.'

'Right you are, but I hope you both have strong stomachs.' Connie handed them spare blankets in which to wrap the corpse.

Pamela and Sally set off, picking their way through tangled heather and spiky gorse and steeling themselves to face what lay ahead. Pamela paused at the spot where she and Connie had discovered Reggie. Her torch beam rested on a small silver object: a cigarette lighter. 'This must have fallen out of his pocket,' she murmured as she picked it up. Shining their torches at the ground, they trod carefully around the concrete base until they found the body just as Connie had described – burned beyond recognition.

Pamela shuddered. It would have been over in a flash; hopefully the victim had been knocked unconscious by the blast, rendering him oblivious to his fate.

'Let's hope it was quick.' Sally covered the dead man's blackened face; a tender, respectful gesture that moved Pamela as she held her breath then raised the man's legs and slid a blanket under them. He'd been a small, slight man – not too heavy. The charred remnant of his sweater suggested that this was no German pilot or RAF engineer.

Sally gasped and rested back on her heels.

'What is it?' Pamela's task of sliding the blanket into position was complete.

The sweater had been hand-knitted in a traditional cable stitch that fishermen wore. Sally knew someone who owned just such a sweater. She stared at Pamela in sudden anguish. 'Look – here, at the jumper he was wearing!'

Pamela forced herself to study the top half of the corpse more closely. The man had been a civilian – the small scrap of sweater was evidence enough. Besides, the remaining hair was long and dark rather than regulation short back and sides. An object hung from a leather strap around the wrist of the bomb victim's raised right arm – an object with a charred wooden handle attached to a heavy metal head. Pamela reached for it with trembling fingers. 'A hammer,' she whispered.

Sick and faint, Sally lowered her head. 'Yes.'

Ron Butcher had met his end in a violent,

ear-splitting boom. He'd been swallowed by a ball of flame.

'Kite balloons are used to defend key ground targets such as industrial areas, ports and harbours and to direct enemy bombers towards anti-aircraft fire. Shaped like a giant fish, a typical dirigible is 66 feet long and 30 feet wide, tethered to the ground by a dozen strong steel cables.' Weeks earlier, Ron had read and retained the exact facts and stored them methodically in his tortured brain. These were the final thoughts that flitted through his consciousness.

'We know who this is.' Pamela's voice was scarcely audible.

'Yes,' Sally said again. Ron had perished in an instant, killed by an enemy he had never fought. Driven by a wild, insatiable desire for revenge, he had paid the ultimate price.

CHAPTER TWENTY-TWO

The one place that Connie longed to be was at Tom's bedside. Pamela and Sally had to use all their powers of persuasion to get her to go back home for a change of clothes before she went to the hospital.

'It's half past three in the morning,' Pamela reminded her as they travelled back to the old town in the commandeered lorry. 'Tom needs a good night's sleep and you could do with some rest too.'

Connie reluctantly took her point. She dropped Sally off in the market square and watched Pamela accompany her to the door of the Anchor.

'You're sure you'll be all right?' Pamela asked.

Sally was in a daze as she looked up at the familiar stone lintel with the date 1756 carved into it. She couldn't believe that Ron was dead – the night's horrific events didn't seem real and she was convinced that she would wake tomorrow from a harrowing dream. Glancing down at the heavy iron door key in her hand as if it would provide a magical exit from the nightmare, she gave her friend a questioning stare.

'Are you all right?' Pamela repeated. She was anxious to get back to Sunrise to reassure her mother and father and to share her experiences with Fred.

'God forgive me, I wanted Reggie Nolan to die,' she would confess. 'I plumbed the depths.' Fred would comfort her and the bitter poison would be flushed from her system. Love would overcome hate.

'I'll have to be all right.' Sally's shaky answer was accompanied by a faint smile. Stone was real; the dated lintel above her head and the doorstep under her feet worn down by the tramp of fishermen's boots, the uneven cobbles of the market square and the massive bulwark of the man-made jetty that had stood for centuries against the fury of the sea. 'The little ones need me.'

Pamela squeezed her hand and watched brave Sally insert the key in the lock. Satisfied, she turned and ran swiftly along the headland path to Fred.

At Elliot Street Connie washed at the kitchen sink in hot water from a kettle boiled by her father, who stood by attentively. She dried her face and hands with the towel he provided.

'Lizzie?' he enquired tersely.

'She's fine. She drove Reggie Nolan to the Queen Alexandra. He was in a bad way.'

Bert nodded. He didn't wish to know more. He listened as Connie went upstairs to change. It had been a long night of waiting and wondering. The whole town had heard the blasts and seen the kite balloons go up in flames, and when his girls hadn't come home at the end of their shifts, he'd feared the worst. 'It put years on me,' he would later tell Vera. 'I'm too old for this game – my nerves won't stand much more of it.'

His sister would tut and tell him off. 'We came through the first war, didn't we? And we'll come through this one if we keep our heads down and do as we're told.' Like millions of others, Vera put her faith in Mr Churchill and the bulldog spirit that kept Kelthorpe going through thick and thin. 'Buck up, our Bert. We do what we always do – keep calm and carry on.'

Upstairs, Connie took off her uniform. Standing in her underclothes in front of the bedroom mirror, she placed her hands on her stomach then turned sideways to stare at her reflection. It was still too early to see any difference in her body but she felt . . . transformed. Yes; that was the word. Outwardly, she looked the same – tall and strong and capable, pale-skinned and with her dark hair loose around her shoulders. Inwardly she welcomed a new soft glow that spread from her core to her fingertips and toes. In future she would be slower, more considered, kinder. Yes; right now this minute, she would lie down on the bed and rest a while.

Lizzie and Bill had done their best. Lizzie had broken the rules by driving through barriers and taking short cuts around gaping holes in the road, turning her headlights on full beam against blackout regulations and often driving on the wrong side of the road around bends or along the pavement if it meant she could shave off a few seconds in the race to get Reggie Nolan to hospital.

In the back of the ambulance, Bill had strapped an oxygen mask to the injured man's face. Though still unable to see, Reggie's panic had lessened and he'd grown more rational. 'I copped it good and proper, didn't I? Go on – give it to me straight.'

'You've sustained fractures to both legs without a doubt. X-rays of your chest will give us the full picture.'

Reggie resisted Bill's oxygen mask. 'I thought my number was up.'

'Not this time,' Bill assured him.

Lizzie pulled up close to the main doors. Within seconds, Reggie was transferred to a hospital stretcher and wheeled away. She slumped forward against the steering wheel and felt the vehicle rock as Bill opened the passenger door and sat down next to her. For a while, neither said a word.

'Just when you think it can't get any worse.' Lizzie broke the silence. She sat upright and inhaled deeply.

'Boom! Jerry proves us wrong.' Resting back in his seat, Bill closed his eyes.

'All those LZs, just sitting there . . .' Strung out across the estuary and lining the coast; each one capable of exploding and raining down destruction on the very people they were designed to defend. Lizzie shuddered. 'One bullet from our own ack-ack guns would be enough, let alone Jerry snagging one and blowing himself up while he's at it.'

Gloom settled on their exhausted shoulders and it was many more minutes before Lizzie gathered enough energy to park the ambulance then enter the hospital with Bill. They discovered that it was touch-and-go for their patient – extensive second- and third-degree burns were proving to be a major problem and it was too soon to assess the extent of the damage.

'We'll hang on here, if that's all right.' Bill hoped their efforts hadn't been in vain. It was true that no one had a good word to say about the wisecracking RAF erk, but when the chips were down, he was one of theirs and you had to hope that he pulled through.

Dawn broke as Connie arrived at the Queen Alexandra. She'd slept for two hours, then got dressed and slipped from the house without waking her father. She'd driven through empty streets. A blanket of hazy smoke obscured the headland: the sole reminder of the previous night's inferno.

It was a bright new day. The sky was suffused with a rosy-pink glow and there wasn't a cloud in sight. She walked into the reception area to see Lizzie and Bill in conversation with one of the doctors. They listened and nodded then shook hands with him before linking arms and walking towards her.

'Have you two looked in a mirror lately?' Connie asked. Their faces were streaked with soot, their hair and uniforms caked with mud.

Lizzie drew her sleeve across her face.

'You've made it worse.' Connie pulled a handkerchief from her pocket. 'Here, let me.' She wiped Lizzie's cheeks then gave the handkerchief to Bill. 'What's the latest on Reggie?'

'He's a tough little blighter.' Bill spat on the handkerchief and rubbed his face as he spoke. 'His eyes were damaged by the blast – probably not permanently – and the docs are treating him for serious burns, but now he's back on the ward and already making a nuisance of himself.'

'Ron Butcher wasn't so lucky.' Connie kept the information to a minimum. 'He was sneaking about up on the headland – wrong place, wrong time.'

'And that's that.' Bill felt nothing – Butcher had had it coming to him, one way or another.

Lizzie gripped his arm more firmly. 'How about the family at number fifty-two?'

'The rescue teams worked a miracle. They pulled all six of them out without a scratch.'

There were smiles all round and sighs of satisfaction. God was in his heaven after all. Bill and Lizzie walked out into the warmth of the rising sun while Connie hurried on to see Tom.

He greeted her with a worried look and a question. 'You haven't changed your mind?'

'About getting married?' She sat beside him in her prettiest summer dress, with her magnificent, shiny hair swept up in a loose topknot. 'Of course not. What makes you think that?'

'It's not too sudden?' He'd lain awake listening to the sirens and the gunfire, seeing a great blaze light up the midnight sky when the kite balloons had exploded. What if Connie had had second thoughts and backed out?

'Sudden, yes,' she agreed, 'but I wouldn't want it any other way.'

'That's good then.' Tom winced as he shifted position. 'I'll be out of here before you know it.'

'Tom Rose, you're the worst patient in the world.' He could barely move, for heaven's sake; his skull was cracked, his arm broken and his face covered in cuts and bruises, yet all he could think about was being discharged. Connie teased him then grew serious. 'The man who did this to you died in last night's raid.'

Tom winced again. 'You're sure?'

'Certain. Sally identified him – she's the only one in the entire town who's even a little bit sorry.'

'Aye.' Tom was silent for a while. 'Good riddance, then.'

She held his hand and stared intently at him. 'I'm going to do as you asked,' she promised. 'After we're married I'll take things easy. You won't recognize me when I put my feet up and start knitting matinee jackets.'

'Bloody hell, Connie.' He sighed in disbelief. 'Don't change too much, though – I wouldn't like that.'

'I promise.' Leaning forward, she brushed his cheek with her lips. 'I'll stay on at Gas Street for as long as I can, but Dad and Lizzie will take the brunt of the bakery work from now on. Vera will lend a hand.'

Tom had been making plans of his own. 'We'll need a marriage licence from the town hall. How soon can we arrange that?'

'I'll wave my magic wand and see what I can do. More to the point, how quickly can I run up a wedding dress? Sally's a dab hand with a sewing machine and she's already promised to help. I decided I don't want to be in white, though, so I've chosen lilac with a cream lining. I'm thinking of asking Sally to be my bridesmaid.'

'Whoa, steady on!'

'What? I thought you'd be pleased.'

'I am – I'm chuffed. But what about setting a date before we run too far ahead of ourselves?'

Connie's eyes gleamed with excitement. 'I've already thought about that,' she confessed. Holding up her hand, she counted off the days on her fingers. 'Today's Tuesday, then Wednesday, Thursday, Friday, Saturday the sixteenth. Five days to prepare – do you think you'll be ready to hobble down the aisle by then?'

'What are you saying?'

'Saturday the sixteenth,' she repeated.

'You mean we could double up with Bill and Lizzie?' Without a second's hesitation, Tom agreed. 'You bet I'll be ready – never mind wild horses, a whole division of Rommel's Panzers couldn't stop me.'

'I love you, I love you, I love you!' Connie showered her fiancé with delighted kisses.

'A double wedding it is!' he declared.

Dresses, a cake, someone to take the photographs – oh, and she must check that Lizzie was happy to share her big day. 'Leave it with me,' she said. 'All you have to do is get yourself discharged in time for the wedding march and the "I dos" at the altar.' *For better, for worse, for richer, for poorer, in sickness and in health . . .*

'All four of us – together?' Lizzie's jaw dropped. Had she misheard or had Connie actually just uttered the words 'double wedding'? 'Me and Bill, you and Tom?'

'Exactly.' Connie was still bursting with excitement. Forgetting all about her resolution to slow down, she'd dashed from the hospital straight to the bakery.

Stooping slightly and stiff from the heavy work of kneading, lifting and carrying, Bert came out from the back room with a what-the-heck's-going-on expression. He used his apron to dust flour from his hands. 'Double trouble, more like,' he grumbled. He and Vera would have to bake a bigger cake. They'd need extra booze for the guests – extra cooked ham and eggs for sandwiches – extra everything. Trust Connie to rush around expecting the impossible.

'Think about it,' Connie went on. 'We're devoted sisters and Bill and Tom have been best friends since they were in short trousers. It'll be perfect to double up on the wedding. Think of us posing for photos in the church porch afterwards – you in white, me in lilac, with Pamela and Sally in blue.'

'Sally will be your bridesmaid?' Lizzie cocked her head to one side.

'Yes – I haven't asked her yet but she's sure to agree.'

'But there's a snag. Who'll be Bill's best man if Tom can't do it?'

'Sam will stand in for Tom. And Tom can ask Fred to step up at the last minute.' Connie had worked it all out in advance.

'Wait!' Lizzie held up her hand. 'Aren't you forgetting something? Fred and Pamela are leaving town tomorrow.'

'Heck!' For a second Connie was flummoxed. 'Not if I have a word with them,' she decided, dashing out of the shop as quickly as she'd dashed in.

Bert pursed his lips then opened them with a pop. 'We could always cheat with the cake.' He was trying to find a practical solution to the rationing problem that a double wedding would present. 'We can do three tiers but the top two would be cardboard covered in royal icing. Only the bottom one would be real.'

'Let's do it.' Lizzie made a snap decision. 'If a fake wedding cake is good enough for Vera Lynn, then it's good enough for Connie and me.'

'Reggie's tucked up in a hospital bed for the duration.' Connie had arrived like a whirlwind on Fred and Pamela's doorstep. Their packed suitcases already stood in the hall at Sunrise and Hugh had promised to present the pair with tickets for the following morning. Harold and Edith had been putting on brave faces and acting as though they knew something that the fleeing pair didn't. Their expressions said, *Top secret, not to be divulged.*

'You know where the tickets are for!' Realizing that her father would be the one to crack, Pamela had cornered him in the kitchen of their bungalow soon after breakfast. 'Tell me!'

'I can't – I promised.' He'd stood at the sink conscientiously washing dishes.

'Please, please, please. Tell me!' Neither Pamela nor Fred knew their destination – only that her uncle had made arrangements for them to disappear without trace.

Harold hadn't replied.

'Uncle Hugh has taken you into his confidence.' She'd thought of Leeds, Manchester, Liverpool, Birmingham – one of the major cities where they could start afresh.

Harold had stacked dishes on the draining board. 'Oh, love, your mother and I will miss you so much.'

'Daddy, what has Uncle Hugh said? Where will Fred and I be going?'

'Not where you think.' Resistance crumbling,

Harold had hugged her and whispered in her ear. 'The tickets are for Vänersborg in Sweden.'

'Sweden?' Across the sea; far, far away.

'Yes. Think about it. Not a soul will know who you are. You and Fred will be safe there.' Harold's heart had ached as he felt the physical ties that bound him to his daughter stretching to breaking point. 'Hugh has contacts in Sweden – there will be jobs and a house for you to rent.'

'Vänersborg?' Fred had listened quietly to Pamela's rapid explanation. Straight away he'd seen the advantages – a new town, a new language, a new world for them to explore together. 'That's very good news,' he'd said at once. 'Sweden is beautiful and the people will welcome us. We must thank Hugh immediately.'

'You're most welcome,' Hugh had told the happy couple. 'But remember, not a word!'

Now, less than twenty-four hours before their departure, Connie was on their doorstep, eager to point out the consequences of Ron's demise and Nolan's serious injuries. 'That means Reggie can't carry out his threats against Pamela, so you two can risk staying on until after the wedding.'

'I could be Lizzie's bridesmaid after all?' Pamela's face lit up as she turned to Fred.

He knitted his brows. What would such a delay do to their plans? True, the Simmons pair would be unlikely to act without their ringleader. It didn't get him and Pamela out of the woods entirely – there were dozens more like them lurking in Kelthorpe's shadows – but if being Lizzie's bridesmaid meant so much to Pamela, then why not risk staying on for a short time? If the tickets could be altered, if Pamela's parents and Hugh agreed, if they could all keep the secret for a few more days . . .

'Tom and I plan to get married on Saturday too.' Connie was breathless with pent-up excitement. 'I want Sally to be my bridesmaid – she doesn't know it yet.'

Pamela pictured the scene – St Joseph's would be bursting at the seams with guests and well-wishers, the organ would play and a proud Bert would walk his daughters down the aisle. Bill and Lizzie, Tom and Connie would exchange vows.

'Say you'll do it,' Connie pleaded.

A new life beckoned but old loyalties between the girls were strong. Pamela clasped Fred's hand and raised it to her lips, hoping, hoping . . .

'Very well,' Fred agreed. How could he resist?

Pamela clapped her hands and jumped in the air. 'Oh yes, Connie! Fred and I wouldn't miss your weddings for the world.'

Knock-knock on the door of the Anchor.

Frank answered it to find Connie looking as if she'd hit the jackpot. 'Sally's in bed,' he cautioned before the visitor had a chance to speak. 'She's having a lie-in.'

'Oh no she's not.' Sally had come downstairs at the sound of the loud knocking. 'She's right here.'

'How quickly can we sew my dress?' Connie asked without preliminaries. 'Can we get it done by this Saturday?'

'Yes, if we go at it hammer and tongs.' Look forward, not back; that was the ticket. Preparing for

Connie and Tom's wedding would help Sally to do just that.

'And can you work miracles and make a bridesmaid's dress for yourself, too?' It was a tall order – Connie crossed her fingers and waited for Sally's reply.

'You want me . . .?'

'To be my bridesmaid – yes, I do.'

Sally let out a loud sigh of wonderment. 'You're sure?' she murmured.

'I can't think of anyone I'd rather have.' Connie squeezed her hands. 'Please say yes.'

'Then, yes – I'd be honoured.' She would be proud to process down the aisle in front of Connie Bailey and Lizzie Harrison – the two women besides Pamela whom Sally most admired.

'Perfect.' All was falling into place. Now to St Joseph's to inform Reverend Greene then to the town hall to secure the licence and from there to Aunty Vera's to rope her in for more food for the reception. 'I'll be back later this afternoon for a marathon sewing session,' she promised Sally. 'When will you be free?'

Saturday the sixteenth of May, 1942.

Bill had offered to buy Tom a wedding ring from the pawn shop on Tennyson Street – a stopgap until Tom and Connie could go shopping for one themselves. It was safe in Sam's top pocket as they stood in front of the altar at St Joseph's church. A bruised and battered Tom had a bad case of the jitters – he felt weak at the knees and he clenched his jaw to stop his teeth from chattering.

On the other side of the aisle, Bill adjusted the knot of his tie. It was blinking tight – he wasn't used to this collar-and-tie malarkey. Fred stood like a rock at Bill's side; firm and steady, taking his responsibility seriously.

Vera and an army of helpers had done wonders with the flowers. The ends of the pews were festooned with white ribbon and sprigs of delicate May blossom, and more blossom stood in brass vases on the pulpit and the altar. There was joy and beauty everywhere you looked. Sun shone through the stained glass as the organist and vicar emerged from the vestry and took their places. The moment had arrived.

Bert fretted in the porch, waiting for the music to begin. Right until the last minute he hadn't been convinced that Connie's groom would make it. Then again, this was Tom Rose you were talking about. And here he was, fresh out of hospital, dressed in his Sunday best, looking pallid and with his arm in a sling, ready to marry Bert's eldest daughter. As for Bill and Lizzie's sudden rush to be wed; well, better to do it before the Royal Navy nabbed him. Them getting married was a two-fingers-up to Herr Hitler and his blasted U-boats. Good on the pair of them.

The first slow strains of the 'Wedding March' reached the porch. 'Ready?' Bert asked Lizzie and Connie.

Connie was in lilac. Sally had worked her magic and the dress was perfect – low-waisted and long-sleeved, with a corsage of cream carnations that matched the trim on her gown. The flared hem skimmed her knees. Her hair was held in place by a satin Alice band adorned with silk flowers. Lizzie was in delicate white silk that swished as she walked, wondrously slim and shaking like a leaf as she clasped her bouquet with both hands. Her face was covered by her mother Rose's short veil, which Lizzie would lift as she reached the altar.

The brides turned to Sally and Pamela. 'Ready?' they echoed in light, breathless voices.

The nervous bridesmaids nodded. Brides and bridesmaids carried trailing bouquets of carnations, also in memory of Lizzie and Connie's mother.

Organ notes swelled to the rafters. All heads turned towards the door.

Lizzie was on Bert's left side, Connie to his right. They slipped their arms through his. 'Let's get this over with,' their father growled as the bridal procession entered the church.

'Smooth as a baby's bottom!' Bert shook hands with everyone in sight. 'Not a single hitch – it's as if we'd been planning it for months.'

The church hall was crammed with guests tucking into a sumptuous spread of sandwiches and sausage rolls laid out on trestle tables. A magnificent cake took pride of place at the centre: the result of Lord knew how many pooled coupons and under-the-counter transactions. Tea urns hissed and cups rattled, while Frank Hopkins stood behind a barrel of his best bitter, serving pints with gay abandon. There was even a piano player, set up on a temporary stage, ready to entice the two newly married couples on to the floor for the first dance.

'Are you sure you can manage?' Connie watched Tom struggle to his feet as the pianist began.

'Watch me,' he told her, wrapping his good arm around her waist and sweeping her free of the crowd for their first dance as man and wife.

'I was dreading this bit,' Bill confessed to Lizzie.

'You'll be fine,' she promised as she pulled him into the space at the centre of the room. 'It's a simple waltz – one-two-three, one-two-three.'

And it was fine. Bill held Lizzie close as they twirled. Thirty-six hours from now, he would step aboard HMS *Northern Lights* for a five-day spell of duty with Harry Tate's Navy. Her crew would sweep for all types of mines, from contact through acoustic to magnetic. Bill knew the drill and in the past had willingly embraced the dangers – after all, the Harry Tate tag was a byword for courage in the face of Jerry's U-boats and low-flying dive-bombers. But this time he had a wife to think about and he would have to do it without Tom.

One-two-three, one-two-three – Lizzie held her husband tight and waltzed him until his head was spinning.

Tom swayed and turned on the dance floor and it hurt like hell. Halfway through the number, he admitted defeat.

'Let's sit it out,' Connie suggested. They passed Lizzie and Bill as they made for the nearest seats. Lizzie looked radiant – her cheeks were flushed and a smile played around her lips. 'We did it,' Connie whispered with a triumphant wink.

'We did.' Lizzie beamed back at her.

Pamela overheard them as Fred led her towards the dance floor. 'Give me a moment,' she whispered to him before grabbing hold of Lizzie, then corralling her and Connie in a quiet corner of the room. 'Well done!' she cried. 'The ceremony could hardly have gone better – I'm over the moon for you both.'

'Come here.' Connie drew Pamela close and gave her a warm hug. 'I doubt that I'll get a chance to do that again before you and Fred set off on your new adventure.'

'But we'll stay friends,' Lizzie promised. 'No matter how far away you go, Connie and I will always be here if you need us.'

Pamela grasped their hands and squeezed them tightly. 'Thank you – that means everything to me.'

The three girls shed glad tears, then Fred came and whirled Pamela on to the floor – round and round until she was dizzy – and Eddie Fraser shyly invited Sally to waltz with him. An embarrassed Arnold protested that he was no sissy, but his mother dragged him into the middle of the room and made him dance anyway. Then Sam Billington and Simon Fraser found more willing partners in Pamela's two fellow lodgers from King Edward Street. Edith in a lilac two-piece and Harold, smiling benevolently, impressed onlookers with their immaculate footwork.

The crowd danced on through the afternoon and only stopped when Bert stood up and tapped the side of his glass with a spoon.

'Speech!' a dozen voices clamoured.

Waiting for the hum of conversation to die away, Bert coughed and cleared his throat. 'I'm not one for spouting, so this won't take long,' he promised. 'I only want to say how proud I am of my two girls and of what they do to keep this town safe.'

'Hear, hear!' Wedding guests clapped and smiled.

'Their mother would have been proud too.' Bert faltered and cleared his throat again. 'So let's wish the happy couples a big dollop of luck, because no one in Kelthorpe deserves it more than Lizzie and Bill, and Connie and Tom.'

'Hear, hear!'

Edith sidled up to Pamela and Fred and took their hands. Soon, she too must let her daughter go. Happiness beckoned from across the rough North Sea.

'None of us has a clue when Jerry will strike again,' the father of the two brides went on. 'It can happen in the blink of an eye. But these young folk are living proof that we can and will come out on top.'

'We will. We'll never give in,' the guests affirmed.

Lizzie and Connie in their wedding finery met each other's gazes and smiled. Bill and Tom squared their shoulders and thrust out their chests. They only did what was asked of them; what anyone else would do. They patrolled the streets and drove ambulances, fought fires and disabled mines. They were not out of the ordinary.

'So let's raise our glasses,' Bert concluded. 'Here's to love and happiness.'

'To love and happiness.' A heartfelt murmur filled the room.

Bert put his glass to his lips and drank long and deep. 'And good health and good luck to one and all!'

My parents on their wedding day in 1947.

A LETTER FROM JENNY HOLMES

'Reader, I married them!'

This is where I say goodbye to Connie, Lizzie and Pamela – and it hasn't been easy.

Looking back over the time since I first breathed life into these three characters, I find that we've been through a lot together.

It all began with a blank screen and Connie, whose lively decisiveness appealed to me from the start. Nothing gets her down for long and even though she sometimes rushes into things without thinking, she rarely feels sorry for herself and always takes responsibility for what she's done. Then there was Lizzie; quieter than Connie but with the same self-reliant, can-do spirit. These girls have a tough energy and dogged determination to die for.

Pamela felt different. At first she acts as a naive, shy foil for the two more confident Harrison girls. She grows in stature as I present her with various challenges. Should she join the ARP and risk her life to save others, and will she break out of the shell of her overprotected childhood to fall in love?

Though I've set the Air Raid Girls books in the 1940s, we're not talking about passive romantic heroines here – my girls are brave and independent and they represent the unbelievable strength and courage of that special generation. Imagine patrolling dark streets with little more than a tin helmet, a whistle and a gas mask for protection. I'm not sure I could have been that brave.

As a writer I do partly live the lives I describe. When I create scenes involving high levels of danger – air raids and violent assaults – it takes it out of me both physically and emotionally. By way of contrast, more gentle, loving episodes bring a feeling of quiet contentment. Big decisions – should a certain character live or die? – are not readily made. In other words, I'm closely involved in every detail from first to last and therefore it's hard to let these people go.

So it's a sad goodbye to Bert Harrison, typical Yorkshireman of those days – taciturn, watchful, wise – and goodbye to lovely Tom Rose, Connie's no-fuss, understated love interest. Farewell to bold, carefree Bill Evans with his passion for the sea and for Lizzie, his bride, and to Fred Miller who survived terrible loss in pre-war Germany and discovers love and happiness and a new life abroad with Pamela.

As well as making a major investment in my characters, I couldn't write these books without a vivid setting to support the action. Yorkshire plays a massive role in the creation of atmosphere and a solid sense of reality. It's my home county and part of my DNA. Kelthorpe doesn't exist except in my imagination, but any reader who's visited Hull, Whitby or Robin Hood's Bay will be able to visualize many of my locations, from timber yard and gas works down to pubs, bread shops and fish markets. And oh, that rugged East Yorkshire coastline!

Now, for my new book – *The Ballroom Girls* – I'm conjuring up new heroines and I'm moving counties! Enter

Sylvia Ellis, Pearl Scott and Joy Hebden. I plan to make these girls dance their way through fierce rivalries and wartime difficulties. The place is Blackpool – yes, Lancashire! Think 'Strictly' and the Tower Ballroom in the 1940s. Think pastures new!

Until next time,

Jenny Holmes

Welcome to the the world of
JENNY HOLMES

Follow Jenny on Facebook and be the first to hear about her writing and research for new books, competitions, and special deals.

Find out more and follow @JennyHolmesAuthor on Facebook today!

If you enjoyed *The Air Raid Girls: Wartime Brides,* you will love the brand-new wartime series from Jenny Holmes . . .

The Ballroom Girls

Blackpool, summer 1942. Meet the Ballroom Girls: Sylvia, Pearl and Joy. Three girls dancing through the turbulence of WWII.

Sylvia is the spoilt only child of an ambitious mother, Lorna Ellis, who runs a dancing school in Blackpool. Approaching 21, Sylvia is under pressure to scoop up prizes by fair means or foul.

Pearl is the oldest daughter in a large, chaotic family who all work on Blackpool's Golden Mile. She often sneaks away to watch ballroom contestants in their glittery finery. She dreams of joining them, but will she ever be anything other than an outsider looking in?

Joy is an evacuee who lost her parents to the Blitz. Now she lives in a shabby boarding house and works as a cleaner. Though shy and modest, she falls in love with the newest dance craze – the American Jitterbug. When Lorna's dance school spots her talent, Joy is given a chance to break away from boarding house drudgery and enter the glamorous world of professional ballroom dancing.

Through blackouts and air raids, the excitement of the ballroom never dims. But competition is fierce. Will the Ballroom Girls find what they're looking for in the joy of the dance?

Available for pre-order now

The Air Raid Girls at Christmas

Book 2 in *The Air Raid Girls* series

November, 1941

Christmas is coming . . . and despite the blackout, shortages and a constant threat of air raids, the inhabitants of Kelthorpe on the Yorkshire coast are determined that war won't stop them celebrating.

The run-up to Christmas sees sisters **Connie** and **Lizzie**, and their good friend **Pamela**, busier than ever. Between their jobs, carol-singing rehearsals with the church choir and night shifts doing their bit as Air Raid Wardens and ambulance drivers, it's all go.

But when Connie and Lizzie's dear dad falls ill, their sweethearts Tom and Bill are called up by the Royal Navy for dangerous mine-sweeping duties, and Pamela's sweetheart Fred is targeted by vicious locals, the girls have to believe in miracles to keep soldiering on.

Can their dearest wishes come true this Christmas?

Available now

The Spitfire Girls

Book 1 in *The Spitfire Girls* series

'Anything to Anywhere!'

That's the motto of the Air Transport Auxiliary, the brave team of female pilots who fly fighter planes between bases at the height of the Second World War.

Mary is a driver for the ATA and although she yearns to fly a Spitfire, she fears her humble background will hold her back. After all, glamorous **Angela** is set to be the next 'Atta Girl' on recruitment posters. **Bobbie** learned to fly in her father's private plane and **Jean** was taught the Queen's English at grammar school before joining the squad. Dedicated and resilient, the three girls rule the skies: weathering storms and dodging enemy fire. Mary can only dream of joining them – until she gets the push she needs to overcome her self-doubt.

Thrown together, the girls form a tight bond as they face the perils of their job. But they soon find that affairs of the heart can be just as dangerous as attacks from the skies.

With all the fear and uncertainty ahead – can their friendship see them through the tests of war?

Available now

The Land Girls at Christmas

Book 1 in *The Land Girls* series

'Calling All Women!'

It's 1941 and as the Second
World War rages on, girls
from all over the country are
signing up to the Women's
Land Army. Renowned for
their camaraderie and spirit,
it is these brave women who
step in to take on the
gruelling farm work from the
men conscripted into the
armed forces.

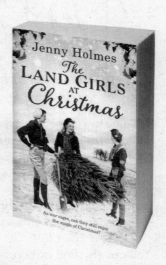

When Yorkshire mill girl **Una** joins the cause, she
wonders how she'll adapt to country life. Luckily she's
quickly befriended by more experienced Land Girls
Brenda and **Grace**. But as Christmas draws ever near,
the girls' resolve is tested as scandals and secrets are
revealed, lovers risk being torn apart, and even patriotic
loyalties are called into question . . .

**With only a week to go until the festivities, can the
strain of wartime still allow for the magic of Christmas?**

Available now

SIGN UP TO OUR NEW SAGA NEWSLETTER

Penny Street

The home of heart-warming reads

Welcome to **Penny Street**, your number **one stop for emotional and heartfelt historical reads**. Meet casts of characters you'll never forget, memories you'll treasure as your own, and places that will forever stay with you long after the last page.

Join our online **community** bringing you the latest book deals, competitions and new saga series releases.

You can also find extra content, talk to your favourite authors and share your discoveries with other saga fans on Facebook.

Join today by visiting
www.penguin.co.uk/pennystreet

Follow us on Facebook
www.facebook.com/welcometopennystreet/